St Heliers Bay B&B

Patricia Snelling

Contact:
patricia.snelling.books@gmail.com
Website: patriciasnelling.com

Disclaimer
This novel is written in British English with
New Zealand colloquialisms or Kiwi slang.

A catalogue record for this book is available
from the National Library of New Zealand

Martin Joyce – Cover Designer
Thoughtfields, Auckland

Judith Little – Editing Support

The Security Guard directed the torch at his wristwatch. It was nearly midnight. Something was amiss on the distant side of the wharf.

Ships arrived at other terminals during the graveyard shift at odd hours, but not on this one. Only skeleton crews worked in that part of the container wharf during weekdays, and this was Sunday.

The port worker knew there was a fresh intake of terminal operator trainees, but not expected on duty until around seven on Monday morning.

Although the LED floodlights could be dimmed, they were only used in stormy weather and during winter mornings. This weekend was dry.

He was perplexed—worried to see a mysterious glow emanating from the far side of the massive wharf. Pulling out a mobile phone from his jacket pocket, he alerted the Maritime Police Unit to the suspicious activity.

It was late spring and there was enough light from the starry sky and a full moon for him to weave his way through the mountains of shipping Conex container boxes to the far side of the wharf without using his torch.

Nearing the spot where a soft glow emanated from between the massive steel containers, he heard the resonation of dulled voices.

While crouched holding the clipboard with paperwork, he scanned the documents with his torch on a low beam. He was right. Apart from him, there should be no one working in that segment at night.

Inching closer, he heard muffled chatting, but it wasn't clear enough to decipher.

In this section of the Port, he knew there were stacks of empty metal shipping crates—evidence of importers having supply chain troubles.

But what was a truck doing there—a Toyota Toyace Box Tail-lift?

The guard rechecked his documentation, suspecting the driver must have used a forged ID to enter the terminal and steal cargo. He noted the name on the side of the vehicle, *Tried-and-True Movers.*

Then it imploded as he watched and waited. A tall figure climbed out of the truck and knocked on the door of a large crate, calling out before lifting the bars on the steel door and opening it. Instantly, a group of people poured out—a dozen—in single file, shuffling behind a wiry, pint-sized but muscly Asian man who appeared to be their leader and escort.

The guard drew closer, keeping out of sight in the dark. When the stowaways came out of the shadows and stood in a huddle, he guessed they were Asian migrants.

Without giving it another thought, the spectator lurched forward, turning up the beam on his heavy-duty flashlight, confronting the truck driver.

'Hey! What's going on here? Show me your ID!' he roared.

The driver stumbled backwards in fright as the Port worker's eyes scanned the terrified group whom he figured had been trafficked. Glancing inside the container, he was surprised to see only rubber mats, sleeping bags and boxes of food packages and water bottles.

'This wharf is off limits at night except for international container ships under exceptional circumstances,' the guard growled.

'I have clearance to access this container for their belongings,' the driver replied nervously.

'Why at night—it's pretty irregular?'

The driver pointed at the migrants. 'They all work during the day and wanted to pick out their belongings themselves.'

'Well, where is the freight?'

'On the truck. I've already taken one load earlier this evening.'

Let me see your papers!' The guard demanded.

'They're in my cab. I'll go get them.'

The carrier waved as the group's leader directed his proteges towards the back of the truck—waiting until the tail lift was low enough to load them onto the truck.

But before they were loaded, a loud crack shattered the tense silence as the guard approached the vehicle and then a sharp, sickening pain in his head sent him reeling. He vomited, collapsed in a heap and passed out.

From behind the truck, the leader had heard the bloodcurdling slam and the clatter of a metallic object dropping as he kept his distance.

The attacker, wearing a black ski mask, bent down to grab the metal bar then took off into the night, disappearing in a maze of container boxes as swiftly as he had appeared.

'Give me a hand over here,' shouted the driver to his accomplice after approaching the limp body, nudging the victim in the loins with his boot.

'Just checking to see if he's still alive. Grab him under the arms and help me turn him onto his back.'

The trucker took the guard's feet, clutching his heavy leather boots tight as they rolled him while his helper lifted the torso.

When they finished, the driver looked up, shaking his head. 'He's gone, all right. Let's get your people into the lorry and out of here.'

Suddenly, his frightened assistant began waving his hands in the air, motioning him to stop.

'Wait—listen! Sounds like police sirens close by,' he blurted in perfect English.

'Steady on—you can hear them in this city twenty-four seven, But just in case, let's get them loaded,' the driver roared.

Suddenly, a shrill whirring sound echoed from the main gate of the huge container terminal. The driver's face paled.

He bolted to the front of the vehicle, jumped in the cab and raced off—disappearing out of the wharf, leaving half the passengers and their escort behind in the dark, gaping with terror-stricken faces awaiting their doom.

A police car raced towards them, stopping in front of the victims with blinding headlights. When a second vehicle arrived from a different direction, the onlookers lit up like a Christmas tree in a town square, as the officers lurched at them.

Two Weeks Later

Summer reached across the table for the lemon curd, spooning dollops onto her multi-grain toast.

'Coffee?' said Tony, her husband, picking up the plunger.

'Yes, thanks. Don't you have to shoot off? You'll be late.'

'No, not yet. I worked all those long hours last night, so that justifies me going in a bit later. There's something I want to discuss with you,' he replied, pouring her coffee.

'Sounds ominous. Hope it's not to do with us.'

'No, not that kind of talk. It's something at work bugging me—I'm unsure what to do.'

Summer knew most things happening in the Strand Police Station Tony usually kept to himself—especially criminal cases, unless the information had been made public.

'You remember the human trafficking case at the Port earlier this month when my team on the graveyard shift had sprung the Thai people in the shipping container? It was all over the news.'

'Yeah—you mean involving the security guard who was killed? You thought the Thai escort was innocent.'

'That's the one. There's something dodgy going on with Rob Dean to do with that case.'

Summer stopped eating her toast and licked her fingers. 'Like what?'

Tony explained what had taken place at the station with his sidekick, Detective Constable Samantha Evans—known by her colleagues as Sam.

'Sam had seen Dean enter the evidence deposit room without Property Officer Williams. She knew the DSS had breached the procedure for handling forensic exhibits by entering the storage room alone and reported it to me.'

'When did she see him do it?'

'It was the day following the murder—after I'd placed the security guard's clothing in the station's evidence storage room after Forensics had finished with them early that morning.'

'Do you think the DSS was tampering with evidence from the Port killing?'

Tony began wringing his hands. 'I can't say for certain, but he was up to something. Later, when I cornered him in the men's toilets and asked why he was in the evidence lockup unattended, he became defensive—outright nasty.'

Summer began picking at a cuticle on her fingernail. 'I've sensed you've been troubled the past few weeks. What's happening at the station now with all this?'

'Since that day, Dean has had it in for me—always trying to find fault. At one point, he insinuated I'd helped a gang member during a drug bust—covering up for him. When I threatened to report him to the

Superintendent for intimidation, he retracted his slur.'

'I thought he was your friend. When you first joined the city force, he often dropped by to visit, but he seems to have lost interest the past few years.'

'Yeah—because he knows I can see right through him after I twigged he's not as straight as he makes out.'

Tony got up to grab his car keys from the sideboard then kissed her.

'Don't concern yourself with all this, my love—I can sort it out. Perhaps after work, we can go over your plans for the guest house. I've got two weeks off from tomorrow.'

'Oh, wait. Remember, I promised Mum I would come and stay with her. The carer said she's able to go for short walks and seems more talkative, but recovery from her recent stroke is slow and I'm worried. Pity Dad isn't alive to help—but I suppose he has been spared from the grief of Mum losing her faculties.'

'Sorry, love. I forgot you were going this week, but I'll still be on leave when you return. Work on your plan and we'll look at it when you get back.'

'Sure, I won't be away for long, and Mum's only in Cheltenham—a stone's throw away.' Her face brightened. 'So you're happy for me to run the B&B now? You said you were too busy to think about it.'

'True—that was last week. But I've mulled it over and realise I'm earning enough now for you to take on staff to help run the place.'

'Oh, wow! I can't believe it's almost happening.'

'I'll also be in for a pay rise when I pass my Detective Senior Sergeant exams, and once you get paying guests, the place will support itself. You can rally around and find someone to help with the cooking and housekeeping and hire a landscape contractor too, but I can sort that out.'

Summer got up and wrapped her arms around him. 'Aw, thanks, darling. I'd hoped you'd give in.'

'I told the guys at work yesterday about our landscaping plans, and I've also put the word out we want quotes for the water fountain.'

'Put the word out—how?'

'By putting up a notice on the community board at our local dairy.'

'Great! I'm so excited. It's going to work—I guarantee it.'

'Must race off now, but perhaps I can start by clearing the old orchard—see you tonight.'

'Awesome—I'll cook something special,' she replied, waving him out the door.

~

Summer had a skip in her step for the rest of the day as she walked along the hallway holding a clipboard and pen, inspecting the rooms one by one.

The house had four double bedrooms each boasting an ensuite bathroom.

There were three single bedrooms for commercial travellers and a common bathroom containing two showers assigned to them.

Tony and Summer slept in the larger double room, which opened into a small lounge. They also had an Ensuite.

Their private accommodation was separated from the remaining part of the guest house.

Summer had thought of turning this area it into a family suite once the B&B got up and running, but she and Tony both needed their own space, and that was their little flat. Her grandparents had once used it for their privacy, too.

The rooms all needed upgrading, and the outdoor areas and garden were also a proper eyesore.

Summer opened the door of the first double room, scanning the dated wallpaper and old-fashioned plaster cornices on the ceiling. Even the wool carpet, although of excellent quality, was 1970s. She could see it was going to take thousands of dollars to refurbish the whole place. But if she did it gradually, Tony won't mind the cost so much.

She finished going through the house itemising a to-do list then flopped into a seat leaning on the dining table, propping her chin on one hand.

The morning had nearly gone while Summer sat daydreaming about house renovations, imagining the place booked out with guests.

She'd definitely have to have a housekeeper and with another person helping with breakfasts and laundry she'd manage but would need to advertise on various hosted websites.

Summer visualised a cascading stone fountain suitable for birds, with a shallow pond below—which Tony had once suggested—together with a path leading to a fruit grove lined with plum and peach trees. She'll have berries too. The various fruits will be used solely in the kitchen, offered at breakfast or with smoothies for the guests during the summer months. And hens with pet names searching for worms in the orchard.

She continued with her pipedreams of various homemade foods she could produce—fresh yoghurt with berries and granola, free-range eggs and her own baked grain bread. Of course, there'll be raspberry jam made from her grandmother's cherished recipe.

Her sweet daydreams instantly dissolved after a call from her mother's carer to say her Mum was incessantly asking when she was coming.

Since her first stroke, the woman had become fretful, and Summer didn't want to cause her any more distress than necessary. That's why she and Tony had moved her from Taranaki into a Rest Home in Auckland to be closer.

Tony rang to say he'll be late home from work and asked Summer to put aside a meal. She'd eaten already and placed a bowl of Spaghetti Bolognaise in the microwave before stretching out on the sofa in front of the television in their flat.

She lay on the couch watching a new crime series. Her friends could never understand why Summer was so interested in morbid TV programs after years of working as a police media advisor and married to a homicide detective. Surely she'll want a break from it.

This TV program was a gangland series following the exploits of a corrupt senior police officer living a double life as a so-called upstanding detective and pillar of the community involved in organised crime.

Her mind started doing somersaults as the plot played out, compounding her hidden anger at what Tony had told her about Rob Dean. Was he capable of living two lives and what if Tony's suspicions were justified while everyone else turned a blind eye to corruption in the Force?

She couldn't relax after the TV program had triggered anxious thoughts about the vulnerable, young, Thai escort who had accompanied ship stowaways and hidden them in an empty shipping container at an Auckland shipping terminal.

Chai was involved in the human trafficking industry, whether he clearly understood what part he played.

But murder was something else. Tony didn't believe the Thai man killed the security guard, so who else could have done it?

Summer had to persuade her husband to pursue the investigation. It was this intense curiosity of hers that had once made her a top police reporter.

~

When Tony arrived home from work that night, he found Summer fast asleep. He realised she must have been exhausted—not from physical activity, but from sitting in bed with her laptop looking at the internet while sketching designs for their newly landscaped backyard. She had fallen into a deep sleep and didn't hear him arrive home. He climbed into bed beside her after closing her computer, which he placed on the dressing table and plugged into a charger.

~

'Wakey-wake!' A blurred figure pulled back the drapes, letting the intense sunrays pierce Summer's brain.

'I've got your breakfast here—just for a change.' Tony bent down and kissed her cheek.

Summer opened one eye, blinded by the light, wondering why all the attention—it wasn't her birthday.

'Wow, a treat—thank you. What's the occasion?' she mumbled, rubbing her eyes while straining to focus them on the bacon and eggs on toast, juice and a mug of coffee.

'You're off to see your mother in Cheltenham later today. I'm going to miss you.' He sat on the bed next to her.

'Aw ... I won't be gone for long—less than a week I hope, but Mum has been missing Dad since her stroke. Anyway—I expected you to do lots of fishing and kayaking with your mates. I'll be in the way.'

'Let's go for a long stroll along the waterfront before you go. We can take a packed lunch and spend time together before you head off this afternoon,' said Tony.

'I'd love that, and we could pick up a coffee-to-go. How about wearing swimming gear under our clothes? It's so warm,' she replied.

'I'm all in. A great way to spend my first day off in a long while,' said Tony.

'Right, and I can have you all to myself.'

Summer loved sharing the breaks Tony could take from his intense job. They had little time together, and she was determined his police work would not impede their marriage.

~

Tony rang Summer later in the week just as she had finished eating breakfast one morning with her mother.

'I've got a surprise for you in the backyard when you come home. I'm dying to show you, but it'll have to wait.'

'Oh—please tell me what you've been doing. You'll have to now.'

'No, I can't do that. It won't be a surprise, will it? There's something else too. A landscape designer phoned me to say he'd seen the advert I had placed on the community notice board.'

'Awesome! I can't wait to get the fountain installed. When can he come?'

'He wanted to drop around late this morning, but I told him I'll be out all day. He'll pop by tomorrow. Funny—his voice sounded somewhat familiar, but his mobile appeared to break up so I could have been mistaken.'

'Oh, okay—what have you got planned today?'

'Not sure yet. I could see if Mick's free to go kayaking or maybe I'll just go hiking alone—take a coastal walk from Achilles Point to Karaka Bay. I haven't done that track for ages.'

'Are you going at low tide along the shore or up the road through the bush and Pohutukawa?'

'I'll take the beach—much less risk of running into tourists or screaming kids.

'Great. You used to like that walk. Just goes to show how much your work has drained the life out of you—it doesn't leave you any room for recreation.'

'Yes, love, you keep on telling me. To be honest—I'm tired of working around the clock all hours. Perhaps I can change all that.'

Summer's eyes widened. 'And do what—stop being a detective?'

Tony dug his hands inside his pockets. 'I could leave the Force—become a private detective working the hours I choose. I'll probably make more money than I'm earning at the station. A couple of my lawyer friends have asked if I would be interested in working with them.'

This was an about turn for Tony. Summer couldn't grasp what he meant, but she had to get off the phone and attend to her mother.

'Let's discuss it when you return home. I hope the landscaper turns up. You know how unreliable tradesmen can be,' said Tony.

'See you back home tomorrow evening, but I'll probably wait until the peak traffic quietens before going over the bridge.'

'Great—perhaps we can go to the fish restaurant down the road for a meal. I'll book a table for eight. See you then ... love you,' Tony replied.

'Sounds wonderful—love you, too. Night-night.'

'Oh, don't forget to give my regards to your mother.'

Summer's eyes sparkled when she got off the phone. This was the beginning of a new chapter in her life, running a B&B—apart from hired help. She had always felt insignificant since relinquishing her role as a full-time police crime reporter, and at last, she could get her teeth into her own business—something a heap less taxing than following macabre criminal cases.

2

Soon after midday, when Tony had finished lunch, he began working on the surprise he had for Summer. While she was staying with her mother, he had slaved away, creating a beautiful brick patio area. It was one of the design options he and Summer had chosen for their new fountain. He had left a circular area of ground unpaved, which he had precisely measured to prepare for the rockery cascade installation.

Two tradesmen had phoned earlier in the day with offers for quotes. Tony told them he would be at the site all afternoon if they dropped by.

He had just started digging the centre well when he was startled by a man who must have entered his gate on foot.

There was no vehicle in sight. He greeted the young tradesman dressed in faded Jeans, a hoodie and muddy leather boots, who handed him his business card.

Tony questioned in his mind whether the fellow would be hardworking and reliable enough to take on the massive landscaping project but took a chance.

He explained to the stranger he wanted to find the water table before starting on the fountain's construction.

'I'll bet it's barely a metre down,' said the man. 'Let me look.' He swept a hand through his unkempt, bushy hair and pulled on his leather gardening gloves.

'You've dug a fair bit of it yourself I see?' said the contractor.

'Yeah—I thought it would reduce the cost,' Tony replied with a half-smile.

The man pointed at an enormous pile of alpine schist rocks stacked nearby.

'For your fountain, are they? I'll bet they set you back a dollar to two.'

Tony nodded. 'Yep, they came from the South Island.'

Once they discussed how deep the foundation should be, the tradesman took the spade and began digging out the topsoil until he hit the hard claypan layer.

'There—see the moisture slowly forming? You'll have to bend down closer and look.'

Tony strained to get his head down into the cavity. 'Yeah, I see it. Thanks.'

It all unfolded in a flash, and Tony didn't see it coming as his six-foot-tall body slammed towards the hard ground. An unyielding object had smashed his skull and the blow to his head was so hard it rattled his jaw, breaking his front teeth. The last thing he could remember was the warm, metallic-tasting fluid leaking into his mouth, making him retch, and his head feeling as though it had exploded. As he lay spread-eagled face-down next to the clay pit, he lifted a hand to locate the pain in his head as blood oozed between his fingers while he fought the urge to pass out. Within seconds, he lay powerless as the bloodied darkness enveloped him.

~

The sun descended under the sea's horizon as Olive Wood left her house, heading next door to visit Summer.

She bustled along the driveway in her fluffy slippers, clutching a small Tupperware container. The sea breeze prompted her to reposition her woollen shawl as she shuffled towards her neighbour's gate, shuddering.

All she needed was a cup of flour, as once again, she'd forgotten to check her pantry before starting baking.

Her friend, Summer, always came to the rescue. Olive hadn't seen her for a while but knew she had planned to visit her sick mother in Cheltenham but couldn't remember exactly when it was—this week or next?

The letter box had been cleared—Olive observed while passing. Now she wished she hadn't worn her slippers while walking on Summer's broken driveway, struggling to keep on the grass edging.

It was nearly six o'clock as the sun began waving goodbye behind the sea. Olive sensed an uncanny stillness as she stumbled along to her neighbour's home.

The windows were open in the kitchen as she went onto tiptoes, craning her neck to look inside.

'Are you home, Summer? It's Olive. Hope you don't mind—I need to borrow a cup of flour,' she called sheepishly. No Answer. It was dead still.

Casting her gaze towards the garage, she spotted Tony's unmarked police vehicle—his Skoda—parked in front. This unnerved Olive.

Strange, as it appeared they were home. Usually, the television would be on for the headline news at this time. Tony often watched it lying back on the couch holding a beer can in his hand while waiting for Summer to serve dinner.

Walking up the front steps and peering through the locked glass ranchslider, she called, 'Are you there, Tony—it's Olive?'

Frustrated, she wandered around to the back and up the steps, pounding at the wooden door, which was also locked. There was not a whisper in return.

She guessed the couple were out in the orchard or working on Summer's elaborate landscaping design.

Olive hesitated, not wishing to disturb them if they were slogging away on the section but decided she must get a cup of flour for the cake she'd promised her granddaughter for her twelfth birthday.

Treading cautiously across the backyard towards the small orchard, careful not to stumble on the clay and debris lying on the path, she called out again.

'Summer, Tony! Is anyone at home?'

In the backyard, from a short distance, she saw a large patch of ground that had been cleared—most likely for Summer's new fountain.

Stepping furtively closer, she spotted what looked like a pile of washing on the ground, lying in the clay.

Having left her spectacles at home, it was much of a blur until she edged closer, making her way nervously towards the mysterious object until suddenly halting.

The shock of seeing her neighbour, Tony, lying prone, caught Olive's breath short. She clutched her chest, gasping.

'Oh, no ... Tony!

She wanted to cry but pulled herself together—aware of her responsibility to alert the police. First, she bent over and saw he had a nasty head wound—his thick, curly hair matted and congealed with dark blood. Olive gagged.

'You poor fellow. What happened?'

She leaned over, checking a wrist for a pulse. His hand was cold and limp.

'Oh no.' She grasped his shoulders, trying to shake him. 'Tony—can you hear me? It's Olive from next door.' He lay dead still. 'I'll go for help.'

Olive, ready to rush inside and use Tony's landline, remembered their doors were locked. She had no mobile phone so hurried awkwardly back down the driveway in her slippers, which were now covered in wet clay.

Arriving home, she called the police.

~

Officers had cordoned off the crime scene. A female constable was busy interviewing Olive next door on her veranda. She was still in a state of shock.

Detective Sergeant Mick Randall from the Criminal Investigation Branch arrived at the scene, stopping his vehicle in the parking lot next to the guest house.

Mick's stomach turned as he edged his way across Summer's backyard.

Anxiously, he approached his friend's lifeless body, which lay next to a freshly dug hole, observing that Tony's clothes were soiled by clay mixed with blood.

Next to the corpse lay a bloodied spade. The assailant must have planned it, Mick assumed—and worn gloves. Otherwise, they wouldn't have left a weapon lying at the crime scene.

'I think he has gone—I called an ambulance,' muttered the constable, standing next to the body, grim faced.

'Forensics are on their way too,' Mick replied. 'They'll have to test the spade for fingerprints in case his attacker was careless.'

Mick struggled to look at Tony—his colleague, and friend who had often confided in him. Just as he spotted something poking out the back pocket of the victim's Jeans, the forensic team arrived with Charles, the pathologist.

Mick pulled a card out from Tony's trouser pocket with a gloved hand and before passing it to Charles, he saw it belonged to a landscape contractor. The pathologist gave it to one of the forensic team who placed it in an evidence bag.

Before leaving the property, Mick sent an awkward message to Summer's mobile.

Reluctant to describe Tony's gory details over the phone, he instructed her to go directly to the Strand Station and meet him there.

He explained that her home was now a crime scene, and she mustn't return until the forensic investigation was completed.

Summer was devastated. She just wanted to see Tony. Mick told her she would get the chance once the coroner was finished with him.

Was this a planned attack, or just a random opportunist walking off the street hoping to steal something?

It's possible the killer had cased the garage for an easy point of entry and was spooked when he spotted Tony working in the backyard.

Mick left the rest of the investigation to Charles and his team and headed back to the station in time to comfort Summer.

~

Beads of perspiration dripped off Mick's furrowed brow onto his face. He pulled a handkerchief out of his pocket, wiping his cheeks dry before pulling into the station's car park. He didn't want Summer to see how upset he was about Tony while she needed his support.

Sam had drawn Summer aside and sat her in the interview room while she ducked off to get her a cup of tea.

The bereaved woman leaned over the table, resting her head on crossed hands. Sam placed the cup beside her on the table and wrapped her arms around the woman's shoulders.

'I have tea and biscuits for you. So sorry about Tony—I'll deeply miss him too. He was an awesome person to work with.'

Sam reached over to pass her a box of tissues. Large half-moons had formed deep craters under her eyes.

'I still don't understand why your team wouldn't let me onto my property.'

Sam stared at the ground. 'Let me pour your tea,' was about all she could muster.

'Thanks—milk, no sugar.'

Before Sam could think of anything more to say, Mick knocked, stepping into the room. The constable hastily retreated.

'I'll leave you to it,' Sam said to Mick. 'There's a pile of work on my desk I have to get through.'

When the officer had left, Mick joined Summer at the table, who had wiped her face dry and started sipping her tea.

'Can you provide me with any information about the days leading up to Tony's death? I believe you were staying with your Mum and spoke to him on the phone that week,' said Mick.

Summer explained that Tony had received a call from a tradesman offering to quote the installation of their water fountain. He was going to drop by, but Summer didn't know whether he had come to the house following that phone conversation with Tony.

Mick cleared his throat and began twirling a button on his shirt.

'Did Tony mention the contractor's name?'

'No, he just said the guy had seen his advert at the local dairy.'

Mick rubbed the stubble on his chin with an index finger. 'Summer, I know this might sound insulting—but is there any possibility Tony was seeing another woman.'

Her face turned the colour of a tomato. She pursed her lips like a trout. 'How can you insinuate such a thing—that's terrible suspecting my husband of playing around? We've always been happily married!'

Mick could see he was only causing her more duress.

'I can't understand anyone wanting to hurt someone like Tony. Everyone liked him,' Summer muttered.

Mick placed a hand on her shoulder. 'We're going to need a statement from you regarding your movements during the past forty-eight hours.'

'That's simple. I was away in Cheltenham staying with my mother who is ill. The staff at her residential home can vouch for me.'

'We'll find Tony's killer, I promise. When we're finished here, I'll take you to the morgue to identify him.'

Summer sat back on her chair, holding the teacup with a blank look in her glassy eyes. She could barely say any more except a feeble, 'Thanks, Mick, you're a good friend. I must contact my family in Australia now,' sobbing again.

3

Three months later

Summer reached over and lowered the roller blinds to block the sun streaming into the conservatory. Jane, her long-standing friend, had dropped by to visit. They were both eager to catch up with their latest news—something which only happened when Jane drove up from Thames to see her family in Auckland.

'Petra's bringing us tea—my extra help in the kitchen.'

Jane flicked her eyebrows. 'Oh, quite the lady now.'

'Wait till you meet my new gardener.' Summer winked.

'He must be the hunky eye candy I passed in the driveway as I drove in.'

'Remember, I told you that my grandparents ran this place as a guest house during the fifties.'

Jane nodded, her eyes scanning the length of the colonial bungalow with its flaking white paint.

'I love the railings with flowers growing up them,' she said, pointing to the sides of the veranda.

'Clematis and old-fashioned roses,' Summer replied.

'I understand, as an only child, you inherited the home from your grandparents. I don't wish to pry, but I wondered why they didn't leave the house to your parents.'

'No, you aren't prying. My grandparents left it in Trust to me but gave my parents a life interest so long as they lived in it. My folks convinced them that with Mum's health being bad, they didn't need the worry of an immense house that needed major maintenance, so they signed it over to me. Also, with this home being a Heritage house, they didn't want the hassle of complying with all the regulations. They said it was better for a younger couple to take care of it. Their judgement was ratified by Dad dying unexpectedly from a coronary embolism not long after they made that decision.'

'Why didn't you and Tony run the home as a guesthouse after you had inherited it? In the heart of St Heliers Bay, it would be a goldmine.'

'There was no way we could do that initially. A detective's life in the Organised

Crime Squad is a killer for togetherness as a couple, so we just lived in the house.'

Jane nodded. 'I get what you mean. Quite stressful.'

'That's right. But prior to his assault, he was ready to complete his exams for Detective Senior Sergeant, which meant he was in for a major pay rise. He'd agreed that once he went up the ladder, we could afford to hire someone to help me run the Bed and Breakfast as a viable business.'

'Oh, no. Poor man. I'll bet he couldn't wait to pass his exams, knowing how much you wanted to start your business. Such a pity for you both.'

'Well—thanks to Tony's life insurance, I'm now able to pay staff and go ahead. I've called my guest house, St Heliers Bay B&B.'

Summer knew Jane didn't have had the faintest clue what she'd been through with having a husband working at the heart of underworld crime.

Despite the limited amount of recreational time they had spent together, loving memories of special occasions spent with him rose in her mind—cutting into her heart and reminding her how much she missed him.

'What's happening with your family in Australia?'

'The two kids have gone ahead in Sydney since we moved back here,' Summer replied.

'What are they doing?'

'Pete finished his law degree and is a partner in an established legal firm. Ava is a qualified social worker.'

'They've done well,' said Jane. 'Neither careers are for the faint-hearted.'

'Exactly! Like the life of a cop. Their lifestyle is no match for New Zealand. They stayed there for the high salaries, warm climate, and cheaper housing.'

Summer knew sensitivity was needed with Jane. After years of a blissful marriage, she had lost her husband, Brandon, to cancer. Material assets were not currently high on her agenda.

'Do you hear much from your kids these days? I would hate it if mine lived in another country.'

Summer looked away, deflecting her regret of living so far apart from her children, especially since she had become widowed.

'Mostly only on WhatsApp, but I saw them at Tony's funeral. They fly over here when they can get away from their work—which isn't often, sadly.'

'It must be dead quiet in this magnificent mansion.'

'Oh no, it's hardly a mansion. I do miss the family, but I'm kept busy now that I have guests slowly trickling in. I recently employed my domestic help Petra—who lives in—and Liam who is here most days.'

'Lucky you! So, what do you get up to when you're not rattling around all these rooms each day?'

'I have grand plans for my acre of land—beginning with the installation of a fully landscaped English country garden with flagstones and a special water feature—a pond with a schist stone fountain. Liam will have a major job clearing out the overgrowth in the orchard and digging up the hard ground before he designs the main plot. I'll keep him on permanently to maintain the rest of the property, including my lawns.'

'It sounds exciting. If I lived in Auckland, I'd offer to help you out too.'

'It's okay, I should be able to manage with two workers—depends on how busy we get,' Summer replied.

'I thought you were doing freelance investigative journalism now—or so I heard. This B&B thing is something out of the box,' said Jane.

'Oh—I only get to do it occasionally now with having to get this place up and running. I still get requests from some newspapers and companies who know me, but my time is at a premium these days.'

Summer wanted to say she could see herself writing a True Crime story of Tony's death but kept it zipped. The timing was wrong.

They sat on the veranda soaking up the sun drinking Earl Grey tea and revelling in

Petra's fresh scones—reminiscing on old times when they got together with their families while the children were small.

By the time her friend left, Summer felt drained, especially as Jane had popped in a few questions about Tony's demise, which disturbed her. She had intended to tell her she suspected corruption in Tony's police unit, but all she had said to Jane was that the case was closed.

~

Summer had a basic idea of how the police force functioned from her past employment as a crime reporter and later a media advisor for the NZ Police.

She had heard stories that could make a person's hair curl.

It was at the station that she had first met Tony—before Dean's arrival—and after a brief courtship they married.

They were both keen to see Australia. Tony had accepted a post in Sydney with the New South Wales Police where he gradually climbed the ranks to Detective Sergeant.

Although Summer was no longer working for the NZ Police as their Media Advisor, she kept her hand in working casually as a freelance Digital Reporter.

While they lived in Australia, Summer gave birth to their two children, Ava and Peter.

It took the devastating shock of a horrific accident that took the lives of her grandparents—the stress of it causing her father's fatal heart attack—and the subsequent rapid deterioration of her mother's health to make Summer realise just how homesick she was for New Zealand.

Tony was offered a position with the Criminal Investigation Branch in Auckland, and they both returned without their children who were living their independent lives.

They had no desire to leave their friends and country to move to New Zealand, so their parents left Australia without them.

After shifting into her grandparents' stately home, Summer often mused over running a guest house, but at the time, Tony hadn't quite warmed to the idea.

~

Summer hadn't seen a soul apart from the patrons of the guesthouse since Jane's visit the previous week until Mick Randall dropped by.

He'd been a staunch friend and colleague of Tony's and a tremendous support to Summer following his friend's death.

'Long time, no see,' Mick said, as he wrapped a muscly, tattooed arm around her.

Summer guessed he was fond of her. But as he was a staid bachelor, she'd always been careful, as a married woman, not to let Mick bear-hug her as he did with most people. Perhaps it was herself she didn't quite trust.

But now Tony was gone. She lowered her defences a little, grateful for Mick's emotional support.

'I guess you have little time on your hands to visit friends these days,' said Summer.

'You're so right. It's a wonder I have any left.'

'Things will change for me soon. I'll be running off my feet, just like you.'

'Oh, so you're serious about the B&B idea?'

'It's not just an idea. You know my grandparents operated it as a guesthouse for decades—I want to carry on the tradition. It's a pity they let it get so run down in their old age.'

'I think it could be a decent money-earner around here. There isn't one for miles along the coast.'

'Coffee? I'll get my new staff member to make it.'

'No thanks, just a cold drink will do if you don't mind.'

'Let's sit out on the veranda. I'll be back in a tick.' Summer went to the kitchen and prepared a plate of cheese and crackers, placing them on a tray with two cans of soft drinks and glasses.

'I've only got Coke and Tonic Water.'

'Coke's fine thanks,' he said, as Summer placed the tray next to him on a small table while he helped himself to the food.

'So, you've taken on staff?'

'Well, I can't run the place on my own. Petra's a genuine treasure,' Summer replied. 'You'll meet her someday. I think she's busy doing a pile of ironing right now.'

They finally got to discussing Tony's case—how Mick had agreed with Tony that their immediate boss, Detective Senior Sergeant Rob Dean, was dodgy, but they couldn't blow the whistle on him without absolute proof.

Mick brought up the human trafficking case and police investigation, which had been all over the news, involving a dozen stowaways of various ages who had arrived at the Port hidden inside a false wall of a shipping container.

They were discovered around midnight by a security guard while a driver was loading them onto the truck. An altercation followed during which the guard was murdered, and the driver took off, leaving some migrants stranded on the wharf with their leader.

Those left behind had given evidence to the police and Immigration officers. The young Thai leader had been arrested for the crime and was currently held in a remand cell. He continued to protest his innocence.

The day after the forensic team had lodged the exhibits for the Port killing in the station's evidence deposit locker, Sam, Tony's partner, had spotted Dean coming out of the room alone without the property officer.

After she had reported the serious incident to Tony, he notified Mick, who warned him to stay out of it. There was no way he could prove anything, and Dean would make sure he could never work with the New Zealand Police again. Mick did say—in his experience—that bent cops eventually tripped themselves up.

Summer listened, perplexed. 'I still find it absurd that Tony had always believed that the wrong person was jailed for the guard's murder. Why would Dean have covered it up?'

Mick rubbed her arm. Not in a creepy way—just kind-heartedly. She accepted his warm advances. During Mick's long friendship with Tony, Summer had always been careful not to encourage him or give him mixed signals. It would be unfair.

Tony had told Summer that Mick was a lonely guy and although a bachelor, had experienced enough broken relationships.

'You've got to let it go, Summer—before it does your head in and drives you mad.'

She tried not to sound irritated by him saying "let go" but annoyance rolled off her tongue.

'If you were in that situation—I mean, if someone you loved was killed you would not be so keen to shut up,' Summer retorted.

'And those poor women who got left behind after the truck driver took off before the police raid. Did they provide any more information about the racketeers?' she asked.

'Although they were terrified, they did speak to the police. It was obvious they were kept in the dark about who their prospective employers were and who owned the illegal migrant scheme. So was their escort, Chai,' Mick replied.

Summer persisted in questioning Mick. She couldn't accept all the injustice.

'You said Chai speaks articulate English. That's unusual, isn't it?'

'Not really—that's why the traffickers used him.'

Mick told Chai's story.

'His late father was British, and his mother was Thai. After Chai was born, they remained in Thailand. When he was a teenager, his father was robbed and shot in front of his mother. Chai left school and took a job to take care of his two younger brothers and his mother until she died of leukaemia. He had spent most of his savings caring for her. Eventually, after leaving home, both he and his brothers went their separate ways, but Chai had heard they were struggling. That's when he accepted contract work as a highly paid chaperone—smuggling migrants into New Zealand and sometimes Australia. He planned to make enough money to support his brothers after his most recent job escorting stowaways from Thailand to Auckland.'

Summer's face dropped. 'That's awful—what a tragic story.'

Mick continued. 'That must have been why he got desperate enough to risk hiding on a boat to come here. He said that his hirers were going to pay him big money for seeing it through once they were all loaded on the truck and delivered safely to their new employers.'

It pulled at Summer's heartstrings, listening to Mick giving a rundown of Chai's story. It was the first time she'd heard it—but now she wanted the detective to focus.

'Mick, you're the only one who believes the assault on the Port guard was an inside job. Tony was aware Dean had it in for him after he pushed to have the DNA found on the guard's boots and safety jacket re-analysed.'

'Yes—and you and I know Tony shouldn't have discussed it with you, but I understand he was at his wit's end when Chai was jailed.'

'Where do you think the truck driver took those people?' Summer asked, ignoring Mick's unsubtle comment.

'I guess you've seen the news. The media has been all over this case. Chai confessed he was to be paid for escorting a group of illegal migrant workers from Bangkok to New Zealand. They first hid on a cargo ship—an inside job—and then transferred to an empty shipping container on the boat before berthing in Auckland. Once in the dock, the box with the stowaways was deposited onto the shipping terminal amongst a heap of empty ones. Chai was to return to Bangkok by plane the following day. His bosses offered him a large sum of money to accompany the people to New Zealand but had kept him and the other stowaways in the dark about the nature of the business. The migrants were to be transported by truck to their dodgy workplaces and lodgings after being promised well-paid jobs,' said Mick.

'What happened to the boat people who were abandoned at the wharf when the police turned up?'

'They've been placed in a refugee centre as they're now seeking political asylum. None of them can speak English and the interpreter couldn't get much sense out of them except that they paid big money to come here for work and better living conditions—what a joke! They were better off where they came from.'

Mick finished his Coke and continued. 'Chai had said the murder weapon was a wheel wrench, but the Maritime Police divers had searched the harbour by the wharves and there was no sign of it. The driver must have disposed of it elsewhere, which makes the investigation even more difficult.'

Summer pursued her train of thought.

'I keep telling you Rob Dean must be involved somehow. Tony wouldn't lie—all our married life I have trusted him implicitly.'

'Okay, okay. Let's go over the facts again and see if there are any flaws in how our team handled it. Tell me what concerns you most,' said Mick, picking up on her desperation.

'Right,' Summer replied. 'This is what Tony had said about the incident.'

'His partner, Sam, had spotted Dean leaving the evidence storage room unaccompanied by the property officer. While she was waiting to give the custodian an evidence deposit from a burglary, the storage attendant wandered off to the men's room after Dean had whispered something in his ear.'

'We already know all this,' Mick murmured.

Summer ignored him and began rubbing her temples. She was tired of this same thread too, but it was important to get it right.

She took a deep breath and let it go loudly then continued.

'Briefly, while the storage locker was left unmonitored, Dean entered it alone and came out just as the property officer returned. Sam reported the incident to Tony who suspected Dean had tampered with evidence.'

'What are you getting at?' Mick's eyebrows snapped together as the tone of his voice changed.

'Please, listen a minute! When Tony told you he suspected Dean was involved in trafficking, which I realise was a hefty burden to place on a police colleague, why didn't you have the evidence re-examined as he asked you?' She blurted.

'Not that simple, Summer. Do you know how risky it would have been for either me or Tony to report him to the Anti-Corruption Unit? You can't do it unless you catch them in the act or have hard facts. I'll get the evidence re-examined once I've got sufficient proof Dean is involved in the racket.'

'But Sam did catch him!'

'No—she didn't go into the deposit room and see him exchange the evidence bags or tamper with the paperwork. When questioned, Dean said he was there to deposit fingerprints for an unrelated case. The property officer had let him in while he rushed to the bathroom, as he knew Dean well and trusted him.'

'Rubbish! It was one brilliant cover-up. The custodian wouldn't have done that for Tony.'

'No, but Dean is the head of his department, so more entitled.'

'Entitled to corruption,' Summer growled. Mick combed his fingers through his thick hair—aged-looking, although only in his late forties. 'Sorry, Summer—I don't know what you want me or anyone to do to help you accept that the case is closed. Perhaps you should have been a detective. You would have been a goer.'

Summer couldn't stop ranting. There was something Mick was missing about the whole saga.

'You know Tony confronted Dean about tampering with the evidence. He denied it, of course, and from that day onwards he rode Tony into the ground—placing him on long shifts, mostly night duty involving the worst crimes.'

'Yes, I heard all about it.'

'I don't care what you say, Mick. I will not stop until I find out what that swine was up to. This is something I'll never let go of until I find answers. Dean's still living a lie while that poor young fellow from Thailand could be locked up here for years with no support.'

Mick gave her a disapproving look and shook his head.

'What about the truck that transported the migrants away from the Port? Surely you can track that down with the mover's name—*Tried-and-True Movers* you told me was caught on CCTV.'

'We did a trace on that vehicle and there is no such company name. It would have been fake, and the number plate was also false.'

'Unbelievable!' Summer sat fuming briefly, then continued. 'You told me you have a friend in the Anti-Corruption Unit. Can't you ask him to be a mole and monitor the activity on the wharves to see if Dean turns up? If he's involved in a human trafficking racket, he's bound to appear at the Port, eventually.'

Mick sucked in a breath, then exhaled noisily. 'They haven't got the resources to do random hit-and-miss surveillance with no sign of criminal activity.'

'Well, if they can't do it, perhaps I can.'

'I wouldn't if I were you. He may associate with hardened criminals or gangs and will soon be alerted if you're spying on him. Anyway—there's no way he'll go anywhere near the wharves after the assault on the guard if he's involved. We need absolute proof before anyone goes digging.'

'I'll get it. As you say, he'll trip himself up one day and I'll be around when he does.'

'Well, lass, it's slightly difficult—don't you think—now that you're no longer an official police reporter? I obviously can't talk you out of it, so be careful. It might just come back to bite you.'

Mick picked up his car keys. 'Thanks for the drink. I'll drop in and see how your guesthouse is coming along sometime soon.' He squeezed her arm and waved as he let himself out.

~

After Mick left the house, Summer wandered out to the backyard to see what Liam was doing. It was a warm day in early summer— too hot for him to be toiling in an overgrown garden. She made allowances for the fact he was strong and young—late twenties, she guessed. His shirt lay on the rock edging at the side of the lawn, and she noticed rivers of perspiration trickling down his back as they talked.

'It's going to take me a while to sort this lot out, I'm afraid to say.' He wiped the drips of sweat running off the end of his nose with the back of his hand before it landed in his mouth.

'Here—I've brought you freshly squeezed orange juice,' said Summer, passing him a glass. 'I keep it frozen all season and when thawed, it makes a refreshing drink.'

She sat on one of the garden chairs at the wooden outdoor table.

'Take a break and join me. I don't want to wear you out before you get to the important stuff.'

Liam chuckled, pulling a seat up next to her.

'Oh, you mean this great landscape design you have in mind. By the way—I've ordered the pond base and fountain you chose. Unfortunately, it won't arrive for a few months. It has to be shipped from Australia.'

'Yeah, I guessed as much, but I'm sure you have plenty of work to keep you going way before it arrives. Anyway, chill out and help yourself to the oat biscuits. I have a few things to do now, so I'll catch up with you tomorrow.'

Summer liked to spoil her workers. She had done a batch of baking while Petra was on her morning off and had enjoyed being in the kitchen.

Although remiss, she hadn't told Mick about her plans to stalk Rob Dean. Mick would go to every length to stop her if he knew.

~

The landscaping took forever, and Summer wasn't happy letting guests stay with the extensive construction underway in the backyard. She therefore restricted her guest list to overnight travellers only.

When the house was empty for several days, the decorators came and promptly completed their work—bar the office—in time for the next intake of lodgers.

Finally, the house was completely refurbished with freshly painted walls and new furniture for the lounge. It had been fun for Summer picking out coordinating fabrics for the family suites with cushions to match. For her, it was like a new beginning since Tony had gone.

Now she could concentrate on the one thing foremost in her mind—how to go about tracking Rob Dean. This required a strategic plan. Was she naïve, or could this work?

~

Before setting out the next morning to track Rob Dean, Summer gave Mick a call.

'I need a favour. Would you mind letting me know what Dean's roster is for this month, so I can at least have an inkling of his movements?'

She heard him sigh into the phone.

'You're at it again, aren't you—despite me warning you off? What part of no don't you understand? Come on, Summer, give me a break. You know I'm not being difficult—just cautious. I can't give out that information—you already know that!'

Just as she expected—Mick wouldn't play ball.

'Never mind. I'll just have to chance it instead.' She hung up on him abruptly, feeling a sense of betrayal from her friend.

That was it—she was now on her own with her decision to probe the secretive DSS.

Summer woke the next day feeling jaded. Hot milk before bed at night had helped, but despite falling asleep, she woke early before dawn, unrefreshed.

Lack of sleep had always affected Summer's mental stamina. Peering at her puffy eyes in the bathroom mirror, she was unsure if today was the best time to watch Dean's movements.

She took a leisurely shower, feeling her tense neck muscles unwind as she let the hot water run down her back. This, followed by Petra's cooked breakfast, set her up for the day.

It was a blessing she had recently traded in her car for a modern second-hand vehicle. Dean won't recognise this one. She and Tony had owned a lime-coloured Suzuki 4x4, which stuck out like a sore thumb. Her new silver Toyota Corolla blended in with the colour of the road—perfect for tracking corrupt police officers.

Summer grabbed her phone wallet off the dining table. It contained all of her electronic cards.

Petra brushed past, carrying a basket full of laundry. 'Off out, are you?'

'Just a few hours. If you can put the roast in the oven, I'll help you with dinner when I get back.'

'Will the guest from Wellington be staying in for an evening meal?'

'Yes, he'll be eating with us. He decided to stay on for another day. The woman in Room Six will be back for dinner too.'

So much for her establishment being a Bed and Breakfast.

When Summer had first opened the guest house, she reluctantly offered evening meals to patrons following requests from her regulars. Now, she was worried it would limit her time monitoring Dean.

'I'll manage, thanks—got it down to a fine art now,' said Petra. 'Don't rush back. Most of it will be done by the time you get back.'

Summer raced into the bedroom, checked her hair and left the house.

About to drive off, she remembered the notes she'd drafted as a plan of action to track Dean, which were on her dresser.

Racing back inside, tripping over the cat, she grabbed the list and then hurried back to the car.

As Summer approached the end of the driveway, she was filled with a sense of excited expectation at finding justice for both Tony and the young Thai fellow in prison, as she was sure both deaths were connected.

Just before she drove onto the street, Mick's unmarked, blue police car cruised past her gateway. Her phone began ringing furiously on the dashboard screen. It was Mick checking her out.

'Hi, there. Sorry, I can't talk right now— I'm about to go on a few errands,' Summer muttered, then hurtled off down the road.

4

Mick followed Summer's car from a distance, every so often hanging back, as she kept him in her sight through her vehicle's mirrors. She lost him when she turned into Dean's street, although Mick had guessed where she was headed and backed away.

Dean's 1930s, five-million-dollar white mansion stuck out like a sore thumb, set back from the road behind a black wrought-iron fence. A pricey possession for a mid-rank police detective.

Dean's home was already familiar to Summer, as she and Tony had visited there once—a stately house near the Rose Gardens in Parnell located amongst other high-end homes in a narrow street with limited parking.

Seeing the house for the first time, Tony had commented how Dean must have had a dollar or two—for a policeman, that is.

When Summer arrived, there were only a few parking spots left, but in luck again, she found one close enough to watch the house from across the road.

Dressed in a navy puff jacket and Jeans, she slunk down in the car seat—feeling like a gangster, pulling a woollen beanie over her head. Apart from the noise from a stranger mowing the lawns, there was no movement coming from Dean's mansion.

Summer continued to watch—baffled why the detective wanted to live in a massive house alone.

After an hour, just as she was about to get out of the car and stretch her legs, Dean's garage door opened. His new unmarked, silver Skoda Octavia car rolled out. The shiny beast captured the bright sunrays, instantly dazzling Summer. For a moment, her eyes couldn't zoom in on the figure at the steering wheel. She was too far away.

'Darn!' she blurted, rubbing her eyes.

As the iron gates opened, a car crawled through the gateway and stopped. The driver stepped out of the vehicle, bending over to check his letterbox. As he stood back up, Summer snapped a mugshot with her phone—triumphant. 'Gotcha!'

Waiting for him to drive off down the street, she fought the fear gripping her torso. Taking a deep breath as the car lurched forward, she kept the Skoda in view, but glancing at the fuel gauge she admonished herself for not checking it before setting out.

She followed him into the city centre, thinking he was going to visit the Port—up to his old tricks—when he veered off to

Karangahape Road, known as K Road. This was a central Auckland business district by day, and at night, a sleazy location Summer wouldn't usually visit. Now it was broad daylight, but at night it would be unsafe wandering around the street alone.

Dean pulled up at a shabby, unmarked building and stopped at the entrance to use a keypad. Up went a roller door and his car disappeared.

Cars piled up behind Summer and began tooting while she blocked the narrow road. There was no point in her searching for a nearby car park, now that Dean had gone into the building.

She recalled once going to a nearby market with a friend several years ago, where there was a public car park by a block of Asian shops and restaurants.

Luckily, the public car lot wasn't full and found a space conveniently near the entrance. She resented paying the five-dollar entry fee for thirty minutes.

'At this rate, it had better be worth the overrated price!' she muttered to herself.

Having forgotten to make herself a cut lunch that day, she ducked into one of the Asian food outlets and bought a bottle of juice and a steamed pork bun, which she slipped into her shoulder bag.

Amongst the food sellers were a mixture of cultures—people racing in and out during their morning tea breaks or for early lunches.

'Excuse me, but do you know what that white, unmarked building is on the corner?' she asked the elderly lady behind the counter of a fish outlet. 'I'm trying to find someone.'

The woman served the customer waiting next to Summer and spoke, lowering her voice. 'You mean the White Lady—we call it. It has a name printed above the door so small you'd need a magnifying glass to see it.' said the woman.

'Oh. What does it mean?'

'White Lady—goodness only knows where they got that from. It should be Red Minx—although they're no ladies. We often see them walk out wearing red cocktail dresses usually clutching the arm of a man in a suit.'

'White Lady is what they call those white trucks you see parked around the city. They sell hamburgers and other takeaways,' Summer replied.

'Oh, yes—there's one at the bottom of Queen Street. Perhaps that's where the name came from. The hungry males go there to satisfy their appetites.'

Disgusting! Summer had listened enough and wanted to pull away.

'There are plenty of people around here who know exactly what goes on inside. I guess you're trying to find a young daughter?'

'Sorry—I didn't quite catch what you meant.'

'You know,' she muttered. 'It's one of those creepy joints, mostly young girls—although they must all be at least eighteen or the place would be shut down.'

Summer shuddered. 'Do you mean an escort service?'

'You guessed right—one of those sophisticated massage parlours. They have a bar with pole dancers, too. I hope I wasn't right about you looking for a young daughter.'

Summer hesitated—unsure how to answer.

'No, absolutely not! I'm looking for someone else who owns a reputable nightclub.'

The woman laughed. There are a few reputable clubs—as you call them—along this road, but the White Lady ain't one of them.'

'How do you know—have you been inside?'

The woman roared with laughter.

'No, not me, silly. Some locals—men, of course—who work at the market ... talk. Word gets around here pretty quick.'

'Thanks for the heads up. You've been a great help.'

Summer purchased a large fillet of fresh fish from the woman, tucked it into her bag and walked to the street corner where she photographed the building.'

Her snapshots, so far, were not for criminal evidence, but to jog Summer's memory of events and work out whether

Dean was on the straight-and-narrow or not—a character analysis.

She needed to know whether the DSS was corrupt enough to be involved in organised crime, which would give her a clue whether he would have seen Tony as an actual threat or not—especially if her husband had caught him out doing something illegal.

She walked back to the car park and sat in her vehicle to finish the pork bun and juice she'd bought at the market.

After lunch, she looked at a Google map of the White Lady's address to see if it pinpointed the business, but just as she expected, it didn't mention the real name except *Massage Parlour* in tiny print.

Satisfied with what she'd seen and heard, Summer called it a day and left to drive home. The first day of her investigations had been a success—but there was more to come.

She was about to head over to Grafton Bridge when she spotted Dean's car exiting the White Lady a short distance ahead of her. Summer had to follow him. Where to next?

Remembering Mick's warning about not getting caught, Summer was careful not to tailgate his car as she continued to bring up the rear.

Dean veered off into Khyber Pass and through Remuera village where Summer thought she had lost him at the traffic lights.

She had got into the wrong lane but in her rear vision mirror caught sight of him turning left at the lights into a street with prestigious mansions. The road was clear enough for her to make a swift U-turn and follow him.

A thought crossed her mind that this was the neighbourhood where the grisly gun murders took place during the 1960s.

Dean pulled up outside a stately colonial villa, turning into the driveway and stopping in what looked like a designated car park.

Summer drove further down the street then parked her car outside a house surrounded by a tall fence, keeping back out of sight.

What if he's just doing normal police work—interviewing suspects or witnesses? She wondered if this was a wild goose chase and whether it was worth so much effort.

What should she do now? On a roll, she decided not to give up prying. What was this place? It appeared too upmarket to be a sleazy outfit.

Summer recalled that Dean lived in a prestigious home in Parnell. *Perhaps this house belongs to his family.*

This time she was prepared to take risks and wandered over to a dairy on the corner by the intersection.

A man wearing a tall turban stood at the counter talking on the phone. Summer was annoyed, thinking him rude, until he looked up and pointed to a woman dressed in a sari and blouse standing behind him.

Summer grabbed a muesli bar and a bottle of diet ginger beer. The woman served her.

'Sorry—my husband is trying to deal with an important order. He should have taken the call at the back of the shop. That will be seven dollars, thanks.'

Surprised at how articulately she spoke, Summer took a deep breath and blurted, 'I don't suppose you know who lives in that massive house opposite? I'm trying to find a friend.'

The woman gave her a scrutinising glance and before she answered, glanced over her shoulder at her husband.

'You mean Angel's Staircase? Hmm … unfortunately … it's not the establishment we want in our street, but what can we do? Nothing! The council won't do anything about it, either.'

'Oh—you mean it's a place of disrepute?'

'We think so. But it must be above board, or it would have been closed down by now. Everything is legal these days—free for all!'

Summer nodded in agreement, grimacing. 'I'm afraid so.'

'You said you're looking for your friend— does she work there?'

Now Summer had to lie, which she hated as she was straight as a die.

'My friend's young daughter—actually, she's gone missing and her mother's devastated.'

'Really? I'm sorry to hear that. Is she the kind of girl to work in such a place? Mind you—they'll tell you they are only escorts who accompany lonely men to dinner or drink at the bar with them. The establishment also has private hot tubs and saunas—it doesn't bear thinking about what goes on in there.'

Summer blushed. She didn't expect this female shopkeeper, who appeared to be Punjabi, to talk of such things.

She kept digging. 'Does it have a restaurant and bar on the premises?'

'I believe so—upmarket, I've heard. It's a private outfit, run as an exclusive businessmen's club. The woman who owns it, Selena Mathers, only takes select guests—mostly wealthy people. Many of her girls are from Eastern Europe and Asia, I hear.'

Summer didn't wish to know any more. She only wanted to get inside and hoped Dean wasn't there.

It was becoming a compulsion. Why would a senior detective patronise such shady businesses? Surely he'd risk damaging his reputation—unless he was investigating a crime. What was his connection?

She sat in her car with an ample view of the entrance to the driveway. It must have been an hour later when Dean's Skoda finally reappeared at the gate, making a right turn through the traffic lights and disappearing onto the main road.

This is my chance. After removing her beanie, she took off her jacket, revealing a smart, floral, cotton blouse, combing her fingers through her hair. Ignoring the swarm of butterflies inside her stomach, she got out, locked the car and then crossed the street—the entire time rehearsing what to say when confronted by the owner.

For a start, Summer would stand out like a sore thumb, as female guests did not frequent the establishment.

She had a vivid imagination, having written dozens of short, true crime stories in the past for one of the major newspapers. In no time, she had mentally concocted an alibi for being there.

Standing outside the closed door, she pressed the bell in trepidation of who might greet her.

A bottle-blond, buxom woman of medium build—likely in her late forties—opened the door.

Summer caught herself scrutinising the woman's heavy, shocking-pink lipstick and dark pencilled brows which didn't match her freckled complexion.

'Hi—what can I do for you?' said the woman with a raucous Irish accent.

'Sorry, I hope this is the right place.' Summer rattled off an alias. 'Trixie's my name. My best friend's daughter has gone missing recently, and I'm trying to help find her. Someone mentioned she may work here.'

The woman squinted at Summer in a scrutinising manner, shaking her hand.

'Selena,' she said. 'Come on in. I've a team of girls who work different shifts. They aren't sex workers—I won't allow it. What they do in their own time is their business. They are escorts, in the true sense of the word. Some just wait on tables in my restaurant or accompany men in the bar. Others are trained masseuses.'

Summer wasn't sure if she was telling the truth but gave her the benefit of the doubt.

'What's her name—I'll look at my register.'

Summer rattled off another phoney name while Selena waved a hand at a curious young woman who stood behind the reception desk. 'I'll attend to this, thanks, Debra. You can go upstairs now.'

Her assistant appeared disgruntled as she walked off, while Summer's eyes scanned the interior of the foyer.

Selena flicked through the pages of a book and then stood at her computer, while Summer took it all in—the elaborate furnishings and lavish decor of the hallway. She could have been standing in the foyer of a luxury hotel had she not known what kind of establishment this was.

'Sorry, I've had nobody working for me by that name. Are you sure she wouldn't have changed it? Many of my girls do.'

Why? A sure sign they were taking part in socially unacceptable activities.

'I doubt it ... although she doesn't tell her mother everything. Perhaps some others may know something.'

'Wait here—take a seat if you like. I may be some time. We have two floors upstairs. I'll go up to the bar and restaurant to ask around. You never know what these girls might come up with, as many of them have worked in similar establishments before coming to me.'

This was Summer's chance to sus Dean out. The minute Selena had gone upstairs, she raced over to the counter.

There was a thick book lying next to the computer. It appeared to be a register. She nervously perused the records for the last two months. Dean's name wasn't there.

Stopping to listen for the elevator, she continued to pry. The PC had a screen open with a program familiar to the booking system Summer had once used when working at a friend's motel.

It displayed the calendar with the current month's bookings, but Dean's name showed up nowhere. She searched earlier dates without success. He wasn't a client or must have used an alias.

Beads of moisture mushroomed on her brow. She was taking a risk. Searching the address book on the PC, she found the name Bobby, whom Summer suspected was an undercover name for Rob Dean with his phone number. It was grouped with the contact details of Selena, Deb and a man called B—all under the heading of KG. How were they each connected and who was B? Summer photographed these details on her mobile phone.

Sitting back down on the velvet-covered bench in the foyer, she heard the elevator making its way down as she darted out the front door and back to her car.

~

Summer phoned Mick, holding her mobile in one hand while loading plates into the dishwasher with the other. She had let Petra go for the evening, once the guests had gone to their rooms.

'So now you're spying on me!' Summer blurted down the phone.

There was a brief silence before Mick answered, obviously unprepared for such a reaction.

'I've no idea what you're talking about.'

'Yes, you do! Careening past my gate earlier today. I thought you were someone I could trust.'

Her voice shook—confused about his motive for following her earlier that day. For a frightening moment, she wondered if he was colluding with Dean and then remembered what a loyal friend he had been to Tony and how he had worked tirelessly to find his killer.

'Wait on—I think you're overreacting. We've had reports of vandals in the area, and I wanted to check that your neighbourhood was safe.'

'You aren't even on duty. Why were you following me into the city?'

'I was on my way back home and saw you turn off into Dean's street—I was concerned. You're taking a risk. I hope he didn't see you.'

'I was careful, don't worry—he doesn't know my new car and wouldn't have twigged.'

'And was it worth your trouble?'

Summer elaborated further on her day's findings in K Road and Remuera.

'Why would Dean go into those establishments?'

'All kinds of reasons, but not what you're thinking. Perhaps he had a tip-off about an underage girl, or he was tracking a suspect. Sometimes detectives withhold information until they're sure it is relevant,' Mick replied. 'It's not a crime for him to go into those places and as police officers, we can't keep tabs on all our colleagues.'

Hmm, he always has an answer for everything. Summer had hoped Mick would give her a lead from what she had disclosed about Dean. Or did he know he know something he wasn't letting on?

'I must get going now, sorry—I have a report to write before I turn in and I'm dog tired,' said Mick. 'I know you won't listen to me, Summer, but once again, I advise you to back off. Goodnight.'

Summer omitted to tell Mick she had captured an image of what she had assumed were Dean's contact details on Selena's PC. When she had returned home from visiting Angle's Staircase, she checked Tony's personal address book stored in her bedside cabinet. He had always called Dean on his work or private phone, but the mobile number Selena listed for the DSS didn't match. Dean must be using a burner phone for his covert conversations.

After the call with Mick, Summer set her phone alarm and placed it on her bedside cabinet before turning in for the night.

Two guests required breakfast early, and she had to be on deck to help Petra. While struggling to get off to sleep, Summer pondered the possibility of the guesthouse making a profit and contemplated employing more people to run the kitchen and laundry. They could do the early starts without her.

At present, she had to help with the meals, cleaning and laundry and when the place was busy, had no time for herself.

She set a goal in her mind—more staff to relieve her load, but it would be further down the track.

~

The guest house stood a fair distance down a long driveway where Liam had spent a week clearing the orchard of old, gnarled or dead trees. Avid gardening friends had advised Summer to remove them and start again with healthy specimens.

Liam showed her the clearing he had done. 'What do you think? I'll bet you don't recognise it.'

Summer stood in the backyard, gaping at the bare section. He had cut out the last of the rotten trees and levelled the ground.

'What about the compost heap? You won't remove that I hope. We'll need it for the new vegetable patch,' she said.

'Sorry—I'll have to shift it out of the way. It'll be more practical to place it near the new kitchen garden over there.' Liam pointed to the patch Summer had designated for her vegetable plot, close to the house.

'Tony didn't want it too near our home as it would attract flies during the summer months,' she replied.

'It needs to be confined in a plastic bin.'

'You're right, Liam. I'll order it once you've finished the remaining part of the fountain—thanks.'

'Let's wait until I've completed the landscaping and excavated the pond. Then we can see where it can best be placed. It's just in the way right now. I'll move it aside soon,' he replied.

As an experienced landscape artist, Liam knew what he was doing, and Summer left him to it.

'By the way—I received an email from the water feature company. My fountain will be delivered next week.'

Liam rubbed his palms together. 'Great news—I'll get to it then. The excavation could take a week!'

'Well, don't bury yourself in it. From what I've read, you'll have to dig down a fair way for the pond at first, although Tony had made a small start on the pit.'

Summer was eager to get all the landscaping done and her fountain installed before the beginning of summer, when carloads of tourists flocked to St Heliers Bay.

The holiday makers converged on the eastern beaches in hordes each year, while retail business along Tamaki Drive doubled during the warmer months.

Once Liam began excavating the cavity for the pond, continuing from where Tony had left off, there was no way Summer could allow guests to stay on the property. Apart from the backyard looking like a bomb site, it was a potential safety hazard for guests.

To pass the time and overcome her impatience, Summer decided it was time to stalk Dean again. Mick had refused to give her a copy of Dean's monthly roster. If he were to find out Mick had breached his privacy, the DSS would have his guts for garters.

Finally, Mick agreed to give her a rundown of Dean's roster over the phone. He knew it was risky, but despite his disapproval of Summer acting as an amateur sleuth, he secretly wanted her to help find answers to Tony's unsolved murder.

It was highly likely he was still feeling guilty about not intervening when he knew Dean had been acting suspiciously in the forensic deposit lockup during the Port murder investigation.

Summer decided it wasn't necessary to wait until Dean was off duty. It was just as likely he was involved in illicit activities, while at work, especially if he was in cahoots with the underworld. She was determined to find dirt on him that would stick so he would end up the subject of a criminal investigation. Or was this purely a flight of fancy in her desperation to find answers to Tony's murder and to prove her husband was not implicated in police corruption?

Dean was a plain-clothed detective who often worked independently, just as Tony had—the perfect cover.

Summer knew that the way she went about tracking him was long and drawn-out— hugely amateurish. But what could she do, not being a police officer, and how else was she going to probe this fellow?

5

The fountain arrived. Liam made amazing progress, creating a pond from the schist rock inside a plastic bowl he used as a platform for the fountain.

He fashioned a stylish, cobblestone path leading to the pond. This was completely orchestrated by Summer who kept a sharp eye on Liam's every movement—her perfectionism taking over.

The young man was fit but straining as he heaved every rock on top of each other, carefully following the diagram he had tucked in his pocket for the schist stone fountain.

By the end of the day, it was finished. The pump supplying the water was working, and the backyard had been completely transformed.

If only Tony were here to see this. Summer's eyes glassed over as she handed Liam a bottle of cold beer to reward him for his more-than-expected efforts.

'I've got an idea,' she said, sitting on the low stone wall next to the path.

'I would like to make this fountain Tony's special water feature, seeing it was originally his idea. Perhaps a little brass plaque that says, *Tony's Fountain.*'

Liam looked at her with an empathetic expression. 'I think that's a cool thing to do. I'll order one through the city engravers. Each time you look out the kitchen window, you'll see his fountain—like a sepulchre.'

Summer was taken aback. 'Oh, no! You mean a memorial—not a sepulchre.'

Liam's face flushed. Oh, sorry—yeah, that's the one.

Summer imagined how guests would react, thinking the fountain rockery housed the dead body of a murder victim.

'You're right, though. It would give me a lovely memory of him. He enjoyed spending time amongst the orchard and garden on his free days.'

~

It was a dream come true for Summer. Her backyard, with an acre of land, had been completely transformed.

The fountain worked superbly with the sun powering the solar pump. Liam had heavily pruned the fruit trees, hoping for a bountiful crop during the summer and had planted blueberries and raspberries.

Thanks to Tony and the life insurance money he had left her, Summer had gone the whole hog. With the redecoration finished— except for the office—the guest house had filled and at least six people were staying each night for bed-and-breakfast.

The high season was almost upon her, and she was now advertising the renovated B&B on a handful of websites throughout New Zealand and overseas. On the property, there was a minor dwelling—a small cottage that Summer and Tony had planned to rent out but never got around to it.

Now she had done it—lock, stock and barrel. It was a surprise when Liam inquired about moving in. After long discussions, Summer came to an understanding that for recognition of his work outside, and minor maintenance jobs inside, she would charge him a very low rent.

She was pleased to have chosen the right person for the cottage. Liam could have afforded to pay the full costs with the high hourly rate he charged for his landscape designs, but he deserved to be well-remunerated for his services as her caretaker.

~

It was late afternoon when Marty, a renowned gourmet chef and food critic—and regular guest—joined her sitting on a garden bench. He was admiring Liam's work.

'This is a fine piece of real estate, you have here. Running it by yourself must be pretty onerous,' said Marty.

'Oh, it's fine. I have a caretaker now and household help. They both live on the property—and I'm also capable, so it's not a problem.'

'I wanted to say ... I mistakenly walked into your office earlier today and couldn't help noticing your family photos.'

Summer wanted to interject. Shouldn't he have just left at once instead of staring at the portraits? She usually locked the office door if she went out. It must have been when she ducked into the kitchen to fetch Liam a drink earlier.

'That fellow with your husband in the portrait on the mantelpiece. I've seen him somewhere before.'

Summer wondered how Marty knew it was Tony then remembered she had pointed him out to the guest from a photo in the hallway, soon after he had arrived. He must have read the story about Tony's assault in the news.

'You must mean my husband's young brother, Jonathan, who is known as Jonny. He has also gone from our lives.'

The guest's face dropped. 'He hasn't been ... sorry.'

'Oh, no. Nothing bad has happened—at least, as far as I know. He went to Australia. Flew the coop suddenly—in fact, shortly before Tony's death. You say you recognise him—from where?'

'I'm sure it was him. Waiheke Island at that fancy vineyard restaurant—Veneto Estate.'

Summer frowned. 'I've heard about it but never been there. When was this—are you sure it was him?'

'It must have been around early May when we still had all that warm weather. I was over there for a week visiting a handful of exclusive restaurants—some of them world-famous.'

Summer wished he would just get on with it instead of name-dropping every elaborate gourmet destination his globe-trotting took him.

It was just before Tony's death. Was there a connection, and why would Jonny have suddenly up and gone to a wretched place in the Australian outback? He returned for Tony's funeral, then flew out the following day. What was he running from?

'I guess it's none of my business, so I won't ask who the blonde woman was, except that I thought she was his mother or an older relative. Her strong Irish accent stood out.'

Marty's last sentence hit her right between the eyes. The only person she knew with such a description was Madam Selena from the parlour. But it could have been anybody in a city of 1.6 million.

'Sorry, Marty, I've got to get going now and help Petra prepare the evening meal. Are you in tonight?'

'No, I'm going into Mission Bay to try out the new fish restaurant. I've already noted it in your day book. I'll be busy tomorrow visiting a few venues in Parnell and Newmarket. That's why it's so handy staying here at your guest house—so convenient, and reasonably priced compared to the city hotels.'

Summer was relieved when he left her to get on with it. There were only two guests for dinner, as most of them only ate breakfast at the B&B, except for the commercial travellers who found it more convenient to eat in for the evening.

Summer had planned special meals during the holiday season such as pizzas in a wood-fired oven, and Liam had offered to help. She would also serve homemade raspberry ice cream—but that was all a little way off yet.

Petra needed minimal help in the kitchen that evening after her beef stroganoff had been slow-cooking all day.

Summer went to her office, closed the door then slumped into her grandfather's soft leather, well-worn armchair. She and Tony had never replaced her grandparents' furniture. This was the one room she didn't want to alter—preserving their memory. But that would soon change.

Sitting gazing at the portrait of Jonny with Tony, Summer couldn't get her head around why her brother-in-law was on Waiheke Island with a much older woman. She knew his relatives. Most of them lived in Australia and the few living in New Zealand were nothing like the woman Marty had described. This was truly a quandary.

She sat staring at the antique, mahogany wall unit full of old books that nearly took up one whole side of the office. Most of them were on New Zealand's history or scenery. There was also a full section of crime novels—Hercule Poirot, Agatha Christie and Sherlock Holmes. They had been Tony's favourites he took to bed at night—better than any sleeping tablet after a hard day at the station, which Summer had always found amusing.

The decorators were finally returning to paint the office. It was the last room to be done, and the tradesmen had agreed to keep the character of the room intact, preserving Summer's grandparents' memory.

But first, she had to get all the books out of the heavy wooden wall unit. Liam said he would help her pull it out from the wall and they would start on it in the morning.

~

The awful Equinox winds that had tormented Auckland in October, deterred many people from staying by the seaside.

But recently the weather had stabilised and bookings for the B&B were coming in earlier than expected, especially for the Christmas holidays.

Liam finished his breakfast, picked up the sandwiches Petra had made him for morning tea and walked to the door.

'When do you need a hand with the bookcase? I've got a couple of jobs on this morning—back here by lunchtime if it works for you.'

'Oh, thanks, Liam. Not sure if I'll be ready by then, but if you're around in the afternoon, I'll grab you,' Summer replied.

'I've got a bit of mowing to do between the fruit trees at the bottom of the orchard first. We won't be able to walk there soon,' said Liam.

'I'm more worried about my raspberry canes becoming overgrown. I need a good crop this year as it takes a lot to make ice cream—my speciality this summer.'

'Don't worry, I'll get it sorted,' said Liam, waving goodbye.

'Okay, see you later.'

Summer trusted Liam and felt secure at night knowing he was on the property, especially when Petra was staying with her family or a friend.

He had installed panic buttons around her house—one in her bedroom and some concealed in a few other living areas. On the roof, he connected the alarm to a megaphone. If Summer pressed any of the buttons, the siren would be heard across the city.

It sounded like overkill, but Summer had agreed to it when Mick once suggested how vulnerable she was in the guest house left alone with strangers.

She had found her detective friend to be over-the-top as far as looking out for her.

He most likely carried misplaced guilt over not being proactive when Tony had accused Dean of tampering with evidence. Or did he have other motives for showing such interest in Summer's welfare?

Once she and Petra had cleaned up the kitchen and there were no guests in the house for the day, Summer resigned herself to spending the rest of the morning clearing out the books in the office which lined two walls. One unit was built in, and the other was freestanding.

By late morning, she had removed the books—stacking them on the oversized, mahogany writing desk that had belonged to her grandfather. Most of the furniture in the office was antique.

She fetched a bucket of warm water with a cloth from the laundry and began wiping the shelves—picking up speed so she would be finished by the time Liam returned home ready to help her shift the movable bookcase.

Summer went to the spacious broom cupboard in the hallway and returned with a small stepladder. She balanced the bucket up top before climbing.

The wall unit was thick with dust. Not good for her asthma, but she ignored it and hurriedly wiped the top shelf clean. It was a wide stretch to do it in one go.

When she had finished clearing away the dust, she held on to the ornamental cornice on the top shelf to secure herself before climbing off the ladder. The ledge suddenly slid across in her hand, sending her flying along with the bucket of water. As she lay sprawled out on the sodden carpet nursing a sore backside, she was more interested in why the wooden ledge of the wall unit had moved.

After mopping the drenched carpet with a towel from the hall cupboard, she went back up the ladder to inspect the strange phenomena of the movable section in the bookcase and discovered a mysterious, hidden compartment.

Fiddling with the sliding door of the narrow hiding place, Summer saw it blended in with the furniture. Her grandfather had never let on he had a secret closet in the office.

There was something inside—a large envelope. It wasn't his Will, as that had been read, so what else could it be?

She grabbed the packet, put the section back into place and stepped down, eager to inspect the contents of her find. Relieved to have the office to herself, she opened the window. Then she closed the drapes, just in case any passers-by looked in, and finally slumped back into the leather armchair, emptying the contents onto her lap.

Summer's eyes scanned the documents. She shook her head. What's this? It appeared to be the information asked when applying for a visa. Then she saw the stamp on the letterhead—*Immigration, New Zealand.*

She understood these were application forms for foreign nationals wanting to work in the seasonal fruit industry in New Zealand.

There were copies of passport photos—men and women from various countries including Thailand. Why would her grandfather be hiding these in his office? Then she read the dates on the forms and realised it could not have been him. Maybe it was Tony, but why?

Another mystery to solve, but she must be careful whom she told. Had Tony been linked with the racket at the container wharves involving people smuggling and, if true, what was his connection to the orchard workers?

It made little sense. Tony had been an upright Detective about to sit his Inspector's exams.

She leaned over her knees resting on her elbows. If only she could discuss it with him.

Her next course of action should be to phone Mick and ask him to drop by. But that would only open up a police investigation, which she didn't want at this stage. What if Tony had been involved in a human trafficking racket—or worse still—in cahoots with Rob Dean? No ... he can't have been.

Summer had never once doubted her husband's integrity. She swiftly put that thought further in her mind.

Her eyes scanned the documents again. There was a name of a company on the visa application forms—a hire company.

Hortihire. She was sure she'd heard that name. But where? It certainly wasn't from Granddad.

Summer was at a stalemate over this. Tony wasn't able to help her solve the mystery, and her grandfather was dead. She dared not tell Mick, so her options were zilch until she could find out more. And it was highly likely that the photographs of migrant workers' passports and their corresponding visa application forms meant someone was involved in illegal dealings. This she would keep quiet, at least for the time being. Something more for her to probe.

Maybe one day she could write another investigative story and hit the headlines.

Petra pushed her head through the door.

'Hi, Summer—I was about to ask if I could make you a coffee before I do the washing. I hear Liam has arrived back—he'll probably want one, too.'

'Don't you worry, Petra. He's going to help me shift one of the heavy bookcases in the office before the decorators arrive. They'll be here on Monday, which is why I've taken no bookings that day. I'll sort it.'

'Okay, I'll come back to lend a hand with the evening meal.'

'Thanks, Petra. It will only be you, Liam and me.'

'Amazing, for once all our guests are eating out tonight,' Petra replied, picking up a basket of sheets and carrying it through to the laundry.

Summer heard Liam banging his heavy work boots to shake the dirt off before leaving them on the front porch. This irritated her, as she would have to sweep up the mess later. She had often asked him not to do it, but he must have had a memory block, as he continued the annoying habit.

She wandered into the kitchen and turned on the kettle for coffee. Liam was there.

'You're back—shall we move the bookcase after lunch? Petra has made a quiche if you'd like a slice.'

'Gee, thanks.' Liam replied. 'I'm ravenous after laying heavy concrete pavers for a woman in Mission Bay. She was rather demanding—I was glad to get out of there.'

'Wash basin,' Summer replied, thinking he must have found her demanding too as she rubbed her hands together—hinting he needed to clean up before eating.

They sat chatting while enjoying a light meal. Summer wished it was Tony sitting with her so she could discuss her mystery find, but kept her mouth shut. Her head was busy with frightening imaginings that her late husband had been hiding something from her. She couldn't wait to get the furniture moved into the office and get rid of Liam.

They finished their lunch and in no time, with Liam taking most of the weight off Summer, they shifted the heavy wall unit.

'Ahh—the carpet is wet? How did that happen—leave the window open, did you?'

'No, I fell off the ladder, and the bucket came down with me.'

Liam stifled a chuckle. 'Oh, no. Are you all right?'

'Yep, luckily. I'll have to leave the window open for the room to dry out though, which is a nuisance. At least it's warm today.'

'Is there anything else I can do in here?'

'No, thanks, Liam. The tradesmen will be here Monday, and once they've finished, I can put the books back—although I'll do an immense cull first, so I won't have to do all this again. The second-hand book shop in Mission Bay will take them—and perhaps the Museum may be interested in several of the Auckland history publications.'

'Right—I'll leave you to it and get on with finishing the lawns. I had to pull out a heap of old roots down the back of the orchard the other day. They kept getting stuck in the ride-on mower, but it's all good now.'

Sitting back in the office sifting through the mysterious pile of documents, she was relieved to know Liam could use the ride-on that Tony had been given by his brother, Jonny, when he took off to Australia.

The lad had got his master's degree in horticulture management, and while studying part-time, he'd worked as a contractor mowing lawns for kiwifruit and avocado growers who mostly employed migrants.

Jonny even had contracts as far away as the Bay of Islands. When he last worked in Auckland during the summer months, before leaving for Australia, he had boarded with Tony and Summer and, while staying with them, had mentioned he was friendly with a girl from Thailand.

Jonny had got to know her while contracting for a kiwifruit grower in Franklin, South Auckland called Kiwi Gold and said the girl had been fruit picking for an orchard in Riverhead until her work visa expired. After that, she was offered employment via a private horticultural recruiting contractor called Hortihire who found her a kiwifruit packing job with the Franklin outfit, Kiwi Gold, where she had met Jonny. They would often eat their lunch together. He had always talked about going to Thailand—enticed by the girl's talk of blue lagoons and tropical sunsets.

Summer remembered him saying how poor conditions for migrants were—low wages and really poor accommodation.

A moment of clarity struck her.

Kiwi Gold had the initials KG. Where had she seen them? Then she remembered—it was on the computer at Selena's Angel's Staircase as a file heading.

Listed underneath the caption KG were the names Bobby, Dee and B. They must have been the big guns involved in the migrant racket—DSS Rob Dean, Debra the administrator and a nameless man beginning with B.

Perhaps Summer had an overactive imagination. Despite this, it was her ability to embellish mediocrity that had once made her an exemplary journalist and reporter.

The decorators had been and gone, with Summer hoping it would be the last time she would need them, as the upheaval while advertising the B&B on multiple websites and fending off guests was a juggle. It was November. The warm weather had finally arrived.

Barbeque season was upon them, and Summer was sure her idea of a pizza wood-fired oven would take off.

She got herself ready to head off to the Bunnings store after noting a *Special* in their latest promotion circular, which hopefully would fit in with what she and Liam had envisioned.

'I'm off out for an hour or two,' she said to Petra. 'I've always wanted an outdoor pizza oven and now we can put one to good use.'

Petra stopped what she was doing in the kitchen. 'Really—wow! Are you going to work it yourself?'

'No trouble at all. My parents had one at their home in Taranaki, but as they got older, they didn't use it much. Tony and I often got it going when we stayed with them. They eventually sold it. Pity, as I could have used it here.'

'Where will you put the new one?' Petra asked, reaching for a wooden spoon to stir the batter in her mixing bowl.

'Liam found the perfect place. He shifted the old brick compost bin from the orchard to the courtyard so now we can sit the clay oven on top.'

'Oh, yeah, I wondered what the red brick stack was. It'll be handy to the kitchen there.'

'Petra ... I was hoping to talk to you, as I thought you should know I may take on one more person to help run the guest house. Just for backup during times you take your holiday breaks and days off.'

'Oh, yeah. I suppose you can't run it on your own, especially once we're fully booked.'

'That's right. We'll be chock-a-block right through to the end of February, although I'm trying to stagger the bookings this month while I'm still setting things up,' said Summer.

'Will you take on a permanent person?'

'No, someone on a casual contract. You're my regular worker. We may not need the extra person during quiet periods, especially in winter.'

Summer spotted Petra's smug smile— being told she was Summer's permanent staff member. It must have made her feel valued.

'I'd best get on now, as I don't want to get caught up in school traffic. Please keep an eye on that roast for me. I turned the oven down, so it should be okay.'

~

Summer took ages, making her mind up about the pizza oven at Bunnings. It was at times like this she wished Tony was with her—he had always been the barbeque whiz and would love to have tackled it.

Since his death, she'd been lumbered with a multitude of decisions to make on her own, and it had become tiresome.

Having baled up the store's expert on ovens, Summer made a choice. Although the model she looked at was a store sample, the shop assistant arranged for a pristine, new item to be couriered to the B&B later that week.

After paying for the oven and arranging delivery, she drove to Sylvia Park shopping centre to do a few more errands.

By the time she'd finished, she was seduced by the delicious aroma of coffee, ending up in her favourite café for a well-deserved Flat-white.

While enjoying her quiet interlude, Jonny kept popping into her mind. The enigma of the mystery documents hidden in the bookcase plagued her. She needed help to unravel the mystery, as it would not happen by contemplation.

There had to be a way she could track down Jonny's female friend from Thailand. The girl might shed light on why he left for Australia unexpectedly.

Suddenly, while images of the mystery passports agitated in her mind like a washing machine—something twigged. Amongst the half dozen passport photocopies, one stood out. It belonged to a Thai girl called Anya Lai.

That's it! She remembered hearing that name somewhere. Anya was the name of the girl Jonny had met at the kiwifruit packhouse, Kiwi Gold, in Franklin—the girl who'd infatuated him.

Summer couldn't get back in her car fast enough to race back home. She was busting to tell someone about her mystery find in her office but even more eager to track down Jonny.

The phone number he had given her at Tony's funeral was no longer in service. But hell or high water, she was determined to find him—and Anya.

~

Liam devoured Summer's continental breakfast—such a mighty spread.

On the table there were baskets of croissants and homemade sourdough bread, cheeses, avocados, ham off the bone and an assortment of Summer's homegrown fruit jams.

After washing his meal down with orange juice and coffee, Liam drove two of the guests into Mission Bay. The couple were elderly folk who couldn't easily walk the distance. They met up with friends who would later bring them back in time for dinner.

While all the guests were out for the day, Summer spent time alone in the orchard—collecting fruit and checking on the berries. Strawberries were on target for Christmas.

After picking fruit, she wandered down to St Heliers Bay beachfront to test the water by dipping her toes in the first waves.

Brrrr—freezing! Just as Summer guessed. Far too chilly for a swim and she had decided at the last minute before leaving the house not to bring her bathing suit. Although it was an extraordinarily warm day for November, the water was like ice. The sea wouldn't usually get warm until January or February.

Summer had thought she could follow in Tony's footsteps who, from early in summer, would take an early morning dip when everyone else thought it was freezing. It was probably the reason he was so fit and healthy.

Her eyes glazed over—plagued by vivid memories of her beloved filling her head.

The conundrum of mysterious documents hidden in her office started living rent-free in her head, stopping her from relaxing. She would have no peace of mind until she'd solved the puzzle.

Pulling out her mobile phone, Summer went to her Notebook app where she'd recorded the contact details for Kiwi Gold.

She had rehearsed a fake story to give to the company as a reason for enquiring about Anya—knowing they wouldn't give out any information but just to hear their reaction when she asked for her.

She phoned. 'I believe you hired Anya Lai through the Hortihire recruitment agency. I need to tell her about an emergency at home with her family. Can you give me her phone number?'

'Anya no longer works for Kiwi Gold!' a woman retorted. 'She left several months ago.'

'I'm a family friend trying to help them. Do you have any details for her, please? It's urgent.' Summer demanded.

'No, I do not,' snapped the woman on the office phone. 'And I wouldn't give it out even if I had one—company policy.'

Summer knew as much. 'When was it she left?' I didn't know she had resigned,' Summer persisted.

The woman finally disclosed that Anya had quit working for the Kiwi Gold packhouse at the same time Jonny had departed from New Zealand. Could she have gone with him to Queensland?

By the evening, Summer felt weary from trying to keep up with the suspicious events in her life which consumed her.

The guest house was quiet as usual by nine in the evening, and she wasn't in the least bit sleepy. For the past month she had trouble falling asleep each night. Was it the Executive B vitamin tablets she had taken, or the fruit smoothies full of sugar?

With all that was going on with her private investigation into Tony's death, her new B&B, stalking Rob Dean and now the mystery of the migrants' passports—it was no wonder she couldn't sleep. Despite all this, it was goodbye to her late night smoothies and comfort snacking.

That aside, it was time for her to be more proactive. She abhorred procrastination in others and was certainly not going to be guilty of it herself.

~

Surely Tony's sister would have heard from Jonny. Summer ferreted around in her office drawers for her old address book—the one she'd used before installing the Calendar app on her phone and computer.

She found it at the bottom of a drawer underneath a pile of items she needed to sort out but never found the time. Famous last words.

Jumping onto Google to search what time it was in Australia if she rang, Summer worked out it would be around seven in the evening, Sydney time, if she phoned Mona, Tony's sister.

Summer had last seen her at Tony's funeral after several years of brief contact between the two siblings.

They had never been close because Tony always thought Mona was jealous of his loving relationship with their deceased parents, with whom she could not see eye to eye. She had always accused him of being a mummy's boy.

But that was water under the bridge now, and they had to get on with the business of living in the day—all except Tony, of course.

Summer dialled the number in her tattered address book, hoping it was still the same as when Tony was alive.

She let the phone ring for longer than usual—desperate for answers. About to hang up feeling dejected, a husky voice answered.

'Hello—who do you want?' a woman croaked.

Summer checked the time on the wall and was sure she hadn't got it wrong. It was still early evening in Sydney. But Mona was an alcoholic—unreliable—and recognisable by her husky voice and paranoia.

'It's Summer. How are you, Mona?'

There was silence on the other end of the phone at first and then the woman answered her curtly.

Summer explained how she urgently needed to contact Jonny and asked if she had seen him.

'He was staying with me for a while after the funeral and then shot through after he got a job as a foreman on a huge macadamia farm somewhere in Noosa. I haven't seen him since,' said Mona.

'He had a girlfriend here in New Zealand—Anya was her name. Was she with him?'

'Oh, yeah. The sweet thing she was—a Thai girl. I let her stay here with him as he was pretty keen on her.'

'Don't you have a forwarding address for him? It's rather urgent.'

'Somewhere ... I think. I'll have to search it out and get back to you. How about I send you a text message when I find it?'

Summer came off the phone exasperated. It sounded as though her sister-in-law had a few too many gins under her belt, which meant it was doubtful that she would get back to her. Summer would have to phone the woman again to remind her.

Within a short time, her eyelids felt like lumps of lead, and she couldn't stay awake. It had been a long day, and the intrigue was getting to her.

~

The cacophony of birds outside her bedroom window woke Summer at first light at 5.30. She hated times like this when she was desperate to sleep until her alarm went off at 6.30 but was woken prematurely. She felt jaded—half alive, and Mona's rasping voice kept resonating in her head.

Summer's phone calls the night before seemed to have been in vain. She turned over, plumped up her pillow and tried to push away anxious thoughts while focusing on her breathing.

Petra stood tapping on her door. 'Are you awake, Summer? It's quarter to seven.'

Woken from a strange dream and struggling to swallow, Summer reached for the drink bottle next to the bed, taking a gulp.

'Yes, I'm awake, thanks. Must have forgotten to set my alarm. I'll be out shortly.'

Her mouth was so parched, that she swallowed a few more mouthfuls of water from her drink bottle, threw on her dressing gown and took a quick shower in her Ensuite. Remembering they had guests for breakfast, she dressed smartly, as always, being the perfect hostess.

There were six guests at the dining table which Petra had set. She and Summer provided the lodgers with their usual choice of a continental or cooked breakfast and got it down to a tee.

After the last person had left the table and the workers were busy in the kitchen clearing up their dishes, Mick arrived in the driveway.

Summer appeared disgruntled. *Darn! He would turn up now ... just when I need to sort this business about Jonny.*

'He probably wants coffee. Would you mind telling him I'll be there soon but have some business to attend to in my office first?

I didn't know he was coming. Thanks, Petra. Oh, see if he would like some sausages and bacon we have left over. That'll keep him happy until I get back.'

Summer dashed into the office and checked her phone. At last, Mona had sent her a text message. 'Marvellous!'

It was good news. Tony's sister had come through for her with the name of the macadamia farm where Jonny worked. *Sheer Nuts*, in Noosa Shire.

She jumped on her laptop and searched the web for the farm. In an instant, she had the location and phone number.

First, she would call the company and ask for him. If they let on he was there, she would take the first flight to Noosa.

Summer flicked her wrist. Now it was time to get rid of Mick and then make the call.

By the time she returned to the kitchen, he was already seated at a table in the dining room devouring a cooked breakfast, with Petra waiting on him hand and foot.

He looked up, wiping tomato sauce from his lips with a paper napkin.

'Summer! Good to see you. Hope I'm not holding you up. Just want to update you on our investigations with Tony's case.'

Her heart missed a beat. Did they finally track down her husband's killer?

'Oh, thanks for the breakfast, too.'

'I'll just help Petra clean up in the kitchen and perhaps we can sit outside and go over it. Or we could take coffee onto the veranda, but it's chilly in the shade.'

'Either sounds good to me.'

Summer wondered how Mick was going to react to her going to Queensland. She wouldn't let on her reason for going there—except that she would visit relatives. At least it wouldn't be a lie—although they were only Tony's relatives, her in-laws.

Later, sitting at a garden table under an umbrella, Mick updated Summer on her husband's murder investigation.

'I'm sorry—we haven't been able to find a motive. As you and his colleagues know, he had no enemies. We now put it down to a random attacker about to steal Tony's Ute or hoping to find a door open so they could rob the house while he was in the backyard.'

'So, where do we go from here—are you going to close the case already?'

'No, of course we won't. It's too soon, but we don't have any suspects or a motive for murder—that's all. You know, motive is an important factor when solving a crime. It's what we look for first.'

Summer felt her blood pressure rise from frustration. No wonder she had taken it upon herself to investigate and follow her gut instinct. She had always been a keenly intuitive person.

'You should have gone straight to the top and made a formal complaint against Rob Dean after all. I don't know why you won't follow it up—tampering with forensic evidence and his defensive reaction to Tony confronting him.'

'Oh, you're not starting all that again, are you? Give it a break, Summer. We've been through this already.'

A black cloud enveloped her. It was as though Mick doubted her integrity. She had the urge to tell him he'd just eaten his last breakfast gratis of St Heliers Bay B&B but restrained herself.

'I thought you were my friend, offering infinite support ... you once said. As I told you a short time ago—I'm on my own in this,' said Summer with a quaver in her voice, bordering on seething bitterness.

Mick leaned over the table and stroked her hand, taking her by surprise. It was the first time he had ever touched her in this way. He was being emotionally supportive, which took an edge off her instantly.

'I'm here for you, Summer—one hundred per cent—and will do my utmost to follow up on all leads we get. But right now, we don't have any. I promise you, if I detect any kind of gross misconduct involving Rob Dean I'll take it straight to the top—to the Anti-Corruption unit—trust me.'

7

Two weeks after Summer had contacted Mona, she was ready to head off to Australia and find Jonny.

Fortunately, it was during a period when the guest house was quieter. Summer put up the *No Vacancy* sign for her time away. She had booked her ticket to Queensland for a three-day get-a-way for Thursday returning Saturday. Mavis, the new housekeeper, had started earlier in the week and had proved her worth. It was obvious she had plenty of experience in the hospitality industry and would be on deck for the weekend. Petra was confident she and Mavis would cope well with the few guests who had booked Saturday, and Liam had agreed to pitch in if necessary for the morning.

~

The three-and-a-half-hour early morning flight to Noosa was uncomfortable as Summer sat between two hefty people. She had never splashed out on a business ticket but imagined what bliss it would be to travel in style—*dream on.*

It was the first time she had been back in Australia on her own and it was odd arriving in another country with no one to meet her at the airport. The suffocating heat was like walking into an electric blanket. Although she had lived in Australia in the past, it was not sweltering like this.

Summer caught a taxi to her hotel in Tewantin town centre. By now she was literally dying for a swim and once her baggage was in her room, she changed quickly and wandered downstairs to the outside pool.

The chilled pineapple juice she'd ordered from the bar on her way through was sent down to her as she lounged under an umbrella.

For the first time since Tony's death, Summer could completely lie back and unwind without finding something to do. Her constant busyness back home was her way of coping with grief.

Having finished her drink, she slipped into the cool pool. It was refreshing—her first dip of the season and certainly better than swimming in the chilly waters of St Heliers Bay.

It didn't take long before she was weary from the flight and the sun. While taking a nap upstairs in her room, she was woken by the phone. It was her daughter, Ava, ringing from Sydney.

'Mum—Petra said you're in Noosa. What on earth are you doing there? I hope you're coming to Sydney too.'

'Not this time, sorry, love. I've only got three days or two nights and important business to sort out with your father's brother, Jonny.'

'What's going on Mum? Are you in some kind of trouble?'

'No, nothing like that. There are some unresolved family matters I must talk about with your uncle, and it's confidential.

'Well, I hope everything's okay. Call me if you need to. If it's a legal issue, Pete can help.'

'I know, dear. Thanks for your concern, but I'll sort it out and get back home. I've left the staff to manage the guest house, so can't stay here long.'

They continued catching up with other news until Summer realised it was time to find the hotel restaurant. She was starving.

Later that evening, following the meal, Summer pulled out an iPad from her suitcase and opened the hotel's prospectus in search of their Wi-Fi password.

Finding the website with the macadamia farm again, Summer noted that Jonny's name was listed as John Martin, Production Manager.

She had rarely heard anyone address him as John. To his family, he was always Jonny.

That's it. She would phone him first thing in the morning—or was that the right thing to do? If he'd cleared out of Auckland because he was in trouble, a call from Summer may scare him away.

Instead, she decided to just front up, and catch him by surprise. In her mind, she rehearsed what she would say, planning to invite him to meet her in the evening for a chat over a meal.

Summer had brought over from New Zealand several family photos and personal mementoes she had thought Jonny might want. This could be the ice-breaker for meeting him at his workplace.

~

The rental car Summer hired was waiting for her at the front door of the Hotel. She signed the documents which the driver handed her in the foyer. Before passing her the key, he gave a run down on filling the petrol tank on return.

It was a thirty-minute drive to the macadamia farm. Summer was grateful for the cooked buffet breakfast she'd enjoyed earlier before heading off, as she expected it would be a nerve-wracking day.

While motoring through the countryside amongst lush forests, there was barely any traffic on the road.

The peace and tranquillity made her uneasy—aware of how manic she'd been since Tony's death. She'd invented a myriad of ways to stuff down her feelings.

Struggling to keep the car on the road while careening around the tight bends, a river of tears meandered down her cheeks finding their way to her mouth. She pulled the car over into a layby to prevent an accident and began sobbing from deep within her gut. It was the first time Summer had experienced any genuine emotion over Tony's passing. At least ten minutes later, having blown her nose several times and filled a small rubbish bag attached to her gear stick with tissues, she started the engine.

Before taking off, the face looking back at her in the car mirror alarmed her. The puffiness around her eyes was an obvious sign she'd been crying and would be difficult to hide.

It wasn't only Tony's death that distressed her. She was also plagued by a dark cloud of angst hovering over her because his murder remained unsolved.

It was just too much, and she felt so alone.

Oh, no. Now Jonny will think I'm in trouble for sure.

Turning the ignition off, Summer reached into the tunnel console for the packet of aloe vera wipes she had placed there. She pulled out a thick wad and placed it over her eyes, letting the healing balm do its work for a few minutes.

Before driving off to her destination, she said a quick prayer. *Please come through for me, God.*

Having regained her composure, she started the engine and followed her GPS out to the macadamia farm.

By the time she arrived, Summer guessed Jonny could be on a morning tea break—that's if managers had them. *What if he's not there—or even out of town this week?*

The company, *Sheer Nuts*, was much more extensive than Summer had imagined. They must have hundreds of acres. She'd read it was one of the largest macadamia farms in Australia. Well done, Jonny!

Her throat tightened as she approached the reception desk.

'I need to speak with John Martin, the Production manager. I'm his sister-in-law, Summer Martin, and must talk to him urgently.'

'Oh, of course. Do you have an appointment?'

'No, I didn't think it necessary, being family and all.'

'Well, usually we wouldn't let anyone in without one, but seeing you are family, I'll bend the rules for you, dear.'

The woman, well past middle-aged, fortunately, had a soft spot for Summer.

'I'll try to call him on the radio phone. He is working in the southern sector organising the planting of new trees. Please take a seat in the waiting room.'

Summer sat, picking at her fingernails, which needed a decent manicure. But with so much drama going on, they didn't stand a chance, just about gnawed down to the flesh. Not a pretty sight.

She didn't expect Jonny would follow through and agree to meet with her, so this was a huge hurdle she'd jumped. Just one more to go.

'Summer! I can't believe you've travelled such a long distance to see me. How are you?'

She was taken aback as he approached quietly from a side corridor.

'I'm fine. Just feeling this heat, of course. It's pretty tropical out here.'

'There's a small garden behind, with a table and chairs under the trees. Let's sit down. I can't be too long, though.'

'Sounds great.'

'How about a cool drink? I can get you one.'

'A glass of cold water would be lovely, thanks.'

He brushed debris and twigs off a wooden garden seat and directed her to sit before going to fetch a drink.

He returned promptly with a glass, taking a seat beside her.

'It must be serious for you to come all this way. I'm dying to know what it's all about.'

Summer took some mouthfuls of water. 'Actually, I hoped you might accompany me for dinner this evening—my shout. There's a lot I want to go over with you.

'Oh, sorry—Anya and I are tied up tonight. We agreed to join friends for our Quiz Night at the Noosa RSL.'

Summer's heart missed a beat.

'Anya! Is she still with you? Your sister, Mona, thought she may have gone back to Thailand.'

'No, she's my partner now. We live together, and she works here as a cook, turning out amazing Thai food. The workers all rave about it.'

'To be honest, it was Anya I wanted to track down, but didn't know she was your partner.'

'Is she in some kind of trouble? What's going on, Summer?'

'What time is your quiz? Perhaps if we went for a meal early, you could still spend time with me, then meet up with your friends. That way, I could explain everything to you both.'

Summer waited while Jonny appeared to be tossing it over in his mind.

'I guess it's possible. Our home is close by here, but the RSL in Noosa is close to your hotel. It's a terrific club with a super menu selection—we could meet you there around five if that suits you. We'll have to leave you soon after seven. That'll give you two hours to talk. How does that sound?'

Summer gulped down the rest of her glass of water, hoping it would ease her tension headache. 'Marvellous, thanks for being so accommodating.'

Jonny glanced at his wristwatch. 'Sorry, Summer. I have to get to a meeting—big workload on today. Promise I'll be there after work with Anya—who'll help if she can. Wonderful girl who wouldn't hurt a fly.'

~

During the drive back to the hotel, Summer recalled her conversation with Jonny—grateful to hear Anya was still around, as she thought the girl would be a key to solving the mystery of the immigration documents she found in her office. Summer had caught a big fish!

A host of scenarios churned in her mind as she tried to figure out the mystery behind the hidden papers belonging to Kiwi Gold employees. She dreaded the worst of these scenes playing out, where she imagined Tony and Jonny had possibly been involved in human trafficking. She actively resisted that last script playing out in her mind.

When she arrived back at the hotel, the idea of relaxing in the pool to cool off was too tempting.

After a lazy soak, there was still plenty of time for her to kill before meeting up with

Jonny—time to lose herself in the Myer department store.

Summer loathed shopping for clothes since living in Auckland. Most of the malls had the same shops and were fitted out mainly for young people or women with bodies like pencils.

She could barely find anything to fit her five-foot-six, pear-shaped stature, and it wasn't because of a lack of exercise, or overeating.

While living in Sydney, the Australian clothing stores had provided her with a pleasant distraction from the humdrum of everyday life on her days off.

Although not an avid shopper, when let loose in Myers or David Jones at Bondi Junction, she went berserk with retail therapy.

In Australia, the dresses were designed for outdoor wear in radiant colours. Even children's garments were an eye feast.

By the end of the afternoon, Summer had purchased two dresses, three blouses, and a sunhat. There was enough room in her suitcase, as she had deliberately travelled light so she could replenish her wardrobe. She chose cosmetic bags for Petra and Mavis with Aboriginal artwork. Before she left the store, an elegant nightdress caught her eye—perfect for her mother. Even Liam didn't miss out. Summer pushed the boat out with her credit card and bought him a brown, leather Jacaru hat. She would give her staff these gifts at Christmas.

'Oh, no. I must be away with the fairies,' she muttered, admonishing herself for not watching the time.

Hurrying down to the underground car park, she jumped in her car and sped off to the hotel to get ready to meet her brother-in-law and his partner.

8

The RSL carpark was full, as this was their busy night. Summer parked on the street next to the club, despite her reluctance to wander about at night alone. One comfort she had was a personal, super-loud survival alarm she wore on her wrist when out in the evening but never had a reason to activate it, as she wouldn't normally place herself in risky situations.

Jonny waved at her from the bar. As she approached him, she felt deflated seeing Anya wasn't with him.

'Hi Summer. Can I get you a wine or beer?'

'Just a diet ginger beer is fine, thank you. I don't drink and drive.'

'Nor do I. Anya is my sober driver.'

'Oh ... so she is with you? I don't see her anywhere.'

He pointed towards the window. 'Over there, see? Would you rather sit outside on the veranda?'

'Sure.'

They wandered over to the table where Anya sat waiting for Jonny. The girl stood up, lunging forward, hugging Summer.

'Hello, Summer. It's so good to meet you, finally,' she said with perfect English. 'Jonny talks about you often.'

Summer was taken aback, assuming he'd never mentioned her name. She scanned the girl from head to toe, comparing her light-weight, short stature with her own athletic build.

'Really? That's nice. All good, I hope.'

Jonny chuckled and directed them to the door leading to a large deck.

'Not too breezy out here for you?' he asked Summer.

'No, I'm okay, thanks. I have a jacket in my bag.'

'Shall we order food first? I'll just get a couple of menus.'

'Good idea,' Summer replied. 'I'm starving. Remember—my shout tonight.'

After almost an hour of eating and catching up, Summer cut to the chase.

'I guess you're wondering why I needed to see you both urgently.'

Jonny darted a glance at Anya and then nodded. 'Yes, it did sort of come as a bolt from the blue. Sorry, I haven't been in touch since the funeral. My life has been rather hectic,' he replied.

Summer leaned over and grabbed her bag off the floor, pulling out a large envelope. She placed the photocopies of the migrant workers' passports and immigration documents on the table under their noses.

Jonny's whole countenance changed. A red flush moved up his neck, forming pink blotches on his cheeks. He took a few loud gulps of ale.

'So, you found them .... I can explain it all, but I hope no one else knows about them.'

It was a long story as the two of them described the trouble they were in with the outfit, Kiwi Gold where Anya had worked before leaving for Australia.

'The information on my work permit application form is false. It's fraudulent. They fill in the forms for us and send them off to Immigration,' said Anya.

Her statement was exactly what Summer had hoped to hear. 'It's just what I thought was happening after I found the papers in my office. You just confirmed my suspicions.'

'They threatened to harm Anya for something I did when trying to help her,' said Jonny.

Anya opened up. 'Yes ... I couldn't stand working for them anymore and they wouldn't let me leave—threatening I would be left homeless and penniless, unable to return to Thailand.'

'Summer frowned. 'Sorry—you've lost me.'

Jonny jumped in. 'I started seeing Anya regularly while I was contracting there. The workers could only leave the premises when they were driven to the Franklin market each Sunday where they could buy all kinds of produce and new or secondhand clothing. They told Anya she had to finish working her twelve-month contract and could not leave until it was over. I kept telling her it was illegal—that she was entitled to a day off to do what she wanted. She just took the ill-treatment as she didn't have the funds to seek legal help.'

Anya told Summer she had worked a six-day week and only received fifty dollars for wages. The owners had told the workers that their weekly rent, food, and transport into the village—a twenty-minute drive from the Kiwi Gold Orchard—was deducted from their weekly pay. That trip was supposed to be a treat courtesy of the management and somewhere they could go for personal shopping. This meant they had only received less than a minimum wage.

Most of the migrant workers had gone to work in the orchards to send money back home to their poor families, but now they were no better off.

'Daylight robbery—you were being exploited!' Summer blurted. 'Only fifty dollars? Where were you living—at the Ritz?'

'Exactly! No, they were cheap and nasty hostels—backpacker dorms—three for the men and two for the women, as fewer females were working there than males,' said Jonny, speaking for Anya.

'Each hostel had two bathrooms—three showers in each and a small kitchen. There was one laundry in each building,' said Jonny.

'How many workers per hostel?' asked Summer.

'Eight—mostly. There were other more sophisticated lodgings—cabins for couples or chalets, even, for those who wanted to pay for them. But not for the employees working under the Migrant Workers scheme—like Anya. They simply couldn't afford it.'

'Okay—getting back to the documents,' said Summer, pointing at the files on the table. 'Can you share any information about the other migrants on these Immigration forms?'

Anya leaned over the files, slowly sifting through them, nodding as she browsed.

'These here are like Lily, from Myanmar, and the last ones are Thai.'

'Did any of the others talk about the false information Kiwi Gold had entered on their immigration forms?' asked Summer.

'No, because none of them could speak English—or if so, poorly. But they knew a little Thai,' Anya replied. 'They had an interpreter there when the hirers from Hortihire got us to sign the forms. We all thought he was dodgy and probably working for Kiwi Gold. Lily and one of the men could read the forms, which the hirers hadn't realised, and Lily told me the information

112

they had written on their papers was inaccurate.'

Summer picked up the passport photo of the man Anya pointed out. 'We need to get Lily and that guy to verify the fraud.'

'I doubt he will open up while still working there. But if you can track Lily down, she may do so,' Anya replied.

'So, how did you get hold of these documents, Jonny?' asked Summer.

He glanced at her sheepishly.

'Anya came to me in tears one day. She'd had enough of slave labour and wanted to escape. I said I would help her, so we discussed a plan.'

When Anya first arrived at the orchard, she spotted the clerk placing the key to the filing cabinet in her desk drawer.'

'What was her plan—to steal them?' Summer asked.

'No, it wasn't stealing. The papers belonged to her and without them, she couldn't stay in New Zealand. They also proved she'd been contracted for work by Kiwi Gold. Anya wasn't smuggled here but had flown in from Thailand after originally being recruited by a Kiwi hirer legitimately.'

'Oh, I see,' Summer replied with a quizzical look. She nodded at Jonny. 'But how did you get into trouble at Kiwi Gold?'

'One afternoon, after the staff in the main building were getting ready to go home, I crept inside and hid in the men's room, waiting. After everything went quiet and I was sure the clerk had locked the door to the building and left already, I made my way into the office. Checking there was no one else around, I went straight to the clerk's desk, retrieved the key and dived into the filing cabinet. It took me no time at all to find Anya's passport and documents. I shoved them in the inside pocket of my leather jacket.'

'You took a risk. Someone could have still been outside the building wandering around.'

'Well, yes, but I'd parked my Suzuki motorbike behind the bushes near Anya's hostel, just in case.'

'Did you get away with it?'

'Well—sort of. I had what I needed for Anya, but there were lots of other files, so I grabbed a few at random. Unfortunately, as I tried to stuff them inside my jacket, one of the senior staff entered the office. He questioned why I was still in the building after the clerk had left, demanding to know what I had hidden in my jacket.'

'Oh, that was risky. What happened?'

'The door was still open—I guessed he had come to lock up—so I made a run for it. Anya was already waiting for me, as planned. I scooped her up on the bike, waited till she did up her helmet and raced off.'

'This sounds like a suspense movie. My goodness, you certainly were sticking your neck out. How did the documents end up in my office at the B&B?'

'We had previously discussed that Anya should stay with one of her Thai friends until we sorted what to do next and that's when I asked if I could come and stay for a few days with you and Tony.'

'We thought something was troubling you, but you said everything was all right,' said Summer.

'I was going to bring it up with Tony and ask if he could get a search warrant for Kiwi Gold—and report it to Immigration New Zealand.'

Summer nodded. 'Definitely—on both counts. Why didn't you?'

'After I rescued Anya and dropped her off at her friend's house, I received a threatening phone call later that night. I believe it was from a burner phone.'

'Oh, No. You never let on. What did they say?'

'I couldn't identify the voice. It was a male saying I'd placed Anya's life in danger and there was no way an idiot like me was going to blow their operation apart.'

Anya continued to explain to Summer that most of the information her employers at Kiwi Gold had entered on her application form for work in their program was fraudulent.

They had got her work visa and subsidy under false pretences. From the look of the other files Jonny had stolen, it appeared they had falsified all the migrant workers' documents and were running an illegal slave labour industry.

Summer looked wide-eyed. 'I can't believe what I'm hearing. You mean you kept this to yourself all the time you were staying with us. If Tony were alive now, he would be devastated.'

Jonny's eyes lowered. He picked up his glass, swirling the dregs at the bottom. 'Actually, I did tell him about the threatening phone call the week before he ... he was killed.'

'What? He never said a word to me.'

'I'm sorry, Summer—I swore him to secrecy. I asked him to investigate, but it was a tricky situation as we thought his boss was involved with exploiting migrants.'

Hearing that last sentence felt like a ton of bricks landing on Summer. Something twigged inside her. She had an uncanny feeling about his reference to Tony's boss.

'You mean Rob Dean?'

'Yes, him.'

'Why would you say that?'

Until now, Anya had kept quiet, furrows forming on her brow. 'I saw him one day arriving in a car with this much older woman who wore heavy makeup—bright red lipstick.'

Summer couldn't make sense of it all.

'Sorry, I don't understand,' she said.

'Anya means Rob Dean. I also saw him at Kiwi Gold from a distance once, driving an unmarked car and thought he had come on police business, which I had mentioned to Tony. I showed Anya a photo of him, and she described the woman who accompanied him. They were met by the managers.'

'Wait—let me show you something.' Summer dived into her bag for her phone and began flicking through her gallery photos.

'Here, see this?' She showed them both a screenshot of the woman her guest had seen at the vineyard restaurant on Waiheke that day.'

'Selena! How did you get that photo—do you know her?'

'No, but you do. I can't go into the entire story, but I followed Rob Dean to Angel's Staircase in Remuera and got a photo of her.'

'Why on earth did you go there?'

'It's a long story, but I believe Dean was involved in Tony's death.'

Summer could have scraped Jonny off the floor with the shock of what had just come out of her mouth.

'Oh, no. This is all such a mess. I'm sorry, Summer.'

'Sorry—for what? You have done nothing wrong, have you?'

'Wait.' He glanced at his wristwatch. 'Another quick drink, will you?'

The women shook their heads. Jonny raced up to the bar while they sat and chatted. He returned, instantly downing a half glass of ale.

'I told Tony about Dean turning up at Kiwi Gold with Selena and we both guessed he was a corrupt cop involved in a racket—and maybe others, too, which we didn't know about,' said Jonny.

'I can guess,' Summer snarled. 'There's more to that awful man than meets the eye.'

'I think you're right. Anyway—I wanted nothing to happen to Anya, once the cat was out of the bag. Our tourist visas to Australia came through quickly. I applied for work in Sydney while staying there with my sister. At first, I got labouring jobs and Anya was offered work in hospitality. Then I applied for the role I have now. They took her on too.'

'Are you still getting threatening phone calls?'

'No, only that once—I changed my phone number and sim card. I'm not putting Anya at risk.'

Unidentifiable, powerful emotions welled up inside Summer—connected to Tony's death.

'I ... do you think, because you left the country with Anya and didn't return her or the illegal documents that they ... um ... killed Tony instead out of revenge?'

When Summer uttered those last words of her sentence, it was as if the ground had opened up and swallowed Jonny. His eyes suddenly glazed over as frozen tears filled them. He was speechless as Anya clutched his arm and snuggled up to him.

Summer could see by his face he concurred with her but couldn't answer. She wanted to take back what she had just said, realising how her statement would impact him—the guilt.

'So sorry, Jonny. Tony's death wasn't anything to do with you or Anya. You did something magnanimous, taking such risks rescuing Anya and moving to another country to save her life. You had no idea they would turn on Tony.'

Jonny shrugged. 'Guess so.'

'I'm doing my best to clear Tony's name. He's blameless—and so are you. Rob Dean must be mixed up in all this, and I'll solve it—just wait and see. With my experience as a crime reporter and police media advisor, I've learnt all kinds of tactics.'

Jonny cleared his throat and sniffed. 'Don't go getting involved. Tony wouldn't have wanted that. Keep out of it, Summer. Bent cops like Dean eventually trip up. He'll get his dues, don't you worry.'

Now Summer was determined to get the complete story from Jonny.

'There's something you haven't told me yet. What were you doing with Selena on Waiheke Island?'

'Oh, that ... well ... before I rescued Anya from Kiwi Gold, I began making waves—questioning the managers on Anya's behalf, why they hadn't paid all of her wages. They didn't like it, of course. I continued asking them about their migrant program, and they quickly removed her from the kiwifruit orchard to the packing shed where they could monitor her and keep us apart. We used to have lunch together when she worked in the orchard, but once they moved her, we couldn't.'

'So, how does Selena come into this?'

'She phoned me one evening, not long before Tony's death, to say she was a shareholder and joint owner of Kiwi Gold and wanted to make me a proposition. She paid for a ferry ride to a fancy restaurant on Waiheke Island to discuss business.'

'You mean, to manipulate you,' Summer snarled. 'That's why she wanted to meet you out of town so no one would see her with you.'

Anya interjected, 'Sorry, I need to use the bathroom,' and wandered off.

Jonny continued. 'Selena tried to tell me how costly it was to feed and accommodate the workers at Kiwi Gold and that they weren't financially exploiting them, as he had alleged. She wanted to pay me off—keep me quiet by offering me a job as orchard manager with a salary package.'

'Conniving cow! Did you take it?'

'No, I didn't. After turning down her offer, I said that blood money didn't interest me when their workers were being ill-treated and made it clear what I thought of them keeping migrants hostage—not allowing them to leave the compound.'

'Wow—I'll bet that didn't go down very well. What was her reaction?' asked Summer.

Before Jonny replied, Anya returned with a carafe of water and offered Summer a glass.

'Thanks, Anya.' She turned back to Jonny. 'Please continue.'

'Selena hit the roof, calling me all the names under the sun and asking why I was working for them if I didn't agree with their conditions of employment. The rest of our lunch date was history.'

'You stayed on there?' asked Summer.

'Yeah—I wanted to get Anya out of that dodgy outfit. She was desperate, and I had to help her. I was just waiting for the right moment.'

'So, you think Dean is involved with their business? I wonder what part he plays,' said Summer.

'Not sure, but at least she's safe over here. I was worried about you, but you're not such a threat to them, although Tony was,' said Jonny.

'What do you mean—in what way? Summer asked.

'After the meeting with Selena on Waiheke, I told Tony I was sure Kiwi Gold was into something suspect—exploiting migrants, at least, and Rob Dean was probably involved.'

'Wow, that was pretty gutsy of you to tell him. He said nothing to me about it. Did he believe you?'

'Yes, I think so. He said he would confront Dean and ask what he was doing accompanying Selena in the car to Kiwi Gold. It was shortly after our discussion that Tony was attacked. That's why I blame myself.'

Poor Jonny. Summer imagined that scenario herself, but if he were to blame, it was unintentional, by default only. It was too poignant for her to sit and watch him suffer like that.

'Do you have to work tomorrow or are you free to have breakfast with me at the hotel? I'm booked to fly out in the afternoon. This will be my shout too. I'm so grateful to find all this out.'

'We're free. Okay, we'll take you up on your offer,' Jonny replied.

'Great! When I go back, I'm going to tell the entire story to Mick, Tony's friend and colleague. I'll persuade him to help me investigate Dean.'

'Wait—there's something else you should know if you're going to investigate Kiwi Gold further,' said Anya.

'Jonny—remember I mentioned to you about my Thai friend, Direk? Summer should know about it.'

'You tell her, Anya.'

She bristled, waited, then opened up.

'Okay ... While I was working at Kiwi Gold, a new crew of workers arrived—supposedly under the Seasonal Migrant Workers Program. They were in terrible shape—skin and bones, some of them. I wondered if they were fit enough to do physical work. As I got to know Direk, I asked how they had travelled from Thailand. He said they'd flown in. He seemed very cagey when I asked more questions about who had accompanied him and so on. Something just didn't sit right with him. He was extremely defensive as though he was afraid.'

Summer was busy getting it down in a notebook. 'What about the others—did you get to quiz them about it?'

'There were a couple of women in my hostel who came on the same boat, but they couldn't tell me the vessel's name. They said the migrant workers' program paid for their travel and arranged it all.'

'Did you recognise any of the names on the immigration documents I showed you?'

'Yes, I did. A few of them were with that group.'

'I'd love to question them to check if the hirers had entered false information on their immigration forms, too. There's no way I can do that—but my friend, Detective Randall, could do it. On second thoughts, not without Rob Dean obstructing him. Mick will have to go in with a warrant and a list of their names.'

Jonny tensed. 'Oh, is that right? Make sure you don't get caught up with that lot. What if they're dangerous? I mean—if they were involved in Tony's death, they'll eliminate anyone standing in their way. Anya was going to be next, but poor Tony copped it instead.'

'I'll keep out of it, but there'll have to be a police enquiry which will be difficult with Dean involved, and it'll be pointless involving the police anti-corruption unit if we haven't got our facts right. We have to be sure,' said Summer, yawning. 'Sorry, but I'll need to go back to the hotel. I'm feeling completely shattered—asleep on my feet.'

'Sure—how about we meet at your hotel for breakfast around eight?' Jonny replied.

'Breakfast is until ten so let's do eight-thirty.'

As Summer headed out the door of the club, Jonny grasped her arm. 'Wait! Let us walk you to your car. I don't want you walking around the street alone in the dark, so let's go.'

9

Anya walked into the dining room dressed in a deep-red silk blouse, a white skirt and flat court shoes. The blouse contrasted beautifully with her sleek, black, long hair.

'Where's Jonny?' Summer glanced around the room.

'We had trouble finding parking, just like you did at the RSL last night. He won't be long.

The women found a small table by a window.

'It's a buffet breakfast, so plenty to choose from.'

'Thanks, Summer ... but there's something I need to tell you before you leave for Auckland. It's really important. I wouldn't say anything, but Jonny talked me into it, and it may help you.'

Summer picked up a carafe of water on the table and poured it into their glasses. Her neck muscles tightened. She wasn't sure if she was anxious or excited as the young woman at last found her tongue.

125

Anya told Summer about Lily, the close friend she had made while working at Kiwi Gold. They had hit it off, although the girl was younger.

'We got on well, but some things Lily had said didn't add up. Once, she told me she'd arrived in New Zealand by ship, then quickly changed the subject. Then another time I overheard her telling someone she'd flown into Auckland, which is what she told most people.'

'Is this what you wanted to tell me?' asked Summer.

'No ... there's something else. After Lily came to work in the packing shed, she spoke about a strange woman who'd phoned her and said she was a director at Kiwi Gold. She offered Lily a job working elsewhere with better pay and conditions.'

Now Summer smelled a rat. 'So what happened—and who was this woman?'

At that moment Jonny finally arrived.

'Gidday, girls. Sorry, I've been so long. Anyone for a coffee? I'm starving—let's eat.'

'I wouldn't mind,' said Anya. 'I'd rather get some food into me first. As you know—I can't drink coffee on an empty stomach.'

Summer picked up her shoulder bag. 'Well, let's all have breakfast, and then I'd like to continue our conversation, Anya, if you don't mind.'

The meal took longer than Summer had expected, as she was dying to find out more about Lily. Finally, they finished eating and sat around the table with their coffees.

Summer touched Anya's arm. 'Please continue where you left off. I think what you're about to tell me may help clinch Tony's case.'

Anya took a few sips of her Flat White and began. 'The woman is called Selena—I don't know her last name. She told Lily that she was a real beauty, and her looks could make her a fortune. Another time when the woman phoned, she offered Lily a waitressing job in a Remuera club that had an upmarket restaurant and said she could also be trained as a special masseuse in her beauty parlour.'

Summer took more notes. 'Do you know the name of the business?'

'She wasn't allowed to say, although she rang me twice after she went there.'

'Oh, so Lily accepted the offer.' Summer shook her head in disapproval. 'Lily was being groomed by her to work in a disreputable establishment. Do you know how she's been getting on since you left New Zealand?'

"I've heard nothing more, but she told me her boss wasn't happy about making calls on the business phone. Selena insisted she would have to save up, buy herself a mobile and pay the cost of any calls.'

'What do you mean? A restaurant wouldn't restrict phone calls. Where was she living?'

'That's the point I was about to make. Lily was so beautiful she was offered a lucrative role as an escort for rich businessmen.'

Summer's heart somersaulted.

'Oh, so it wasn't just a restaurant?'

Finally, Anya let it all out.

'No. The last time Lily phoned me she said her workplace was a massage parlour run by Selena who is the same woman who contacted Jonny. It is also an escort service which Lily knew nothing about. She is mainly in the restaurant and accompanies men to dinner or the bar.'

'Sounds dubious, to me,' said Summer glumly.

Anya continued. 'She lives upstairs in a luxurious bedroom with an Ensuite bathroom and a small lounge area for entertaining, but she told me she wanted to leave there, as Selena had tried to persuade her to allow men into her bedroom, but she refused. After that, her boss demanded she stay and pay off all her living expenses from the past year on top of what she has to pay now to keep herself—working for nothing!'

'I see,' said Summer. 'I've heard that story before.'

'Don't you see?' said Anya. 'They trapped her just like they did me and others at Kiwi Gold with the same ploy.

'So, Dean's friend, Selena, has a big finger in both pies—Kiwi Gold and Angel's Staircase. Busy woman!' Summer scoffed.

Until now, Jonny had let Anya do most of the talking, but he suddenly interjected. 'We both felt bad fleeing the country in a hurry and leave Lily behind. She sounded in a bad way—powerless—but we couldn't get the police involved. We told her we would get her out of there and bring her here. Since then, we've heard nothing, and it hasn't been safe for either of us to return to New Zealand while those thugs are still roaming free.'

'Mmm,' said Summer. 'Perhaps I can ask Mick to help get her out. It sounds like organised crime with Selena at the helm. She'll have other cogs in the wheel too and one of them is a bent detective. I'm going to see if Mick will get warrants to search both Kiwi Gold and Selena's parlour. We'll get Lily out—trust me.'

Summer couldn't wait to get back to Auckland and tell Mick about her findings.

If only she could speak to Lily at the parlour. Strangely, she could sense the young girl's pain. Empathy was something Summer didn't lack, but now she carried the burdens of both Chai and Lily in her heart.

'How about we take you out to the airport? Bring your luggage down to the foyer and I'll get the car,' said Jonny.'

'That's kind of you, thanks.'

'Be there three hours before your flight, so we can carry on talking while you wait. We want to do everything we can to help our friends get out of those awful sweatshops.

'Great! I've put the meals on my account. I'll shoot upstairs and get my suitcase then meet you at the front entrance after I've cleared my bill.'

~

They arrived at the airport earlier than necessary, as Summer had completed her check-in on her phone app.

'Sorry, you guys,' said Summer, glancing at her wristwatch. 'My flight's not until three in the afternoon. It's going to be a long wait as I've already checked in online.'

Jonny muttered something to Anya who nodded in agreement. 'No worries. Let's grab another drink and talk some more. It'll be a while till we see each other again, I guess.'

They ordered their beverages and unexpectedly, Anya dropped another bombshell.

'I guess if you are going to rescue Lily and my friends at Kiwi Gold, there's another important detail you should know. But you must promise you won't let them be sent to jail and deported.'

'Sorry, I'm not following. Have they committed a crime?'

'Not really, but they have broken the law, I suppose.'

Anya told Summer about a group of workers arriving at Kiwi Gold one night while she was staying in the hostel. She had heard the racket—people speaking a foreign language she couldn't recognise, and others speaking Thai. Lily was amongst them.

After some time, when Lily could trust Anya, she opened up to her, explaining how she had arrived in New Zealand. on a cargo ship with other stowaways.

Before the vessel had docked, they were transferred to the wharf in an empty shipping container, aided illegally by shipping staff.

'So is Lily a Thai girl?'

'No, she is a Muslim from Myanmar, although she abandoned her faith when her parents were killed in the riots there. Lily speaks quite good English as she is well-educated, like me.'

'They must have been smuggled in by traffickers. So, was the entire group who were in the shipping container Burmese?' asked Summer.

'I know nothing else … you'll have to find Lily and ask her. Please, Summer, try to get her out of there … please.'

'I promise I'll do what I can. But I'll have to involve Mick. It will not be easy for him as he can't go in there all guns blazing with Rob Dean at the helm, but we'll do our best.

'Anya reached into her handbag, pulling out a notepad and pen. She wrote something on a piece of paper which she passed to Summer.

'Here, please give these contact details of my friends in Newmarket to Mick. Ask him

to get it to Lily. I'll organise refuge for her
with them. They'll help anyone who needs
asylum.

10

The flight home was far more comfortable than the plane trip to Noosa a few days earlier. This time Summer had elbow room as the middle seat was empty and she sat next to the window.

She dived into her shoulder bag and pulled out a sizable diary to record her investigations into Tony's death while they were fresh in her mind.

'Tea, coffee or water?' asked a female flight attendant with red lipstick and a skirt that was too tight, revealing everything.

'Oh—coffee please.'

'You'll need to lower your table,' the woman said, still with no warmth in her voice.

Summer let it down and slid the book onto her lap.

'Chocolate Chippie biscuit or mini crisps?'

'The crisps, thanks.'

Summer downed the lukewarm, burnt coffee so she could have her table free for writing and nibbled on her snacks. After an hour, she felt overwhelmingly tired. The hype and intrigue of the last couple of days had taken its toll and now she relaxed it was obvious.

After adding to what she had written during her stay in Noosa, Summer shut the diary and slept until mild turbulence shortly before landing in Auckland woke her.

'Put your table back up please and secure your bag under the seat. We're preparing to land,' said an equally stoic male air attendant. Summer passed him an empty paper coffee cup.

She felt there was always something unnerving about landing at an airport and not having anyone to meet and greet. When Tony was alive, she often used to fly back and forth to Australia, visiting Ava and Pete alone when he couldn't spare the time to accompany her on the trip. He would always drop her off at the airport and be there to collect her with an enormous hug on her return. His beaming smile was an obvious sign of how much he had missed her. Memories of this brought tears to her eyes.

The travel had taken a large part of the day and Summer still had to wait for the airport shuttle into the city and then get a taxi home.

It was well after dark by the time she had retrieved her luggage from the baggage carousel. She was dying for a home-cooked meal and the light snack on the plane had not done it for her.

There was a long queue going through customs and by the time she had made her way to the arrivals exit into the airport, she was shattered.

'Summer—over here!'

It was a voice she recognised. Her face lit up suddenly to see Liam waving at her.

'Have you eaten?' he asked, pushing her luggage trolley. 'The car's parked just across the road.'

'Earlier, but I'm starving now.'

'Petra's kept a meal for you.'

'Aww, that's sweet of her. How did you know my flight number?'

'You left it with her, remember?'

'So, I did. Well, thanks so much. I don't think I could have faced hanging around in the dark for a shuttle full of passengers going to the city and then a taxi home. I'm exhausted, so really appreciate you coming to get me.'

Liam loaded her baggage onto the trolley, and they headed out to the car park.

While he drove her back to St Heliers Bay, Summer felt as though she was coming home to a family, as her staff were so caring and always looked after her.

'We've only got two guests staying tonight—an old couple. They are leaving early in the morning and have asked for a continental breakfast. Petra said you may as well sleep in as she and Mavis can manage.'

'It's good of her. To be honest, I could do with the morning off to get my head straight. It has been a hectic few days.'

'Perhaps you had better rest up. The place is completely booked out the rest of the week.

'Wow, that's great. Don't worry, I'll get my act together by then.'

When Liam pulled up in the driveway, the security lights lit up the backyard. Summer was thrilled to see he had completed the paving and landscaping. She couldn't wait to view it in the daylight the following morning.

'Amazing, Liam! You must have worked your butt off doing all this while I was away.'

'I did, rather, but wanted to surprise you.'

'Thanks so much for going the extra mile for me. Don't think it goes unnoticed.'

As a sign of appreciation for her staff, Summer often rewarded them, giving Liam meals to take home and allowing Petra and Mavis extra time off.

It was late at night by the time Liam drove through the gate of the B&B. Petra had left Summer a meal on the bench ready to heat in the microwave and had gone to bed.

'Goodnight, see you tomorrow. I've got a job on in the morning, but we can catch up later in the afternoon,' said Liam, as he wandered down the pathway towards his cottage.'

'Night, see you tomorrow. And thanks again.'

Summer knew she shouldn't have eaten the lasagne so late at night. She had to take an extra reflux capsule to settle her stomach, but finally drifted off and slept soundly until the early morning light. The familiar symphony of birdsong outside her bedroom window had woken her.

She still felt overtired. Puffing up her pillow and pulling it under her neck, she dropped off again.

Feeling more refreshed two hours later, Summer stumbled into her Ensuite for a shower. After dressing, she made herself breakfast—a bowl of muesli with a chopped banana. There was hot filter coffee, which Petra had left on the element.

Petra was outside, hanging up the sheets after stripping the bed of the guests who had just left. Mavis was in the vegetable garden picking herbs and greens for the evening meal.

Summer wandered outside for a brief catch-up with both the women and then took her breakfast on a tray to her office.

She finished eating her muesli and revelled in the stillness while she drank the remains of her coffee. As she sat in silence, Summer contemplated how she was going to question Lily or get her to confess about the boat passage to Auckland and her account of what happened on the container terminal the night the security guard was killed. She could be a prime witness. If only Mick would bring her into the station for questioning. But would she talk, or shut down in fear of intimidation by Selena and her cronies—especially Rob Dean?

Summer felt she must tell Mick the complete story—everything Anya and Jonny had told her. But it had to be in such a way to maintain their safety and Lily's—if they could get her out of there—although she wasn't eligible for the Witness Protection Program in New Zealand.

With Lily's testimony, the illegal workers at Kiwi Gold could be granted refugee status.

~

It was time for Summer to get back to the business of running the guest house and catching up with her devoted workers. She made herself useful by getting the place ready for the onslaught of tourists who had booked for the week.

Mavis was carefully moulding the dough for her savoury scones into precise symmetrical squares—patting them into shape and when she had finished, wiped off the excess flour from her hands on her blue floral apron, which was clean on that morning.

'What are all those colourful bits in the dough?' Summer asked. 'Looks interesting.'

'All from your veggie garden out back—red and yellow capsicum, Italian parsley, basil, spring onion. I added fresh garlic and a pinch of curry powder.'

'Mmm, sound delicious. I wondered what you were doing out in the garden. When are you thinking of serving them—the guests have already left today?'

A pink streak ascended the older woman's neck. 'Oh, they're not for eating now. There's nothing wrong with freezing them and when we're ready to dish them out, a few minutes in the microwave after thawing, they're as good as freshly baked.'

'Well, I never would have guessed. That's a great tip to know,' Summer replied.

'You can do the same with muffins—especially the berry ones. They also turn out incredibly moist.'

'We'll have plenty of blueberries and strawberries this summer. Can't wait.'

Mavis had proved she would be a great asset to Summer's business after years of culinary experience behind her.

Together with Petra's positivity and Liam's flexibility, the staff had the makings of a successful team.

Summer sat at the dining table where Petra had served her a pot of tea, then joined her.

'Whew. I got the laundry up-to-date despite the cursed, squally weather we keep getting. 'How was Noosa? Hope you had a relaxing break over there,' said Petra, pouring herself a cup.

If only she knew the truth. 'It was great to touch base with everyone again, but not long enough. I was a tornado for a few days and arrived back exhausted.'

Mavis removed her apron and sat alongside her. 'Oh, that's such a pity. Did you see all your family?'

Summer had to think what to say as she detected a hint of a busybody in Mavis, although sweet and harmless.

'Not family, this time—just special friends. I'll see my kids when I get over there next time—for longer, I hope.'

Summer nodded at Petra. 'Thank you for passing on the message to my daughter that I was in Noosa. I had a lovely chat with her after she phoned me.'

They exchanged ideas about a summer menu for the guests and other useful anecdotes to enhance the running of the B&B for which Summer was grateful—thankful she wasn't running the place on her own and that she had two loyal and honest staff in-house.

'Your detective friend called yesterday morning asking when you were getting back,' said Petra.

'You mean Mick, don't you? The man with the gorgeous thick reddish-brown hair and hazelnut eyes.'

Petra threw Mavis a wry smile, who smirked behind her hand. 'I hadn't got that close to him to take any notice—but yes, it was the detective who comes around to see you now and then,' replied Petra, trying to keep a straight face.

'What did he want?' asked Summer.

'He asked how your trip went, that's all. But he wants you to phone him as soon as you can.'

'Oh, okay. I'll do that later. Let's go over the menu again. And Mavis—I love your idea of placing a small vase of fresh flowers in the guest rooms with a pretty cup of chocolates.'

By late afternoon, Mavis had left for the day. She was still on a casual contract and only employed as and when needed. Summer gave Petra the afternoon and evening off to rest before the next day when they had heavy bookings. The girl was keen to meet up with a friend in Mission Bay for a meal.

While the place was quiet, Summer phoned Mick. He asked if he could come over to see her and bring take-aways. She agreed, despite being weary and jet-lagged, as she was keen to see him.

Summer knew she had to tread carefully, telling Mick her news, while not dropping anyone in the muck. Although he had once been her late husband's close friend and confidante, things had changed now. She wondered how far Mick would go to protect his career, as he, too, was busy climbing the ladder, like Tony had done.

11

When Mick arrived with a bulging packet of fish and chips under one arm and a bottle of non-alcoholic cider in the other, Summer didn't see him at first. She was lying stretched out, revelling in the peeps of the sun that struggled to find their way through menacing clouds.

When he tapped her on the shoulder from behind, she almost fell off her canvas deck chair—one of a new set she had recently purchased to match the umbrella at the table.

'Straining to get some sun, I see,' said Mick, glancing at the heavens. 'Are you going to stay out here—forecast says showers this evening.'

He placed the cider on the table, still clutching the packaged meal under his arm.

Summer didn't savour the idea of fish and chips mixed with sweat from a man's armpit—dirty habit, but she dared not send him back down the road with an admonishment. She needed his alliance now and kept it shut.

'Bearing that in mind, we'd best get inside and sit at the dining table,' she replied, quickly grabbing the food package out from under his arm. 'There's nobody here. The women have gone out for the evening and Liam is in his cottage watching TV.'

'Great—all to ourselves,' said Mick.

Summer wondered what he meant by that. She had never thought of him in any other way except as Tony's colleague.

He washed his hands at the kitchen sink, drying them on a hand towel. That raised his hygiene a notch, in Summer's mind.

'I'll grab some plates. You sit there and relax,' he said to Summer as he laid her brightly coloured Batik placemats on the table.

'There's tomato sauce and mayonnaise in the first cupboard on your left. Pepper and salt are here. Can you bring cutlery?'

Before they started eating, Mick poured them each a glass of cider.

'So, how was the family?' he asked. 'Did you have a pleasant break?'

Summer instinctively knew that Mick, like Mavis, was sniffing around, sussing out her real reason for going to Australia.

Now she was between a rock and a hard place, as he would be the only one who could set the wheels in motion and get search warrants for Selena's business and Kiwi Gold.

For the next hour, she spilt her guts, blabbing about the long story Jonny and Anya had offloaded on her. Mick said nothing while taking notes in his day book after Summer consented.

When she told him everything, Mick started questioning her, as he struggled to assimilate it.

It was late in the evening by the time they finished talking and discussing Mick's plan of attack.

He leaned over the table and eyeballed Summer, checking he had her full attention. For the first time, she noticed he had soft, brown eyes that smiled. He slicked his fingers through his wavy fringe as she smartly dismissed the strange tingling feeling rippling through her spine.

Summer's cat, Petal, walked in and rubbed itself against Mick's legs. He bent over to pat it, scratching her under the chin then continued.

'I'm so sorry, Summer, for doubting you and not taking seriously what you told me. It sounds like your suspicions were correct, but you must realise the position I'm in now with Rob Dean.'

'Sorry. I don't understand. Do you need his permission to get search warrants?'

'I don't need warrants to sniff around Kiwi Gold and Angel's Staircase. Especially now they are both suspects in the port murder. But once Dean knows what I'm up to, he'll be like a raging bull and make my life hell by doing everything he can to stand in the way.

'And he's going to know what you're to, up if he's thick as thieves with Selena,' Summer replied.

'Exactly! We'll have to make sure we get sufficient evidence he is involved, or he'll put up roadblocks using his position of power,' he added, his eyes gleaming with determination.

~

Mick Randall struggled to get off to sleep after leaving Summer's house that night. His head throbbed from the tension of knowing he had undermined her by not taking her suspicions seriously. He was now in a deadlock—cornered between his loyalty to his late friend's wife who was becoming a tad more than that—and putting his job on the line, just when he was on his way up the ranks.

Something in his soul sat askew. Was there a connection between the Port murder, Tony's death, Dean and Selina?

If he opened an investigation into these allegations made by Summer, Jonny and Anya, it would normally not fill him with angst. But having to point the bone at his boss, was something he hadn't had to do— ever.

He jumped out of bed in his boxers, revelling in the cool night air wafting through the insect mesh at the kitchen window while heating a mug of hot milk and honey. The night toddy was a private pleasure he enjoyed but told no one, as he thought it minimised his so-called hard-boiled façade—carried by most city detectives.

This was an advantage of living alone—the freedom of doing what he wanted when he wanted was a bonus of the single life. But now, at nearly fifty, that line was wearing thin.

He brought the mug of milk back to bed. Seeing Summer's cat at her house that evening had made him wonder whether he should get a pet of his own. He chuckled as he imagined a tough cop sitting in an armchair drinking hot milk, stroking a lap cat. What he was coming to terms with was his loneliness. Because of his job—being a slave to his career—none of his relationships had worked, despite a generous supply of women who had fallen for him in the past. He had grown so accustomed to being unable to fully commit to a woman because of his job, it caused him to give up dating.

Before climbing back into bed, Mick placed the mug of milk on his bedside table and then rearranged the turmoil of blankets that he'd dragged half onto the floor while thrashing about in his sleep. This was a regular habit and another drawback to relationships.

He still couldn't relax, trying to sort out in his mind how to tackle the allegations

Summer had made, but he couldn't let her down. He was aware, since Tony's death, of his heartstrings being pulled whenever in her company. Was it only because he felt protective towards her, or did he have deeper feelings for his friend's widow? Now he was confused, denying hidden notions of any other connection with Summer except in a professional capacity as a witness giving evidence, or just a friend.

~

Two days later, Mick phoned Summer with surprising news that he'd brought home a cat.

'It's a young female from the Animal Refuge in Glendowie. A white Persian—cute and fluffy. She was found abandoned during the school holidays.'

'Sounds adorable. I hope they advised you to keep her indoors for three weeks to familiarise herself with your home,' Summer replied.

'Yes, and put butter on her paws,' he replied.

Summer was amused at her conversation with this rough-and-ready city cop. 'Do you have a name for her yet?'

'She looks like talcum—white in contrast to her clear, blue eyes—so I call her Powder. Seems she's already house-trained.'

'Gorgeous, Mick! But why would she be unwanted and at a cat refuge—a beautiful animal like that?'

'The sanctuary owners think she has run away. She wasn't micro-chipped, and they have contacted all the local vets in the area. Nobody has reported her missing and nothing on Facebook either.'

'I hope further down the track the owner doesn't turn up. Don't get too attached to her, Mick.'

'I know what you're saying. Still—one day at a time she and I can keep each other company.'

Summer was impressed. She couldn't wait to meet his newfound furry friend.

'That's not all my news. I've something even better to tell you.'

Mick carried on explaining to Summer how he had gone, accompanied by Sam, to visit Selena's parlour in Remuera, checking first that Rob Dean was at the station.

He told Summer he used the excuse that he had received an anonymous tip that underage girls were working for Selena, which wasn't true. But it gave him a valid reason to go snooping around. While Sam kept Selena busy downstairs, pummelling her with questions, Mick found Lily upstairs. He slipped her the cash Summer had given him along with contact details of Anya's friends in Newmarket and, as a backup, Summer's phone number and address. He had told her to pack a few things and take a taxi to Anya's friends who expected her, as he had already been in touch with them. They would help her seek political asylum since she had fled from Myanmar after both her parents had been killed during the countrywide rioting.

Selena wouldn't allow any of her girls to leave until their contracts ended, so the police had to liaise with Immigration in getting Lily refugee status as she had been brought into the country under false pretences.

Mick knew Dean wouldn't be happy about him poking around Selena's parlour, and she would have been on the phone to him the minute Mick had left the building.

'What time did you expect Lily to arrive at Anya's friend's house in Newmarket?'

'I left Selena's outfit a little before midday,' said Mick. 'Lily had agreed to pack a small bag of things and then leave. She said she'd be at Reception after midday while Selena worked in the back office doing accounts. This allowed her to slip out the door and disappear up the road where there was a nearby taxi stand.'

'Please let me know as soon as you hear she has arrived safely at Anya's friend's flat later today.'

'I will do. In the meantime, I'll organise police officers to search Kiwi Gold. But first, I have to have a conversation with Lily once she's free of Selena's spider web and use her evidence to compel her boss to surrender

Lily's passport. I'll take it one step at a time to avoid mistakes.'

'Thanks so much for all this, Mick. I know you're sticking your neck out taking risks, but we can't let them get away with it—all those vulnerable people coming here in droves and getting trapped.'

12

The B&B was busier than usual. But the mounting pressure of investigating Tony's death, made it difficult for Summer to focus on her business.

Although loyal staff helped prop her up, she still held the responsibility of keeping her guests happy and handling the accounts and bookings.

Summer had stayed up longer than usual one evening watching TV while waiting for Mick to call with news of Lily. He must have been side-tracked by another critical case.

After switching off the telly, she checked the kitchen was ready for early breakfast guests before taking a brief shower.

While standing in a nightdress brushing her teeth and staring in the mirror, she was shocked at the puffiness under her eyes from sleep deprivation.

A strange noise emanating from the front of the house startled her. As far as she could remember, the last guest had turned in for the night, as she'd checked the day book before leaving the lounge.

Rinsing her mouth out, she wiped her face with a towel and then crept down the hall to the main lounge to see what the tapping was. For a moment she thought it was a branch Liam had forgotten to prune, flapping around in the breeze. Suddenly, she nearly jumped through the roof seeing a face at the window.

'Summer, it's Lily—help me, please open the door!'

A sick feeling rose in Summer's gut, sensing fear in the girl's voice. She rushed to the door to let her inside.

'Lily! What on earth has happened? I thought you were with friends tonight.'

Summer gazed horrified at the state of the girl who stood trembling, although it was a warm night in November.

Lily was speechless, traumatised.

'Why don't you come and sit at the dining table? Have you eaten?'

The girl shook her head. 'No ... he was after me. It's all gone wrong.'

'You're safe now—I'll help you. How about a bowl of chicken soup with sourdough toast? That'll fill you until the morning when you can join us for a nourishing breakfast. After we've talked, I'll get your room ready.'

Summer raced down the hallway to her flat and pulled on a dressing gown in case a guest caught her in flimsy night attire. She returned to the kitchen and heated soup in the microwave, made a pot of tea and toasted the bread.

Once Lily had eaten and was more at ease, she offloaded on Summer a detailed description of the frightening event which had caused her to be in such a state.

'Your friend Mick gave me your cash, thank you. He said that Anya had insisted you help me escape from that place and that he was your friend. He told me to pack a few things and get out of there, directing me to a taxi stand about a hundred metres from the corner dairy. It was late afternoon before Selena finally settled in the back office to do her accounts and I could get to the front door. I bolted as fast as I could but missed the last cab, which took off before I got there. I was scared, as there wasn't much cover around, and I'm sure Selena had phoned that awful police friend of hers to chase after me.'

Summer studied the girl's face which was etched with deep distress—her appearance resembling that of a woman a decade older. She had experienced far too much hardship for her age.

'Why do you say that—was it a police car or an unmarked vehicle?'

'It didn't have "Police" written on it. The car was silver, a modern one ... a Skoda ... I think, but I recognised the man. He's Selena's friend who often visits the parlour talking business—not a client.

Summer's eyes narrowed. 'Are you sure about that? You think he's involved with her business.'

Lily took a moment, then continued.

'Selena had promoted me to the front desk reception area to cover for Nadia who helps with administration. Special clients had requested her presence upstairs in the parlour.'

'So, what do you know about this policeman friend of Selena's?'

'One day I heard her call him Bobby … I'm sure that's what she said. On the computer, Selena books his business appointments with her in that name, although I've never seen him in a police uniform.'

'What does he do there?'

'Police business—security—Selena says, looking after her girls.'

'That's highly unlikely,' Summer muttered, recalling seeing the name Bobby in Selena's address book on her PC.

She scanned Lily's face where deeper crevices had appeared under her eyes than when she'd first arrived.

She had to get this wound up right away and offer the girl a bed for the night until they could sort out safe accommodation for her.

'Sorry, please finish what you were saying about Rob Dean arriving in his car. What did he do?'

'He pulled up alongside me and said he knew I was one of Selena's girls and offered me a lift. He ordered me to get in. Without answering, I ducked away behind a building and ran for my life down a pathway between some houses in the next street, keeping off the road and out of sight.'

'Oh, you poor girl—thought for a moment you were going to say he had arrested you.'

'Reckon he would have done if he had the chance. I just kept heading East for miles until I got to a garden centre in Orakei Bay. I bought food at the café there and studied a map of Auckland, which a client had given me. That's how I found my way to your house along Tamaki Drive.'

'That was an enormous distance to walk. Your poor feet. How did you know my address?'

'Your friend, Mick, the detective, said to go straight to your house if I got into trouble—so I did.'

'Thank God! He wouldn't have been able to give out his phone number while he's investigating Selena and that creep, Rob Dean.'

Lily's eyes drooped. She wilted, yawning.

'Let me show you one of our guest rooms and get you a towel. You're welcome to take a hot shower. Tomorrow I'll get Mick to come and get a witness statement from you, if you don't mind. We can help you get political asylum, but we need to find you a safe place first. Rob Dean will come poking his nose around here, before long, so we need a plan.'

It was midnight before Lily finally got settled into bed, but before that, Summer phoned Mick to update him on the latest events. He agreed to drop by on his way to work in the morning.

Summer was much more relaxed when she finally hit the hay, knowing for the first time they were a huge step closer to finding out the truth about Rob Dean and his dark secrets.

But for now, keeping Lily safe was at the top of her agenda—and herself, too, once Dean twigged onto her connection with Selena's runaway.

~

Mick arrived the next morning pronto, ready to tuck into a cooked breakfast which Summer had provided—a reward for risking getting Lily out.

When he sat down at the table, Petra left to clean the guest rooms and attend to laundry. Summer had asked her for privacy while she sat talking to Mick.

'Where's Lily? Is she still here?' Mick asked, licking buttery fingers while eating toast.

'Yeah, she's still asleep—probably exhausted. I've left her something to eat in the kitchen for when she wakes.'

'I was hoping to get a witness statement from her.'

'Goodness, you don't let the grass grow under your feet,' Summer replied, pouring their plunger coffee.

'You know, in this game, we have to seize every opportunity when it arises.'

'Don't worry, Mick. I explained you might ask her, but I also suggested she sleep in. Perhaps you could come back later today.'

Mick's expression became intense. 'I'm worried Dean may get wind of her being here and put you in danger, too. There's no telling what he might do to protect his booty if he's involved in racketeering—of which we still have no actual proof.'

There were footsteps in the hallway. Summer was sure the last guest had left the building and was surprised to see Lily standing in the dining room doorway, already dressed.

'Lily, you're up out of bed earlier than I expected. You've already met Detective Sergeant Mick Randall, I gather?'

She darted a smile at Mick. 'Yes—and thanks again for coming to get me out of that awful place. It wasn't the money I needed so much as Summer's contact details. That man-friend of Selena's would have followed the taxi to Anya's friend's house in Newmarket.'

Mick gazed at Lily's exceptional beauty. He'd noted it when he'd searched for her at Selena's premises before she escaped.

Right now, Summer, too, observed Lily properly for the first time. Her skin was like porcelain—translucent—although she was Asian. She had long tresses of silky, black, straight hair to her waist which contrasted with a white, cotton lace dress as a background.

Her most unusual brown, almond-shaped eyes with long lashes were unlike any Summer had ever seen. It was like peering at a living, ceramic doll. No wonder Selena had chosen her as a premium stock-in-trade.

'Sit at the table, Lily. I'll heat your eggs and make fresh toast. Help yourself to the orange juice on the table. Would you like coffee, too?'

'Oh, yes, please. That's kind of you doing all this.'

Mick and Summer gave the girl time to finish her breakfast before getting down to business.

'Do you want to tell us what went on at the parlour?' Summer asked, before hearing voices behind her, realising Mavis and Petra had finished preparing the guests' rooms.

'I think we should go to my office and shut the door. Walls have ears and we don't want this leaking out. Bring your coffee with you, Lily,' said Summer as she walked down the hallway, with Mick following behind the two women while they left the domestic staff to finish in the kitchen.

Lily revelled in stretching back in a deep leather armchair that was another of Summer's grandfather's antiques, while they sat discussing the shenanigans at Angel's Staircase.

At the end of her interview, the girl appeared wrung out.

'Thank you, Mick. I feel so relieved to tell someone what I've been through. I hope you can shut Selena's place down. Those poor girls are trapped,' said Lily.

'Don't you worry, now. I think you should let your friends in Newmarket know we don't think it's safe for you to go there—at least not until we've finished our investigations. We'll find you a safe place, but until then, you mustn't breathe a word of this to anyone. Otherwise, we won't be able to stop the illegal exploitation of migrants and more people will get hurt, just like you.'

Mick told Lily about a safe house she could stay at temporarily in Waikato, near Cambridge, with his friends. They were an ex-police officer called Dougie—who had taken early retirement—and his wife, Elma.

'Two female police officers will take you there tomorrow after you've had time to unwind. It'll be lovely in the countryside on a horse stud farm—that's if you like horses,' Mick said to Lily.

'I love animals,' she replied, beaming.

'You said you like kayaking and they own canoes. They might take you out on Lake Karapiro. You'll enjoy that,' said Mick.

Summer added, 'It won't be for long—just until we can get your asylum arrangements with Immigration New Zealand sorted.'

Her mind wandered while listening to Mick consoling Lily. She pondered his humane qualities then suddenly caught herself, worried Mick could read her mind.

Summer was captivated by Mick's eyes as they caught the light from the window, reflecting the gentleness in his soul.

'Don't you agree, Summer?' said Mick.

She raised her eyebrows. 'Sorry, I've lost you.'

'About Lily staying in the Waikato. An excellent move, don't you think?' he reiterated.

Summer caught herself. 'Yes, of course. You'll love it there, Lily—such a peaceful farming community and the village has excellent cafes.'

Mick questioned Lily on a variety of things. She finally spilt the beans and told them how she came into New Zealand illegally on a ship.

'After my parents were killed in Myanmar, relatives helped me get to Thailand on a boat and then I transferred to another ship from there, heading for New Zealand. It was all paid for by my Aunty and Uncle whom I said I would pay back one day.'

'Of course, this was all done illegally, stowing away,' said Mick.

Lily nodded. 'My relatives knew people on the boats who could help. Before the ship docked in Auckland, some of the crew moved me and the other stowaways to a shipping container to hide until it was loaded onto the wharf. There, a truck arrived to take us to our new workplace and accommodation during the night.'

Lily opened up a huge can of worms, telling how the people on the ship were transported to Kiwi Gold. She had witnessed the killing of the Port security guard, but the police had blamed their Thai escort. Lily hadn't heard what had happened to him but said he wasn't the killer.

'Goodness, no wonder Rob Dean doesn't want you to wander about telling all and sundry about this. You're a prime witness in a murder, Lily,' said Summer, looking sideways at Mick who cast her a sheepish glance.

'That's why we have to keep you in a safe place, for now. Your testimony has stirred up a massive hornet's nest.'

13

Before Lily left for the safe house in Cambridge, Mick had got a meaty witness statement from her, exonerating the Thai chaperone, Chai. But he had also explained to Summer that it was too soon to use Lily's testimony, as he wanted to dig up evidence that Rob Dean and Selena were in the frame—so long as it didn't take too long, otherwise, Mick would be obligated to get Chai released, pronto.

Now that Mick was clearly on her side, Summer felt more confident of his support in piecing everything together. She had got witness statements from Jonny and Anya which fortified her ammunition against Dean. All they needed now was for Mick and the officers he trusted to carry out a raid at Kiwi Gold—proving they employed and exploited illegal immigrants.

But was it so easy? Mick didn't think so. A man in Dean's position would always have a backup plan—if he was guilty.

Summer would now have to stay clear of it, according to Mick, and remain neutral now that Selena had seen her. Dean would eventually discover her identity.

~

By early December, the B&B was fully operational and booked out until the end of January. Except for Christmas Day. Unless Summer wanted to take a breather and pamper herself.

That was not a time to have her nose in police business, no matter how relentless her obsession was to track Tony's killer.

She would have to trust Mick to pull the whole thing off—get Chai out of prison and put Rob Dean behind bars. That's after proving he was involved, of course.

Patience wasn't a virtue Summer was born with, which meant this was going to be a struggle for her to keep out of it, after all her efforts at trying to solve everything.

~

Strolling between the rows of blueberry bushes, Summer plucked the succulent fruit, carefully dropping each one into a large bowl. When it was full, she went back inside and placed them on the kitchen bench before going back outside to collect ripe strawberries in a second container.

'Mmm, my mouth is watering,' called Mavis from the laundry. 'I've put a large bottle of fresh cream in the fridge. Are you making a blueberry pie?'

'Not this time. I thought I'd keep them to serve for breakfast with granola and yoghurt. I'll make a pie once more berries ripen,' Summer replied.

'What about the strawberries—are they for breakfast, too?'

'No. They're to go into the fresh fruit salad tonight. I found huge cherries at the market along with a pineapple, rock melon and papaya. We could have the fruit with your lemon cheesecake.'

'That'll be a hit. Just keep the leftovers for yours truly,' chuckled Mavis, as she carried a basket of sheets back inside.

Summer noticed the ground was drying out along the rows of berries and made a mental note to ask Liam to do extra watering during the warmer weather.

An entire morning out in the strong sunshine was enough for Summer's fair skin. Although she'd worn a sunhat, the penetrating sunrays still beat down on her head, so she called it a day.

It was warmer than usual for this time of the year. The headline news had bombarded everyone with alarming stories about El Nino in England and Europe—and to expect a long, hot summer in New Zealand. It felt as though it had already arrived.

Petra and Mavis had the guest house under control, although this week it was almost booked out.

~

The case involving the migrant workers continued to plague Summer—especially the incident at the Port. How long was Mick going to let this drag out? He had told her he needed more evidence before using Lily's testimony to get Chai out of prison.

She rang him on his burner phone.

'What's wrong, Summer? I said I'd be in touch when it all blows open. Be careful about what you say with your guests hanging around. You never know if you have a stool pigeon in your midst.'

'There was something I forgot to pass on to you about Kiwi Gold—information Lily gave me before she left here.'

'Oh, really—about what?'

'The illegal migrant workers—how they bring them into Auckland.'

'Oh no. Not again. This is getting out of hand.'

'It's something she told me about a girl staying in the hostel at the orchard.'

'Look, Summer. I can't talk about this over the phone. There are too many big ears around. I'll meet you tomorrow morning at the Seahorse Café in Mission Bay around ten, if you can get there.'

'Sure, I can arrange it. I'll see if Liam can help the women clean up. I think you're going to be blown away by what Lily told me. Perhaps now you will go ahead with the police raid on Kiwi Gold.'

'You do realise, Summer, my team has three criminal cases on the go right now that are potentially all interconnected. If the common denominator is a senior detective such as Rob Dean, it's going to be a huge quagmire—and, for me, like walking on a great minefield with my hands tied behind my back and blindfolded.'

Summer felt Mick had been short with her—as though he blamed her for dropping him in it. The investigations were taking longer than she'd expected and the more they dragged on, Chai would have to spend unnecessary time behind bars while his family suffered. She had to speed things up.

~

Mick sat reading the local rag at a table in the Seahorse Cafe without spotting Summer walk in. She went straight to the counter, ordered a Flat White coffee then joined him.

He looked up and put the paper down.

'Oh, you're here. Have you eaten?'

'No, not yet. I was running late and stayed back to help the women clear up after the guests had left the dining room,' Summer replied.

'Well, I haven't either and I'm starving. How about I shout you today, as I've eaten gratis from your fine establishment too many times to count—it's my turn?'

Summer's face reddened. 'You did the honours with fish and chips not too long ago, I remember.'

'Yes, that was nothing compared to all the full Kiwi breakfasts I've eaten at yours. What will it be?'

Mick handed her the menu. 'I know you're partial to hotcakes with maple sauce and bacon. They're on the list.'

'Mmm, you're right—exactly what I feel like eating this morning. Something sweet to give me a lift.'

'And then, perhaps a walk along the promenade before you head back?'

Summer hesitated before answering.

'I guess so but must be back on time to help my staff get the rooms ready for new guests arriving this afternoon—promised Petra I'd be there.'

'Sure, We don't have to go far.'

They didn't have long to wait for their meals. Mick polished off a Kiwi breakfast, with all the trimmings, while Summer looked on amused, thinking he couldn't have had a decent feed in days. She had also made quick work of her hotcakes and coffee.

'So, let's have it—don't keep me in suspense any longer,' said Mick, glancing furtively around making sure none of the other customers were in hearing distance while they sat at an outside table.

Summer began, 'Lily had made friends with Mae, a young Burmese girl at Kiwi Gold and had assumed she'd been smuggled here the same way as Lily had been in a shipping container. Mae had arrived at Kiwi Gold about a month after her—on a ship, too. But one day, she described to Lily how the ship she'd travelled on from Thailand stopped out

167

at sea, not far off the east coast North of Auckland. The group of girls were then transferred to an old, white wooden launch with a blue stripe down the middle that smelt disgustingly of fish. It carried the passengers to a long pier in a bay near the city.'

'It was probably a converted fishing trawler,' Mick commented.'

'Yes, exactly what I thought,' Summer replied.

She continued. 'As Mae walked towards a black Nissan Elgrand 4WD with tinted windows awaiting them at the end of the pier, she saw in the poor street lighting it was parked on the roadside near a building that appeared to be an eatery. Above the building was a signboard that read Okahu Bay Pancake House, which Lily had noted in a small pocket diary she had been keeping.'

'Goodness, you've been doing your homework. I assumed you were going to take a break from it all. In all honesty, I'm glad you didn't. Continue,' said Mick, winking. 'This sounds intriguing.'

'Sorry, I need to visit the Ladies' Room. Back in a tick.'

Summer was glad to get the chance to draw breath. Her head was spinning from trying to remember everything Lily had told her.

When she returned, Mick had a glass of water for her. 'I can't let you dry out before getting to the end.'

'Yeah, well—I'm trying to remember it exactly as Lily told it. I'd hate to get it wrong.'

'I wouldn't worry. This young woman is going to be another prime witness and fill in the gaps if she testifies.'

'Well, just in case she refuses, I'd best get it right.' Summer gulped the water down and carried on.

'A man bundled them into the vehicle and drove off, but on the way, two of the girls were offloaded at a massive white house. It was dark. In the dim light on the driveway, Mae saw a woman scurrying outside to greet the girls and rush them indoors. Afterwards, the rest of them were taken to Kiwi Gold.'

'Is that everything? It's remarkable that Mae told her all this. Did she contact Lily after that?'

'No, Lily has heard nothing from her since she left Kiwi Gold to work at Angel's Staircase.'

'So, I guess there'll be other girls working for Selena right now who arrived here with Mae,' said Mick.'

'That's what I thought. Lily was frightened of leaving, so those girls would be too.'

Summer flicked her wrist. 'The time! I'd best be getting back soon. I wondered if you could monitor the jetty at Okahu Bay somehow. If the criminals have been bringing illegal migrants in on smaller boats since the bust at the Auckland Ports, it would be worth trying to trap them, wouldn't it?'

'You're right—technically—but for anything to stand up in Court, it has to be conducted legitimately.'

Summer let out a sigh of frustration, resting her face on her palm.

'There may be a CCTV camera on the jetty. I'll check when I leave here,' said Mick.

'And if not? Can't you plant undercover police officers there, or a police camera?'

'No, it won't work. Whatever surveillance is done, it has to be without Rob Dean's knowledge. It's too easy for him to come up with alibis why he was visiting Angel's Staircase. Our team has been monitoring the place for years—ever since a couple of underage girls were found working there,' said Mick. 'That's what he'll say.'

'What about Kiwi Gold? Does he have the right to frequent their premises, too?'

'Unfortunately, he does. He can also use the "upstanding policeman" cover and say he was following up on missing persons. And apart from his assumed tampering of evidence, I have nothing on him—understand? That's why I can't accuse him of anything without concrete proof.'

Summer was sure she'd heard Mick hammer her with that statement before—more than a dozen times.

'Look—I don't doubt Kiwi Gold is employing illegal immigrants on false passports, and Selena too. That's difficult enough to prove—the hiring contractors are clever. But a high-ranking officer hand-in-glove with them is far worse, and ten times harder to prove. Bent cops cover every loophole observing all the golden rules the higher up they climb.'

Summer sagged. Half her brain wanted to take on board what Mick said, but the other half of her neurons egged her on to pursue her private investigation and finally tie up Tony's assassination with Rob Dean.

'I could ignore the sleazy business going on at Kiwi Gold and Angel's Staircase, if that's all it is, but a double homicide is a huge reason for me not to give up. Especially when I believe the killing of the Port guard is associated with my husband's murder, and somehow, I believe Selena and Dean are involved,' said Summer, wanting to add that she would not rest until she could prove it, but held her tongue.

'I need to get going. Can't let the girls down and we're having a busy time this week—we're full up.'

'I've got to get on too,' said Mick. 'I'll see if there's CCTV by the jetty at Okahu Bay. If not, I'll think of who I can plant there, but it'll have to be someone outside the Force, and that won't be easy. I'll work on it. The boats may only come into the harbour infrequently.'

Summer appeared disgruntled. 'What are you going to do about Mae? She's a prime witness.'

'I'll have to hold off until the right time and ensure Dean is out of the way at a conference or something. Then I'll go in there with a warrant,' said Mick.

Summer was once again exasperated with the detective and felt out of control. It was agonising for her every time Mick used delay tactics, but he was an experienced officer and she had to trust him.

'Wait … I remember something else Lily told me which may help. It was apparent to her that once a month Kiwi Gold and Selena replenished their stock of employees by bringing in new migrants.'

'You mean people smuggling?' Mick replied.

'That's right. In Queensland, Anya had told me some workers are only here on three-month seasonal contracts, others longer, but they have to keep replacing them frequently.

'That makes sense.'

'So, they could still bring another lot into Okahu Bay, as they will avoid the container wharf now.'

'Okay, Summer, I see where you're heading with this.'

'Look, Mick. I've got a little time left—let's check out that jetty now to see if there's a camera there.'

Mick looked at his watch and sighed. 'Okay then—we can shoot across in my car.'

14

When Mick pulled up in Okahu Bay at the end of the jetty, it was just as Lily had described it. Summer remembered going fishing there with her grandfather as a schoolgirl, although they caught nothing. In those days there was just the wharf and years later, Kelly Tarlton's Aquarium appeared. She had spent many happy days staying with her grandparents by the beach.

'Darn! There's no CCTV to be found,' said Summer.

'Of course, organised criminals wouldn't pick a spot to conduct their illegal business if there was a camera—I knew that. I just wanted to let you see for yourself,' Mick replied, giving her a wry smile.

Summer wasn't sure whether to be furious at his unintentional patronising. She soon realised he was right.

'That's okay—there are plenty of other ways to skin a skunk.'

Mick gave her another sideways glance, frowning as they got back into his vehicle.

'I'll bring you back to your car so you can get ready for your next onslaught of guests. Frankly, Summer, I don't know how you can run a guesthouse as successfully as you do and get involved with all this police business,' said Mick, driving along Tamaki Drive.

'Well, if you had experienced what I had when I returned from taking care of my mother, you might be as zealous as I am to find my husband's killer—especially if one of his colleagues is involved.'

Mick said no more and dropped her back to her car.

'Thanks for taking me to the jetty. Come for breakfast sometime soon,' said Summer. 'You might like to try my pancakes with fresh berries from the garden and mascarpone cream.'

'I'll take you up on that. Sounds like a real treat, though I'll have to watch my waistline,' he said, winking.

Summer chuckled. 'Thanks, Mick. See you again soon.'

~

Climbing into bed that evening, Summer got out a notepad and pen from her bedside table. It was time to plan another strategy and hasten the investigation.

She could hear the last guests returning through the back door whispering in the hallway before entering their room. Liam always did his security round at eleven each night when he locked both doors.

Summer's mind wandered back to the jetty at Okahu Bay. If only her father were still alive. He would help her by being an eagle eye staking out the wharf during his regular, night fishing sprees. He would do a far better job than one of those upmarket CCTV cameras.

That random thought gave Summer an idea, and she was sure it would work. At first, she had thought of involving Liam, but it had to be someone completely separate from St Heliers Bay B&B.

It had been ages since Summer had been to see the Repia family. She had gone through school with some of them. Most were adults now who, like Summer, had children, but she often saw various members of their whanau driving past the guesthouse in the evening in a Ute loaded with fishing rods. Her grandfather had helped them when their home had burnt down, and they were deeply indebted to him. He had offered them shelter for months until their house insurance came through and a new home was built.

Before sleep captured her mind, Summer rehearsed what she would say to the Repia family during her visit, hoping their family members who had once stayed in the guest house would still be there. Whatever reason she would give for her intended request, it must jeopardise none of the investigations, and this was a tremendous risk for her to take. In her mind, she had no choice.

~

The path to the Repia's home was overgrown with old-fashioned rambling roses. Summer stopped to smell the fragrant blooms.

She recognised the familiar face of a tall, strapping male who greeted her at the door holding a baby.

'Oh, my gosh ... Charlie, isn't it? You've hardly changed after all these years.'

The man who appeared as toned as an All Black called out, 'Aroha, Summer's here,' and invited her into the living room.

Summer spotted a neatly placed row of shoes at the front door and removed her own before stepping inside the house.

'Come in and sit down,' said Charlie, as he gently nudged his brown Labrador dog out the front door.

'Hello, Summer, good to meet you. I'm his other half, Aroha.' The woman held out a hand to their guest.

As Charlie directed Summer to a seat, a delicious aroma wafted through from the kitchen.

'Homemade Maori bread. Unfortunately, it's not ready yet, but I've got some scones if you'd like one. Tea or coffee?' said Aroha.

'Sounds lovely, thanks ... um ... tea with milk would be fine.'

After mulling through the niceties and small talk, Summer was ready to get to the point. But before she said anything, an elderly couple entered the room.

'Is this the lady you said you went to school with, son?'

'Yes, Dad, this is Summer. She's the granddaughter of Mr Martin who put us all up in that big house when our whare burnt down.'

Charlie's father gaped at Summer who was admiring the tattooed moko on his wife's chin. The old lady stood squinting at her as she sat down on the couch.

'You're right. I can see some likeness there,' said the man. 'Kia Ora—Tane Repia is my name, and this is my wife, Pania. I've seen none of your family since your father's funeral. That's kind of you to visit,' he said, joining his wife on the couch.

Summer had a sudden thought. Perhaps they wouldn't be so kindly towards her once she told them the reason for her random visit.

'I hear you have got the guest house up and running since you lost your husband. It must be a lot of work for you,' said Tane. 'But I have to say, I'm so pleased you haven't ruined the house, keeping it in its original state. We all have fond memories of staying there.'

'Oh, I try to keep it up to scratch. Recently I had it redecorated, but only paint and paper—haven't changed the structure at all.'

'We would love to come and see the place one day, if you don't mind. No rush though. I'm sure you'll be running off your feet throughout the summer,' said Tane.

'Of course, I'm sure I can arrange it. I'd love you to pay a visit,' Summer replied.

Aroha served the tea with scones and jam while Charlie put the baby to bed. Summer enjoyed catching up with old times and chatting with Tane and Pania.

Charlie returned from the nursery and hoed into the scones. When they had all finished their tea, he muttered something quietly to Aroha.

'Yeah, go on. I'll bet she could use them,' his wife replied.

'Would you like a few fillets of fresh fish? We caught half a dozen big Kingis off the wharf the other day. Kept them on ice.'

'Sounds wonderful, thank you both.' Summer replied. 'Except … I've never filleted a fish. Wouldn't know where to start.'

Tane laughed. 'Charlie can soon teach you—can't you, son?'

Charlie chuckled. 'Dad's just teasing. Of course, we'll fillet it for you.'

Summer drew a deep breath and then fired. 'Actually, I have a huge favour to ask of you. It's pretty tricky, and you can say no—I won't mind. But I need help with something.'

Pania glanced at Tane and then nodded at Charlie and Aroha while Summer cautiously told the story about the boat arriving at Okahu Bay at night delivering migrant workers—how they were being exploited and abused. She never mentioned Rob Dean. It was a risk, but if Charlie and his father agreed, they would be the perfect plant to act as informants—on a jetty often frequented by night fishermen.

'How often do you fish there?' Summer asked.

'At least three times during the week or the weekends.'

'What do you think—are you able to help me?'

'I guess it can't do any harm, but we wouldn't want to be involved in anything that might put my baby granddaughter at risk,' said Tane. 'As long as we can do it anonymously.'

Summer felt like hugging the man. 'Of course, we'll keep your names out of it. You could be the key in helping the police catch the smugglers.' Summer felt guilty leaving out the fact that she suspected Tony's murder could be tied up with human trafficking. She knew it would put them right off. She would have to ensure this family would never be identified as informants.

'Thank you so much, both for the excellent scones and for helping me with the migrant

business. I'll have to make my way back to
the guest house soon.'

'Wait—tell us how you want to do this—I
mean, if we see a fishing vessel dock at the
jetty and drop off Asian workers. Should we
ring the police or you?'

'Oh, don't phone the police. I have a
detective friend who is right onto it and is in
charge. If you phone me immediately, I'll
alert him to come right away.'

'We can take photographs and videos as it
plays out. That will be evidence for you.'

'Of course, thank you!' Summer had
forgotten to give the men those instructions.
Charlie appeared right up with the play.

'Wait—before you go. Aroha has finished
filleting the fish. All ready for breakfast
tomorrow for you and your guests.'

'Look—I can't thank you all enough and I'll
return the favour—make it worthwhile for
you.'

'That's unnecessary,' said Pania. 'My boys
are always ready to help our community—no
matter who it is. And we owe it to your
granddad. It's called "paying forward".
Haere ra—we'll be in touch as soon as we see
anything happening at the jetty.'

When Summer walked down the rose-
lined path with a bag of fresh fish, her heart
was full of gratitude. Someone had been
smiling down from above that day. Perhaps
this was the breakthrough she had long
awaited.

It was two weeks since Summer had visited the Repias, and she'd not heard from them. It was a gamble. Maybe the smugglers had smelt a rat and chosen a different drop-off point, or they had enough migrants for now and would not bring in another group for months.

Patience eluded Summer, but this time she had to wait it out and not interfere any further. She knew that if the Repia's covert surveillance succeeded, it would blow the trafficking operation apart.

The phone ringing in her pocket brought her promptly back to the task at hand as she cleared up the breakfast dishes after the last guest had left for the day. It was Mavis calling to say she had gone down with a nasty virus and didn't expect to be back on deck for at least a week.

The news wasn't received well by Summer, but this was the risk she took in high season with a skeleton staff. Mavis was supposed to be Petra's backup, and if she got sick, Summer would be well and truly up the creek with no domestic staff.

Mick had once told Summer about a reputable hospitality staff hire agency. Fortunately, the company's calling card was still in her wallet.

She called them and hired a casual worker to help with breakfasts and laundry. Then she had to let Petra know the new arrangements.

'Are you there, Petra?' Summer poked her head around the door of one of the guest rooms. 'Have you got a minute?'

Summer explained to her that Mavis was on sick leave and a new woman from the hire agency would soon arrive. Mavis mostly worked from mid-morning until three in the afternoon to help clean up the kitchen and carry out laundry duties.

As Petra lived in, she was the one who usually lent Summer a hand with breakfasts.

'Oh, poor Mavis. I hope we don't get it—the virus, I mean. Is she okay?'

'She lives together with a daughter who fusses over her,' Summer replied.

'I'm glad you're getting help. I know you need to get away from here often to attend to ... you know.'

'What do you mean, Petra? I have errands to run for this place. You know I can't always be here twenty-four seven.'

Summer's mind went into a whirl, thinking Petra was referring to police business. Had she overheard her talking to Mick?

'I know it's nothing to do with me, but I know that Mick, the detective, is sweet on you. I understand if your mind has been elsewhere—you deserve to have someone.'

Summer's mouth dropped open. A flush of blood raced up her neck. She would never have guessed that Petra had such a notion.

She was now aware her staff had a quiet snigger whenever Mick visited, but she was even more full of angst that Petra may have overheard her conversations with Mick about the police investigations.

~

It had been strenuous for Summer to orientate a new person to the guest house routines, and the casual worker was more casual than expected. Everyone was relieved when Mavis finally recovered and came back on deck after a week.

Summer could barely cope with a worker operating half-mast during the busy season, as did the agency girl.

On Mavis's first day back—despite Petra and Summer being eager for her to be on board—her obvious pallor showed she was still not ready for a full day's work, so the women made sure she paced herself.

During most evenings, the guests either turned in for the night or went out on the town. Most evenings, Summer usually took a mug of chamomile tea to her living quarters and chilled out in front of the telly or sat there surfing the net on her laptop.

One of her favourite pastimes was watching videos on YouTube about exotic destinations. She had always dreamed of going on a Pacific cruise. Tony had promised that once he passed his Detective Senior Sergeant exams, he would take her on such a holiday. He had often talked about a second honeymoon.

But now her hopes and dreams were in tatters, and she may as well kiss goodbye to her nightly meanderings Googling holiday destinations.

Summer was getting ready to call it a night. To her utmost delight, it was Charlie Repia ringing.

'You've got to get your detective friend to come now! The white fishing boat you described with a group of young Asian girls came to the jetty tonight, just like you said. I took a video, but I couldn't get right up close. I got some mugshots of the girls as I zoomed in but not of the blokes who were with them. They were all hooded up and dressed in black.'

Adrenaline raced through Summer's veins. She slowed down her breathing. 'When was this—are they still there?'

'No, they left swiftly while I videoed them getting into a Nissan Serena.'

'What did the men look like? Any remarkable features?'

'Sorry, I couldn't get any closer. They would have twigged I was stalking them, but I did notice the driver was wearing a black, woollen beanie. It was too dark to see the number plate at night, unfortunately.'

'That's okay, you did well. It's amazing what the police can do with digital technology nowadays,' said Summer.

'Wait—I wanted to get more evidence, so I followed them with my Dad out to South Auckland. First, they stopped at an address in Remuera—I noted the name of the street—and kept pursuing them to Drury where they headed out to Franklin.'

'Really? That was pretty gutsy of you.'

'You're telling me—they almost saw me. I thought it was game up as they suddenly pulled up at a petrol station. One of the girls must have needed to stop and use the bathroom.'

'Great! I think I know where they were headed—I won't go into it right now.'

'Hold on, I haven't finished yet. I was going to leave it there, turn around and head home, but Dad stopped me. He wanted me to follow them.'

'Really—what did you see?'

'They eventually turned into the entrance of what appeared to be an orchard with a heap of packing sheds we could see through the fence. The sign at the gate said Kiwi Gold Orchards. We drove past and parked on the road with our lights turned off. I got out and ran down the driveway behind the sheds while Dad waited in the car.'

'Jeepers, you took a risk,' said Summer.

'I wanted to get closer to film the girls before they entered a building, but I heard another vehicle coming down the driveway and had to duck out of the way.'

'You should be a detective, Charlie. Well done. Keep going.'

'I hid behind a tree and filmed the car with a man at the wheel and a woman passenger beside him. The driver got out and stood at the entrance of the building where the girls had entered while talking on his phone. When he finished the call, he and the woman both went inside. When the coast was clear, I thought I'd best get out of there.'

'I know you've recorded it, but what kind of car was he driving?'

'Ah … let me think … I know, it was a silver Skoda. I remember because my uncle drives one just like it.'

'Thank you, Charlie. You don't know what a great help you've been by putting your neck on the line for me.'

'I hope I've been of some help.'

'You're a Godsend. I'm sure my detective friend will use the videos. Can you send them to my phone?'

'Yes, for sure. But what's all this about? Who are these people?'

'Sorry, it's complicated. This is an ongoing police investigation into the illegal trafficking of migrant workers for sweatshops here in Auckland.'

Summer was careful not to mention about Rob Dean being involved.

'How about coming for dinner sometime soon, Charlie? It's pretty quiet on Sundays, although it's nearly Christmas. Perhaps we should wait until after New Year and I'll get my friend Mick to join us. I'll let you know.'

After Summer finished the call, Charlie sent through his videos and photos. She couldn't believe the breakthrough she had but was frustrated he didn't phone Mick directly and have the traffickers arrested on arrival at the jetty.

A sudden bleak thought. What if Charlie was wrong, and it was an innocent group of tourists he'd seen disembarking from the launch?

With Charlie's videos, Summer was optimistic that Mick could finally crack the case and solve Tony's murder, which was undoubtedly linked with the killing of the guard at the container terminal.

Such intrigue. Summer could write a book about how she solved her detective husband's murder.

There was no way she could sleep that evening. Before turning in, she rang Mick to report the evening's events, then emailed him Charlie's videos and photographs from her phone.

This was going to be a long night, and with all the excitement, Summer's adrenaline levels were going through the roof. Her head was overloaded.

At such times, when her tinnitus returned, Summer could hear a dozen locusts living rent-free in her ears. And there was nothing she could do but wait.

15

During Summer's conversation on the phone with Mick the night before when she'd sent through Charlie's photographic footage, he surprised her by saying Rob Dean was on leave, taking an early Christmas break and heading off to Fiji the next morning.

Summer was ecstatic. It was a miracle. She'd expected nothing to ensue from Charlie's videos overnight, but Mick said this was the one opportunity he'd been waiting for to swoop on Kiwi Gold.

Today Mick would drive out there with Sam and use Charlie's evidence to identify the trafficked Asian girls.

He felt confident, he told Summer, that the testimonies of Anya and Lily were enough for him to storm the building with a warrant to search their records and locate Mae.

This would be the first time Mick stuck his neck out, encroaching on Rob Dean's territory. He now had a sound reason for carrying out a detailed search at Kiwi Gold, and whatever it produced, would be sufficient to incite Dean to retaliate. He was bound to hear about Mick's visit as quick as lightning. But Mick planned to be one step ahead of Dean. He intended to take Mae back to the station as an eyewitness, persuading her to tell him about others who had arrived at Auckland harbour on the same boat as she did. Once he was sure illegal migrants were employed at Kiwi Gold and that Rob Dean was involved, he could go straight to the Detective Superintendent with concrete evidence.

Now Summer was worried. She had pressed Mick to tell her what would happen if his probing of the company was unfounded. All he said was to trust him—that he had everything in hand.

~

Sam accompanied Mick as he drove out to Franklin.

'The turnoff should be near here,' she said, pointing out the window.

'There it is,' Mick replied, veering off onto a side road.

'What will you do if Selena is there? According to my friends, she visits the premises often with Dean.'

'Yes, I know. I'll just say I've had an anonymous tip-off about people working there without permits—that's all. Not only Selina, but Dean will be livid. But as long as the DSS doesn't twig we suspect he's implicated—he may just believe I was routinely following up a random lead.'

189

'Poor Mae won't be able to return to work after coming back to the station. The staff will persecute her—or worse, scare her into keeping quiet,' said Sam.

'I realise all that—have been in this game long enough to have a plan worked out but didn't want to announce it until now. I've arranged for Mae to join Lily in Cambridge where she'll be safe, and we can help them both seek political asylum,' said Mick.

'What will we do when we arrive at Kiwi Gold?'

'While I wave the warrant at the office clerk and demand to see all the office records and passports of their overseas workers, I want you to ask the packers in the shed to take you to Mae.'

'Oh, okay,' said Sam. 'What then?'

'Go with her to the women's hostel and help pack her bags, as she'll be coming with us when we leave here. Explain how we're going to a safe place where I can question her and reiterate that she's not in trouble.'

'I think Mae's going to be terrified,' Sam answered.

'So it's your job to pacify her. I have arranged for her to stay overnight with Summer at the B&B. You can best return to the station.'

Sam shrugged, obviously put out that he didn't need her to follow through.

'Don't you want me to accompany her on the trip to Cambridge?'

'No, sorry. I'm going to ask Summer to assist me. Lily trusts her and she has already gained some insight from Anya about what these girls have been through. Now that we've been sniffing around at Kiwi Gold, the heavies will notify Dean. He'll want to come back—even if he's on Mars—once he finds out, so I need you back at the station to keep the dogs at bay.'

'Humph! So you're dropping me in it well and truly,' Sam mumbled.

'You'll be okay. I'll be back this evening and can take it from there. You don't have to be involved. If I'm right about my suspicions and can rake up sufficient evidence, I'll be going straight to the top—Detective Superintendent Hayley Winters—and request that the anti-corruption unit conduct an internal police enquiry.'

'Sam glared at him sideways. 'Man! That's pretty heavy. What if Dean has a mob of followers? He'll be out to get you.'

'I'm not afraid of him. His feet won't touch the ground before I have him arrested once we connect him with this trafficking racket.'

Sam went quiet until they finally bumped their way down the drive, arriving at the Kiwi Gold site. When they pulled into the visitor's carpark, her eyes hastily scanned the area. 'Looks like Dean's car isn't here, thank heavens.'

Mick chuckled, sensing her insecurity. 'I told you he's on his way to Fiji—although once he hears I've been turning this place over, he'll be back in a flash.'

~

While Sam followed Mick's directions and sought Mae in the packing shed, the DS stormed the main office holding the search warrant, explaining to the office clerk he would need to take all the immigration documents and passports held on file.

'Wait—I'll have to get permission from my boss before you go poking around in here!' the woman stammered, reaching for the intercom and shouting the name Byron.

'Oh, no you don't. Just read the warrant and let me do my job. I'll be talking to your manager soon enough.'

The clerk was livid—her face bright red, puffing up like a stonefish.

'Hand me the key to the filing cabinet where you keep the immigration documents,' Mick snarled.

By this time, corals of moisture had appeared on the woman's wrinkled forehead. She snatched a key from her desk drawer and slung it at Mick. He had planned to wait until he had Mae safely in the police car before phoning for backup, but Sam returned with her faster than he had expected, so he made a quick call. Mae carried a backpack that was almost as tall as she was.

'Sit in the car while my colleague and I sort out your papers,' Sam said to the girl, whose face was riddled with fear. 'Don't be afraid. We're going to take you somewhere safe.'

While the constable settled the girl, Mick stood tall, eyeballing the office clerk. 'I need Mae's visa documents, passport and everything relating to her employment here,' he demanded. 'She'll be leaving with me after you pay her in full what she is owed to date,' he snapped.

'I can't do that. I'll have to notify the payroll. You should know that.'

'Well, it had better go directly into her bank account tonight and I'll be following it up. Your head will swing if it doesn't happen,' he replied again curtly.

The flustered woman stood back as Mick and Sam rummaged through the filing system, her eyes agog as they gathered various immigration documents.

Mick pulled out Mae's dossier and walked over to his car with this and the remaining files while Sam remained guarding the office worker, ensuring she made no phone calls. He asked Mae to check her papers, which left the girl baffled.

'It's not what was translated to me when I signed these documents after I arrived. They had their Burmese interpreter, but he hadn't given them the correct information. This is all wrong, especially where it says I told them all my family is dead—that's a lie! I certainly don't want to remain at Kiwi Gold for two years. They promised me twice the pay I receive now and set me up in a house with one other person, not sleeping in a barn with a dozen others, which isn't even a hostel!' Mae burst into tears.

Mick rubbed her shoulder. 'Don't worry, dear. We know what's been going on—Anya and Lily have informed us. I am taking you to be with Lily this evening where you'll be safe, and we have a strong case against these people who have robbed you and many others. Please wait here a little longer until I get back up from other police colleagues. Wait—I think that's them coming through the gate now.'

While Mae wiped her eyes and sat patiently in the car, Mick spoke to the officer in charge of the team, who was ready to search the property. Mick's Detective Senior Sergeant friend from the Franklin Police cooperated with him, agreeing for Mick to interview witnesses at their station nearby and drop him back to the city afterwards. It was going to be a long day, and he still had to get Mae down to Cambridge.

He rang Summer to ask if she could take care of Mae until he could get there late afternoon, and then accompany him to Cambridge. Summer was delighted.

'Of course, I'll look after her and I'd love to join you. Have been feeling a little cooped up here lately. Mavis is back on deck and we've no guests booked for the evening meal tonight.'

When Mick came off the phone, he suggested to Sam it would be easier all around if she took his car and delivered Mae to Summer, who was waiting to receive her. Then she could leave the vehicle at their station where he would collect it before heading out to the B&B.

~

It was late evening by the time Mick arrived at the guest house after collecting his vehicle from the station. Summer was thrilled to see him, and he was grateful for her help with the girl.

'Where is Mae—isn't she going to join us for a meal? Mick asked.

'She ate not long before you arrived and is just now taking a shower before our trip to Cambridge. I'll eat with you, though.'

'I need to take a written statement from her before we head off, as there won't be much time when we get down there, and she'll be much too tired to think clearly.'

Summer passed him a glass of orange juice.

'I'll also be knackered, but we must drive straight back here, as I told Charlie I would be over to interview him. That means we can't hang around too long.'

Summer shared a ham and cheese frittata with Mick and when Mae returned to the dining room, she left her alone with the detective to complete the witness report.

She closed the door before clearing up the dishes in the kitchen, wishing she could listen in on Mick interviewing Mae, but Summer was not permitted, although she knew a fair amount about the fugitive already.

Before Mick arrived back at the guest house, Mae had disclosed a great deal to Summer about her covert arrival into New Zealand.

First her voyage by ship and then a fishing boat with other trafficked migrants arriving at Okahu Bay.

Mae had described at length the abuse she and other workers had received at the hands of the contracted hirers and the staff at Kiwi Gold—modern-day slavery.

While Mae was being interviewed by Mick in the guest house office, Summer changed her clothes, preening herself for the trip. She couldn't resist squirting her new Chanel No. 7 perfume around her neck and applying lipstick and blush. It was not as if she were intending to catch Mick's attention—or was it? Summer smartly banished the thought, revelling in her denial. She still sorely missed Tony, and loneliness constantly plagued her—especially at this time of the year.

It appeared Mae's interview went on for hours, although it had been just over an hour when Mick exited the room with the girl in tow.

'Sorry, it took rather longer than I had expected. I certainly didn't realise it was so late.'

'No problem. It was your key priority to get it done before dropping Mae off to Lily. Shall we leave now?' said Summer, with an elated twinkle in her eyes. Then her face dropped.

'No—forgive me for mucking you around, but I'm afraid we'll have to leave it until early in the morning. The poor girl was practically nodding off to sleep in the chair while we chatted.'

'Oh—so what's happening now, then?' Summer said, trying to hide the quaver in her voice, which was mainly embarrassment for getting all dolled up.

'Well, I was … um … I wondered if you'd mind letting Mae stay overnight and I'll pick you both up after breakfast if that suits you.'

Summer swallowed her hurt pride. 'Of course. I'll have breakfast ready, and we can all eat together when you arrive. I'll send my helpers a text and hopefully, both of them will be on deck bright and early in the morning.'

'Thanks, Summer. Sorry to inconvenience you at such a busy period for the guest house.'

'Liam is also available this week to assist. The staff can call on him if need be.'

'It'll be worth it after this, as we've caught a few big fish now that we have these girls' testimonies. I've phoned and asked Charlie if

I can interview him tomorrow evening at his house after we return from Cambridge.'

16

Mae woke with a tap on the door. 'Are you awake in there?' Summer said quietly.

'I have breakfast ready, and Mick will be here soon,' she said, holding the bedroom door ajar.

'The girl stumbled out of bed rubbing her eyes and shaking her head, suddenly realising where she was.

'Sorry—I seemed to have overslept. Do you mind if I take a quick shower? I'll be there shortly.'

'Of course not—go ahead. The guests have already eaten and left early so there'll just be you, me and Mick. See you in the dining room in a jiffy.'

Summer and Petra began clearing dirty dishes and cleaning the tables. Mavis had arrived early to help with the laundry and Liam had poked his head in the kitchen door to see if he was needed, but the women appeared to be coping. He ducked back to his cottage.

'Thanks for coming in at short notice, Mavis. It's bad timing for me to leave

Auckland—I know—but it can't be avoided, sorry.'

'No worries—I can stay until the evening if you wish.'

'It won't be necessary—thanks, all the same. No one has booked an evening meal. Most guests eat out in Mission Bay or down the road near here as there are such amazing restaurants and cafes within easy walking distance or five minutes in a car. That makes it easier for us, except for breakfast, which is always busy.'

When Mick turned up in the driveway, Mavis and Petra had a quiet giggle together and made themselves scarce.

'You're driving an unfamiliar car,' said Summer, her eyes scanning the vehicle.

'Mick patted the bonnet, as though it was a racehorse. 'No, this is my private SUV, Outlander. I thought there was less chance of anyone at the station spotting me on the road with Mae in the back.'

~

The traffic going south was bumper to bumper, even though there were still a few days until Christmas. Summer had reapplied her lipstick in the morning and even tried a different hairstyle. It was as though she was rediscovering—in her forties. A mid-life crisis.

'I suspected the traffic might be like this. It'll take longer than normal to get to Cambridge,' said Mick, glancing at Mae in the rear vision mirror. 'It usually takes around two and a half hours from St Heliers but not today, I'm afraid.

'No matter—I'm sure Mae hasn't seen a lot of our lovely countryside,' she said, glancing back over her shoulder at the girl.

'No, I've seen little of anything apart from the place Kiwi Gold had taken us shopping. They wouldn't let us go out on our own and didn't leave us with enough money to do it even if we could.'

Her answer enraged Summer to think that modern-day slavery did exist in New Zealand, although rarely.

'Well, that's all behind you now. It was your past and now you have a whole new future awaiting you,' said Mick.

The detective's compassionate reply melted Summer's heart.

'You'll love Elma and Dougie,' Mick added. 'They have adult children who do aid work in Southeast Asia. They're all familiar with the hard trials you've been through.'

Mae smiled back at him but said little apart from, 'Thank you, Mick.'

When they finally arrived at the farm, Elma and Dougie were in the front yard tidying the garden. They beamed as Mae got out of the car. Mick carried her backpack as she followed behind him and Summer to greet her hosts.

After being thoroughly welcomed, the couple invited them inside, taking Mae to her room.

The girl found her tongue suddenly. 'Where is Lily?'

'She's in the bathroom. You'll see her shortly,' said Elma.

Just as the woman spoke, Lily came out smelling like a rose and threw herself into Mae's arms.

'Oh, my gosh—you're finally here! Can't wait to show you around. You'll love it.'

Both girls broke down. Rivers of tears streamed down their cheeks as Elma thrust a box of tissues at them.

'Come on everyone. Just in time for lunch. I've got cold chicken and salad if you're hungry,' said Elma, showing them the way to the dining room while Dougie chatted with Mick.

'Sorry—Summer and I won't be able to stay long. I have a witness back in Auckland to interview and the traffic on the motorway is heavy,' Mick replied. 'We can have a quick bite before we go, though.'

Summer was delighted to see Mae and Lily relaxing together catching up on old times during the meal. She was even happier to see they were both in excellent hands with Elma and Dougie who fussed over them constantly as though they were their children.

After finishing lunch, Mick explained to the girls that he may need them as anonymous witnesses when Kiwi Gold's trafficking case ends up in Court. He explained how the two girls could give evidence from a remote location via CCTV with courtroom screens remaining blank.

'Anya has agreed to take part. I'll name you as witnesses A, B and C and go over the process with you before it happens.'

The girls both nodded in agreement and thanked Mick and Summer for rescuing them.

As they headed towards the front door, Mae ran up to Mick and threw her arms around him. Lily followed suit. Summer held back tears as she followed Mick out to the car.

~

Just as Mick had described to Elma and Dougie, the traffic on the motorway returning to Auckland City was heavier than their trip down.

'This is going to be another slow ride.' Mick sighed. 'It always happens leading up to the Christmas Holiday break even though many people have already left. It's getting late, so I'll have to drop you straight home and head over to see Charlie.'

Summer was sad she would be alone after Mick dropped her off and winced at the realisation that for the first time, she would have to suffer Christmas by herself.

Ava and Pete hadn't planned to visit their mother, as they had recently been over for their father's funeral. This time they would spend the holidays with their partners' families in Australia.

The children had invited Summer over to spend Christmas Day with them, but this was the worst time of the year to leave the guest house. It wouldn't have been fair on Mavis and Petra—especially as Summer had recently taken a trip to Queensland and left them both to it.

There was an awkward silence in the vehicle when Mick drove onto the main highway and Summer couldn't resist. 'So—are you going away for Christmas? I've never asked, but do you have siblings or parents around to spend it with?' What she meant was did he have a girlfriend?

'No siblings, unfortunately.'

'Oh—and your parents?'

'Mum died of a heart attack shortly after my father had passed away.'

'I'm sorry to hear that, Mick. My father also had heart trouble. It's what killed him not long before Mum had her first stroke in her sixties.'

'We're just peas in a pod then, aren't we?' Mick answered with a comforting smile.

Although Summer had been through the mill, she felt real empathy for Mick. Trying hard to restrain herself, she let rip.

'Well—you're always welcome to spend Christmas Day with me, if you're not rostered on,' then instantly regretted putting her neck out.

'Funny you should ask. I usually opt to work Christmas day, but this year I felt like taking it easy and just enjoying it. The Police Club put on a luncheon for those on their own. I was going to book it today and clean forgot. Other than that, I'm not doing anything.'

Summer felt confused. He didn't give her an answer. She had to ask again, and this was difficult.

'I don't quite understand. Did you say yes to my invitation, or would you prefer to go to your club?' She felt awkward and didn't want to sound desperate, which she wasn't. Just the thought of spending the day on her own in the empty guest house would make it the worst Christmas ever.

'Oh, so sorry—my mind was wandering. I meant to say thank you for thinking of me—and yes, I'd love to spend Christmas Day with you, if we can make it a little later in the day. I've been looking forward to a long-earned sleep-in.'

Summer didn't know what else to say and changed the subject.

'What do you think about the awful experiences Mae and Lily both had? I was wondering if their witness statements will do the trick.'

'Definitely. Tomorrow I'll get an update on the police search at Kiwi Gold, including the

PC they took from the administrator. The managers will be furious, so now they'll do a proper cover-up job of how they treat the rest of their employees.'

'What about Rob Dean? We know he's involved.'

'The top brass has been going through everyone's visa applications and employment records with an immigration officer today. I'll get those updates tomorrow.'

Summer felt a shot of adrenaline race through her veins. 'Wonderful. At last!'

'Once we have concrete evidence that Selena is involved with a human trafficking organisation, we'll get a warrant to search Angel's Staircase thoroughly, including her PC.'

'Humph! It's about time that woman is brought to account.'

'And any hint that Rob Dean is complicit with her criminal activities, I'll have him arrested.'

Once Mick drove onto the Waikato Expressway, the monotonous drive caused them both to lose their tongues. Finally, they arrived at the beginning of the Southern Motorway.

'Are you into ice cream?' Mick asked. 'We're about to pass the best outlet in the whole of Auckland. 'I'll take you there if you like—my shout.'

'I'm addicted to the stuff,' Summer replied, chuckling. 'Where is it?'

'Pokeno village. I'll take the turnoff at the next motorway exit. It usually stays open during the warmer months.'

'Tony took me here once when we were on our way back from our honeymoon in Tauranga. Gosh, that sure takes me back a few years.'

They were fortunate enough to get a parking space outside the shop and it wasn't so busy.

Summer was amazed at the size of the sweet treats that were half the price of any ice cream sold anywhere in Auckland, and she was a seasoned connoisseur.

It was almost uncanny, sitting with a stoic, bordering on austere detective casually eating ice cream in his car—just like an old couple. Once again, she dispelled all thoughts of such intimacy.

'I guess you must miss him—Tony, I mean. Hanging out doing this sort of thing.'

Summer felt a twinge of guilt, mixed with sadness.

'You're right—especially at Christmas,' she replied, her voice crackling.

Mick pulled a packet of baby wipes out of the car's front consul handing one to Summer. He licked his fingers, wiping them on a moist towelette dropping it into a small rubbish bag next to the gear lever. Summer did the same.

'Better get going or we'll be right in the thick of peak-hour traffic.'

It was another dreary drive back on the motorway, heading into the city and then out to St Heliers Bay. This part of the trip would take at least an hour and thirty minutes.

Their conversation dried up. Summer struggled to start anything, but again she couldn't stand the silence. She was prone to fill the gaps by babbling when feeling awkward.

'Do you mind if I ask if you've always been on your own—without a partner? You must get lonely.'

Mick hesitated, clearing his throat. He was treading on eggshells.

'I've had little luck, I'm afraid. Not like you—as Tony once told me—love at first sight,' he muttered wistfully.

'I was engaged to be married twice. The first woman wanted children fairly quickly, and I wasn't ready. We were only in our early twenties. The second one cheated on me twice with her ex-boyfriend during our rather tumultuous relationship. I haven't been interested in anyone else since—learnt to guard my heart.'

Now Summer understood his aloofness bordering on a hard exterior. But she also knew he had a heart of mush.

The only words she could muster were, 'I'm so sorry to hear that, Mick.'

'It's okay. I've learnt to enjoy my independence—rather like a cat.'

Following his confession, Mick went quiet while Summer sensed his hidden embarrassment about revealing his inner soul so readily. She kept her mouth shut.

When they finally arrived back in Auckland city, he dropped her home without staying for his usual cuppa.

'Sorry, Summer. I'll have to take off to see Charlie. It's getting late. Once I have a signed witness statement from him, I'm going to take it along with those of Lily, Anya and Mae to discuss the case with Hayley Winters. I think at least I could convince her to bring Selena into the station as a suspect for questioning and hope she weakens and spills the beans.'

He took her hand before she stepped out of the car, then abruptly held back. 'It won't be long now, Summer, and this will all be over. It'll be a happy New Year.'

'Let's hope so,' she replied with a heavy sigh.

17

'I'll be off now unless you want me to do anything else before I go,' Liam called from the front steps, standing tall in the leather hat Summer had bought him back from Noosa.

She stood at the ranch slider. 'No, I'm sorted here, thanks. 'You've got some driving to do to get to your family in Taupo in time for lunch. The traffic won't be too bad, being Christmas Day.'

'There's no hurry. We usually eat later in the afternoon anyway, after my sister's kids have opened their presents. I'll be back on New Year's Eve when I'll meet a few friends at night in Mission Bay to let off fireworks and cook marshmallows on the barbeque—coals in a ceramic slow-cooker. Works well.'

'Sounds fun. I may check out the firework display around here myself if I can stay up that late, but I can't count on it.'

'Well, whatever you do, enjoy and take care,' said Liam, hopping into his Ute and driving off.

Summer was at a loose end this year. Her emotions were in turmoil, and she was still feeling like a charity case having asked Mick to spend Christmas Day with her. He must have seen her as quite needy. Still, it beat doing Christmas on her own and she didn't have the grit to be alone.

After the trip to Cambridge, Summer couldn't resist predicting the outcome of Kiwi Gold's investigation, which was now called Operation Sea Wolf.

According to Mick, the investigative team had chosen that name because the traffickers worked from the sea. They were predatory pirates.

But he had not yet come back to her with the outcome. He had only texted about their lunch arrangements for Christmas Day. She had decided not to pressure him about it, guessing he would let her know in due course.

~

There was still an abundance of berries in the garden on Christmas Day, despite Summer having picked buckets of them before Christmas and made ice cream and smoothies for the guests.

This season had been a mighty harvest and Liam had given her a large container of ripe cherries as well. A fruit platter fit for a king—or should she say, for a Detective Sergeant.

Summer enjoyed pottering around in the kitchen on her own. Mick said he would bring a bottle of bubbly and cooked ham to go with her roasting chicken. Turkey had never worked for her.

Wandering into the garden, she gathered an array of vegetables to bake with the roast. It was a matter of keeping it simple, for Summer, as she felt at a loose end without Petra and Mavis's support in the kitchen.

'There you are!'

She was startled to the point of nearly jumping out of her skin as Mick suddenly appeared behind her in the strawberry patch.

'I knocked on your door several times and thought you were out but saw your car in the garage.'

Summer stood clutching a basket full of garden treasures—a wide grin beaming across her face.

'You frightened me. I'm running behind after having breakfast with my mother—although I expected you a little later.'

Mick reached over to take the basket off her as they walked inside the house.

'I'll duck out to the car to get the ham. It's all ready to go into the oven for warming later. I already glazed it this morning,' said Mick.

Summer admired his level of domesticity in the kitchen. He returned with the ham and a four-pack of mini Prosecco bottles, placing them on the kitchen bench.

Summer was annoyed she hadn't dressed in her Christmas garb or combed her hair before Mick arrived. She left him sitting in the lounge and disappeared into her bedroom.

Finally, she returned to see him with his head stuck in a newspaper. He looked up, scanning her from top to toe.

'Wow! If you don't mind me saying—you look sensational.'

He hadn't yet seen Summer smartly dressed for a special occasion. This time she wore a strappy, blue, three-quarter sundress with white sandals. A styling product made her short hairstyle shine, catching Mick's eye even more. He sniffed the air, detecting a sweet fragrance wafting in his direction. For seconds, he couldn't take his eyes off her, until he caught himself, blushing.

'I've put the bubbly in your fridge, and the ham is on the bench ready to go into the oven.'

'Okay, thanks. How about a cool drink to start, with zero alcohol? I made up a jug of soda water with elderflowers, lemon zest and raspberries. It's quite refreshing with ice.

'I guess I could try something different,' Mick replied.

'It's such a perfect day we could sit under the umbrella in the courtyard until the meal is ready. I'll peel the root vegetables and pop the chicken in the oven first. It's nearly ready to go—stuffed it this morning,' said Summer.

'Well, I certainly can't just sit around like King Farouk, leaving you to do everything. Let's get it ready together.'

Summer was flabbergasted. He was the last person she expected to be helping her in the kitchen at Christmas.

'Oh, okay. I'm feeling peckish. I'll get a few things out for us to nibble on while the food's in the oven and then we can sit outside.'

Summer placed bowls of mixed roasted nuts and potato crisps on the bench while they busied themselves.

Mick followed her instructions peeling vegetables while she took the prepared chicken from the fridge and placed it in the oven.

'We won't need to heat the ham until the last half hour before serving the rest,' she said.

They finished in the kitchen and then sat outside.

'I've got our snacks here but thought we could save the wine to have with our meal later,' said Summer.

'I won't drink much tonight. Not a good look if one of my team breathalyses me on the way home. You can enjoy it, I'm sure.'

After sharing small talk for a short time, Mick dropped a bombshell.

'Summer, I've got you the best Christmas present ... something you've been longing to hear.'

Summer could hear her heart pulsating in her head, assuming the police must have found Tony's killer.

'Tony!' she blurted.

Mick sensed the pain in her eyes. He had hoped to surprise her pleasantly, not disappoint. He wanted to stroke her arm in sympathy and restrained himself.

'Sorry, not Tony. But I have good news that should put a smile on your face. Just as we speak and even though it's Christmas Day, my team has brought both Selena and Rob Dean into the station for questioning on suspicion of illegal trafficking of migrants. They caught the DSS at the airport when he arrived back from Fiji last night, and he was livid, of course. Selena was hosting a Christmas party at Angel's Staircase with high-paying guests. She got quite a surprise Christmas present.

Summer's eyes widened. 'Marvellous! Things sure are beefing up.'

'I'll be there first thing tomorrow to interview them with their solicitors present. The anti-corruption unit is interrogating them at the station as we talk. I've got sufficient evidence to charge the culprits, now that we have eyewitness statements from Charlie, Anya, Lily and Mae.'

'That's marvellous, well done, Mick,'

'Our South Auckland team who searched the property and buildings at Kiwi Gold also have evidence to suspect Dean of his involvement.'

Summer stood up and threw her arms around Mick. 'Thank you so much. I knew you could do it. This is the best Christmas present ever!'

'Whoa! Take it easy. Let's just take this one step at a time, shall we? A corrupt senior police officer like Dean will have alibis stacked to the hilt. Such cops are experts at finding an angle. They use their power and positions of authority to take advantage of others—using deception, giving and receiving bribes and turning a blind eye to evil. They usually have a line of dodgy colleagues to cover them.'

Summer's face dropped.

Mick had burst her bubble, but he instantly regretted letting her down so hard.

He reached for her hand. 'Look, Summer. Dean may be pretty shrewd, but I am too.'

She managed a half-smile as Mick continued to explain his angle.

'During my long stint in Glasgow fighting organised crime in the drug squad, I came face to face with expert corrupt officers and brought many of them to justice. I have no fear of Dean—I assure you—he will get his comeuppance. Now shall we change the subject, just for the rest of today?' he said warmly.

Summer pulled herself together. 'Sure, of course. I'll just pop into the kitchen and check the roast. It should be almost done by now.'

'Give me a yell and I'll get the ham into the oven when you're ready.'

~

Summer was worn out by the time she saw Mick out the door after a long drawn-out Christmas Day.'

'It has been extremely pleasant, and I couldn't have thought of anyone else I'd like to spend it with. Thanks a heap, Summer.'

Mick leaned over and gave her a warm, lingering kiss on the cheek—startling her somewhat, as she wasn't accustomed to this level of intimacy from her late husband's best friend.

Summer couldn't help feeling guilty, despite it being only an innocent peck on her cheek—his smooth, close-shaven face, with a hint of Dior Sauvage aftershave, next to hers.

Once again, she forcibly banished her unexpected desires triggered by his supposed romantic advances.

Maybe she'd just had one too many glasses of bubbly.

'I thoroughly enjoyed this evening, too, and would have been alone this Christmas. Although I could have spent the day with my mother in the rest home. We had breakfast together, and it completely tired her out. So I appreciate your company. Thanks, too, for giving me an update on Dean and Selena.'

'I'll be in touch with you once they've both been interviewed. We'll have to wait for Immigration NZ to go through the migrants' visas and corroborate the statements Mae and Lily gave me about their hirers making false declarations and forcing them to become overstayers—threatening to have them sent back to their own country if they didn't comply with Kiwi Gold's demands. That may take a while,' said Mick.

'Well, I've waited this long. I'm sure I can ride it out.'

'If this goes to Court, you'll also be required as a witness. We'll bring Anya and Jonny out here for any trial if we can get it that far,' said Mick, stepping into his car. 'At least you'll feel a lot safer now Dean is no longer under the radar.'

'Thanks, Mick. I appreciate your support.'

'I know you do,' he replied, smiling, nudging her with his elbow.

After he drove off, Summer ran a hot bath, which was unusual for her. She preferred a shower, but now her body ached from the nervous tension caused by the case involving Rob Dean. It had been a hectic week for her. Now she was glad of the peace—having the house to herself. She knew she'd have to get a good night's sleep in readiness for the onslaught of tourists booked Boxing Day through the New Year.

Mick's Prosecco had gone straight to her head and made her sleepy. Despite them being mini bottles, Summer had drunk most of it.

The perfumed soap-suds spumed around her neck tickling her face. This time, she decided not to play her relaxing classical music on Spotify—Litvinovsky's Le Grand Cahier: La Forêt Et La Rivière, as it was bound to put her to sleep. Mick wouldn't have appreciated her drowning on Christmas Day after he'd shared bottles of sparkling wine with her.

What had impressed her most about Mick was how he'd remained the perfect gentleman even though she was quite tipsy.

Summer's mind wandered back to the latest drama with Dean. Could the mongrel wriggle out of this one? Selina might trip herself up and dob him in. They would both have to get their stories straight. And, as Mick had discussed with Summer during lunch that day, neither of the offenders would have had enough time to swap notes before their arrest.

Summer closed her eyes, trying her best to empty her mind and meditate. She should have played her classical music, as she struggled to unwind.

Ensuring Rob Dean got his just desserts had become an obsession with Summer, but when she stepped out of the bath and stared at her face in the mirror, she could see how much it was taking its toll.

Deep cavities under her eyes and more crow's feet had appeared. But there wasn't much chance of her being able to relax until Tony's killer was found. She was holding her breath, hoping that Rob Dean was not only the instigator of the human trafficking ring—but also her husband's murder.

18

The puffed-up Detective, Rob Dean, leaned over a table in the interview room completely flummoxed.

With his sudden arrest at Auckland International Airport, he had no time to get his story straight or to compare alibis with Selena.

During his interview, joined by the head of the anti-corruption unit and the Detective Superintendent, Dean tripped himself up several times.

When Mick and Sam produced files with witness statements from the people they had rescued—including those from other migrant workers from Kiwi Gold—he shrivelled into his shell.

Dean was lost for words and whatever false alibis he conjured only pushed him further into the muck—enough for Mick and Hayley Winters to charge him for his involvement in a trafficking ring. He was suspended from work and remanded in custody until the outcome of his Court hearing.

Selena had dropped Dean well and truly in the quagmire. She had denied any connection with him, but Charlie's video of her arriving at Kiwi Gold together with Dean when the migrant girls came off the boat proved she was lying.

The witness statements from Lily, Mae, Anya and Jonny had painted Selena into a corner.

She and Dean were both held on remand at the Mt Eden Correctional Facility in Auckland until their first Court appearance.

Mick drove Sam back home from the station after the interviews while they shared their views on what had just taken place.

'So, Dean is likely to go down for his part in the trafficking—but that's only just the beginning, isn't it? I mean ... the murders. What about the dead guard at the Port? We know it was the same group who smuggled the Asian people in via the shipping container. I'm sure Dean won't tell you the identity of the truck driver who killed him,' said Sam.

'I get you, Sam. But now we know who they are, we'll track down the hitman. Tomorrow, I want you to carry out a search on both Selina's and Dean's family members. There might be someone they're related to or connected with. In the meantime, I'll get permission from Hayley to have Forensics conduct another analysis of the evidence we hold from the guard and Chai. While

Operation Sea Wolf is underway, we'll continue to hold Dean and Selina on remand as prime suspects, as neither of them was granted bail.

'Sure, boss. At last, the pieces of the puzzle are all coming together, thanks to you,' Sam replied.

'Listen here. We all play our part and without one, the rest crumbles. So, don't underestimate your valuable contribution.'

'Thanks, Mick. That means a lot.'

'Remember, before you dig around about the truck driver, familiarise yourself with the witness statements of the victims who had arrived at the Port, including Chai's testimony,' said Mick.

'I thought you have our tech team to do that probing.'

'You're right, I do, but I would rather it was something we kept to ourselves at this point. With a senior police officer involved in serious crime, I'm not sure who to trust at this point.'

Sam took it on board and for the rest of the journey home, they talked non-police business until Mick pulled up at her gate.

'Want me to pick you up tomorrow?'

'No, thanks,' Sam replied. 'The mechanic said my car will be ready tomorrow morning. He'll drop it off.'

~

It was head down, bottom up, until the end of the week. Summer was of two minds whether she enjoyed the guest house being so full as there was no lull in the busyness, but she was glad of the boost in her income as she had planned to take a trip to Australia to see her children the following winter.

Liam's barbeques were an immense success as was Summer's homemade berry ice cream. It was so hectic she barely had any mental space to focus on Operation Sea Wolf. But once a week she would make time when the tide was in and the beaches weren't so crowded, to have a most welcome ocean swim.

Tony and Summer had bought identical kayaks, which they had often used on his days off. Now Summer occasionally allowed her guests to use them for free, but whenever she got the chance, would paddle herself out to Brown's Island or along the coast to Mission Bay.

~

It had been a week since Summer's cosy, bordering-on intimate feast with Mick Christmas Day, but she'd heard nothing from him.

Was he now feeling threatened by their deepening friendship or thinking he'd betrayed Tony by wining and dining his wife?

Summer was worrying she had scared him off.

19

When Mick finally got back in touch with Summer, he said he would drop by her house that evening, as it was his day off.

'Stay for dinner, if you like,' she said, trying not to sound over-enthusiastic. 'There's no one booked for a meal. We're encouraging guests to go out to the local restaurants and cafes at night, as breakfasts are pretty busy enough these days.'

'I suppose I could come, but I'm sorry it won't be until late—around eight, if that's okay for you,' Mick replied. 'I've got business to attend to during the day.'

Summer longed for a break from her usual routine of cooking meals, cleaning, laundry and sharing small talk with the guests. Although she had her helpers, Petra and Mavis, the burden of work was still heavy, and she had to pitch in each day or employ an extra staff member.

She hurried off to her office to get the list she'd made of the things she wanted to check out about Tony's case and Operation Sea Wolf. With all Mick's focus on nabbing Rob

Dean, she wondered if he'd lost interest in solving Tony's mysterious death. Why hadn't he been in touch with her since Christmas? Did he think Summer was too involved with police business—or worse—had she got too close to him?

Either way, it irked her he'd been so avoidant. But tonight she intended to discover whether he was losing interest in her involvement in the criminal cases—and most of all—their deepening friendship.

~

Seeing Mick get out of his car clutching flowers in one hand and a bottle in the other gave her palpitations. The tension in her head hurt. What was going on—was he giving her strange, mixed messages, or was it just a figment of her wild imagination?

Thankful that she'd tried to spruce herself up, Summer glanced at the hall mirror, ensuring she'd not overdone it.

Dressed in knee-length denim shorts, a floral blouse and white sandals, she answered the door. After swapping pleasantries, Mick passed Summer the gifts. Instead of a posy, it was a bright orange Begonia pot plant.

'The plant is gorgeous, Mick. Thank you, but you'd best keep the wine. My stomach didn't cope with our session at Christmas. I've been taking it easy lately.'

Mick plonked himself down into an armchair while Summer sat opposite him.

She guessed he didn't want to share the couch with her.

'Don't worry—it's only sparkling grape juice. I must be careful too. I'm driving,' he said, winking.

Summer served a simple meal at the table of chicken pasta with mushrooms and spinach, which they ate while discussing the criminal cases. She poured the grape juice.

'Some of my berry ice cream before we move on?' Summer asked, poking her head around the kitchen door after the meal.

'That would be awesome. I've tasted it before—it's great.'

Summer handed Mick his dessert and joined him to eat hers. After the meal, they returned to the lounge and got down to brass tacks. It was a long and drawn-out discussion.

'So, you're saying the divers have retrieved the missing wheel wrench they didn't originally find in the harbour?'

'That's right. After we'd arrested Dean and carefully considered the victims' witness statements, Hayley Winters ordered a more extensive dive search of the harbour near the container terminals. The team then decided this trafficking case was serious enough to do a widespread probe.'

'What did the sea turn up?'

'We found the wheel wrench was one of several with a serial number showing it was produced in New Zealand. We have investigated everyone who has purchased such a tool and discovered one of them was Selina's father, but he died three years ago, so it couldn't have been him.'

'What? That's so strange. How would the truck driver at the Port have got hold of it?'

'Perhaps the old man pawned it at a second-hand shop or gave it away to a friend. The trouble is we can't question him to find out.'

'Selena has been under intense interrogation over it but denies having any knowledge of her father's toolbox except that a charity near his home in West Auckland came to collect his stuff soon after the funeral. She can't remember if any of them took the tools. There were a lot of them, and they were also offered to family and friends. Her mother is dead, so no help there.'

'Oh, no—what a shemozzle. So close and yet so far from finding the answers,' Summer replied. 'It seems to be the very key to solving the Port killing,' she added. 'Perhaps Selena took it from there and gave it to one of her cronies in the crime syndicate. She could be buddies with the truck driver and have given the wrench to him. Can't you use that as circumstantial evidence against her at least?'

It was clear to Mick that Summer direly needed answers—hoping for a reason to nail Selena and Rob Dean.

'That's not how criminal investigations work. We've already been over this. If

Selena's father had owned one of those wrenches, it may have had no connection with her. But we'll fully investigate her family, don't worry.'

Don't get ahead of yourself again, Summer reminded herself. 'Sorry, Mick. I understand.'

'There has been a recent development though regarding the Thai fellow, Chai. You know he was released from prison and taken to a secure refugee centre until this case goes to Court. With the approval of Hayley, I had the guard's clothes and boots re-examined—and investigated for tampering with evidence. In the pathologist's original report, DNA samples were taken from skin and sweat under the armpits of the guard's jacket which Forensics matched DNA from Chai. During his police interview, the suspect had said that the driver had directed him to clutch the body under the arms while he took the feet, then they turned the guard over onto his back to see if he was still alive.'

Summer's face fell while Mick continued.

'But when we had the clothing re-examined, they only found DNA from Chai on the guard's jacket and there was none on the leather boots—it had been removed.

'Oh, no. What does this mean?'

'Good news for him. Remember the trafficked victims who were left on the wharf when the truck driver took off? Well, we interviewed them in the refugee centre, and they testified in written statements that the driver had hold of the guard's boots. The pathologist has now confirmed that the forensic evidence was tampered with—that the footwear had been cleaned since the forensic testing, so we can put that one on Dean. The stowaways witnessed the guard being struck on the head by a mystery assassin using a wrench of some sort—testifying that it was neither Chai nor the driver who attacked him.'

'See, Mick!' Summer's complexion instantly changed from peaches and cream to tomato red.

'I kept telling you right from the beginning. Tony knew Dean had tampered with evidence. If only someone had believed him, or me—you could have been a lot further down the track long ago.'

Mick scratched his nose, clearing his throat. Momentarily, he was lost for words, thinking he would have to pacify this irate woman. He'd always thought she was secretly blaming him for the slow progress in solving Tony's murder, which she believed Dean had carried out.

'I'm sorry if you think I rubbished your judgement—or Tony's. Perhaps I should have pushed to have the guard's forensic evidence re-examined at the time Tony had pointed it out. But in the policing world, things are not that straightforward, Summer. The thing is, it's happening now and we're going to lay this one on Dean. Sam is our witness and we're also going to corner the property officer who has been charged with perverting the course of justice. We'll sufficiently pressure him to squeal.'

'So, do you have enough dirt to put Dean away now for good?'

'We have a problem proving he is directly involved in trafficking, although Dean has a weak alibi for why Charlie saw him with Selena at Kiwi Gold that night. We can't just lay it on him. His alibi is that Selena had been in the car with him earlier in the evening while they searched for Lily—which we know is false—and, according to Selena, the girl had stolen a considerable sum of money from her before leaving Angel's Staircase. Dean raced to Kiwi Gold after he alleged he'd received a tip-off that an employee knew of Lily's whereabouts. He admitted Selena was a silent business partner in Kiwi Gold orchards, so she had the right to question their employees. Of course, none of the migrants cooperated, leaving Dean with no proof. But what we do have are several testimonies from workers there who often saw Dean and Selena arrive at Kiwi Gold together and meet with Management.'

Summer got out of her chair. 'Are you going to finish your drink, or will you join me for coffee? I rarely drink it this late, but I'm reasonably hyped up and can't see myself getting much sleep tonight,' she blurted.

Mick could sense the ire in her voice. He was in deep thought about how he was going to undo the damage he had done by his past decision to protect his status at the police station and not rock the boat. He had made such an effort in trying to change all that by going the extra mile to appease Summer by privately investigating both cases, but she had not let it go.

'Coffee is fine, thanks. Plenty of milk.'

She dashed off to the kitchen and returned, finding him in deep thought. She passed him a mug.

When she sat down with her cup, he turned to her with a serious expression. 'Look, Summer. Once again, I'm sorry for not taking seriously your persistence about getting Forensics to re-test the evidence from the Port killing. It's not that I doubted your integrity. I guess I was weak and was more interested in protecting myself—my ambition—than defending Chai. It just shows how selfish one can become living on your own—oh, except not everyone—you're not.'

Oh, no, I've put my foot in it again. 'What I mean is … I've become one-eyed, living in a world of self. I hope you can forgive me,' he said, looking down at the floor.

Summer nearly choked, gulping down her coffee. It was harrowing listening to Mick humbling himself. Suddenly she saw him in a different light and felt guilty putting him through the mill—struggling to find words to turn things around.

'Well, I think we're a noteworthy pair of crime-fighters, don't you think? We work well together,' she said, smiling but thinking how clumsy that sounded.

Mick's eyes twinkled. 'You can say that again. I think you would have made a brilliant cop. Ever thought of changing vocations?'

'Not on your Nelly. I saw enough when I was working at the station as Police Media Advisor before I met Tony. Look at the long hours and gruelling night work you all have to do—not to mention the frightening situations you get into. And the last one finished my husband.'

Mick gave her a sheepish look. She was right.

'Summer, listen. I promise you, before long, your husband's killer will be locked up for good. You'll have justice for Tony. In the meantime, once we track down the truck driver, a trial will be underway for the traffickers. It's a long and drawn-out process battling organised crime on that level—especially with possibly a top police officer in charge or high in the pecking order.'

'Thanks, Mick—sorry I snapped. I don't blame you, as I've said before. I know you'll solve it eventually, so let's move on from here. How about I get Charlie and his Dad around as promised to share a meal sometime soon?'

'If you don't mind, I'd rather not. As he is a key witness, it wouldn't look right for me to be fraternising with him. Perhaps one day when the trial is over. I've already got his witness statement.'

'Okay, I understand.'

'Do you want to take a walk along the beach in the fresh air? It's a warm night, and the sky is so clear you can see the stars.'

Summer jumped at the idea. 'I'd love to join you. I'll just grab a jacket.'

20

It was midnight when Mick had seen four missed calls on his cell phone—two from the station and the other two from an unknown Caller ID. When he had spent the evening with Summer earlier, he'd left his mobile phone in the car while walking under the stars chatting to her. After accompanying her to the door, he'd gone for a drive around the waterfront and sat parked on the wharf at Westhaven, watching the fishermen sending ripples through the calm water while sitting on their fold-up chairs. The air was muggy and close as he revelled in the cool breeze wafting through his car window.

Mick's hand had barely touched the phone to check his voice messages when it rang, startling him. As usual, during his days off, he rarely paid much attention to his mobile— peeved at how much it dominated his life.

'Mick! For goodness' sake, man. Don't you ever answer your calls? It's Pete Rogers.'

Pete was his buddy and the Fire Chief of his local Fire Service.

'Happy New Year, mate. What's up? It's my day off. Keeping the darn phone at arm's length today,' Mick grumbled.

'Well, I'm sorry, friend—you've picked the wrong day for that. I've got awful news. You'd better get your butt over to your property. Your home is on fire and we're still there. Everyone has been trying to reach you! I'll wait for you to arrive.'

Mick froze, like a stunned mullet. His throat tightened with angst. He could barely speak.

'Are you okay, friend?' said Pete.

'I'm under the harbour bridge in the carpark thinking I was chilling out. I'll ... be there in a flash.'

He didn't bother checking the rest of his messages, as he gathered they were from his colleagues alerting him to the crisis.

Arriving in the street where his property was cordoned off, he was directed by fire officers to park his car. He stepped out, flashing his ID under their noses, but they had already recognised him. He took off down his driveway and stood staring at the apocalypse. It was as though he had been transported in time to another planet. The once charming, character-filled 1960s villa he owned was nothing but a pile of wet ash and charred rubble. The odour of burnt debris scoured his lungs as he stepped out, racing up to Pete, a senior fire officer, who hugged him. 'I'm so sorry, Mick. There will be a full investigation, but from the burn pattern, it appears to be arson. There are considerable remains of gasoline around your property, too.'

Mick's house had been located down a long driveway. He stood mesmerised at the holocaust that left only an unrecognisable shell. Even the roof had caved in.

He was about to crumble in a heap when Pete took his arm and led him down the driveway to a grass berm by the road where he sat by the curb, holding his head in his hands while Pete kept an arm around his shoulders.

Mick raised his head, wiping his eyes with his sleeve. 'Can't believe the timing—it's uncanny. Been busy all day with my lawyer and the bank rearranging my finances after finally paying off my house loan. I'd been doing a heap of overtime this past year to make this possible. I thought for the first time in my life I was financially independent. Now it's as though I've been jinxed.'

Well, congratulations, anyway. That was a huge milestone. I gather your house was insured?'

Mick wondered why he would have to ask that question. 'I'm not worried about the house, right now. It's my new cat, Powder. I kept her inside the house until she was familiar with it to stop her running away—and now she's gone, anyway.'

Pete was lost for words as he listened to his desperate friend. He wasn't used to seeing him in such a vulnerable state.

'I'm sorry, mate. I'll find some guys to help look for her. Perhaps we should start with the neighbours. We'll inform them in case she turns up in their garages or sheds.'

Mick wasn't permitted to go onto the site to search the remains of his house with a suspected arson at play. The timing meant it was now a forensic case, as he could have been asleep inside.

He followed the fire officer, looking for his cat, calling her name with a shaky voice, throwing all pride and his macho image out the window. He had become like a small boy who had lost a pet.

After spending more than an hour leaving no stone unturned, Mick's neighbours came out of the woodwork—some of whom he had never met—clutching containers with meals. Kind old ladies invited him to dine with them during the week and offered him solace, promising to help find his beloved cat.

Mick was a broken man wrecked by the loss of something worth far more to him than a house—a delicate, white Persian cat with a cute face that melted his heart.

Pete received a call from the Detective Superintendent. 'Hi Hayley ... yeah, he's with me now. Do you want to speak with him?'

She declined, saying Mick needed time to process what had happened and said he could call her the next day. Hayley discussed alternative accommodation for Pete and hung up.

'Come on, Mick. I'm taking you to the Police hostel. I'll bring you some clothes. You're about my size.'

Mick wasn't in a fit state to negotiate, but he stalled him. 'No. wait! I'll get someone to bring me there later. I want to keep looking for Powder.'

The Fire Chief shook his head. 'I think you're still in a state of shock, Mick. There are plenty of neighbours keeping an eye out for the cat. She'll turn up when she's hungry. It's nearly morning.'

'The poor thing will be terrified. That's if she's still alive,' Mick groaned.

He begrudgingly accompanied his fireman friend out the gate to where his vehicle was parked.

'You're not looking that great, mate. How about I drive you over there? Someone can bring you back later in the day.'

'No, I'll take my car. Thanks, Pete. I'm okay—just a heap bereaved.'

21

The hot weather and chaos in her life caused by the two criminal investigations had wrecked Summer's sleep patterns. She got into bed each night and just lay there—although overtired—wide awake until three or four each morning. This wreaked havoc with her health and ability to cope with the running of the B&B and handle the guests—some of whom were occasionally difficult.

Had she made the right decision to manage a guest house on her own? Regardless of having staff to help with the domestic chores, she still had to handle all the business side of things for the first time in her life, including the maintenance.

Summer missed Tony dearly and somehow felt a degree of misplaced guilt that his murder had not yet been solved. She couldn't even lay his memory to rest not knowing what terrible horror he'd suffered. Had he lain there long in the cold, hard clay maybe even trying to raise his voice to alert help? Olive hadn't tried to resuscitate him. She just rang the police, but if she had given

Tony CPR or even called an ambulance first, he could have been saved.

There was no way a woman—likely to be in her eighties—could bend down to the ground and revive him. Olive didn't own a cell phone. Instead, the poor woman had staggered in shock all the way home to use her landline. She had done her best.

Summer was worn out from arguing with her mind about the chain of events which had robbed her of Tony on that dark day.

Another humid afternoon, and all the guests were out. No dinner bookings, which gave her some relief.

She searched for Petra and found her folding sheets in the laundry.

'I'm taking myself off for a swim. Mavis is still here, isn't she?'

'Yes, she's making the beds for the new guests who arrive tomorrow. We'll be okay— not much to do this afternoon.'

'Thanks, Petra. I won't be long. Just need to blow away the cobwebs and get some fresh air.'

Summer changed into her swimming togs and took off down to the beach with a zip-up towelling beach robe covering her. She carried a beach bag containing a towel.

To her delight, it was high tide. During the week, it was usually busy on the beach with families and children tearing around everywhere. But today it was quiet, with only a handful of people walking along the pathway and others sitting under the trees.

She left her beach bag and towel on the sand, headed straight for the water and dived under. Summer revelled in the warm water current, which was a strange phenomenon and often occurred at that beach during the summer months—like taking a warm bath.

After staying in the water longer than planned, she got out and spread her towel on the sand. Lying on her back gazing at the fluffy white clouds, she let go of all unwanted, worrying thoughts.

'Hi, there! Fancy seeing you here. I thought you were always too busy in that guest house of yours to have time for such pleasures.'

It was Charlie walking along the beach barefoot, carrying a bucket. 'I've been out in my kayak today and thought I'd come here and collect seaweed for my garden.'

'Oh—I wondered why you carried a bucket.'

Summer suddenly remembered she was going to invite Charlie and his family for a meal.

'How about dinner at mine—you and your family this Thursday? I owe you still.'

'Aww, you don't owe me anything. Remember, after the way your granddad took care of us, we're forever indebted to you and your family. It's the other way around.'

Summer realised it was the truth, but she hated to make promises she couldn't keep.

'Tell you what,' said Charlie. 'I know how busy that guest house is, and you must get tired. Surely things quieten down after the school holidays. How about calling me when the kids go back in February?'

That's what Summer liked so much about Charlie—ever so humble and caring.

She thought twice about entertaining others with so much stress in her life. 'Okay, you win—it's a date. I'd best get back now before the girls knock off for the day. I'll be in touch, Charlie.'

When Summer arrived home, she was about to take a shower when Petra caught her.

'Your phone has been ringing continuously from your bedroom. You must have several missed calls. I could hear it going off from the hallway while I was putting the linen away in the cupboard.'

Summer remembered she had left her mobile behind deliberately so she could completely relax.

'Thank, Petra. I'll see to it once I'm dressed.'

When she finally got to her phone, the calls were from Mick, with one voice message asking her to call him urgently.

Listening to Mick's troubling news about the house fire and losing his cat gutted Summer. She didn't know what to say to him.

'I can't believe it. So have you ... lost everything?'

'Yep. Just the skeleton of my home—charred debris—remains. All my belongings were vamoosed. Thank God I saved all my documents to the Cloud—even my photos are backed up there, and my laptop was in the boot of my car.'

'That's a relief. Where are you living—are you okay?'

'At the police hostel. There is accommodation for officers on call or night duty who live a distance from work, and they have spare rooms at present.'

'That's great, Mick ... so what about Powder—did you find her in the end?'

'Yes, thank goodness. She was micro-chipped. Someone in the next street found her hiding in the woodshed next to their house and they took her to the vet. I couldn't believe it,' he said, his voice crackling. 'One of the elderly neighbours is caring for her until I get a more permanent place to live.'

Summer thought he was about to burst into tears. Instead, he instantly changed the subject.

'Come for dinner tonight. I want to hear all about it and see if I can help.'

'That's kind of you, Summer. But I'd like to take you for a meal instead, for a change. Give you a night off.'

Mick's invitation was unexpected. 'Oh, I'd like that. Where shall we go?'

'I know you're partial to pizzas. How about the new restaurant—Pizza Palace? They make the best-woodfired pizzas on the coast. I'll pick you up at seven.'

'Great—look forward to it. I still haven't got the knack of making them yet, although we have our clay oven in the backyard.

~

Pizza Palace was full. Mick had forgotten to make a booking. They stood at the front desk while a waitress found them a table.

'If you wouldn't mind taking a seat in the foyer, there is a table with a couple by the window about to leave. I'll come and fetch you.'

It took longer than expected for the table to become vacant. Mick and Summer were about to leave and look elsewhere when the waitress returned, directing them to the spot where they had a view of the sea.

'Sorry about the long wait—I should have booked first,' said Mick.

Summer was miles away, staring out at the billowing surf. A strong southwesterly blew, wafting the branches of a nearby palm tree.

Mick passed her a menu. 'Shall we order? I'm famished.'

During their meal, Summer couldn't help commenting on the deep hollows under his eyes and a pallor she hadn't seen.

'How are you? Looking a little pasty on it. Sleeping okay?'

Mick took a mouthful of mineral water.

'Actually, I haven't had a decent night's sleep since the fire. It's the hostel. I have a room of my own, but I'm not used to living in the city centre. It's noisy and there's a bright street light outside my bedroom window.'

'What about your insurance—can't they help with emergency housing?'

'It's as impossible as getting blood from a stone. I think I'll have to find alternative arrangements.'

'Why don't you come and stay at my guest house? I can offer you a reasonable discount. The school holidays are almost over so the busyness should slow down now.'

Mick took his time to answer. 'I'm not sure that's a wise idea, Summer. If the arson had something to do with me putting Rob Dean away, it may put you at risk too.'

'Do you think so—where could you go then?'

'I have a beach house—a bach—up north at Coopers Beach.'

Summer was confused. How could he work from there? She wouldn't get to see him, thinking how used to his companionship she had become.

'Isn't that rather far for commuting to work?'

'Oh, I don't plan on living up there. I thought about renting it out and with that money, I can lease a property near the station until my new home has been built using the insurance.'

Summer let out a breath of contentment. She was overjoyed Mick wasn't about to disappear just like her husband had suddenly.

'That's a marvellous idea. But just remember, there's always a spare room here if you get into trouble.' Summer was disappointed he wasn't about to take her up on the offer. Loneliness had caused her to become a secret fantasist.

22

A week after his house fire, Mick sat opposite Sam at a table in the police canteen, yawning loudly.

'Are you sure you're up to getting back into the thick of things at work yet—it's too soon isn't it?'

'It's okay Sam. What else am I going to do? I'd be bored otherwise. By the way—well done! All that research you did into Hortihire has paid off. Immigration will make certain the owner and his accomplices will never again work in the industry.'

'Thanks, Mick—all in a day's work. I can't believe they've been operating for so long, defrauding labour contracts. Their foreign language interpreters sure have some gall risking prison by aiding the trafficking of migrant workers.'

'Yeah, I know. But this kind of thing has been going on for years—although not only with trafficking gangs. Other people are arriving from overseas, too, hired by dodgy recruiting agencies and falsifying their employment documents.'

Mick pointed at the food cabinet. 'Let's grab something to eat—my shout.'

They got their meals on trays and brought them back to the table.

'Sam, I want you to phone all the second-hand dealers in West Auckland as a process of elimination. If what Selena says is true, a shop must have a record of receiving a toolbox, and if not, she must have passed it onto one of her friends when she cleared out her father's stuff.'

'Yeah, I can do that. It shouldn't be too difficult to trace it, surely. I'll find a way. Are you going to question Selena's family? Maybe they know something about her we can use.'

Mick poured tomato sauce over his pie and took a mouthful of orange juice. 'Yep, I'll be checking out her family once you get back to me about the charities.'

'By the way—did you have an enjoyable time with Summer the other night? I saw you both strolling along the promenade in Mission Bay on that gorgeous, warm evening.'

Mick was taken aback, being a private man.

His neck flushed. 'Stalking me, are you? I needed to give her feedback about the progress of our investigations into her husband's murder. It was too stuffy inside, so we took a walk.'

Anyway, why should I justify myself to you?

Mick held his tongue, knowing his sidekick was not being intrusive but pleased to see he had found a friend in Summer—regardless of his denial.

'Well, I must be getting off,' he said. 'If you can get onto those charities, I'll be preparing evidence for Operation Sea Wolf when it goes to trial.'

23

Mick's rental townhouse in Newmarket overlooks the Auckland Domain. Today he sits perusing documents in the case file for Operation Sea Wolf, which are spread out on the dining table—although he knows he should be resting.

Since the fire, he has had great difficulty focusing, as he still suffers from Post-Traumatic Stress Disorder.

Superintendent Winters ordered him to attend therapy with the police psychologist who reported that recovery from such a horrifying incident would be slow.

While Operation Sea Wolf continued, Dean was remanded without bail in Mt Eden Correctional Facility as the prime suspect for the port worker's murder.

Selena was also in custody there, charged with her involvement in the trafficking ring.

Mick mulled over the files he'd just finished reading, endeavouring to digest the summary of events.

Selina and Dean both vehemently denied they were in any way connected with the Kiwi Gold slave labour business.

Dean had insisted he only got involved with Selena in Angel's Staircase when there were major problems with "her girls". And Selina trusted the DSS to be discreet.

The DSS had lied to the police, saying he occasionally carried out security checks on Selina's business premises. She owned the massage parlour in K-Road called the White Lady, which he monitored along with Angel's Staircase. Mick suspected he may have had other more undesirable motives for frequenting these shady outfits but had no proof.

Selena finally admitted to owning shares in Kiwi Gold, which meant the team was now busy investigating whether her investments were legitimate.

Socially, she was friendly with the head shebang, Byron, the owner, and Mick had strong misgivings about him—thinking he was one of Selena's old clients when she worked as a call girl. Her "investments" may have been a pay-off—a bribe for keeping her mouth shut about his dodgy business dealings. Kiwi Gold supplied her with cheap labour through selected girls they sent to Angel's Staircase.

Dean refused to confess any involvement with Kiwi Gold other than having a "friend" in management called Byron to whom he was introduced on a social level through Selena, with her having shares in the company.

How did the axiom go? Mick pondered—*you are known by the company you keep.*

A buzz on his phone startled him. It was Summer texting to find out how he was going. He found it more and more difficult to answer her questions about both criminal cases she had involved herself in. With most suspects in custody and full investigations being carried out by his team—particularly those involving a bent cop—Mick clammed up and would not disclose any further police dealings to Summer. The dynamics had changed.

He phoned her. 'I'm taking it slowly, Summer—thanks for asking—but I'm not sleeping well. Both Powder and I need time to adjust to our new abode.'

'You poor things. Are you free this evening—come for a meal?'

'That's kind of you. If you don't mind, I have an enormous pile of reports to go through following our interviews with the suspects of Operation Sea Wolf. We've also arrested the trafficking ringleader—Byron— the manager of Kiwi Gold and his associates, but I can't discuss it with you further, at this point.'

Summer sagged. She was used to discussing the cases with Mick until recently. But having been married to a police officer for so many years she knew the drill. Mick would have to be careful divulging information now they had made arrests.

Summer tried to hide her despondency as she preferred his company in the evenings—the loneliest time of the day for her.

She promptly reminded herself of the stress Mick was under both at work and in his personal life.

'Hey! Get off there,' Mick blurted, lifting his cat off the keys of his laptop and placing her on the floor.

'Oh, for a minute I thought you were telling me to get off the phone,' said Summer, humouring him.

'I wouldn't speak to you like that. Every time I'm on the laptop she rubs up against my neck and plonks her furry body down onto my keyboard. So frustrating.'

It melted Summer's heart hearing this. Mick, whom she'd once thought was an aloof, stoic detective, was now being controlled by a white, fluffy kitten. She chuckled.

'It's my turn to cook something, anyway. Once I get this place looking how I want it, you'll be the first person I'll invite around for one of my fancy knock-up meals,' said Mick.

'Cool, I'll look forward to trying out your expert cooking and seeing your new feline companion. She sounds very cute.'

~

Mick had not long finished his call with Summer when Sam rang.

'Never a dull moment in this game,' he muttered quietly under his breath.

'Partner! What have you got for me? Something to put a smile on my face, I hope. Any progress?' he asked. 'Give me the good news, first.'

Sam got right to the point. 'None of the charities Selena used to offload her father's belongings have ever received a toolbox. We've come to a stalemate in that department, but the good news is that we now know that her father must have given it to someone.'

'Or she did,' Mick replied. 'Which makes more sense. I'm sure Selena knows the truck driver—you can almost guarantee she's in cahoots with him. It also means we'll have to do a background check on her previous jobs, and her friends and family. Can you help with that lot please, Sam? I'll do some research but see what you can come up with, too. Well done on your work with the charities.'

'No worries, Sarge. I'm as keen as you are to catch the psycho who killed the guard. Have you heard any more about how Chai is getting on?'

'He's in good health but will need to stay under police protection in the Refugee Resettlement Centre until Byron and his associates go to trial. We have two officers on site there twenty-four-seven.'

'What about the migrants who were picked up by the truck driver when the guard was murdered—where are they now?'

'They're still in the Refugee centre and will soon be allocated housing once their papers are through. Some of them have added to their witness statements. You can have a read if you like. There's a copy in the case file.'

'What are they saying?'

'When the truck took off, they're certain they were hastily and covertly transferred into another heavy-duty vehicle, which took them to Kiwi Gold during the night. None of them could see anything. The transfer must have taken place in a darkened warehouse.'

'I won't bother reading the report. Hope the court hearing will be soon,' said Sam.

'Not until I've rounded up all Byron's associates. What I wheedled out of him was that his administrator—the woman who gave us the key to the immigration documents in her office—is his daughter-in-law. Rhonda is her name, and she is married to Byron's son, Chester. I'm thinking maybe we can put him in the frame for either Tony's murder or my house fire. Either way, it will be one of Byron's cronies, I'm sure. It's just not so easy to get sufficient evidence to prove beyond reasonable doubt that they are the culprits.'

Sam sighed, leaning back on her chair appearing downcast. 'I hope we can get it.

There must have been some stone they've left unturned.'

'Exactly—why do you think I've been sitting at my dining table up to my eyeballs going over all the witness statements and my interview recordings? Sorry, Sam, but my head is spinning now—I'll have to get off the phone now.'

'Meet you for lunch tomorrow?'

Mick didn't want to give her the brush off as the young constable seemed keen to talk things over with him. 'Not tomorrow, unfortunately. I have made other plans but how about this Saturday evening? We're both rostered on.'

Mick had thoughts of inviting Sam for dinner at his townhouse but instantly changed his mind. Rivalry between two women on account of him was more than he could cope with right now.

How about we slip down to that popular Thai café on the corner near the station?'

Sam beamed. 'It's a date. Whoops—forget that—I mean, it's all locked in.'

~

Summer began offering guests a seasonal special for their evening meal on Saturday nights.

Tonight it was a Mystery Meal, and she had planned a barbeque of chicken satays with homemade peanut sauce, shellfish—which she had purchased from Charlie—and gourmet sausages.

The day before, she'd texted Mick, inviting him to join her but was gutted that he was rostered on duty till eleven that evening. She wondered if her repeated invitations had scared the staid bachelor off, but he invited her to come to his home on Sunday afternoon for lunch instead, which lifted her spirits.

Shopping was a real bugbear to Summer— a necessary evil.

She loaded the groceries into her car. 'Darn! I forgot the garlic bread.'

Slamming down the car boot, she ran back into the store. There was now a long queue in the supermarket, which infuriated her.

A friendly old gentleman let her go before him. She smiled, explaining how she'd finished her shopping and packed it into her car boot, only then remembering she'd missed an item—showing him the garlic bread.

'Sorry, I'm a little deaf,' he replied, waving on the next person in line to be served.

Summer had expected a barbeque to be daunting, as Liam wouldn't be there to cook the meat as he normally did, saying he had a call-out for work.

She was inexperienced in cooking shellfish in any shape or form but could handle the sausages and satays.

Mavis said she'd often watched her late husband cooking muscles on a BBQ hotplate and would have a stab at it.

Checking the clock in her car as she arrived home in the driveway, Summer panicked. *Oh no, we're going to have a late dinner. The guests will be annoyed.*

Petra spotted Summer unpacking the groceries from her car.

'Hi there. Let me help you bring them inside,' she said with a wry smile.

As they brought the groceries along the path towards the house, Summer was surprised to see the handful of guests who said they would be in for dinner, sitting outside under the umbrellas at the outdoor tables.

'I offered them all pre-dinner snacks and a glass of beer or wine like you always do. Hope that's okay.'

A delicious aroma emanated from outside. Summer was in awe to see Liam standing at the woodfired oven, cooking.

'That's fine, thanks, Petra, but what's Liam doing over there? He said he couldn't help with the BBQ today, so why is he using the pizza oven?' Summer said as they trundled up the steps into the kitchen.

'His customer cancelled the job. Liam told me some time ago that he's an expert in woodfired pizzas,' Petra replied.

'Well, he's a dark horse,' said Summer, unpacking the groceries and putting them away into the pantry.

Petra dived into the food bags. 'Here, let me help. He said that when you had pizza nights, he would love to surprise you and make them to his special recipe.'

'Unbelievable. He's so talented.'

'Absolutely. He's a gem,' said Petra, handing Summer the meat packets to put in the freezer.

'But what am I going to do with this fresh shellfish? I can freeze the meat and chicken but not that.'

'Liam wants to do seafood, tandoori chicken and a spicy sausage. He's making a small herb and garlic one for starters to eat with drinks as an appetiser.'

'Goodness, what an asset to have around here. I hope he doesn't move away,' said Summer.

'Me too,' Petra swiftly replied, although Summer wondered if there was more in Petra's quick response than meets the eye. It was the girl's tone of voice and mournful expression.

'Liam won't have much time to make all these pizzas. The dough is fiddly and takes a while. How is he going to manage?'

Petra pointed to the dining room. 'Look in there.'

Summer popped her head through the door to see an array of pizzas.

'Great! I have olives to go on the sausage one and fresh tomatoes and herbs from the garden. They're going to be delicious.'

'Mmm, I know—can't wait to sample them.'

'Petra, why don't you join Liam in the garden and pass the garlic pizza to the guests? He has just taken it out of the oven. And then you can pour more drinks and look after everybody. You can do a half-day tomorrow. I appreciate you staying on to help now—life savers—both of you.'

'Thanks, Summer. I wanted to stay back and get to sample Liam's culinary delights after he told me what he was going to do.'

Summer was convinced Petra had developed a real soft spot for Liam. She looked forward to seeing how that played out.

After Liam cut the garlic pizza bread and Petra passed it around to the guests, he went inside the house to talk to Summer and gave her a test piece of his gourmet delight.

'It's delicious! How do you get the dough so puffy and soft?' asked Summer.

'Sorry, culinary secrets from way back,' he replied, winking. 'Hope you don't mind me interfering in your dinner plans. I can stop if you like ... only ... you kept saying for ages you wanted to fire up the pizza oven and try it out, so I thought I'd surprise you.'

'No, of course, I don't mind you doing that. I'm over the moon, and I can't fathom how a landscape gardener came to learn the art of pizza making.'

'My grandmother is Italian and married to my Kiwi granddad. She passed the art down to my mother who taught me—anyway,

261

designing landscapes is akin to creating decorative dishes, don't you think?'

'It's marvellous, but you're going to waste in the garden scene. You could set up your own pizza business,' Summer replied as she stood back and watched the well-organised amateur chef set about covering the dough with fillings.'

'What's on the menu?' Summer asked.

'This one here is Italian with gourmet sausage, tomatoes, Moroccan spice, cheese— oh, and if you don't mind, I'll use some of those black olives you put on the bench.'

Summer smiled, passing him the jar.

'For the next one, I'll use the chicken breast you bought with, brie and your cranberry compote. The third will be one of my special seafood pizzas.'

'Don't forget to use the fresh basil and oregano from my herb garden. Also, there's fresh garlic in the pantry, but if you run out, I have plenty hanging in the garage.'

'Thanks, Summer, but I'm sorted—the herbs are in the fridge all ready to go.'

'Let me help you. Tell me what to do, just to speed things up. How long will all these take to cook?' Summer asked, raising her eyebrows and looking out the window at the guests waiting for their Mystery Meal.

'No time at all—each one only two to three minutes at the most, considering they are extra-large pizzas.'

'Wow, that's incredible! Can't wait to sample them,' she replied, remembering she had only eaten once during the day and now felt ravenous.'

Summer put on her apron, washed and dried her hands and got busy helping the gardener prepare the meal. When the naked pizzas were 'dressed', they each carried one out to the oven which Liam had installed onto the brick fireplace he had set up for her.

The chef cooked more pizzas while Petra attended to refreshments and dirty dishes, enabling Summer to mingle with the guests.

A more than scrumptious aroma emanating from her new oven overwhelmed her. The kiln was tried, and tested, and it worked! Finally, one of her dreams for her B&B had come true.

After helping Liam bring other pizzas outside onto the table next to the oven, in between passing around the pieces he had sliced with an over-sized cutter, Summer ordered Petra to sit down and eat. Soon afterwards, she and Liam joined the guests to enjoy the fruits of their labour too.

While sitting there feeling suddenly weary after walking back and forth to the house, together with the headiness which only one glass of wine had given her, Summer was disheartened Mick couldn't join them. He would have enjoyed it. Glancing over at her beautiful, seven-foot high, stone water feature with a ceramic sparrow sitting on top promptly reminded her of Tony, whose favourite pastime at home was feeding the birds.

Now, many varieties flocked daily to the bird bath at the top of the fountain, which Summer had intended as a memorial for her beloved late husband. While reminiscing about Tony, she had a twinge of guilt for being distracted by another man who was pulling her heartstrings.

Summer finished eating and walked over to the table where Liam had placed the remaining pizzas he had left for the guests so they could help themselves. She kept one segment aside from each of the gourmet treats that had been on the menu to give to Mick on Sunday.

24

Mick congratulated his team on doing a superb job raking up enough evidence from files which the Franklin Police had taken from the office at Kiwi Gold during their raid—enough to charge Rob Dean with protection of the trafficking ring and slave labour industry.

While the DSS sat slammed up on remand until trial, Mick and Sam worked tirelessly trying to nail him, but his involvement with the Port guard's murder was much trickier to prove. Like most corrupt high-ranking cops, he had all loopholes covered.

'The fire chief has completed his report from the remains of my house, and they have spent weeks searching for the arsonist to no avail,' said Mick to Sam over morning tea in the canteen.

The constable spooned a mouthful of cream from a large glass of iced coffee into her mouth. She wiped her lips using a serviette while savouring the moment of her favourite indulgence.

'A moment on the lips, a lifetime on the hips,' Mick said, winking.

Sam rolled her eyes at his poor attempt at playful teasing and persisted with more questions.

'Do you mean we might never find out who burnt your house down with all your belongings? That's horrendous!'

'It's often the way with arson—difficult to track the mongrels. But I discovered something in my interview with Chester, Byron's son. He also doesn't have a watertight alibi for where he was that night. It's possible he did his father's bidding after Byron heard through the grapevine that I had Dean arrested.'

'Jeepers! This gets murkier by the day. It sounds like a family mafia racket with a high-ranking police officer as protector.'

'You've hit the nail on the head there, Sam. It's how mobs work. It could well be that Chester is our arsonist.'

'So, what was his alibi the night of your house fire?'

'He and his wife had argued that evening. Chester drove to Sky City casino and met a friend whom I interviewed and who confirmed Chester was there with him but left Sky City shortly after eleven. Chester reckons he drove straight home to Drury where his wife was in bed asleep when he got there, but she didn't hear him come home that night as he slept on the couch.

'Do you believe him?' asked Sam.

'No, not likely. He's a shifty character and I can see him as an assassin—ruthless. No wonder he doesn't get on with his wife. I can't imagine any woman living with him.'

'Why can't the firemen pin it on him, then?'

'The perpetrator left no trail, which is common in arson cases.'

Sam became agitated. 'So that's it then. The monster gets away with it! What if it were a family with children burning in the house?'

'We can't just arrest him on an assumption, as you know. Although, if he's involved in trafficking, he'll eventually trip himself up. We'll keep tabs on him, don't worry.'

Mick understood Sam's frustration—although it wasn't half of what he'd been suffering.

I'm sorry, but we can't nail Chester for either Tony's murder or the killing of the port guard at this point. He was out of town on both those days for which he has concrete alibis.'

Mick was a true-blue detective, accustomed to the roller-coaster of success and failures in his job. The night before Tony's death, part of the reason he had confessed to him he was leaving the Force, was his increasing disenchanted with police work eroding any joy in life.

25

The Mystery Meal had been a great success and Summer wanted to give Petra the Sunday morning off, the day after the BBQ, but the loyal worker knew Mick had invited Summer for a late lunch that day and wanted to make sure she got there. Mavis would be in after breakfast.

By now, both Petra and Mavis suspected their boss had developed a deep affection for Mick, although she wouldn't admit it.

Summer ran her finger down the B&B's day book to see which guests were arriving later in the day. Most of the people who had attended her Mystery Meal had left that morning. Although it was still the school holiday period, families with children rarely stayed in a B&B. They usually preferred motels or holiday parks on the outskirts of the city.

Summer didn't want to leave her workers in the lurch, but she needed regular breaks to prevent burnout, which was the reason she employed both Mavis and Petra to work weekends when the guest house was fully booked.

'You should manage until I get home,' Summer replied. 'Why don't you take the rest of the afternoon off after you've both finished the guest rooms and laundry? I'll help Mavis with the rest when I get back.'

'Are you sure?'

'Yes—we've only got one couple arriving around four this afternoon. They're going into the city for dinner. The weather forecast isn't too great for tomorrow, which has put most of the punters off. I think these people are just passing through on their way back to Wellington from up North.'

'Okay, thanks—if you insist.'

~

This time it was Summer's turn to be waited on hand and foot. She lapped it up like a cat discovering a dish of cream for the first time.

Mick had pulled out all the stops to impress her. Although he was only renting, he had added his special touch, as the townhouse had a homely atmosphere and was impressively appointed.

Mick had texted Summer earlier to check if she was still coming and to say he'd received interesting feedback about Selena's brother from Sam who had been going to great lengths researching his background.

Summer wanted to get past all the trivia to hear what Mick had to say, but he was too busy showing off his domestic skills standing in the kitchen wearing a BBQ apron while stirring a pot on the stove.

'Come and take a seat at the end of the bar there. I won't take long and then we can relax on the balcony with a drink. I've got your zero-alcohol cider in the fridge, seeing that you're driving.'

Summer gazed through the open kitchen window, looking over the Auckland Domain in Grafton. Directly below the building was a row of Rimu trees lining the park. It was unusually quiet despite being in the central city.

She stood up and scanned the panorama. 'Gorgeous view you have up here. It's priceless to be surrounded by so much greenery in town.'

'Let's sit outside. This sauce is nearly ready, and we can take our drinks out there,' Mick said, removing his apron. 'Would you mind taking the bowls out onto the balcony, please?'

Once seated at the table on the small deck, Summer was busting to press Mick about the progress of the criminal investigations but wasn't sure if he was ready to talk shop. Instead, she just quizzed him about his personal life.

She helped herself to the nuts and crisps and then passed them to Mick. 'How are you getting on with renting your bach at Coopers Beach?'

'A retired couple has settled in it already. They're building a house up there which won't be finished for at least a year. The Title has been delayed,' Mick replied.

'That's marvellous—such a relief for you, I'll bet.'

'It sure is. The rent covers what I'm paying for this place, which is great.'

Summer cast her eyes through the ranchslider at the interior of the townhouse. She didn't ask Mick how much rent he paid for the upmarket rental property but guessed, by the modern fixtures and fittings, it would be pricey.

'The insurance claim for my house fire will take ages now with the ongoing forensic investigation for arson.'

Summer's gaze traced the circles around his eyes, which were deeper and darker than when she had seen him last.

'I'm sorry to hear that, Mick. At least you and Powder are safe.'

'So true. Let's go inside and eat—creamy Beef Stroganoff in red wine served on buttery egg noodles.'

'Sounds delicious, and to be honest, I'm famished now.'

The two carried on their light conversation while eating until they were about to start on the second course—a homemade raspberry and apple crumble served with pouring cream.

Summer couldn't wait any longer and came right out with it. 'You're quite the cook. You certainly kept that from me.'

'Oh, just one of my hobbies when I get the chance. Cooking, but not baking. Every cake I ever made was a flop.'

'You're going to waste living a bachelor's life.'

Summer appeared agitated as she gulped a mouthful of cider. 'Hope you don't mind me bringing up work while I'm here ... it's just that I'm in terrible suspense about how you're getting on with Operation Sea Wolf.'

She decided against adding that she also wanted to hear about the progress of Tony's murder investigation. One case at a time was enough for the evening without spoiling the atmosphere.

'Oh, you just took the words out of my mouth. I was about to tell you the latest nitty-gritty. Sam has been marvellous and made a lot of headway.'

Summer breathed a quiet sigh of relief as she finished eating, wiping the remnants of cream from her lips before she sat back and listened.

'Selena's brother, Sonny, was living in Canada and has returned to New Zealand. We can't track him down anywhere right now. He is a loner, according to his only aunt who always thought him to be eccentric. She called him a little weird and said he has a volatile temper.'

Mick knew, theoretically, he shouldn't have been discussing the case with Summer, so he'd breached police confidentiality. But he trusted her to keep whatever they discussed just between themselves. She was part of the investigation—a valuable witness—and Mick used her as a kind of informant.

'Do you think your team can trace him?'

'I hope so but can't say for certain. If he is a guilty party, men like him can be very slippery. But for some strange reason, his aunt had heard through her relatives' grapevine that he had been back living in New Zealand around the time of the Port killing.'

'You just stay here while I pop these into the dishwasher.' Mick stood and took their empty plates to the kitchen.

Summer felt as though she was always left hanging—getting no real conclusion.

That Sonny could be perfectly innocent, was the reason Mick got up and walked away, not wanting to drag on the conversation. But why did he tell Summer on the phone he had news which would give her a lift?

'Coffee or tea? I've put the kettle on if you'd like a hot drink,' said Mick. 'Let's sit in the lounge.'

Summer settled into a cosy armchair while Mick sat on a couch opposite, just as Powder entered the room.

'So there you are, you little gadabout.' Mick gathered the fluff ball up in his arms and sat holding her on his lap.

'There's a cat door which makes it easy for her to roam. I think she meets up with a secret admirer in the park but doesn't like to go out for too long.'

Summer loved seeing Mick interact with his cat. He was a soft-hearted pushover—at least with cats, that is. But she couldn't resist quizzing him at every opportunity.

She continued to plug away. 'Sonny couldn't have been staying with Selena, as you told me she denied having seen him for years.'

'Yes, but from what we know about him, he doesn't appear to have a motive.'

Summer screwed up her face. 'Humph! I still reckon it reeks of Rob Dean. He certainly had the motive all right.'

'It's possible the guard's slaying wasn't a calculated, ruthless killing. Perhaps the culprit—possibly Sonny—panicked and lost control when our team arrived at the scene, just as Chai told us at the interview. Rob Dean was the chief investigating officer, and he wouldn't have been complicit at the scene with other officers present, no matter how clever he is.'

'What about Tony's murder—do you think it's tied up with the trafficking?'

'I believe that his killing may have been an organised execution to get him out of the

274

way, and it's still possible Dean used a hitman to do it—although we've got no way of proving it.'

'It still could have been Dean then.'

'Sorry, Summer, the DSS couldn't have done it, as I've said. But it's possible he hired someone else to do it. Do you mind if we let this go now? Both these cases are still ongoing investigations, and I really shouldn't be discussing any of it with you at this level.'

Summer remembered they'd had a similar conversation before and detected a hint of irritation in Mick's tone. She was fed up and desperate for a breakthrough. The discussion had left her deflated—again.

A cloud of heaviness descended upon her.

'I'll have to head back now, Mick. I've got an elderly couple arriving late this afternoon and need to make sure their room is ready.'

She felt dejected and just couldn't enjoy the rest of the afternoon with Mick. This ongoing saga of Tony's unsolved case had worn her down, and she didn't have the tolerance to cope with the long, drawn-out criminal investigation.

Mick walked Summer to her car and before she stepped into her vehicle, he gave her a peck on the cheek. She was confused about whether it was a sign they were dating. Or was she just one of a long line of female friends with whom Mick fraternised platonically?

This she was yet to find out. But now was not the right time for her to allow more drama into her life, however lonely she was. Until Tony's murder was solved, there was no way she could settle into an intense, romantic relationship—at least, not for now. For some time, she'd felt as though her life was spinning out of control and she would hate to bring another man into her life in her present state of mind. It would be a roller-coaster ride and not fair to any male admirer.

26

Back at the station, Mick sat at his desk with Sam sifting through the folder with witness statements and forensic reports, ensuring the evidence for the prosecution of Kiwi Gold and Hortihire was watertight. Rob Dean, although not directly involved with trafficking, had been charged with accepting bribes to protect illegal immigrants. But both Mick and Sam were convinced that the DSS had covered up the Port guard's murder, and he was directly embroiled in the trafficking ring. The police team continued to suspect Dean had interfered with the evidence.

Mick ran his index finger down the page of the file lying under his nose. 'Chai had said in his initial interview that when he was given prison garments at the station, it was Dean who took away the clothes he was wearing. Tony told me he knew the DSS had taken them to the storage room as evidence.

'Yeah, and a few days later, I saw him go back into the evidence room unaccompanied by the property officer,' Sam replied.

Mick wanted to say they had been down that road several times but held his tongue.

He continued. 'Apart from not being able to directly prove Dean interfered with the DNA testing on the clothing, we already have him on money laundering and trafficking protection for Kiwi Gold. We're holding Selena on remand until trial for her part in racketeering and people smuggling, as well.'

'Is that since Chai and the other witnesses recognised Dean in the photos they were shown?'

'Yes, Sam, together with the hordes of information which the Serious Fraud Office and Forensic Accounting investigators have dug up on him.

'They have proof that the DSS has hidden investments with Kiwi Gold—Protection Payments if you like—that he had concealed under another name.'

'Oh, so you mean the owner was paying him bribes for covering up their crimes?'

'Exactly—that's how organised crime works. The offenders usually have officials in high places shielding them—police officers or government officials.

'So, it seems the only thing we can nail Dean with right now is the protection of an organised trafficking ring,' said Sam with a sigh. 'Not his involvement in the guard's killing.'

'We have that covered too—sufficient circumstantial evidence to get him on that account—at least as an accessory to murder.' Remember, he was the first at the scene when the guard alerted our team. His timing was suspect. He arrested Chai without even giving him a chance to explain what had happened and he'd already hung him out to dry before he was interviewed.'

'Thank goodness we have it sewn up. Now I guess we need to concentrate on whether poor Tony was directly involved too ... or targeted for poking his nose in after I suspected Dean of tampering with evidence.'

Mick nodded. His face dropped. 'We sure have to get onto it—Summer is slowly going around the twist with this case dragging on for so long.'

'I know what you mean. She must be going through hell on earth.'

'Sam—that's going to be our focus, now that we've got Selena and Dean locked up with sufficient dirt to put them both away for ages.'

The Detective Constable sat flicking through her day book while listening to Mick.

'Wait—what's the latest rundown on Selena with her fingers in the pie getting payoffs from Kiwi Gold? Did she have legitimate shares in the company like she told us or were they dodgy too?' she blurted.

'Both she and Dean had hidden their profiteering under other company names which our Forensic Accounting Division—or FAD—has uncovered as classic money laundering.'

Sam shook her head. 'Sounds complicated to me. I don't understand.'

'People smuggling is an extensive business for corporate companies, involving high profits for low risk. Our people are completely focused on bringing down the traffickers and mob bosses, one of whom they now believe is our very own DSS Rob Dean.'

Sam listened in disbelief. 'Wow, this has become unreal—something you just read about in crime novels. I didn't realise how deep in the quagmire that shifty bloke has stepped.'

'Yep—he's got himself into a corner and won't get out this time,' Mick replied. 'I'm sure of that.'

Sam frowned a little. 'How can you be so sure?'

'Because I've been recently informed by the Anti-Corruption Unit they've had him under surveillance for the last few years and have a lot more on him than we do. That's all I can say. Just keep it between us at this point. At least until he has been tried and sentenced.'

Mick fingered through the file on his desk and sat back in his chair. There's another matter I need to discuss with you.

'Oh, I was going to shoot off to the cafeteria for lunch—I'm starving. Running late this morning and didn't have time for breakfast.'

'Fair enough. How about letting me give an update about tracking the murder weapon used on the Port guard and then I'll buy you lunch. How does that sound?'

'A free shout is not to be sneezed at—especially from my boss. Go for it!'

'The southern police have just located Selena's brother, Sonny, in a remote part of the South Island in the Mackenzie country. And guess what he's doing there? Truck driving—servicing those massive sheep stations. Police officers have taken him in for questioning. I'd love to be a fly on the wall.'

'I thought as much. He had to be involved,' said Sam.

'He doesn't have an alibi for where he had been that night. So, if he was guilty, Selena hadn't prepared him enough to face the music.

'Ah, so the missing wrench used to kill the guard could have been Sonny's after all.'

Now Mick could see his Detective Constable's inexperience showing, but he was patient with her as Sam had continuously shown unusual competence in other areas of investigative work.

'I think the wrench is of no consequence now that we know he drives trucks. It would be logical for his sister to take advantage of him. Selena being the ruthless, hard-nosed businesswoman she is, I think it would be easy for her to exploit him for her selfish end.'

'Wouldn't you like to interview Sonny yourself?' Sam asked.

'Absolutely, and that's why Southern Police are holding him as a suspect and transporting him to Auckland. It will take a day or two to get him up here.'

'So, it's also possible he was involved in getting rid of Tony Martin.'

'It's quite on the cards Selena and Dean could have brainwashed Sonny to do their dirty work by removing Tony from the equation, as he had become a prime witness.'

'Oh, wouldn't that be great—killing two birds with one stone?'

~

Two weeks after Mick had invited Summer to dinner, the lack of progress in Tony's case had been gnawing at him. He believed he had let her down after insisting several times he would get the perpetrator. It was a wonder she still trusted him.

He knew, that if he had the slightest notion of entering a serious relationship with Summer as opposed to his more flippant, superficial encounters with previous female friends, he would have to solve Tony's murder.

That night, he was more mentally fatigued than normal. Despite his team making headway in the slaying of the Port guard, the prolonged case involving Tony's death had left him completely demoralised. Mick was aware he continued to suffer from PTSD.

And the nature of his work, day after day, did not aid his healing.

Hopefully, once they found Tony's killer, he could take a long and overdue holiday abroad.

Would it be presumptuous to invite Summer to go with him—just as a platonic friend, of course?

Mick's brain worked overtime and each night his over-active mind took hours to shut down before he fell asleep.

27

A soft tap at the door startled Summer who was busy in the kitchen preparing a dessert for the evening meal.

'Hi Olive—come on in. Time for a cuppa?'

The woman removed her sunhat and shoes before she stepped inside. Petra nodded at her while walking down the hallway with a basket of laundry.

'I don't want to hold you up,' said Olive. 'I know you're all flat out. It's a bad time for me to visit.'

Summer rinsed her hands under the tap, then dried them on her apron. 'No, it's not that busy today. We've only one guest staying for a meal tonight and he's gone out for the afternoon. Most guests don't stay around during the day. If they're paying for meals, they usually eat and disappear.'

'If you don't mind, I'd like a word with you in private. It won't take too long.'

Summer scanned the old lady fleetingly, observing she appeared more anxious than usual.

'Of course. You go on down to my office and I'll get Petra to make a pot of tea.'

'To be honest, a glass of something cold will do. I had tea not so long ago.'

Olive shuffled along the hallway to the office and slumped into one of the old armchairs, making herself at home. Summer poured two glasses of sparkling water with a splash of fresh lime juice and carried them into the room where Olive sat flicking through a book she'd found on a nearby shelf.

'Sorry, but it's important,' she said, taking the glass from Summer and taking a few mouthfuls.

'How can I help?' Summer replied.

'It's rather how I may assist you—in your quest to find Tony's killer.'

Summer suddenly froze until she realised she hadn't answered the anxious woman. 'Please ... go on.'

'Well, I know you've been seeing a lot of that handsome detective fellow who was Tony's friend.'

Summer's face reddened. She grinned. 'Oh, you mean Detective Mick Randall.'

Yes—well, I've been concerned he had spent the night in your home with your husband before he was killed.'

'I don't get it. Tony had been chatting with me on the phone for days prior and never mentioned Mick staying over. How do you know this?'

'I wasn't actually at home—it was my nephew Jeremy who told me. He was

285

supposed to be at his sister's house, who lives nearby, while I was staying overnight with my cousin in South Auckland. I returned after lunch the next day.'

'Let me get this straight ... when did Jeremy see my Mick with Tony?'

'He had left his iPad at home and went back for it that evening when he spotted the detective's car pull into the driveway around dinner time. Jeremy stayed at my house overnight and saw Detective Randall drive away around seven the next morning.'

'I don't understand why Jeremy has waited so long before coming forward. So Mick left our home at daybreak?'

'No, Jeremy left the house early for his usual morning jog and spotted his car still in the driveway.'

Summer frowned. That last comment worried her. Mick had said nothing about spending the evening with Tony.

'Is that so? I'll have to question my friend about it.'

Olive cowered. 'Please don't tell him I said anything. Just say someone has offered information.'

'He'll want to know the source, sorry. The police may need Jeremy to make a statement. Anyway—where is he these days? I haven't seen him around in ages?'

'He may be at his father's house. Usually does the rounds with the family until he outstays his welcome. Bought himself a

Moped scooter and has a part-time job at the ferry building cleaning the tour boats when they arrive at the dock. When he's not working, he stays in his room at my house and reads or plays computer games—keeps to himself. He's not interested in women or socialising much.'

Summer wondered why Jeremy was still living with his aunt. She was annoyed he had not reported it before now—especially when the police had made continual pleas for the public to come forward if they had any information.

'Thank you for being so brave and telling me, Olive. I'll repay you somehow for your kindness.'

'Don't worry about that. I just want to help put your mind at rest and hopefully, this information will help you come another step closer to putting this whole dreadful thing behind you.'

~

Summer's mind was in turmoil after Olive had left. Not only from hearing that Mick was the last person to be in Tony's company before he died, but there was another even more pressing question mark over this new information.

Was Mick the man with whom she was becoming smitten able to be trusted, or was he now a prime suspect in the equation?

Although the banana smoothie she had before Olive's visit curdled in her stomach, she resisted heaving its contents.

Summer rushed off to the medicine cabinet in her Ensuite and swallowed two Paracetamol tablets to quell her looming headache. Looking herself in the eye in the bathroom mirror, she wondered if Mick had taken her for an idiot. Was she so gullible? What if he was also in cahoots with Rob Dean?

She vaguely remembered how persistent he had been in thwarting her attempts at tracking Dean the week she followed the DSS from his home into the city. Each time she discussed with him her determination to do this, Mick tried hard to deter her from feeding her obsession.

There was only one thing for it—to confront him and test his reaction. But she had no backup. What if Mick was Tony's killer and wanted to get her out of the way?

It had taken all this time for the police to solve the mystery of Tony's death. If Mick had masterminded that, he might try knocking her off, too.

But despite all her confusion right now, Summer found it extremely difficult to follow that line of reasoning—that the new man in her life with a soft touch for his little cat, "Powder", was a serial killer.

She would have to prove that theory wrong—perhaps at her peril.

Summer texted Mick, saying she needed to speak to him urgently and could meet him at the small cafe next to St Heliers Bay Yacht Club.

She rang Petra to remind her she was the only one on the morning shift the following morning, with just one couple having breakfast before checking out. Summer said she would be available to help, but once Mavis arrived, she would leave to attend an appointment.

Mick had agreed to meet Summer at the Yacht Club cafe at 10 am. She omitted to say she wasn't comfortable meeting him at the guest house or his home. As he was on duty, it was more convenient for him to drop by the cafe.

~

Although Summer had no appetite the following morning, Petra clucked over her, whizzing up a banana milkshake which she drank before seeing Mick.

'I'll be back to give a hand with the beds. We've got two singles, and a couple arriving after three o'clock,' said Summer.

'That's okay,' said Petra. 'I'll be fine until you get back. Whatever your urgent meeting with Mick is about, please take your time. New relationships can't be rushed,' she added, with a twinkle in her eye.

If only Petra knew how those words pierced Summer's heart. It was as though her entire world was collapsing on her. She just managed a half-smile before walking out to her car.

Mick sat at an outside table under an umbrella, waiting for Summer to arrive. He gazed out to sea, watching a kayaker far in the distance, appearing to be in deep thought as Summer approached. He smiled warmly, pulling up a chair for her.

'Let me buy you coffee. How about a Danish to go with it—I'm partial to those fresh almond croissants?'

Summer thought she would be sick if she ate but said nothing.

'No, thanks. I've only just had breakfast.'

'Okay, I'll just grab a coffee and pastry. Back in two ticks.'

Summer didn't like lying, although it wasn't untrue—a milkshake could be classified as a breakfast of a sort.

Mick returned and began eating while she struggled to swallow the constricting lump forming in her throat.

'Now, what's up that's so urgent? Good news, I hope,' Mick asked, with raised eyebrows.

It was now or never. Summer had to find her tongue and hoped the words would come out right.

She eyeballed him. 'Mick, I want you to be straight with me, if you value our friendship.'

As she spewed out the words, Mick stopped eating, wiping his mouth with a paper napkin.

'Why didn't you tell me or your colleagues that you had been with Tony the evening before he was murdered? I don't understand why you would conceal that. You were his best friend and possibly the last person to see him alive.'

Mick's pupils dilated. He stuck out his bottom lip and before he could answer; she continued. He took a deep breath and let it go loudly. Summer glared, seeing his embarrassment at finally being caught out.

'Who on earth told you I was with Tony?'

'A neighbour saw you arrive in the driveway the evening before, and your car was still there the next morning.'

'Really? Well, they took an awful long time to come forward,' Mick grumbled.

'You had better have a good alibi, as I'll take this straight to your boss, Hayley Winters.'

Summer was on the verge of tears—not so much from disappointment but overwhelming anger at possibly being betrayed by someone for whom she carried a candle.

'Hold your horses!' Mick cried. 'You're barking up the wrong tree. Just let me speak!' he replied curtly.

Summer was taken aback at his sudden outburst, curbing her tongue while allowing him to defend himself.

'I dropped in on Tony around dinner time to see if he had eaten—which he hadn't. Then he invited me to stay for a beer and a bite to eat. I had the following day off and wanted him to come fishing with me, but he said he was planning on doing his favourite coastal walk in the morning and would be busy after lunch getting quotes from various tradesmen who had contacted him about the installation of the fountain.'

'So, you went out walking with him that morning?'

'No, I didn't feel like exerting myself and had been looking forward to spending the day relaxing fishing. I left soon after breakfast.'

'Where did you go fishing—somewhere local?'

'No, there's not much activity around here. I went to my favourite spot at Music Point.'

Mick was right on the trigger with answers to her questions, but Summer was well-versed in interview techniques with her past career as a police reporter.

'Did Tony cook you a meal that evening?'

'He offered, but I raced down to the Takeaway shop and brought back fish and chips.'

'What did you talk about all evening that it was so important to stay all night?' Summer snapped.

Mick's brow furrowed with annoyance.

'Actually—you mostly. Tony had said how he was tired of the job and the way it drained him so much he had no time for you. He was considering giving up police work and helping you run the B&B. He even talked about the possibility of operating kayak sea tours out to the little islands in the Gulf such as Brown's Island—or Motuihe. There is a camping ground where we could take participants overnight. I chipped in and said I had also been toying with the idea of running a B&B myself. Then Tony added perhaps we could run the kayak tours together as a business sideline.'

'Is that right? I guess he was going to talk to me about all these plans—but he didn't get the chance. At least it would be a lot safer than chasing psychopathic criminals, I suppose.'

Mick continued his confession. 'By the end of the night, we had drunk a few too many, so he offered me a bed in a guest room, and I left with a hangover the next day.'

Summer had her face cupped in her hands and began shaking her head.

'I can't believe what I'm hearing. You of all people—not a word to me! So why didn't you report this?'

'Can't you see that's just what Rob Dean was counting on—slipping up indirectly— dropping me in it so he could set me up as a murder suspect? It was much better for you if I kept quiet.'

Summer felt out of control, not knowing what to believe.

'So, Tony mentioned he was expecting to get tradesmen to drop by for quotes that day?' Summer asked icily.

'Yeah, he did say something about it. I can't remember what time they were coming, but he had a few lined up.'

'I suppose it does put you in the frame as a suspect—even if what you say is true.'

Mick was enraged at her reaction.

'What! What the .... you honestly think I could have killed my best friend? What motive are you now accusing me of?'

'I'm trying to think,' Summer said feebly. 'When I heard about this for the first time, I was honestly worried that you may be in cahoots with Dean and the racketeering with Kiwi Gold. Perhaps you were another member of their syndicate. If there was one bent cop, there could also be others.'

Mick's eyes clouded over with frozen tears. When he spoke, it was now with a husky voice. His gaze met the floor this time.

'Well, I can't believe that you genuinely believe I could be a cold-blooded killer. I'm sorry it has come to this, Summer. I guess the best thing for me to do is to tell Hayley Winters myself the reason I was reluctant to come forward. At least Dean is locked up and can't put me in the frame.'

'Would you really ... tell her the truth, I mean? Please do it, Mick. I'm sorry, but I knew you would have a logical explanation about why the neighbour saw you at our

294

house that day. You should own up. If you don't, it would be worse coming from him.'

'I guess so. Look, Summer, I'm going to fix my bill and get off now. You did the right thing checking all this out with me, but I'm not happy that you had me lined up as a killer.'

Summer was astonished at his reaction. She had done the right thing, and it was brave to confront him like that, but she was gutted he acted so negatively towards her. It was as if her entire world had just caved in.

She sat stunned as Mick ducked inside the cafe to pay his bill and left through the other side of the building without even saying goodbye. He left her feeling distressed—wondering if he would follow through on fronting up to the Detective Superintendent.

It had been two weeks since Summer had bravely approached Mick about his covert behaviour. That night, she cried herself to sleep—broken-hearted after believing her long-time, loyal friend had betrayed her trust while unbeknown to him she was falling for him. Now it was over.

Petra and Mavis had spotted the dark, half-moon shadows under their boss's eyes—fresh signs of sleepless nights and worries, but they never asked her why—knowing their place as employees.

Summer was desperate for someone in whom she could confide in and offload. Once, it was Tony, but since his death, Mick had filled that gap. Her mother was not in a fit state to hear her woes and she'd learnt years ago not to dump her problems on her kids.

The anguish of keeping doubts about Mick to herself was more than she could bear. What if he was involved in Tony's death? The murder remained unsolved, and the police were no closer to finding the killer. It made sense to her that Mick had been the last person to speak to him. Surely a tradesman such as a landscaper would visit a client in his Ute and not by foot, as the police team suspected.

The sick feeling in the pit of her stomach just wouldn't let up—dark thoughts of Mick having shrewdly set her up, grooming her into believing he was her companion and confidante, all the while fending suspicion away from himself.

Were her misgivings about him true and to whom could she turn in such a disconcerting predicament?

Summer should have gone to Detective Superintendent Winters with her suspicions.

She sat in the courtyard, holding a basket of fresh herbs she'd picked from her kitchen garden. She held a bunch of sweet basil to her nose, inhaling the pleasant aroma which reminded her of a time past with Tony when he turned up delicious Italian pizzas at the weekends, which they enjoyed in front of the TV.

The new stone fountain had attracted many birds. Summer was ecstatic.

While she sat watching the tui and waxeyes at the top, cascades of water glistening in the sunlight mesmerised her as they bounced over each tier, finding their way home in the rock pool below.

A stunning tui, proudly displaying its bright blue and green plumage, perched at the edge of the stone cavity up top. It puffed out its chest, singing loudly before flying into a nearby bottlebrush tree.

Is this what Tony had visualised while creating his special mosaic masterpiece in the courtyard before he began digging the pond base? If only he could see it now—the fruits of his labour.

He had toiled so hard to surprise Summer, only to miss out seeing the delight on her face when she returned from her mother's house.

Instead, she arrived home to a living nightmare and didn't even notice the mosaic artwork Tony had designed. Not until much further down the track when she was over the shock of his death.

Glancing at the fountain area, Summer pondered over the crime scene—imagining Mick approaching Tony who was busy digging the clay foundation.

Did she truly believe he could grab his friend's spade and smash it down on his skull? Cringing at such dark images, she struggled to imagine Mick could be a cold-blooded killer.

Regardless, she would never open her heart to him again until she was convinced of the truth.

~

At the end of a busy day at the guest house, Summer stepped out of the laundry with a heavy basket full of sheets she had put through the drier.

'Do you need a hand out there?' Petra called as she hurried out to take the basket off her. 'There's a call for you,' she said, passing her the cordless phone. 'I'll take the sheets inside.'

Summer thanked her and sat on a chair in the garden under an umbrella, checking her voicemail. It was a woman—a stranger who said she needed to talk to her urgently.

'How did you get my number?'

'I'm sorry, but your late husband had placed an advertisement in a shop window giving his landline and his mobile number,' said the woman.

'Yes, that's right—looking for a landscaper. Did you call him—what's all this about?' Summer asked.

'My name's Connie Edmonds—it's about your husband. Can we meet somewhere—not over the phone, please.'

Summer felt uneasy—shocked by what she said.

'My husband is dead. What do you mean?'

'I need to speak with you... something you will want to know about. That's why I rang your landline.'

Was this stranger about to tell her that Tony had been unfaithful?' Could she be an ex-lover—the worst news ever. First Mick, now Tony!

Her heart sank heavily, *but* she had to face it, no matter how devastating it would be.

'You can meet me at my guest house—St Heliers Bay B&B. Do you know where it is?'

'Yes, I've seen the place—a little way along from the beach. There's a sign outside.'

'Can you be here tomorrow afternoon at three? That's when we have a bit of a lull while the guests are out, and I have my two domestic staff who can hold the fort for a short time while we talk.'

When Summer got off the phone, bile rose in her throat with the shock of this woman coming out of the blue. Was she going to hear that two decades of marriage were about to be erased? Just when she thought her life was coming together since Tony's death.

She looked down the hallway to find Petra who had taken over the laundry from her.

'Oh, there you are. Let me help you,' said Summer.

Petra looked up from folding the sheets on a bed in an empty guest room. 'I've just finished, so don't worry,' she replied, seeing despair engraved on Summer's face.

'We've got a couple arriving tomorrow morning who have booked this room. I'll finish getting it ready—it has been a hectic day. You and Mavis haven't stopped, so you get off now.'

'Thanks, Summer—I will. I have grocery shopping to do, so I appreciate being able to go early. Mavis has already left.'

'Yes, she has. I was thinking it might be time for me to offer her whole days instead of part-time hours, as this place always seems to be full and there's so much to do with providing cooked meals. Sometimes I wish I hadn't made that service available,' said Summer.

'You could always stop doing it. Most B&Bs don't offer that anyway—they usually only provide a continental breakfast these days.'

'I guess you're right. I'll give it some thought. Perhaps I could just offer pizzas on Saturday nights instead.'

She omitted to add that most of her energy had been spent helping Mick with his police work.

'I think that's a good idea extra hours for Mavis. Is everything alright, Summer? It's just that I detect a tremor in your voice. Are you feeling okay?'

Petra had triggered something in Summer who was now in tears while her domestic worker placed a comforting arm around her.

Summer got a grip on herself. She wasn't sure how to reply to her question. 'The phone call was from a woman who talked about Tony, which upset me.' She didn't elaborate and changed the subject.

~

This was the most nerve-wracking experience Summer had endured since being told Tony had been murdered.

She was sure Connie was about to break the news that Summer's precious marriage had been a farce—a mockery! It was going to

301

be more than she could bear. Would Mick have known about this? And what about the rest of Tony's colleagues at the station—had they been laughing behind her back, too?

She hadn't eaten all day, and the two coffees she'd consumed that afternoon were now living rent-free in her throat, triggering her reflux again. She should have taken a stiff whisky—that's if she had been a spirit drinker, but she was not. The best she could handle was a fine wine or cider but had never started drinking through the day. This time, she may very well learn how to drink spirits after the woman drops the bombshell on her, but for now would settle for an antacid tablet.

By the time Summer had visited the bathroom twice in a row and taken more than her usual dose of Quick-Eze, the doorbell rang. She peered surreptitiously through her bedroom window to see a gaunt, pale-faced woman, much older than her, standing at the door biting her nails. She rang the bell again as Summer sauntered along the hallway, wishing she'd made an excuse to back out.

'Oh, hello—thank you for agreeing to see me, Summer.'

'Connie, is it? Come on in, Summer said, directing the woman into her office rather than the living area as she didn't want to curse it if her worst nightmare was about to come true.

'Take a seat,' she said in an officious tone. 'Can I offer you tea or coffee, or would you prefer a cool drink?'

'That's kind of you. It's so warm outside— something cold would be fine.'

Summer begrudgingly hurried off to the fridge, irritated by the delay in getting straight to brass tacks. She poured two glasses of her elderflower and raspberry cordial and carried it back to the office on a tray.

'Here you are.' She passed Connie a glass. 'Raspberries are from my garden,' she continued nervously.

Connie took a sip. 'Wow, that's wonderful, thanks.'

'Now—tell me why you are here,' Summer blurted clumsily, refusing to delay the inevitable. She was not prepared to exchange the slightest congeniality with this woman who was about to destroy what was left of her life.

'I guess Tony never told you how he knows me—a police officer and everything being sacrosanct or confidential.'

'No, I don't remember him mentioning your name. If it's police business, he wouldn't have discussed cases with me unless they'd been already publicised by the media.'

'Your husband had quite a lot to do with my ex-husband, Jake, when he was alive. He came to our house several times when I phoned the Strand Station reporting domestic violence.'

Summer was taken aback. It was not what she had expected to hear.

'Oh, I see … carry on, please,' she said in a much gentler tone than earlier.

'Jake has a drinking problem—alcoholism. It got really difficult to cope with when he used to come home drunk and lay into me either verbally, physically or both.'

'I see—I'm so sorry to hear this. How was my husband involved?'

'He was the Detective Sergeant who charged him with Male Assaults Female and got him locked up. When it went to Court, the Judge felt that the suffering I'd experienced when Jake kicked me in the belly, causing me to miscarry, deserved a six-month suspended sentence. This was contingent upon him completing a three-month residential alcohol rehabilitation program.'

'Well, I guess he got what he deserved,' Summer replied, touching the woman's hand, still confused about why the visit and waiting for the bombshell.

Connie continued. 'When Jake finished his rehab and subsequent home detention, I'd already filed for a legal separation pending a divorce. He was livid and blamed your husband. I had a restraining order against him, so he took off to Australia for a while—first on a holiday visa and then got labouring work, in Sydney, I'd heard.'

'Is he still there?'

'I'm not sure where he is now, but earlier this year he appeared at my door pleading for me to take him back. When I found out about his drunken fights in Sydney from a relative, I pressed home he must never darken my doorstep again and threatened to involve the police.

'Sorry, Connie, but my husband is dead, and no longer able to help you. I don't understand why you're here.'

'It was something Jake said when I told him our marriage was over for good. He condemned Tony, saying he had stuck his nose in once too often and would regret it. When I asked what he meant by it, he said he would make sure that bastard cop would get his comeuppance.'

Her last sentence slammed Summer's chest with a piercing jolt. 'Did you call the police?'

Connie began fiddling with an earring. 'I wasn't sure if he was just blowing hot wind. He'd been drinking. I threatened to call them while shutting the door on him. Soon afterwards, I learnt he'd returned to Sydney, but when I heard through the media that your husband had been killed and the case was unsolved, I got worried. The police were asking for people with any information to come forward.'

'You mean you were concerned because Jake said he would get his revenge on Tony? Did he say how?'

'He'd threatened several hateful things—violent—about your lovely man, which worried me, but I never expected he could follow through.'

A shudder reverberated through Summer's spine.

'Connie, I hope you don't mind me asking, but would you mind if I got a friend of Tony's—who is another Detective Sergeant—to take a witness statement from you about the threats? Even if Jake has done nothing, perhaps he needs to be interviewed.

'Sure, I don't mind at all—had the same thought. I've never been able to have peace of mind knowing he was possibly involved in your husband's death.'

'Why have you left it until now to come forward and say something?'

Connie's eyes darted back and forth, avoiding eye contact with Summer. She stared downwards.

'I had secretly hoped that after Jake had completed his alcohol rehab, he would be reformed—a different person—so we could start again. But nothing changed. He went straight back to drinking and lying. Lately, it has been playing on my mind—I just had to contact you and talk it through.'

'I understand. It's not your fault—please don't beat yourself up over it. He did enough of that and now you're free.'

'That's kind of you.'

'I'll help, all you want. 'Where is Jake now—in New Zealand still?'

'I don't know. I've heard rumours he's back in Sydney.'

'Don't worry, the police have ways and means of finding that out.'

'Well, I don't want him coming near me again. Next time I'll call the police, as he'll be in breach of my restraining order. I won't give him any more chances!'

'Thanks, Connie, for your help. I'm sorry, we'll have to finish now as my staff will need me to help with our guests. I appreciate you coming to see me, and I promise your honesty won't be in vain. Give me your phone number and I'll be in touch.'

Connie passed her a calling card which had on it. *"Connie's Crystals"*.

Summer raised her eyebrows in surprise. She didn't look like a businesswoman, but the card in her hand suggested the reverse.

'Do you have a business?'

'Yes, I make jewellery from crystals and agate stones. It's very popular these days.'

'Oh, that sounds interesting.'

'I'll show you one day—perhaps when you've got through this awful business of finding how your husband died.'

Before Connie stepped into her car, she lurched forward at Summer, throwing her arms around her.

'Please call me if you have any further information,' said Summer, before waving goodbye.

After Connie left, Summer was completely drained—shattered both emotionally and physically. She needed to sleep and let her brain recover from all that was said. Mavis and Petra said they would cope for the rest of the day.

She went to her room to take a nap, hoping that after a rest she might be brave enough to phone Mick and update him about Connie's visit. Hopefully, then, he might forgive her for offending him.

29

Summer woke from a long nap peering into darkness. She had overslept, and the sun had gone. Her head hurt as if she were hung over.

The deep sleep resulted from all her pent-up emotions surrounding Connie's upsetting visit. If Jake was Tony's killer, her relief would be indescribable, but now she had to get him investigated—she must speak to Mick.

Dread gripped her as she contemplated how to arrange a meeting with him. The last time they talked he had virtually said he was washing his hands of her.

Hunger pangs gnawed away at Summer's stomach. Having freshened up in the bathroom, she wandered into the kitchen. As it was now late, both the girls had tidied up and left for the evening.

There were no guests, apart from a young couple who had gone out for dinner.

Feeling relieved she had the entire house to herself for the evening, Summer braved it and phoned Mick to invite him for a meal.

He was on a day shift, and when he answered the phone, Summer was surprised to hear the anger she had sensed at their last meeting had left his voice. Had he finally forgiven her?

'Funny you should call right now. I was about to abandon all efforts at cooking myself a meal as I've had a hell of a day. You saved me from buying greasies, especially when my doctor has suggested cutting back on cholesterol.'

'Well, I'd hate to jeopardise your health. How about cold chicken and salad with boiled potatoes from my garden—I'll even skin it for you?' she replied, half-joking.

'You don't have to go to all that trouble. Whatever way the chook comes is fine.'

Within minutes, their meeting was all signed and sealed. She would see him again and on a much more amicable note.

When she got off the phone, Summer battled to ward off the butterflies flitting around inside her as she tore into the bedroom, hurriedly going through her wardrobe for the right clothes. She was careful not to over-dress yet appear alluring to Mick.

Summer was now more inclined to trust him, now that another suspect for Tony's assault had surfaced.

It gave her hope that she'd been completely wrong about Mick but wanted to keep her reservations about him without it being obvious. She would now have to play her cards close to her chest.

Summer chose something demure—a dark blue skirt with a matching short-sleeved merino top and white sandals. It crossed her mind that if it were later discovered that Mick was the killer, she wouldn't be able to live it down if she had dressed seductively for this occasion. The idea gave her goosebumps. She'd just have to stay aloof while discussing Connie's visit with him and watch his reaction.

The food was laid out on the table much more classy than other times when Summer had shared meals with Mick.

She had to keep control, and this was the best way to stay detached.

As Summer heard Mick's car rumble down the driveway and stop by her garage, she wondered how he would have the nerve to continue visiting her if he were Tony's killer. She just couldn't see him as a cold-blooded psychopath.

Or was she falling victim to a hopeless romantic's rose-coloured glasses?

~

Mick stood at the door without a bottle of bubbly or flowers—no peace offering. He didn't even give her his usual peck on the cheek.

But this was the least of her worries.

'Come on in. The food's ready, so you may as well sit at the table. Would you like a cool drink?' Summer gestured towards a bottle on the kitchen bench.

'Sure.' Mick fetched the homemade ginger beer and poured it into the glasses at the dining room table where they both sat down to eat.

First, he updated Summer on all the latest progress of Operation Sea Wolf as far as he could without crossing the line concerning police confidentiality. He explained how far they'd got with solving Tony's murder.

Mick leaned on the table with crossed arms, raising his eyebrows at Summer with a half nod.

'Now—What's this business about the mystery woman who visited you? Let's hope it'll be a good lead.'

Summer began telling the story— determined to describe every detail told by Connie, hoping Mick would use the facts to trace Jake and hopefully bring an end to the unceasing, wild-goose chase.

'I'm going to have to record all this in my day book, sorry, Summer—when we've finished eating of course.'

Summer had prepared a small strawberry tart with cream for afters, as she knew Mick was partial to desserts.

'Let's go sit in the lounge. It's much more comfortable in there and I'll go over Connie's story again,' said Summer when they had finished eating.

Mick began collecting up their plates. 'Let me help clean up the dishes first.'

'Oh, don't worry—I'll stack them in the dishwasher after you've gone,' she replied dismissively.

Once they were seated in comfortable armchairs, Summer reiterated what she had already told Mick as he took notes.

When she had finished, he put the book down. 'You know—this may well solve Tony's case and put his killer away for a very long time.'

Summer breathed a sigh of relief while Mick continued.

'And hopefully—in your eyes—let me off the hook!'

She was irritated by his last remark. Why did he have to ruin a pleasant reunion with such a snide comment?

'I hope so. How will you find him if he's back living overseas?'

'We'll use Interpol to help us. If Jake's still drinking, I doubt he has all his ducks in a row, and he'll be careless about covering his tracks. We'll get him.'

Summer wasn't sure whether to apologise to Mick for insinuating he was involved in Tony's demise or to wait until Jake had been detained for questioning. Although that was going to take time, she held back, keeping her reservations about Mick—for the time being, at least.

He must have detected the coolness in her voice and made no attempts at any romantic gestures, likely twigging she still had misgivings about his innocence. He wasted no time in winding up the meeting and heading off to his car.

'Well, thanks for the meal. I'll keep you up-to-date with the progress in locating this fellow, Jake, and will be in touch once we've traced his whereabouts. It's best not to discuss it any further with Connie, as we don't want him finding out we're on his trail if he's guilty.'

As Mick drove off, those last words of warning gave Summer hope Mick was innocent.

Unless he was as expert at covering up a crime as his colleague, Rob Dean had been.

~

Mick got in touch with his good friend, Detective Sergeant Keith Moss from Interpol, early the next morning, who chuckled loudly on hearing about Jake.

'Not him again! When will the fellow learn? It's not so long ago since he was arrested in Fiji.'

The detective explained about the trouble Jake had inflicted on the Sydney police by engaging in many drunken fights and causing grievous bodily harm to another ruffian—thereafter scarpering off to the Fiji islands.

Interpol had spent weeks tracking him down until he was caught by the military in Fiji. He was extradited to Australia where he served three months in jail. He is now living somewhere in the outback, but his exact whereabouts are unknown.

'We'll get on to this right away. I think, based on him now being a person of interest in a murder enquiry, he will eventually be deported back to New Zealand. But let's wait and see.'

After Mick had sent through Jake's police records to DS Moss, the Interpol detective promised he would keep him in the loop.

~

It had been a fruitful day for Mick. Lounged back in a recliner chair after his evening meal, he scrolled through the Netflix app for a movie that would help him relax and forget about work for a while.

When the doorbell rang late, he looked mystified at Sam standing at the door before she began ranting excitedly—explaining the reason for her unannounced visit.

'Come on in. I'll turn the TV off,' Mick muttered, frustrated at the sudden intrusion.

'Anything to drink?' he asked, directing her to a seat.

'Yes, I will, thanks. I'd rather have a beer, but I'm on duty at eleven tonight—awful graveyard shift. Just a can of your flavoured sparkling water if you have any left.'

'Sure, I've got plenty—back in a tick.'

Mick returned, pouring her drink into a glass while topping up his ale.

'Sorry, I should be on duty with you. I know there's a stack of paperwork to catch up on, but you're best at that. You can call me in anytime if I'm needed … so … what's this critical news you have?'

'You know Bernie Wright? Well, we had an extremely interesting conversation over a drink last night and you wouldn't believe what he told me.'

'What's this all about, Sam—can't it wait? I was hoping for a night in without having to think about work—just for a few hours.'

A cloud burst over Sam's face.

'Sorry, boss. Should I wait until you're back on duty?'

'Goodness, no! Not now—get to the point, woman.'

Sam gave him a disapproving glance at his sexist remark, then opened up.

'Bernie Wright, who just passed his Detective Sergeant exams, has come forward with a heap of ammunition against Rob Dean that you would not believe. He had been working with the DSS on the beat.'

Mick was about to call her out on repeating herself but held his tongue. 'Go on,' he replied.

'It's about the attack on the Port guard. It appears it may have been a complete set-up by Dean who could have collaborated with the truck driver.'

'How … what proof do you have?'

'The night of the homicide, Bernie was on the graveyard shift with Dean who'd ordered him to stay back at the station and write up reports while he slipped out for takeaways. I found this rather irregular not allowing his partner, who was also a senior detective, to accompany him on call-outs.

'A call came in from the Maritime Unit alerting the officers to suspicious activity at the container terminal, requesting help. Bernie rang Dean on his mobile who said he'd picked up the call on his car radio downtown and would check it out himself first.

Mick stood up, pacing back and forth. 'But there were two patrol cars at the scene of the crime.'

'Yes, I know—wait. A little later, Dean called for backup and two other officers raced off to the Port, and insisted Bernie join them.'

'Although it sounds suspect—Dean keeping his side-kick out of the way—it's not mandatory for a detective to attend call-outs with their partners, although safer. But carry on, thanks,' Mick said, sliding back into his chair.

Sam continued. 'When the other officers arrived, Dean was already at the scene of the crime. He must have planned it carefully— hiding his patrol car out of sight while creeping through towers of container boxes before attacking the guard and swiftly returning to his vehicle. He would have quickly changed his clothes and then raced back to bust the stowaways. The backup patrol car which Bernie had travelled in arrived a short time later.'

'So, what are you getting at, Sam?'

'Don't you see? Dean had picked up the call from the Maritime Unit and made sure he got there first. That's why he had gone off to fetch takeaways near the Port before the call came in, as it gave him an alibi for why he was near the container wharf. Bernie truly thinks Dean was involved in the attack on the guard—somehow.'

Mick slid into his chair and poured himself another beer. 'Wow, this certainly puts another slant on things. I mean it does sound possible—fits the puzzle—the way Chai had explained how the truck driver had instructed him to take the body under the arms while he only had hold of the guard's boots.'

'Exactly!' said Sam excitedly. 'It's just where I was heading. That's why Dean had altered the evidence to incriminate poor Chai. It also means the driver is an accessory to murder.'

'Yep—he's probably Dean and Selina's *Yes Man.*'

'Where do you go from here?' Sam asked.

'We have written statements from Chai and other migrants who were abandoned by the truck driver on the wharf. They had all witnessed the first police car arriving with Dean at the wheel. And, from the opposite direction of the wharf, a second vehicle with

318

police officers, which had raced through the main gate a short time after. Strange, don't you think? I mean—why was Dean hanging around the docks in the first place?'

'Yes, I expect he'll just say he was busy stalking the offenders. It could put another nail in his coffin, as he certainly was *Johnny on the spot*. We need a written statement from Bernie.'

'Of course, I'll get onto it.'

30

With everything going on with the police and her recent fallout with Mick, it was difficult for Summer to cope with her mother's issues.

Although the ailing woman had not deteriorated, she'd made very little recovery since her stroke.

It didn't help that despite the rest home having an above-average reputation; the caregivers changed around often, which unsettled her.

Summer had often felt guilty about not caring for her mother at home and giving up the B&B, but Ava and Pete had advised her not to take on the heavy role.

Despite her misgivings about whether she'd made the right decision, the rest home staff had been most insistent that her mother was much better off in a proper care home where she could receive around-the-clock care in a safe setting.

It was late morning when Summer returned from the rest home, and the house was quiet. Autumn had arrived, and although days were still warm, the sea had cooled down considerably.

She was disappointed she'd found little time for swimming and recreation during the summer, and now it was too late.

Packing a small day bag with food and drink, she let Mavis and Petra know she would be out for an hour.

When she arrived at her favourite patch on the beach under the pohutukawa trees, the new seaside vendor who sold real fruit ice cream in a waffle cone caught her eye. It was exactly what she fancied.

Approaching the kiosk, she spotted Mick's Skoda driving by. Her heart jumped as she lurched forward, waving.

Mick's passenger window was open. He tooted but continued driving. She was taken aback as his siren wasn't sounding. He just seemed to be taking a leisurely spin along Tamaki Drive—most likely heading home.

He could have stopped and given her a friendly greeting. It was as though all the closeness they'd once shared—even though not overly intimate—were thrown back in her face. He had virtually cast her aside like a dirty rag.

Maybe it was better that way—at least until Tony's insufferable criminal case had been solved.

There was no time for romance in this precarious set of circumstances, and Summer was dreaming, if she thought it was possible. Still—she couldn't help but stay hurt.

The fruit ice cream was just what she needed—a sugar rush to soothe her anxiety around Mick's standoffishness.

After eating her sweet treat, Summer removed her shoes and then walked over to the edge of the waves as they gently lapped onto the shore.

The water was unexpectedly warm, and she was annoyed she'd forgotten to pack her swimsuit.

Glancing at her wristwatch, there wasn't enough time to race home for it. She was also expected back at the guest house to relieve the staff so they could get off duty.

Summer sat back on the grass where she had laid her towel, drying her feet.

She wondered what would happen if the police never found Tony's killer. Would that mean that Mick was still be in the frame? Maybe she should forget the fun times they'd shared and keep a distance—at least while Tony's assault remained unsolved.

That was it. From now on, she would have to follow through on her resolve and completely steer clear of him.

Realising her thoughts had drifted off for far too long, she packed up her things, put her sandals on and headed back to the house.

~

When Summer walked up the driveway, to her consternation, Mick's Skoda was parked in front of her garage.

What game was he now playing? Why didn't he let her know he was dropping by—the fact that he didn't even stop to talk to her by the beach was weird!

Mick sat at the dining table chatting to Mavis who had kindly made him a coffee. When Summer entered the room, he only gave her a half-smile.

'There you are—I told you she would be home soon,' said Mavis. 'I'll leave you to it,' she said, winking at Summer who, although annoyed, blushed as Mavis removed herself.

Summer sneered at Mick. 'So why did you pass me by the beach earlier and not stop? It's strange, don't you think?'

'Sorry, Summer. I was on my way to interview a witness for a fresh case, but they weren't home. I knew you would be back, so I came around and waited for you.'

'Humph! So what brings you here?' she retorted, sitting at the far end of the table—this time—guarding her heart.

'We've got Jake North—or should I say, Interpol has tracked him, and he is now in the custody of the Melbourne police.'

This was music to her ears. 'What? That's great news—at last! Don't you mean Jake Edmonds?'

'No—his wife is Connie Edmonds. It's her maiden name. She went back to it after divorcing him.'

'Oh, I see. What will happen now—will they question him, or will he have to return here?'

'He was offered a choice of coming to New Zealand under police escort to be interviewed by us or deported, which amounts to the same thing. Except—if he's innocent—he wouldn't want to be deported if he now lives in Australia.'

'When is he flying back?'

'Tonight. As he's a murder suspect, we'll need to get him here as soon as possible.'

'Boy, that's unbelievable—great news.'

'Mmm,' Mick murmured. You're so right. I guess I'm keener than you are, seeing I'm under scrutiny—don't you think?'

Summer glared at him, grasping his subtle innuendo. Was he just being outright sarcastic after she'd judged him not so long ago? It was time he got over it! Besides—he was the last person to see Tony alive.

'I'm not sure what you mean by that,' she said bravely.

Mick suddenly softened. 'Look, Summer. I'm just super keen to prove to you—above anyone else—that I'm innocent. I know you still harbour doubts about me and will do until Tony's murder is solved. That's even more reason behind my determination to find the killer now. I can't stand the thought that you may have any doubts at all that I could be in the frame.'

Throughout the rest of their meeting, there was a coolness in the air—an uncomfortable tension between them, although Summer had experienced relief hearing about Jake's arrest.

But there was still a lingering doubt in her mind that Connie's ex-husband might not be involved in Tony's death. He just could be an unfortunate scapegoat to apportion the blame—and so easy for a cunning, corrupt policeman to do exactly that—Jake being a troublesome drunk with a police record.

~

Summer was in greater turmoil after Mick had left. She was perplexed. It was as though any gut instincts she had before about both Tony's murder and her once budding relationship with Mick were dead-ends and all she felt now was *FEAR*—what Tony used to call *False Evidence Appearing Real*.

If only she could run it past her beloved husband—he would have solved the mystery of his demise, by now. But the reality she faced was the fact of her powerlessness.

She prayed to God in whom she had always believed, but since Tony's death had neglected. Perhaps it was time to go back to her old church where she could find answers—by listening to the still, small voice within.

'Penny for your thoughts,' said Mavis, placing a plate of sandwiches in front of Summer.

'If you don't keep up your strength, how are you going to keep looking your best for Mr Loverboy?' she said, beaming.

Summer's face fell, trying hard not to voice irritation at the woman's careless remark. As she'd never disclosed to Mavis and Petra the cooling of her relationship with Mick, the women continued to act as though Summer still held a candle for the handsome detective.

Perhaps it was time she put them in the picture, saying nothing about Tony's murder investigation.

'Where is Petra? I have something to discuss with both of you.

'She's finishing the last of the towels, before knocking off. I'll put them through the drier once they're done.'

'Would you mind getting her in here? I'll help with the laundry and then she can go.'

'Her boyfriend is picking her up at the gate. He's taking her somewhere special tonight.'

Summer secretly envied Petra—as that was something Tony used to do. He was full of surprises and would often treat her.

She sat with the girls at the dining table to tell them about her awkward predicament.

'I can't get into the nitty gritty of my issue with Mick, sorry. It involves police business, which I mustn't disclose. But he betrayed my trust significantly for it to affect our relationship.'

Mavis leaned over and stroked Summer on the shoulder.

'You poor thing,' Petra added. 'At least you didn't tell us he cheated on you with another woman. It's sad, as you both appear so right for each other.'

Summer shrunk. 'I wouldn't say we were in a proper relationship. I guess we had a few dates before I discovered he had deceived me about a critical issue.' Her voice broke.

Mavis took her hand. 'Forget about him, Summer. There's someone special out there for you. Give him a wide berth.'

Not that simple, Summer wanted to say. She dearly needed someone onto whom she could offload her many troubles. Especially about Mick and the unsolved crimes. Mavis was the loveliest, motherly sort who would be ideal for lending a sympathetic ear. But for the time being Summer would have to bury her pain and stay bottled up.

'You're so kind, girls—I appreciate your concern. Unfortunately, I'm involved with the police regarding Tony's case and Mick is the leading crime scene investigator. Who knows—in time he may redeem himself,' she muttered through gritted teeth.

'I hope so, for your sake. You deserve fun times and not just a hard slog.'

Summer eyes clouded over as she struggled to silence her gut-wrenching disappointment.

After the staff had knocked off, she went to her room to pour out her grief in private.

Lying down with her face in her pillow, she let it all out. Nothing but discouragement and letdowns. It had dragged on far too long and now she had no more inner reserve. Everybody she had grown close to and relied on had been taken out of her life one by one. She had jumped the gun far too soon with Mick, thinking, as a close friend of Tony's, she could trust him with her heart and soul. That was now down the lavatory.

She missed her kids living so far away. And now, her mother, who had recently deteriorated following another stroke, barely recognised her.

Summer wasn't one to feel sorry for herself. She always saw the glass as half full and had passed this mindset on to her children. But right now, it was as if the glass had smashed against a wall and not a drop of inner strength remained.

Troubled thoughts tormented her until she unintentionally drifted off to sleep.

~

Before long, there was a knock at the door, and Summer woke to find herself in darkness.

'Sorry, I don't mean to intrude. But it's dark outside, and your doors and windows were still open. I was wondering if you're all right?'

It was Liam, standing outside the door. She reached for her bedside lamp, switched it on and slid off the bed. After combing fingers through her hair and a glance in the mirror, she stumbled into the hallway.

'Goodness—thanks, Liam. I must have been exhausted and fell asleep.'

'That's okay, I shut them anyway. Just wondered if you were okay.'

'I'm fine—and thanks for doing that. Have you eaten?'

'Yes, thanks. I must get going as I need to do an estimation for a quote on a landscape job in Glendowie.'

'Oh, you'd better get off. We'll catch up another time.'

Liam went out to his cottage while Summer trudged aimlessly into the kitchen to prepare a light meal. She had little appetite, and the more she thought about how sour things had become between her and Mick, the less she felt like eating.

She was determined not to let any man suck the life out of her and forced herself to prepare a nourishing omelette with fresh herbs, tomatoes, mushrooms, courgettes and cheese—an old favourite.

The daily ritual of preparing and eating a meal on her own each evening would get her down if she had no guests to join her. Sometimes the staff ate with her when it was quiet and there were no guests staying in for dinner. For that, she was grateful.

Instantly she changed her focus to flipping her nearly burnt omelette.

31

Mick sat at his desk at the station, checking the witness statement Bernie had placed in front of him.

He closed the file. 'Well done, mate. You know Superintendent Winters and I have your back. This seals it for Dean. Don't worry—he's been under suspicion for years and now it has come home to roost.'

'Thanks, Sarge. What about that Sonny fellow—the one who was in cahoots with Dean—have you interviewed him yet?'

'Yep—yesterday with his lawyer. He buckled after finally confessing to his involvement in the attack on the guard but not killing him. Dean had previously primed Sonny about what to do if there was an altercation with the security staff at the port. He had instructed him to ensure that any DNA found on the corpse would be from Chai and not Sonny.

'So what are Sonny's charges?'

'He is convicted as an accessory after the fact in the murder. Dean had devised the plan and colluded with Selina, but Sonny will do jail time along with both of them.'

Bernie's eyes widened. 'Wow. So, apart from being in the frame for murdering the port guard, is the DSS also the kingpin in the trafficking ring?'

'Not exactly. He was involved in a protection racket accepting bribes from Byron, the owner of Kiwi Gold.'

While Bernie sat constantly racking his superior's brain, Mick perused another report which had arrived on his desk. It was the forensic results from the investigation into his house fire.

Following up on a comment made by his aunt, the forensic team searched Sonny's truck and found a huge number of empty potato crisp bags stuffed in a small cavity under the driver's seat. According to her, he was hooked on them. The fire investigators reported it was highly likely Mick's house fire had been started deliberately by igniting packets of crisps—the fat and contents forming an instant blaze. It is a common occurrence with house fires. They're highly inflammable.

'Unbelievable! My house burnt to the ground using potato crisp packets,' Mick blurted. He could not question Sonny about his house fire because of a conflict of interest, so Hayley Winters elected to stand in for him. The truck driver had no motive nor alibi for where he was the night of the fire.

With Dean out of the picture, Bernie had no one to work alongside, until Marta

Robins, a senior detective from down south, was transferred to the station.

Superintendent Winters thought Marta and Bernie would make a good team, and this meant that Sam, who was worried she would be moved to another station to accommodate Bernie, had her fears allayed.

After Bernie left Mick's office, Sam was dying to get an update and stuck her head through the door.

'Ah—I was about to call you. Good news,' said Mick. 'We've got Sonny Mathers—boots and all. As well as an accessory to the Port murder, we also have him for my house arson.'

'Goodness! How many is that now?'

'Well, it's a substantial organised crime ring with many factions. I hope this isn't just the beginning, as I'd like to get this whole syndicate closed down. Otherwise, we'll have no room to take on other cases.'

'I know what you mean,' Sam replied.

'But we're almost there. Once the ring leaders are in a corner, the rest of them often squeal.'

'I was going to ask you ... I mean ... can I apply for leave next week? It's time I visited my folks down the line.'

'What? Sorry, Sam. I need you around while I interview Jake North—Connie's ex-husband. He has arrived back from Australia for the court hearing, and we need to both interview him.'

Sam sank into her chair. 'Oh, I forgot about that. It's just that Mum and Dad want to take their motorhome down south and have asked if I would house-sit their pets—a dog and cat.'

Mick looked perplexed. 'Sorry to let you down, Sam, but this case has been hanging over me ... er ... us for so long. I want it over. I'll give you as much annual leave as you're entitled once we have Tony's killer locked up.'

'It's okay. They know I'm tied up with my work. I want to see an end to the case and Summer's suffering too.'

This last sentence of Sam's put acid in Mick's throat. It weighed him down heavily and triggered emotions he had buried deeply.

He would wait until he and Sam had interviewed Jake and then let the constable in on the latest update—even if they slipped up and discovered they'd made a mistake and the man was innocent, leaving Mick still with a question mark hanging over him.

~

Summer's life fell to pieces after she'd received troubling news twice on the same day.

Petra had come to her that morning announcing she was moving in with her boyfriend, giving one week's notice. Summer was gutted.

'Oh, really?' She tried to hide her shock. 'I guess I expected it was going to happen ... eventually.'

'I'm not resigning ... or at least ... not yet.'

Summer didn't know how to take that. Did she mean it was on the cards she could leave the job further down the track as well?

'I've got no hold over you, Petra. You're young and have to live your life as other young people do. Please don't feel bad.'

It took Summer hours to get over the first lot of unpleasant news when another whammy hit her. Just after both her staff had left for the day she received an upsetting call from her mother's rest home.

'Summer—it's Lara, the coordinator. I'm sorry to break this news to you ... it's your Mum ... she has had a massive stroke.'

Summer lost hold of the phone but grabbed it just before it reached the floor.

'Are you still there, dear?'

'Yes ... what happened? She was fine when I was in last.'

'I'm so sorry ... she has passed away.'

Summer was speechless.

Although her mother had recently suffered several minor strokes, reducing her short-term memory even more, she could still recognise her daughter and hold a lucid conversation with her.

'I'm afraid that this time there was nothing we could do.'

Summer thanked her and waited until the woman got off the phone before she broke down in tears. She felt all alone, and this coupled with Petra's news floored her. She couldn't even seek comfort in Mick's arms.

Was this the rod to break the horse's back? What she needed was a long, overdue break in Australia with her children. But they had demanding jobs and weren't able to spend time with her.

There was nothing else to do but carry on. That's what Tony would have wanted—to see her following her dream of running her grandparents' guest house, which she had talked about for years.

It was going to be hectic for her to plan a funeral while running the business. When she told her staff the following day, Petra promptly agreed to stay on living in the B&B until after the memorial service.

~

Ava and Pete, Summer's two children, flew in from Australia for their grandmother's funeral but could only stay with her three days. They both had to return home straight afterwards, but Summer was grateful for their support—even if their time with her was brief.

The event was supposed to have been a small family affair with only several close relatives and her mother's friends present, but to Summer's astonishment, the church was packed out.

A handful of Tony's police friends unexpectedly arrived—including Mick.

Summer was delighted to see Ava and Pete taking over—greeting people at the door and offering small talk, which she wasn't in any state of mind to cope with.

For the after-service gathering, there was a large table piled high with sandwiches, savouries and cakes provided graciously by church friends together with Mavis and Petra. Summer had agreed to foot all costs.

Although Mick continually tried to catch Summer's eye, she intentionally avoided him—worried she would lose her composure, which would have been inappropriate at her mother's funeral.

But as the congregation left the church, and she followed the last of the guests out the door, Summer felt a tug on her arm.

'Hey there! I've been trying to catch up with you. I'm sorry to hear about your mother. It must have been difficult ... are you free this evening?'

Her children heard him, and Ava smiled sweetly. 'Mum, it's okay. If you two want to talk, we'll wait in the car.'

Summer nodded at her daughter who whispered in her brother's ear as they both turned and walked out to Summer's vehicle parked on the roadside.

'I could spare a few minutes. The guest house is closed this week, but the kids head back to Australia this afternoon. I have to take them to the airport.'

Summer glanced at her wristwatch. 'They need to be there at four to check in and don't want me to wait so I can miss peak traffic. It's bedlam, as you know, travelling across the city.'

'I'd offer to drive you there, but they may not appreciate me hanging around,' Mick replied.

'Probably not but thank you, anyway.'

'Summer, I want to put things right between us. Perhaps you'll give me the benefit of the doubt when I tell you we have arrested a man we believe to be Tony's killer.'

Her face flushed a deep red. 'Oh, my gosh. Really—who is it?'

'Allow me to take you to dinner tonight— as a way of mending the rift in our friendship and I'll tell you all the news—where we're at with both the cases you've been involved in.'

Summer tried not to scowl but nodded her approval. 'I suppose it sounds okay. What time do you want to do this?'

'Let me pick you up by taxi when you get back from the airport. How does seven sound? I want to take you on one of those Penguin dinner cruises.'

'What? They cost an arm and a leg. Why would you want to do that?'

Mick appeared awkward. 'I just think that after the pain of today, you could probably do with a bit of a lift. You're always waiting hand

and foot on others, which makes me think you deserve a treat or two yourself.'

'It does sound amazing. You must have won the lottery.'

'Actually, I've just received a substantial bonus for the part I played in bringing Rob Dean to justice. We have a handful of big fish locked up and their ring leaders. Although it'll be a while before they go to trial, they'll all be going down for a very long time.'

'Sounds incredible.'

'And I have you to thank for much of that. It's the reason I want to share my bonus with you. There have been rumours around the station that I might leave, so it was a ploy to keep me on.'

'Leaving—is that true?'

'Not quite, but let's talk about it later.'

'Sorry, Mick—the kids are waiting. I must get going, but I'll see you at seven. Bye for now.'

As Mick drove off, he received a disheartening call from Hayley Winters, who had accompanied Sonny to his first court appearance. She said he had pleaded not guilty to being an accessory to the guard's murder.

This plea would likely drag the case out, which frustrated Mick greatly. He wanted the investigation to be over so he could move on—in several respects.

For the rest of the time Summer had left to spend with her children before they flew out, it was difficult for her to focus. Apart from the whirlwind few days that had flown by with the kids staying such a short time and her mother's death to contend with, she was now troubled by Mick's parting words about the possibility of him leaving.

Was this what his dinner arrangement with her was all about—wanting to put things right with her before leaving Auckland?

32

Mick appeared larger than life when he arrived at the door in the evening to collect Summer with a taxi waiting in the driveway.

He looked at least ten years younger with a recent haircut—slick, short back and sides—clean, auburn hair glistening under the front door lamp.

She had never seen him so dressed up, with a navy and white floral shirt and newish, blue denim Jeans. On his feet, he wore leather Birkenstock sandals.

Mick ogled Summer from head to toe as he looped his arm in hers. She had chosen a pink tailored frock and carried a mauve parka, as she knew it could be breezy on the boat.

'Wow', he said, walking her down the steps to the waiting taxi. He opened the car door for her to which she was unaccustomed.

Mmm ... He's certainly extending himself tonight.

'Good idea bringing a jacket. Your dress may not be warm enough. Although it's a calm evening, the wind can blow up suddenly on the harbour. We'll be inside though, so should be fine.'

The cruise was magnificent, and the food was more than Summer had expected. They enjoyed a plentiful buffet with a choice of quality wines.

While the boat cruised around several islands in the harbour, the sea was calmer than usual, which pleased Summer, since she'd over-indulged in the Pavlova dessert with her meal.

'Let's go sit at that small table in the corner where we can talk in private,' said Mick, directing Summer to a quieter place.

They had no sooner sat down when he gave Summer a rundown on the murder investigations.

'First, I'm sorry for not taking your suspicions about Rob Dean and Selina seriously right from the start. Perhaps if I had gone straight to the top right at the beginning, it wouldn't have been such a long and drawn-out case. As I once said, you're in the wrong game. You would have made a brilliant detective.'

Summer wanted to tell him not to waffle on so much and get straight to the point.

'Our team firmly believe we have apprehended the top dogs involved in Kiwi Gold's trafficking ring. They're now all under arrest, facing long sentences. Rob Dean's career is over—the only job he'll have left will be inside a prison.'

'That must be an immense relief for you. I guess you had to be sure before mouthing off to the detective superintendent about Dean. I do understand.'

'Now, there's another biggy to tell you, which I think will put a smile on your face.'

That's about time, Summer muttered under her breath. 'At last!' she responded.

The waiter topped up their wine glasses as they continued their discussion.

'We also have Jake back in Auckland on remand charging him with Tony's murder. We know he had the motive, as Connie gave evidence he had issued threats to her about Tony getting his comeuppance.'

'I hope they throw away the key, the mongrel!'

'Exactly. I can understand your anger. I would be the same if I were in your situation.'

'What if he doesn't plead guilty? Do you have sufficient proof to put him away?'

'I'm sure with the circumstantial evidence we have from his ex-wife, it will be enough.'

'Didn't you say you had other news for me, too?'

Mick beamed and then opened his top shirt buttons while Summer spotted beads of perspiration on his forehead.

'Remember, I told you how I had discussed with Tony the night before his death I was thinking about chucking in police work and letting my house out as a B&B?'

'Yes, I remember ... you also talked about operating kayaking tours out to the islands together.'

'Well, I'm seriously thinking of resigning once these two cases have wound up.'

Summer's face dropped. Now that Tony's killer had been caught, she imagined that Mick, Tony's closest friend, would always be around—especially to exchange cherished memories about her late husband.

'Are you serious? I thought it was just a passing whim when you said you had discussed it while you were both drinking.'

Mick leaned over, trying to make eye contact with her.

'Listen, Summer—I have an idea. If you think it's ludicrous, just say and I'll speak no more about it.'

Summer's stomach muscles tightened. What bombshell was he about to drop?

'You told me earlier this evening Petra is moving out, which leaves you rather short. I was wondering how you would feel if I moved in to help you run the business.'

Mick's unexpected offer confused Summer. Their friendship had completely swung from teetering on the edge of oblivion to a live-in situation.

She couldn't answer right out. There were all kinds of matters to consider—including her children. They would have something to say. And did Mick intend for them to cohabitate? She hoped he meant to share the house, not a bed. Besides, he'd not so long ago referred to their relationship as platonic, and she wouldn't let him, or any other man, take advantage of her—especially while grieving her mother.

'It sounds quite logical, I suppose, Mick, but I need to give it more thought. I mean— would you expect to be paid a wage along with the other staff, or were you hoping to become a business partner in the guest house? There are all these issues to consider.'

'Of course, you must think about all the implications, but if you're worried, you could seek legal advice if it frightens you.'

'I would anyway. Your offer's worth mulling over now that Petra's moving in with her boyfriend. She probably won't be working for me much longer and Mavis is only part-time.'

'There you are. We could give it a trial and see how we get on. If you give me free lodgings, I could pitch in and help whenever you want.'

Summer hesitated before answering.

'I guess we could give it a go. But if it's not working for either of us, we must each have the option of calling it quits, and then you must move out.'

'The other avenue I've considered is to establish my own B&B, as my insurance money has come through and I'm looking for a new property. I could purchase one such as yours and hire staff too.'

Summer didn't expect Mick to have another plan up his sleeve. This completely threw her off balance.

'I've also been headhunted by Interpol who've offered me a private role allowing me to work from home. If I only do it part time, that income would equal what I now earn full-time.'

Summer struggled to know how to react. Should she be happy for him or disappointed he had so many options available? But she wasn't desperate, and if his intentions were only based on self-ambition, then he didn't have any concern for her well-being. It remained to be seen.

'I've also been asked by Hayley Winters to take my inspector's exams now Dean isn't around. A new officer is coming up from the south, but she needs another senior detective at the station in the interim.'

'Oh, so many opportunities. I guess you have to go where your heart leads you,' Summer answered wistfully.

'I know where my heart is leading me. Haven't you guessed by now?' he asked, placing a hand over hers.

Summer, taken aback, stared at him with her bright blue eyes that now appeared like flying saucers.

'What are you saying, Mick? I hope you aren't playing games with me.'

It happened in a flash before Summer could get her head around it, as he lowered his voice and asked, 'Mind if I kiss you?' Mick leaned over the table towards her.

She could hardly hear herself speak, murmuring, No, it's okay, go ahead.'

Her mind went into a spin as Mick planted his soft, warm lips over her mouth, mesmerising her so she became speechless, but her spine tingled.

It took a while before her feet touched the ground after floating to heaven and back. She hadn't felt this way since she and Tony had first started dating, but right now, she shrugged away the guilt of enjoying another man's touch, for right now she needed comforting.

'Boy—you sure are full of surprises,' was all she could muster.

'I'm sorry if I took you unawares. It's how I've felt about you for ages, Summer. Even when you mistrusted and falsely accused me of hurting Tony, I wanted to be with you. That's why I suggested moving into the guest house.'

Summer didn't know how to answer. She was always afraid of getting into a whirlwind romance, but Mick had just ignited something inside her she couldn't control.

'I have those feelings for you also—or at least I did until we fell out. Perhaps it's best to decide exactly what it is you want—to be a live-in companion or a business partner,' she replied assertively.

'I know what you mean, and I'd like to see how we'd go under the same roof as friends and not as lovers—I know you wouldn't approve. But at least we could see how we get on together. I've been living an independent bachelor's life, and you're a self-reliant woman, so it won't be easy.'

'I've also been thinking along those lines,' Summer replied. 'Shall we wait until after Petra moves out? Then we could continue to date and spend more time in each other's company.'

Mick took her hand again and softly kissed her fingers. Summer craved his touch but restrained herself.

'I can wait as long as it takes. I'm not going anywhere and I understand you're grieving,' he replied.

When Mick accompanied Summer home in the taxi that night, he kissed her again. This time it lingered long enough for her to have to fight the urge to invite him inside to see where his amorous advances would lead them. She resisted—being true to herself in not being one to sleep around, conditioned to being a one-man girl after decades of being married to a wonderful, faithful man.

Mick left his mark on her lips, which she savoured while waving him off in the taxi home.

That night, something had changed in her. Until Mick's first, unexpected kiss during the boat cruise, Summer had, until now, slept alone without feeling someone was missing. But now there was a yearning in her soul— for comfort, warmth and love.

~

It had been three months since Mick's romantic advances on the harbour dinner cruise. He'd been steadfast in dating Summer regularly, which led her to agree finally to let him move into her guest house as a live-in staff member on wages just as Petra had been.

He had not yet resigned from the police, which he planned to do once the investigation into Tony's murder had closed. Once that was out of the way he would work freelance as a Police advisor for Interpol, giving him a sizeable income.

Hayley Winters didn't give up trying to get Mick to sit his inspector exams, but he continually reneged, knowing his days with the police were numbered and he didn't want to lose Summer.

There was still the problem of getting Jake behind bars, who had now pleaded not guilty. The circumstantial evidence which the prosecution had presented could not prove his culpability beyond a reasonable doubt.

During his hearing, Jake told the court he'd been drinking heavily in St Helier's Bay the morning of Tony's death. He vaguely remembered being turfed out of a small, licenced café after lunch. His defence lawyer had offered evidence given by the owner that Jake had ordered a pizza and a lot of alcohol around eleven. Two hours later, having made a nuisance of himself with some customers, the manager eventually ordered him off the premises. He didn't leave straight away and one of the waitresses witnessed she had seen him lying on a park bench in front of the café until late that afternoon with a bottle of whisky until the sun went down. The owner was about to call the police when Jake finally moved on just in time. His alibi was watertight. He hadn't left the area all day and had several eye-witnesses.

~

When Mick left the courtroom that day, he didn't know how to pass this bad news on to Summer. She would be devastated.

He waited until they were both seated in the lounge and were alone before breaking it to her.

When he had finished delivering the blow, Summer crumbled onto the couch. Her face turned white, while Mick felt helpless. It took him most of the evening to soothe her and get her out of an almost catatonic state.

'So, where is he now?'

'We've had to let him go. We've no more grounds to hold him.'

'But are you sure his alibi is waterproof?'

'Absolutely. The evidence from the cafe owner and waitress has only just come to light. They corroborated his story.'

Summer sank deeper into her seat.

'Does that mean the police are back to square one?'

Mick nodded. 'I guess so. We don't have any other suspects.'

'I just don't believe this. How could the case drag on so long and all you get is false suspects?'

'It's the name of the game, unfortunately. Why do you think I want to get out? Such investigations can be soul-destroying.

~

Mick gave Mavis a hand as best he could for the rest of that week because Summer appeared to have numbed out, completely losing all motivation. It finally came to where Mick attempted to persuade her they needed to take on another employee to help, but she adamantly refused to admit anything was wrong.

Meanwhile, Hayley Winters had agreed to Mick working part-time until Tony Martin's murder investigation was over. This meant that he could be at Summer's guest house when the staff were busy elsewhere and give her the support she badly needed.

Another bonus was the budding romance between Summer and Mick as their relationship continued to grow and blossom. He was in every way a rock for her.

Mick was a keen cook and never faltered at doing domestic chores. There was no need to replace Petra, after all. He was a more than exemplary substitute, in Summer's eyes.

The substantial, two-storey house Mick owned in Devonport consisted of seven bedrooms. Each had an ensuite bathroom similar to those in Summer's guest house.

There was a family already living upstairs in the extensive suite—a couple with a teenage student.

Mick kept a downstairs room for himself as a backup plan, just in case his relationship with Summer didn't work out, but he preferred not to give that a fleeting thought. If they did end up getting hitched, his home in Devonport would prove to be a substantial retirement nest egg for them both.

Summer and Mick enjoyed spending most evenings huddled together on a couch watching the box after their guests had retired, with Powder at one end and Summer's cat, Petal, at the other.

Most guests preferred not to relax in the public lounge, as they all had a TV set in their rooms. Sometimes they drank tea in the living room mingling with the guests, but most of the time this space was empty.

~

One night, as Summer lay with her head on Mick's shoulder dozing, almost asleep, a loud crash and the splintering of glass shook the daylights out of her as a brick hurtled past them within inches of Mick's head. He ducked just in time.

'Oh, no! What the heavens was that?'

'Get down, Summer. Stay on the floor away from the glass while I check it out.'

'Be careful!' she hollered back at him, as he raced outside the back door, searching for the intruder.

Summer lay on the floor, waiting for the next onslaught as she gazed at the layer of glass shards lying near her. The attack was short-lived but dramatic.

When Mick returned, he rescued Summer from the floor, stretching out his hand to help her up.

'Come on, love. You'd better get out of here while I clean up that mess.'

'Who was it—did you see anyone?'

'No, they bolted. I've let the station know.'

'I expect you're frustrated in situations like this when you can't take charge.'

Mick shrugged. 'Sometimes.'

'Here we go again—another repeat,' Summer mumbled.

'Don't worry. I'm here to protect you this time. Take no notice. It's probably a group of misguided youths letting out their discontent.'

Although Mick had downplayed the incident, he felt sick to the core that the brick could have cracked Summer's head open like an over-ripe grapefruit hitting concrete, when he was sure it was meant for him. Summer had no enemies he knew of, but he was well aware several villains would certainly have a grudge against him.

While Mick called his team, Summer sat quietly, counting her blessings amid her shocked state, and when he came off the phone thanked him for coming to her aid. She then went off to her room—half-wishing he was going to join her for comfort, but they had both agreed—no hanky-panky. They were still testing their relationship, and neither of them was prepared to break their end of the bargain.

33

Mick had stacks of reports to write up and worked from home in Summer's office.

He wanted to keep an eye on her in case the brick thrower had singled her out, and he found it difficult to concentrate. His thoughts continued to wander off as he struggled to find a motive for why Summer's home was earmarked.

It was first thought Tony had been the only person who was a prime target during Operation Sea Wolf, but maybe it was Mick whom the culprit was after.

The police had been at the B&B all morning and luckily no guests were booked in that day. Although the place had emptied by the afternoon, and the house was deathly quiet, they were heavily booked until the weekend.

Forensics had found no trace of evidence from the perpetrator. The police team were convinced it was only bored teens carrying out a prank and did not take it seriously. But Mick thought otherwise, and he worried Summer could be in danger.

He wondered—could it be Tony's killer on the loose again? All of Dean's associates were now locked up, so the incident must have been unrelated to the trafficking ring.

Summer brought a tray with coffee for them both and sat next to Mick at the office desk.

'Something has been playing on my mind. Remember, I told you about Olive's nephew, Jeremy, who works at the ferry wharves? Well, I wondered whether there was any way he could have harmed Tony.'

'Goodness—this is one for the books,' Mick replied.

'I mean it. Last night I lay in bed recalling the times when Tony and I used to stay with my grandparents. Jeremy was still a schoolboy. He used to climb through a gap in the low wire fence behind the orchard. When he got older, it happened with more regularity, arriving uninvited. I remember Tony mentioning one day that Jeremy was becoming like a stalker.'

'As an adult, do you mean? That's serious. Tony should have reported it.'

'No, I'm talking about when he was an adolescent at high school. He's in his twenties now—old enough to be my son. He looked upon me as a motherly figure.'

'I don't get it. I thought you said Jeremy was Olive's nephew. Why was he living with her?'

'He is Olive's late sister's son and has been living with her on and off since his mother died when he was at primary school. He had contracted encephalitis from an outdoor heated swimming pool, which left him with some brain damage. Olive said he was always very slow afterwards and his father couldn't cope. That's why the lad used to stay with his aunt on and off. His father sent him to a boarding school, but the boy hated it. When he left, he started working—mainly doing labouring jobs. He tried going flatting for some time but couldn't relate to his peers, so that type of accommodation never lasted long. Eventually, he moved back to live with Olive as a working adult. It was close to his job with the ferries.'

Mick glanced at his wristwatch. 'I think I'll put the kettle on.'

'Hold on, let me finish.'

Summer continued, irritated at his impatience.

'After he moved back next door, Olive sometimes sent him over to us with a plate of scones or fresh-baked biscuits. Tony occasionally complained about him coming through the back fence of our orchard uninvited, saying he was making a bit of a nuisance of himself.'

Mick became agitated 'So where are you going with this?'

'I've been pondering on various scenes that Tony and I had together here at the house.

When we first moved in, he said more than once that Jeremy was obsessed with me, but I always thought it was just a mother complex. If he had turned up unexpectedly while I was staying with my mum, I think he and Tony may have had some kind of altercation.'

'Well, this is an unexpected lead—carry on,' Mick replied with sudden interest.

'I should have notified the police who could have interviewed Jeremy while they were here following up on Tony's death, but I didn't want to upset Olive further who was already in shock having discovered Tony's body—and don't forget I was gutted, too.'

'I'll get onto it. The team will have to search his room—and computer—if he has one and see what they can find.'

'Really? Poor Olive will be so distressed. He's like a son to her.'

'The fellow's in his twenties—not a child anymore, Summer. He's a full-grown adult.'

'I know—it's just hard to believe Jeremy has a violent bone in his body.'

'You said he was backward, and the brain damage has changed his personality. Perhaps he's unstable—a loose cannon.'

She frowned. 'I didn't call him backward! I would never say such a thing. Olive had referred to him as being a little slow because of the encephalitis. That's what I'd told you,' she retorted.

Mick's propensity for insensitivity since dealing with brutal crimes for so many years abruptly gave him a twinge of conscience.

'Sorry, Summer, you're right—wasn't thinking. I'll get my team in there as soon as possible. Hopefully, tomorrow. I hate to say it, but this may be the one stone that remains unturned. Jeremy's motive could have been his fixation on you and if Tony stood in the way, perhaps it was enough to cause him to flip and attack him.'

Mick's last comment caused a pain deep in Summer's soul. The thought of Olive's nephew being carted off by police in handcuffs and ending up behind bars would finish the old woman. She regretted telling Mick but knew he was now determined more than ever to eliminate Jeremy as a prime suspect in Tony's murder.

Mick pondered his last visit to the station. Although Hayley had taken him off Tony's case because of his conflict of interest, he could still read the reports and follow up on the investigation.

During the initial inquest, Summer had said at her police interview that while staying with her mother, Tony had discussed getting quotes from landscapers. He told her that three tradesmen had phoned to enquire about the job. The police had traced their mobile phone histories and all three tradesmen had concrete alibis. Only one had visited Tony's property that day. His name was Ali Knight, and he ran a landscaping business in Mission Bay.

Ali and Tony had discussed the proposed dig, and Ali had shown Tony how deep he should shovel out the clay to reach the water table for the fountain. Everyone knew this local landscaper, and he had not the slightest motive for injuring anyone. One of his employees was waiting for him out on the road in his Ute ready to head out to another appointment, so Ali had given Tony his business card and left.

What this tradesman did tell the police was that he thought he had spotted someone behind the trees in the orchard, but didn't take any notice, thinking it was Tony's wife picking fruit. The police were convinced someone else was on the property watching while Tony met with the tradesman. Whoever it was, they must have tried setting Ali up as the killer.

~

That night—tossing and turning—Summer's mind went ninety to the dozen. She was agonising over the impact it would have on poor Olive having a team of police officers marching in overturning her home. A gentle woman who minded her own business.

That's it! Summer knew exactly what she must do first thing in the morning. She would head on over there before the boys in blue arrived—thinking that if Jeremy was so besotted with her, he might talk before the heavy machinery started on him. Having met up with Olive earlier in the week, Summer knew it would be her nephew's day off. She had to do something—and fast.

Every other suspect, until now, had an alibi about their movements the day Tony was murdered. The only person who didn't was Mick. He had been one of the last people to see Tony alive and could easily have made up the story about inviting his best mate to go fishing with him at Music Point.

There was no proof that anyone had seen Mick that afternoon and Summer had to be sure about him, too, now that he had moved into the guest house with her.

It was exhausting—rehashing in her mind all the information she had extracted from Mick about the case. It spun like a tumble dryer in her head—regurgitating what she already knew about the case with the limited extra facts he had given her.

Sleep finally came at last, but this was going to be another restless night, for sure.

~

Summer woke the next morning with a heavy head and her throat feeling like she had swallowed a handful of tacks. She took large gulps of water from her pump bottle.

Fortunately, Petra was living nearby and could still help Summer with the morning duties. To give her time to get to work, they had moved the meal time from its earlier start so that it was now officially eight until ten. Patrons were offered either a Continental or Full English breakfast.

Having extra help meant Summer could take a break now and then, and today she asked Petra to hold the fort until Mavis arrived later that morning.

Earlier, she had called Olive to ask if she could visit and talk to Jeremy—hoping the woman would not allow him to duck out.

~

When Summer arrived mid-morning, Olive had just made a batch of pikelets covered in jam.

'This is the lovely strawberry confiture you gave me last summer. It's delicious!'

'Mmm, fresh pikelets. You know they're one of my favourites,' Summer replied.

When they finally got down to brass tacks to discuss Summer's reason for the visit, Olive became flustered.

'Olive—the police may arrive soon and turn your place inside out. They want to eliminate Jeremy from Tony's homicide investigation and before they come, I'd like to get some information from you regarding Jeremy's recent activities.'

Olive threw Summer a suspicious glance and shrunk half her size.

'I wondered when the police would eventually come,' she replied. 'Jeremy is in his room. I didn't warn him—just said you may have morning tea with me today.'

Olive's hand shook as she poured the tea from a floral china teapot and handed over a plate of pikelets. The crockery reminded Summer of the bone china her mother had given her before moving into the rest home.

'I remember you told me Jeremy stayed with you most of last year until now. I need to know from you if he ever said anything about my husband chasing him off our property. Tony said he would sometimes just

363

appear at the fence unannounced or even turn up in the orchard unexpectedly. I thought nothing of it until recently.'

Olive gaped at her. 'You suspect Jeremy, don't you?'

'I don't know what to think, Olive. But we need to solve it. If Jeremy was in our garden that day, I need to find out. Perhaps something happened—an accident of some sort. Forensics think Tony was bashed over the head with his spade, but there were only his own fingerprints on it.'

'Well, isn't that your answer? Maybe Tony tripped and fell on those cobblestones he had laid. There was blood all over them when I found him. Perhaps no one smashed him over the head after all,' Olive replied, desperately.

'I don't think it was an accident. The coroner said the type of injury signified a heavy blow from a blunt object, as Tony's skull had caved in.'

This last statement made Olive cringe. 'Ooh, no,' she said, wrapping her arms around her body.

'Did you ever catch him spying on me at the fence or in our garden, Olive? This is important.'

'He has that OCD condition called obsessive-compulsive disorder which the counsellor at his boarding school had diagnosed. It all started when his mother died. While at college, he got into trouble gawping at females in their changing sheds. He also stalked a girl walking home from school. But the counsellor said he wasn't a predator. It was his condition which kicked in when he was under stress. He even did it to female teachers.'

'Wow, that's so sad.'

'It was the reason his father couldn't cope and sent him to the boarding school.'

'Does he still have the disorder?'

'I guess so, but he isolates now—stays away from people so he can't get into trouble.'

'Suppose that would explain why he hung around me. One day, while wearing shorts, I was busy hanging washing on the line and spotted him near the orchard, staring at me. I had wondered then if he had a problem but gave him the benefit of the doubt. I always thought he regarded me as a mother figure,' said Summer.

'He's not a pervert, you know. A psychologist said he is just infatuated with women's bodies but not sexually. He feels nothing when he does it, his therapist says.'

Summer was now feeling uncomfortable with the idea of his fixation. Not that she was afraid he might harm her, but more so that she didn't know how to approach him now. Was it possible to reason with someone who had a mental health disorder and couldn't control his behaviour? Was he going to own up to having an altercation with Tony—if it were true? She would be the one person in whom he might confide.

'When you've finished your tea, I'll knock on his door and say you would like to talk, as it's such a long time since you've seen him,' said Olive.

Before they walked along the hallway to Jeremy's room, Summer's phone rang. It was Mick. She asked him to hold for a moment.

'I just need to take this call first, Olive. Can you wait before you speak to him?'

Summer didn't tell Mick she was about to talk to Jeremy. That would have to wait until their evening meetup, after the fact. For now, she would just have to play amateur sleuth.

'Sorry, Summer, but my team won't be able to search your neighbour's house until tomorrow. They're tied up with a new homicide today.'

~

Jeremy sat at his computer desk with his back to the door, wearing headphones.

'He can sit for hours, when he's not at work, playing computer games. He won't be able to hear us,' said Olive.

She gently approached, waving her hand in front of the screen startling him. He looked up and smiled at her. When he spotted Summer standing behind him, he tensed and removed his headphones.

'Jeremy, you know Summer. She has been enjoying morning tea with me—I have a plate of pikelets for you.'

He waved at Summer, directing her to take a seat while wolfing down the food in no time at all. Olive left him the plate. 'If you need me for anything, I'll be in the lounge.'

Summer began reminiscing with Jeremy about the times he had spent with her and Tony during his youth and even drew reference to her grandfather who often gave him jobs in the orchard for pocket money, with Olive's approval.

'I remember when your grandparents had that big plastic pool in the backyard, and you used to stay with them.'

'Oh, yes, I remember. That's before I was married—you were about ten years old.'

'And you wore a really pretty bikini—with red ladybirds. Your grandmother growled at you for sunbathing too long—remember?'

Summer could see what Olive meant by the fetish or fascination he had with women—especially recalling what she had worn many years ago.

As they sat talking, she caught sight of multiple photographs on the wall in the corner of his room. She was sure she saw one of herself.

'Jeremy, I hope you don't mind, but there's something I need to ask you. Your aunt said the day my husband was killed, you had seen my detective friend's Skoda police car pulling into the driveway in the evening and you also spotted his vehicle still there the next morning.'

'Oh, she's on about that again, is she?'

'No, it was me who asked her. She said I could talk to you about it. Do you remember seeing any tradesmen or their vehicles that day? It's possible Tony had some visits from landscapers to offer quotes for our fountain project.'

Summer watched Jeremy's face change colour. His rosy cheeks earlier paled, leaving him looking pasty.

'I don't know—it's such a long time ago.'

Yet you could remember the pattern on my bikini when you were ten years old. She restrained herself from spitting it out.

'Did you stay at home that day, after you saw the detective's car?'

'I went to my father's for the morning as I had a day off from work. I keep some of my gear there as Aunty Olive can't store everything here.'

His father would need to vouch for that in an inquest, Summer noted mentally.

'So you can't help me with anything that happened that day?'

Jeremy's tension grew. He began grinding his teeth, which sent shivers up Summer's spine.

'Jeremy. The reason I'm so desperate to know is that—apart from wanting to solve the case—the detective you saw with Tony that morning was a very dear friend of his. He is also like family to me. And the way it stands, he has no proof to say he didn't attack

368

my husband. That's how it looks, although nobody who knows him would believe he was at all guilty. I need to find out what happened that day.'

Jeremy just shrugged and stared at the floor nodding. He struggled to give her eye contact.

Summer got out of her chair and walked over to the prints on his wall. She spotted more than one photo of her—far too many to be appropriate. 'Why do you have all those photographs of me?'

Her blood pressure rose, her face turning hot and prickly.

'What are you playing at, Jeremy?'

'Please, don't tell anyone. Aunty Olive keeps asking me to take them down, but I've told her they're harmless and there's no harm in me looking at pretty girls. It's natural.'

'But I'm a woman now, Jeremy. And when you took the photos, I was married to Tony.'

'Didn't mean you any harm. I don't have a girlfriend and you were always so kind to me. Just enjoyed looking ... you know ... nothing dirty or anything like that.'

'Did Tony ever catch you staring at me or taking photos?'

Jeremy looked down again, this time looking distraught.

'He saw me filming you, soon after you both moved into the guest house—standing in the orchard or your garden.'

'Tony never told me—not a thing, but he must have been furious.'

'Yeah, he was pretty angry. Once, when he went off at me, I moved out of Aunty Olive's house and went to stay with my sister, but she and I argued a lot. Dad also used to get annoyed with me, so I always ended up coming back here.'

It made sense for Summer now. She couldn't understand why Tony had never mentioned it. Perhaps he didn't want to worry her.

'Jeremy—did you get very upset with Tony the day he was killed and hit him over the head with a spade? You must tell me the truth, or the police will find out. It could end up a lot worse for you if I don't explain what happened first. My detective friend can help you.'

For the first time during their long conversation, Jeremy caved in. Tears began rolling down his face.

'I'll die in prison! Please don't let them lock me up. I didn't mean to do it.'

Summer's head hurt, although she was unaccustomed to headaches. What she had just heard was beyond belief.

'Are you saying you did bash Tony over the head that day?'

Jeremy stammered. 'No, not that! It didn't happen like you're saying,' he hollered.

'You'd better tell me quickly, Jeremy. The police are coming tomorrow, and I want to see if I can help you first.'

There was a tap at the door. Olive must have heard her nephew raising his voice. 'Everything okay in there, Summer?'

She answered swiftly to keep her out of the room. 'Yes, please give us a little more time. We won't be long. Thanks, Olive.'

When Summer knew the coast was clear to continue, she pressured Jeremy once more.

'Was it the spade you killed him with?' eyeballing him close up.

'No—I told you—it wasn't like that. I've been wanting to come and see you, but Aunty told me to stay away as you were under a lot of stress with your Mum being sick. I know that wasn't the only reason. She didn't like me going over to your house unless she was at home.'

It was like pulling teeth, but Summer pushed on. 'You haven't answered my question, Jeremy.'

'I'm trying to—just wait!' he snapped.

'What did you want to talk to me about?'

'I was looking for more work. The ferries only give me casual work and it's not regular. Aunty had told me all about your dreams of starting up a B&B and would need a caretaker. That's before Liam started with you, of course.'

'I didn't know you were looking for a job.'

'That's exactly why I came over that day. Aunty said Tony would be at work in the backyard, wanting to surprise you with a project ready for when you came home from visiting your mother. I climbed over the rickety back fence that had almost fallen over and as I hid behind a tree in the orchard, I could see Tony was talking to someone. He had already mentioned to Aunty that he was getting quotes from a tradesman to do the dig for your fountain. I told her I could give him a hand, but she wouldn't have it. Anyway—the guy who was talking to Tony that afternoon took the spade off him and began digging out some of the clay while I hung back and watched. Then they stood talking for a few minutes before the guy handed Tony a business card and walked off out to the road.'

'Where were you at this point?' Summer asked, the tension causing a band of pressure across her temples as if her head would burst.

'I just waited in the orchard for the tradie to leave, then I walked up to Tony. I guess he got a fright as I came through the trees behind him. He waved his spade at me and swore—yelling to get off the property. I tried to calm him, saying I had only come looking for work and asked if I could help him dig the footing for the fountain.'

Summer was shocked that Tony had reacted so badly—if it were true.

'That's when it blew up. He lurched at me, tripping over the pile of rocks in the courtyard and hit the ground spread-eagled, face down still holding the spade. He must have smacked his head on a rock as he fell, bleeding like a stuck pig all over the paving.'

By now, Summer felt like heaving her stomach contents but daredn't budge.

'Why didn't you call an ambulance?'

'Tony was lying with his face on the spade. I pulled it out from under him, placing it nearby. As he was on his front, it was hard to see if he was moving or breathing. I panicked, thinking with your husband's ill-feeling towards me, you might blame me for his death. I fled back home, packed my things and raced off to my dad's house.'

Summer racked her brain, trying to remember what Mick had said about the forensic reports.

'There were only Tony's fingerprints on the spade handle. If you'd pulled the spade out from under him, your prints would have been on there too.'

'No—just like the contractor, I wore leather gardening gloves hoping to help Tony dig out the foundations for your fountain so I could impress you. I thought if I'd done that, you might have given me a job as caretaker or gardener at your guesthouse. It would have been so handy living next door to my work.'

'You should have rung for an ambulance, regardless. That was very self-centred of you—no excuse!'

By now, Jeremy was in tears again. He cupped his face in his hands, saying, 'Please forgive me, Summer. I didn't murder him—I would never have done that. Believe me—I'm so sorry for the trouble I've caused.'

'Was it you who chucked a brick through my lounge window recently too?'

Jeremy lifted his tear-stained, ruddy face, frowning at her. 'What? No, of course not! I would never hurt you.'

Summer didn't know whether to get angry or have empathy for him. Still, if he had phoned an ambulance that day, there was a possibility that Tony would be still alive.

'Where are the leather gloves you wore that day?'

'I washed them and put them to dry in Aunty's garden shed.'

'The police will have to take them for analysis. I'll have to let them know,' Summer replied.

She got up, feeling like a stunned mullet and walked out without a word to him. Olive stopped her before she got to the front door.

'Everything all right, Summer. You're as white as a sheet. It seemed like an eternity you were there with him. What happened?'

'I'm sorry, Olive. Don't let him disappear. He was present when Tony died and will be a key witness, although he didn't kill him. He could have saved my husband's life, although it was an accident.

Olive tried to stop her from walking out the door and clutched her arm. Summer glared at her, pulling away. 'You can ask Jeremy exactly what went on. He needs psychological help, but right now, he will be required for the investigation into Tony's death.

As Olive crumbled in a heap against the front door, Summer staggered home—numb and bewildered by what she had just heard.

35

Following Summer's tumultuous time with Jeremy—squeezing a confession from him—she collapsed into Mick's loving arms the minute he walked through the door when he returned from work.

'I told you not to talk to Jeremy with our team going there tomorrow. You could have frightened him off. Luckily, he told you the truth, and to be honest, I'm thrilled you've solved the case, and we can now put closure on Tony's death.'

Mick poured himself and Summer a glass of wine. 'Get this into you. I guess you're drained after all that drama.'

Summer lay back against him, letting the terrible tension she had experienced the whole time she was with Jeremy unravel. She found it unbelievable that this long and drawn-out saga was finally at an end.

'What do you think will happen to him? Will he go to prison for not coming forward and reporting what happened?'

'Although he has perverted the course of justice, there are mitigating circumstances. I think the forensic psychologist will suggest treatment for his OCD and make a recommendation he get a non-custodial sentence. He'll take into consideration the fact that the bloke lost his mother as a young boy. He or his family may have a fine to pay.'

'It doesn't seem much justice for Tony who has lost his life, although it was an accident—anyone can fall and hit their head. We're such fragile human beings,' Summer muttered half-heartedly.

As she lay back exchanging views about human frailty, Summer quietly thanked God she no longer had to harbour hidden suspicions about Mick.

~

The case was nearly at an end. Summer was impatient to get it all behind her and at last concentrate on her life with Mick—a new beginning.

While the police team and Forensics spent hours searching Olive's house, Hayley Winters and Detective Inspector Marta Robins interviewed Summer in her office at the guest house.

The investigative crew seized Jeremy's laptop, camera, and phone and also collected photos of Summer he had displayed on the wall.

After they had finished, the officers took Jeremy to the police station for questioning.

When Hayley and Marta had finished interviewing Summer, they asked her to write a witness statement and then Summer invited both the women to stop for a cup of tea.

'Sorry, but we must get on,' said Hayley. 'We'd like to wind this up and I need to be back at the station while the evidence is being analysed.'

Summer darted a glance at Mick who had hung around all day to support her.

'That's understandable—we also want to get this wound up. You've no idea the nightmare it's been for me not knowing who the killer was,' she replied.

'Yes, and we're also trying to get a lead on the brick flying through your window. That's if your friendly neighbour is telling the truth and didn't hurl it himself,' said Marta.

Summer shook her head. 'I'm certain he was honest about that. But it does creep me out thinking it could be unsafe living here. I would hate to give up the guest house. That's also why I was so determined to know if Tony was linked to the trafficking. It could mean that I might be the next one on the hit list.'

Mick wrapped an arm around her waist, pulling her close. 'There's nothing to worry about, now that we know it wasn't Dean or an assassin who attacked Tony. You can relax.'

'Well, I'll leave you to it and will get in touch if we need any further information. You do realise that you're a key witness in the trafficking case.'

'It's okay, Hayley. I've already prepared her for that,' Mick cut in.'

'Right then, we'll get going. Please stay in the vicinity, as we may need you again,' Hayley replied as she and Marta left to return to Olive's house.

~

Summer had closed the guest house for the rest of the week. It was becoming all too much for her—especially following the previous day's showdown with Jeremy, but she was grateful to have Mick at her side. Most of all, it was a relief for her to know he was not involved in Tony's death. If what Jeremy said was true, it was an accidental death and no longer a murder.

She was still suffering from the stress brought about by having believed for so long that Tony had been brutally slain and left to die in cold blood. But now it was no longer the case.

Knowing her husband had not been murdered by a psychopathic killer, was much easier for Summer to digest.

It would have been intolerable carrying on living in the guest house, after hearing Tony had been viciously bashed in their backyard. This was why it had become so important for her to uncover the truth.

~

Summer finished stacking the breakfast plates in the dishwasher while Mick wiped down the table.

'Let's go for a walk along the beach before the sun goes down. It's almost Easter and the days are closing in now—daylight saving will soon be over and I'm dying to blow the cobwebs out.'

'Sure, good idea,' Mick replied.

'I've given Petra and Mavis the rest of the week off on paid leave, but it'll be hectic next week.'

'Are you sure you can cover their wages if you have no guests? Perhaps I'd better pay you for lodgings,' said Mick. He took her hand and kissed it.

It was this sudden charm of his that made Summer putty in his hands, but she kept her wits about her.

Despite being tempted to say yes to his offer, she secretly hoped for so much more— that their progressive, budding relationship was heading to something more permanent. And then it wouldn't be right for Mick to be a paying guest.

'No, but thanks for the offer. The guest house has flourished these summer months, and this wee blip won't bankrupt me. Anyway, Jeremy's father has phoned, offering compensation for the duress Jeremy has caused me. He's well off, I believe.'

'Really? Okay, if you insist,' Mick replied.

'And if I accepted, I wouldn't be able to ask you to do extra maintenance around here— such as repairing the wire fence at the back of the orchard,' Summer added, chuckling.

Mick reached over to ruffle her hair. 'You minx. I always knew I'd have to stay one step ahead of you.'

Summer headed along the hallway. 'Come on. I'll grab a jacket and let's do that beach walk. Perhaps we can stop at the kiosk for an ice cream on the way back. I just fancy one right now.'

It was a windless, sunny day with a clear, blue sky. When they arrived at St Heliers Bay beach, Summer removed her sandals. She was the most carefree she'd been in a long while.

As they walked along the foreshore chatting, Mick took her hand. This was the first time they'd done that, and Summer felt secure—something she hadn't experienced since losing Tony.

Now and then Summer dipped her feet in the sea as frothy waves gently stroked the shore and after their walk, they sat down on a grassy berm. Mick dried her feet with his jacket.

'Let's get one of those fruit waffle cones before we go back, and then I won't have to do much for dinner tonight.'

Mick smiled. 'Is that right? I thought you might have had an ulterior motive for wanting ice cream. It's okay, you don't have to prepare a meal. I reckon we could get fish and chips later. I'll ring and order them when we get back and then shoot down the road to pick them up.'

'It would be lovely to have a break from cooking. I'm all for it!'

They had both left their cell phones at home. Mick always said how much digital gadgets controlled his life, but then he remembered the night of his house fire when he had deliberately left his phone in the car and had missed the urgent calls from his fireman friend and colleagues.

'I should have brought my phone with me—although I'm not on duty today. It's just that I have this awful foreboding always that I might miss something critical.'

Summer precisely understood what he meant, as they had both undergone deep traumas and recovering from the resulting stress.

'Wouldn't it be wonderful not to rely on mobile phones, though?' she replied. 'Remember when we grew up, and we only had landlines? It seems like a lifetime ago.'

Regardless of his reticence, the first thing Summer did when they arrived home was pick up her phone. There was a voice message from Connie, Jake's ex-wife. Summer returned her call.

'I was going to ring you, Connie, but thought I should wait a little longer to be sure. I have good news, but it may be better for you to talk to the detective who was handling the case. He's here—just a moment.'

Summer asked Mick if he could talk to Connie about the outcome of Jake's police enquiry. He agreed and took the phone, outlining the eyewitness statements that had given him his alibi.

'I suppose it's of no consequence to you, but apparently, Jake is clean and sober at present doing well in a rehab centre down country and has a job lined up when he finishes. He wants to pay you back for the trouble he caused.'

'I want nothing from that scumbag,' she replied bitterly. 'I just want to hear he has finally faced consequences for killing our baby.'

'He sure has, Connie. Now that he's sober, he has to live with the constant memory of causing you to miscarry. He is immensely sorry for his behaviour and will do anything to put it right.'

'Putting it right will mean staying away from me and never making contact again.'

'He wants to make amends, but I'll tell him you're not ready.'

'You tell him I'll never be ready! But please tell Summer I'm glad the police have found the cause of her husband's death. I'm sorry I was mistaken for thinking it was Jake.'

When Mick got off the phone, Summer waved her wristwatch under his nose.

'Oh, yes—fish and chips. I'll phone them now.'

While Mick was away fetching takeaways, Summer received an upsetting call from Petra, saying she was giving two weeks' notice as she had been offered an opportunity to train as a manager at one of the large city hotels.

Before working at Summer's guest house, Petra had gained a Diploma in Hospitality Management but had been unsuccessful in getting a suitable position anywhere.

'I understand, Petra. This is a great chance—I don't begrudge you. I've loved having you living here with us, but we all have to do what's right for ourselves—especially at your age.'

'I feel so bad leaving you in the lurch like this. How will you cope while Mick is still doing police work? Mavis won't be able to manage on her own and Liam is flat out with his landscaping business.'

'Don't you worry about us. Mick and I will muddle through while we look for another helper.'

~

By the time Summer had got off the phone, Mick had arrived with the food. She took the heated plates out of the oven.

'I've just had some unpleasant news, but let's eat first while it's hot.'

'Oh, no. I hope it's not too disastrous,' said Mick, pouring them both a glass of apple juice. They sat at an outdoor table in the sun before it disappeared and halfway through the meal, Mick pressed her about the news she'd received.

'It's Petra—she's just given her notice. Of course, she'll give me a formal letter of resignation but has just told me over the phone.'

'I see. I wouldn't be too alarmed though, as it was going to come, eventually. She's a bright girl and at her age would want to extend herself. What's she going to do?'

'Hotel management training. I guess I never told you—the girl has a Hospitality Management Diploma. The Sea Quest Hotel overlooking the harbour is taking her on.'

'Well, I guess that's great news for her. Don't worry, we'll cope—we can always get someone else in to help with the breakfasts, but let's wait and see what happens when they close Tony's investigation. I might have some good news for you.'

36

A week later

Mick arrived home with feedback on the outcome of Tony's investigation, to Summer's delight. They discussed the results over dinner while Mick explained Jeremy had been held for 72 hours under Section 4 of the Mental Health Act while the police awaited a full psychiatric report. Afterwards, he was sent to stay at his aunt's house on home detention.

Mick had asked Hayley to show Charles, the forensic pathologist, Jeremy's witness statement.

The physician confirmed Tony sustained a blunt force injury when his head struck a protrusion in a rock pile as he fell.

The impact had caused a compressed, open fracture to the side of his skull. As Tony hit the ground he must have landed face down onto the spade's steel blade, which would account for blood on the garden tool, and clay on his face.

It also meant that Tony's skull had bled out profusely onto his artistic mosaic work in the courtyard.

With the full disclosure of what took place, including his admission of failure to call an ambulance because of sheer panic, the psychiatrist deemed Jeremy to be sane and responsible for his actions, but not a threat to the public.

He was given a non-custodial sentence of home detention involving Community Service of one hundred hours to be served within six months but was required to attend a three-week program for his OCD and voyeurism.

'That's a fantastic outcome!' said Summer, beaming.

'I knew you'd be pleased. The bloke doesn't have an evil bone in his body—it appears— just damaged from the traumatic loss of his mother. But he still needs treatment. You must be wary until he has had a satisfactory report back from the clinic.'

'I'm not afraid of him—he has never caused me to believe he would do me any harm.'

'No, I don't think he would, either. He has a probation officer whom I can ask for a progress report. Her name is Carmel, whom we all call Caramel.'

They finished their meal and cleared up the dishes together before relaxing in the lounge. Once seated in front of the TV, Mick had something else to tell Summer.

'I've formerly resigned from the police pending the trial of Rob Dean and his associates. Hayley has allowed me to use all my annual leave as part of my termination so long as I agree to give witness statements during the court inquest for Operation Sea Wolf. I can stand in for Petra now.'

'That's marvellous!' Summer blurted. 'But don't you think you'll be bored helping me run the guest house after such a high-paced job living on the edge?'

Mick grinned. 'It's exactly what I want right now. I'm over with working all the long hours eating on the run and being socially isolated—completely over it. Boring will do me,' he said, ruffling her hair affectionately.'

'Sounds wonderful,' Summer replied, although harbouring doubts about how he could make such a lifestyle turnaround.

'Are you still interested in running the kayaking tours and camps?' she added.

'Funny you should ask that. Liam bailed me up early this morning and asked if I still wanted him to join me on the tours. First, he wants to talk to you about a few changes going on with his work before he commits. Can you go over to the cottage this evening to discuss it? Sorry—I should have told you earlier.'

Summer was eager to find out what was on Liam's mind. With all the upheavals going on in her life lately, she was having trouble keeping up—especially with Petra finishing the following week.

When Liam moved into the cottage after Summer had taken him on as her caretaker and gardener, he created an impressive pathway from the courtyard in the back garden to the front door of his cottage with old, recycled bricks. On both sides of the path, grew tiny borders of thyme groundcover and its fragrance emanated all the way to the guest house.

~

When Summer knocked at the door, Liam shuffled to greet her with a beer can in his hand.

'Sorry, just relaxing after a hot day shovelling concrete. Come on in—something to drink?'

'No, thanks. I had one earlier.'

She sat down in the only armchair in the room while Liam lay stretched out on the couch.

'I guess Mick mentioned I wanted to talk to you.'

'Yes, he did—everything all right, I hope?'

'There's no problem ... except that my business has stepped up and got rather busy lately—so much so that if I don't increase my hours, I'll have to employ some extra help. Paying wages will cripple me.'

Summer's face dropped. Was this another of her trusted workers who was about to leave? She had got used to Liam being in the cottage—who had been great security while she and Petra had been alone in the house.

'Are you leaving too?' she asked feebly.

Liam could see the daunting expression on her face.

'Well, no—not exactly. Now that Mick is living here, I wondered—instead of being your caretaker, I could take him up on his proposition of running a kayaking tour operation. We don't have to be business partners, but I could do it on wages unless it's a partner Mick wants.'

Summer shrugged. 'I guess you would need to sort that out with Mick. He'll have to help with the maintenance of the property, and I don't know how much time he'll have to spare.

'Yes, he told me ... I'm sorry to let you down, Summer.'

'Never mind—can't be helped. But what about this cottage? Do you still intend to stay on the property?'

Liam sat up straight, combing his fingers through his hair. 'There's something else I wanted to ask you. I don't suppose you know, but I've been seeing a girl for the last six months. I said nothing, as my relationships rarely get past the first post. But I think this time it's serious.'

'Oh? Good on you.'

'The thing is ... I would like her to move in with me and if it works out, we'll save for a house. How would that suit you? I know you'll like her. She could even help in the guest house—perhaps with breakfasts—as she's a real morning person.'

'Doesn't she have a job or anything?' Summer said smartly.

'She's doing a Master of Accountancy degree and is looking for part-time work. It would suit her down to the ground to work here while she's studying. I've discussed it with her already.'

Summer raised her eyebrows at him. 'You have—have you?'

'I hope you don't mind. How do you feel about it?'

'Of course, I would have to meet her and discuss it with Mick first. What's her name?'

'Rosie—Rosie Andrews. How about I bring her around tomorrow to meet you after work?'

'I think that should be okay. Let me check with Mick and get back to you. I'd like him to meet her too.'

~

Later that evening, after Summer's visit to Liam, she and Mick discussed the new arrangement at length.

'To be honest, if she fits the bill, it will suit me to have an extra pair of hands in the kitchen. Let's face it—I'm not exactly the epitome of domesticity and I need some time to attend to my own B&B in Devonport,' said Mick.

'I thought you have Paula, the guest paying rent and looking after it for you.'

'I do, but I can't leave everything to her. Although I have a housekeeper who goes in there after the guests have left, I need to make sure there are no maintenance issues, and the place is in proper order.'

'Honestly, Mick. Don't you think you're taking on a bit too much with working here— your own guest house and managing our lawns? And now you've agreed to operate a kayaking tour business with Liam.'

'You're right, and I've been giving it all a great deal of thought lately.'

Mick leaned towards Summer on the couch and wrapped an arm around her.

'If we're to have a successful relationship and life together, we need to create and maintain togetherness. I've been a virtual workaholic most of my life to compensate for long periods of living alone ... It was my way of coping. Now I have you in my life and don't want to ruin it or lose you. I want us to both enjoy a full life and relationship.'

Summer was taken aback by the depth of feeling in his words.

Before she could respond, he turned, taking her hand, and maintaining eye contact.

'I'm sorry if this is coming out awkwardly, Summer, but I have given this much thought lately and have no doubts. Will you marry me?' he said, as he dug deep in his pocket and pulled out a small box containing a sparkling diamond ring.

He gently slipped it onto the delicate ring finger of her left hand. Her mouth dropped open. She was momentarily speechless.

'Mick … I didn't expect … so soon. I don't know what to say.'

'You know I've always loved you. Even when you suspected I was Tony's killer. I knew I had to regain your confidence and now it has gone full circle. You trust me now, don't you?'

Summer melted in Mick's arms, embarrassed she had suspected him, even if only briefly. It was time to forgive herself and as her eyes moistened, kissed him warmly.

'Of course, I trust you. I feel the same way as you do and want us to get married,' she uttered with her voice breaking.

They spent the rest of the evening making plans—discussing the kayaking tours and how they could work the guest house better.

'Mavis is due back tomorrow. She's going to get a tremendous surprise at all the changes that have been going on. I hope she won't pack it in as well.

Mick pulled her closer, beaming. 'Don't you worry about anything. We've got it all under control, and if that happens, we'll work it out together. We're a proper team now,' he said, kissing her with a passion she had not experienced in a long time.

~

That night Summer went to bed alone. Both she and Mick wanted to enjoy a proper engagement before jumping in head first and agreed to wait it out before sharing a bed together.

Struggling to fall asleep, she battled with nagging misplaced guilt about having a new man in her life.

Although others—including her children—had said that Tony would have wanted her to move on, it was now well over eighteen months since his death. The sense of disloyalty towards her late husband hadn't left her.

It's possible it will never completely go.

Regardless of these unwanted thoughts, Summer wouldn't allow them to erase the ecstasy she'd felt the evening Mick had taken her in his arms and proposed.

It was a night she'd wished would never end, including his passionate kisses and firm embrace. Because he'd taken her to heaven and back.

37

Rosie was a delight and had taken to life at the B&B as a duck to water. She and Mavis worked well together, and everything got back to normality for the first time since Petra and Liam had left.

The kayak tours to the islands were a great success. Liam accompanied Mick on the weekend jaunts around the Gulf and they both revelled in it. Summer, too, proved to be a dab hand as a kayak guide. The overnight camps were an adventure—reminiscent of camping with her family as a child.

They rejuvenated her so much that she was tempted to display the *No Vacancy* signs some days to give herself a complete break outdoors.

Summer closed the guest house after the Easter Holiday period so they all could take time off. At the urgent request of Hayley Winters, Mick had been back working part time at the station before Operation Sea Wolf went to trial, but she had agreed that he deserved time off, too.

For autumn, the weather on Motuihe Island was marvellous—brilliant, cobalt blue skies, warm temperatures and no wind. It was idyllic, although the campground was busier than Summer had expected in such an isolated spot.

Despite the number of campers, there was plenty of space between the trees to pitch a tent.

Mick and Summer had shopped for tents together and bought identical ones, erecting them next to each other.

'Here, let me help,' said Mick, picking up a handful of steel pegs and pushing each one into the ground as Summer held down the loops.

When they had finished, Mick pulled out his small gas barbeque. 'Hungry? You must be after all that paddling. It always gives me an appetite.'

'Yes, I am. But I've only got boring food with me. I have canned beans, corned beef, rice and dehydrated vegetables—oh, and a packet of wholemeal rolls.'

'Sounds alright to me, but how about a few venison sausages? I brought a packet along and they won't keep, so let's have a good feed.'

'Mmm. you're right—I'm ravenous.'

'I'll bet this is a change from cooking at the guest house. I can boil water for your rice and vegies if you like.'

As the sun sank behind the pink horizon— a replica of an artist's pallet—a group of young people formed a circle sitting cross-legged on blankets. Two had guitars while the rest were singing nineties lyrics to their music.

Summer relaxed on a blanket she shared with Mick, listening to the group singing *Candle in the Wind*, while Mick stroked Summer's hair, making her sleepy.

His phone buzzed. 'I should have left this in my tent, sorry.'

Summer pushed herself up on one arm, leaning on her hand. 'Aren't you going to see who it is?'

'It'll be the station. Won't be urgent as they know I'm on leave. Surprisingly, we can get a cell phone signal out here.'

'I know—it even has flush toilets and barbeques,' Summer replied.

'What about hot showers?'

'No, I'm afraid you'll have to jump in the sea to wash. I hope you brought your swimming gear.'

Mick pretended to be surprised. 'What? Oh yeah, I did bring them, but it's far too cold for me.'

'Well, I can't have you stinking in the tent next to me, so you'll have to jump in the tide.'

Mick pointed to his tent, beaming. 'There's a great little solar shower bag in there. I'll hang it from a tree in the sun, and Bob's your uncle.'

'What do you mean?'

'I'll hold it up while you stand underneath it,' Mick said, with a chuckle.

'Oh, is that why you brought it along? No hanky-panky, we said. Anyway—I'll duck into the tide first thing in the morning. I'm used to the sea.'

Mick rubbed her head as he got up. 'I'll just move away from all the singing and listen to the voice message on my phone.'

Summer knew he wouldn't be able to resist his mobile—especially with the pending trials bothering him and his desperately wanting both cases to be closed.

He was away for a short time while Summer revelled in the nostalgic music carried by the breeze in her direction. Delicious aromas wafted around the camp from barbeques.

Mick startled Summer approaching her from behind after he finished his phone call. The disturbance slightly irritated her as she basked in the relaxing atmosphere.

'You frightened me! Is everything all right?'

'Absolutely. I guess I can tell you the news—and it's unexpectedly gratifying.'

'Come on, quick—out with it!'

'It was Hayley. Apparently Sonny has changed his plea to guilty of being an accessory to murder, after the fact, and made a meal of it, saying he was coerced by his sister. He also confessed it was Dean who had murdered the Port guard. They had both threatened Sonny that he would end up with the same demise. For his promise to keep quiet, they had paid him a small fortune and encouraged him to move to the south island as fast as he could. With this additional evidence, the Court changed the charges against him to aiding and abetting.

'So what happens now?'

'After he changed his plea, he wanted to alter his statement. He told how Dean and Selena had treated him as a lackey, and he ratted on them. That's the very evidence we've been waiting for—an eyewitness to Dean killing the guard. This is unbelievable and our lucky break.'

'Not lucky,' Summer muttered.

'What do you mean?'

'I don't think it's a coincidence, but more like divine providence.'

Mick screwed up his eyebrows, waiting for her to continue.

'Not so long ago, when everything seemed to go wrong and there was no light at the end of the tunnel during both these investigations—Tony's and the Port killing— I started going back to church.'

'What brought all this on? I didn't know you were religious.'

'Not religious, but I do believe in God. Guess I got a nudge in the right direction at Mum's funeral at the church after realising how far I'd drifted away from the faith of my youth. You also have faith, don't you?'

'Yeah, but like you—I've become cynical over the years and pulled away after being involved with fighting darkness for so long dealing with the underworld. I guess it kind of got to me.'

'Is that why you have resigned—to find yourself again?'

'I think so. It was also when I thought my little cat had got burnt—all because of the thugs I had upset. She has become like family to me, and I couldn't bear the thought of such a loving, gentle creature suffering a terrible, torturous death. I'm sure that it was divine intervention when she was saved because that night I had prayed hard for the first time in years. The love from that little cat broke me.'

Summer wiped her face as tears flowed down her cheeks. She had never heard a man say such heart-rending things in all her life—not even Tony—and she knew it wasn't a coincidence she and Mick had formed a bond. It was a god-incidence.

~

After arriving home from camping on the island, Summer was taken aback by the huge number of emails in her Inbox from people wanting to make bookings for the following short week.

'Sorry, Summer, but you did say we'd be okay if Petra resigned. Look at this lot. I'm not sure we'll cope. Even with Mavis back next week, we'll be super busy.'

'Don't worry. I've stopped serving evening meals except for weekend pizza nights, and Liam helps with those.'

Summer knew he was a man of his word and would go the extra mile to help her run the guest house. But she did not believe he could keep up the pace. Up till now, Mick had not taken all the guest house chores onboard.

Petra had been a real boon to the place and with her gone, Summer had doubted she could manage without replacing her.

Summer scrolled through multiple emails in her Inbox that had piled up while she was away camping.

There was a message from Connie who had written to say that, although they weren't getting back together again, Jake was clean and sober.

Since recently completing a successful alcohol rehabilitation program, he had gone to great lengths to make amends to Connie for all the harm he had done and had paid her reparation from an inheritance his mother had left him.

With Jake's money, Connie had purchased a holiday bach at Cooks Beach and invited Summer and her family to stay there at no cost. This was a way of saying thank you for her support.

'What do you think of that, Mick?' Perhaps I should take her up on it—but when? I can't imagine being able to take a proper holiday.'

'Why not? You can choose a period during the low season or shut the place up for two weeks over Christmas. You're entitled to a holiday just like anyone else.'

'I guess you're right. It has four bedrooms, which would be great if Ava and Pete could come for a family holiday.'

'Whoa! You're getting way ahead,' Mick replied.

'Not really. Christmas will be here in a flash, and I would have to make proper arrangements with the kids, as they have busy jobs.'

'Okay, I'll leave it up to you. For the time being, we've got all the camping gear to clean and store away tomorrow.'

'Summer heaved a sigh. 'We'll do it together—I'm tired out now. How about I take a couple of meat pies from the freezer, and we can have them with a tossed salad?'

'Suits me. You know I'll eat anything when I'm hungry. After all that camp food, I'm ravenous.

~

Mavis was back on deck the first day of a busy week the following morning and Summer was so relieved, after being worn out from the camping trip. She wasn't used to paddling so far and the muscles in her arms ached.

A couple arrived that morning and another three people booked in the following day.

Summer hurried around the rooms, putting fresh flowers in miniature vases and her usual welcome pack of homemade chocolates in cups wrapped in cellophane with colourful bows.

While the women were flat out inside the house trying to get it in order before the guests arrived, Mick darted about the property on the ride-on mower. After finishing the lawns, he hurried up the steps, removed his boots and placed them at the side of the deck just as a car drove into the driveway.

'Don't bring that grass inside!' Summer called down the hallway. 'The new guests have arrived.'

Before anyone could see him in his grubby gardening clothes, he shot off to his bedroom and changed.

Summer greeted the new guests and then showed them through the house to their room. She recited the house rules, discussed their breakfast requirements, and left them to it.

'What do you want me to do this afternoon?' Mavis asked.

'The new couple would like afternoon tea in the lounge. It'll be busy tomorrow when the rooms fill up, so why don't you go off early after you've done the tea trolley? Make the most of the downtime.'

Later that evening, after taking a hot shower, Mick joined Summer watching TV in their flat while guests rallied around in the main lounge, making themselves hot drinks from the supper trolley.

'You seem tired out tonight—everything okay?' Summer placed a hand on Mick's forehead. 'Hope you aren't brewing anything.'

He gently lifted her hand away. 'Stop fussing woman. You know I'm tough as old boots. But to be honest, there is something I need to discuss.'

'Oh … alright … fire away.' Summer didn't like the sound of this. She hoped it wasn't upsetting news, which had become innate in her psyche now.

'I know I told you I didn't want to do police work anymore, and I meant it. But to be honest, I'm not sure if I'm entirely cut out to be a gardener slash caretaker of this extensive estate. Even though it's all done on a ride-on, I've found it hugely tedious riding up and down the rows of trees in the orchard and all around the house.'

Summer, about to take a last mouthful of lasagne, grimaced, holding her fork in mid-air. 'Sorry, Mick—I don't get where you're going with this,' she said, her neatly waxed brows snapping together.

'After we took our well-needed break camping, the grass and weeds got out of control here without Liam taking care of everything … I mean, when he was caretaker he virtually kept your lawns manicured, the orchard in pristine condition and maintained all the flower gardens.'

Summer shook her head. She still didn't get the gist of where his conversation was heading.

'But you haven't been doing the role for long. It'll take some time before you're up to speed and become fully adjusted to Liam's routine and proficiency. Ease up on yourself, Mick—please!'

'Hold on—I haven't got to the point. I've been feeling inadequate lately—not up to scratch as Liam's replacement. Then today I was head-hunted by a global organisation called *Unchained*, who fight human trafficking and labour exploitation.'

Summer's face fell. Lately, she'd been getting excited that Mick would soon be at her side running the B&B as a team, just as he promised. Was he now going back on his word?

Unpleasant memories made her tense, sending her neck muscles into spasm—a rehash of the time when Mick had let her down after he'd withheld the fact that he was with Tony the day of his death. When all that unravelled and she had forgiven him, Summer had hoped it would be the last time he would let her down. Was it happening all over again?

'What? I don't understand. For weeks you've been leading me to believe you were giving up crime work and going to help me run the guest house—we'd be a team, you said. You didn't stop talking about it and I've been counting the days until you're completely out of there—the New Zealand Police, I mean.'

'No, wait—let me explain! Mick blurted. 'You've got it all wrong. When I said I wanted to give up police work, I really meant it. I don't want to go back on the beat working those awful shifts messing with the underworld ever again. But I also don't want to end up bored and wishing I had kept my hand in investigative work, which I enjoy.'

'You seem to contradict yourself,' Summer grumbled.

'No, I'm not. Recently I'd been thinking of working part-time as a freelance private investigator but then realised it could involve me being away from home, which is not what we had discussed. And then I got this call from *Unchained* to offer me a role as an investigative consultant and advisor. They're a leading organisation combatting trafficking and migrant slavery—which is where my heart is. The beauty of this is that I can work from home—not hands-on. It's all done on the computer and over the phone. I can operate my hours, so when the guest house is busy I can pitch in but also allot part of the day to my consultancy business during the downtime.'

'I suppose it sounds alright, so long as you can handle maintaining our grounds and jump in when we're really busy at meal times.'

Summer wrapped her arms around him. 'I'm sorry I over-reacted—jumped the gun, assuming you were going back to the police station.'

'Look, Summer—promise I won't let you down. I'm just as keen to run this place together as you are,' he said, pulling her close. 'But there is another idea up my sleeve. I'm getting a substantial income from the Devonport B&B and by winter, I expect to have saved up enough to cover the cost of a Transpacific cruise—Hawaii, Fiji and other islands. What do you think?'

'Oh, I haven't thought about taking an extended holiday, but I've never been to Hawaii.'

'Just imagine all those pure white sandy beaches—sipping cocktails under a palm tree.'

'I guess it does sound very romantic. It would have to be before December, as it gets extremely busy from then onwards.

'Okay, it's a deal. The cruises are usually between April and November, so that should suit us well. We could go in October.'

Summer didn't want Mick to think he was bound by the decision he'd made to *keep his hand in it*, but she was disappointed he was taking on extra work—only because she thought it would take him away from her. She remembered how it was when Tony was a senior detective—often ships passing in the night. And she didn't want a repeat of that in her new marriage.

Keeping her thoughts to herself, Summer wondered how Mick could continue the upkeep of the grounds and help jolly the guests along while running his business as an investigative consultant at the same time. It sounded over-the-top.

She persuaded herself to have more faith in the man and let it all develop one day at a time—despite her annoying misgivings.

38

A fortnight after Mick had discussed with Summer his new role for the organisation, Unchained, they were back on an even keel.

The busy period after they had both been away at Easter had finally calmed down.

Although Mick was fully involved with his new role which was mostly online, it only took him away from Summer for an hour two a day—sometimes less. It was no longer an area of contention.

Today was quieter than usual for a Friday, and Summer had let Mavis go off earlier in the afternoon.

Mick was busy with a new assignment, so Summer spent time in the garden watering her vegetable patch. A short time later, as she turned to go back inside the house, Jeremy appeared in the courtyard.

'Jeepers! You startled, me creeping up like that,' said Summer. She instantly regretted her nervous reaction after seeing Jeremy's probation officer standing behind him.

'Carmel, isn't it? Mick told me about you. How can I help?' Summer asked.

'I hope you don't mind me springing it on you like this, but there's something I'd like to discuss—In private, if you don't mind.'

'Sure. Would you like to come inside? If you need some privacy, we could go into my office.'

'I don't think that will be necessary. We could just sit out here,' Carmel said, pointing to the wooden garden table.

'Can I get you a drink—tea, coffee or juice?'

'No, thanks, Summer. I can't stay long,' Carmel replied. 'I'll just get to the point.'

Summer prepared herself for bad news as the probation officer continued.

'Jeremy completed his therapy program with an excellent report and he's ready to return to fulltime work. Unfortunately, because he took too much leave from the ferry job, they sacked him.

'Oh, no, I'm sorry to hear that Jeremy,' Summer answered, wondering what this had to do with her.

Carmel continued. 'Olive had heard that you lost your caretaker and suggested Jeremy could help. Two years ago he completed a horticultural certificate and has never been successful in finding any gardening employment. It would suit him down to the ground if you could offer him something—wouldn't it, Jeremy?'

The fellow's face lit up. 'Absolutely. It would be a dream job for me.'

'He could assist with the orchard and if you get stuck, give a hand in the guest house too.'

'Oh, that won't be necessary, as we have Rosie and Mavis. But I could talk to Mick about taking Jeremy on as our caretaker. Leave it with me and I'll get back to you tomorrow.'

'Thanks so much, Summer. I won't let you down,' Jeremy blurted excitedly. 'Promise I won't make you ... you know ... feel uncomfortable.'

'Let me discuss it with Mick and see what we can do.'

~

Mick got called out all day on an assignment with Interpol. It involved a drug ring bringing contraband into New Zealand on a cruise ship.

After arriving home that evening, he told Summer that a major shipping company had sought his expertise about a drug trafficking problem.

She threw a wobbly.

'You resigned from the Police burnt out from working with organised crime. What you were involved with today isn't any different!' Summer snapped.

Mick had made a pot of tea and poured her a cup.

'It's not what you think—far different from working with the Crime Squad. But it's normal to meet my clients in person for the first time. From that point, I can work behind the scenes.'

'Well, so long as it isn't dangerous. I don't want to spend sleepless nights worrying that you might not make it home through the door.'

'I promised you that when I resigned—remember? And I'll stick to it ... you must trust me.'

'There's something I need to talk about, too.' Summer said, rubbing her eyes.

'Are you sure? You're looking tired. Can't it wait until tomorrow?'

'Not really—it won't take a minute.'

Summer expounded the virtues of employing Jeremy as part of his Community Service.

'I don't want you to feel offended, Mick. if you would rather I said no and you'd prefer to continue doing our property maintenance, I'm sure Jeremy will understand. Perhaps there's something else he could do around here.'

'I think it's a perfect idea. At last, I won't have to motor around on that darn ride-on mower any longer. I guess that makes it win-win all round.'

'You mean, you won't mind? I thought it might put your nose out of joint.'

Mick reached for her hand. 'Look, Summer. I went along with doing the lawns just to keep you happy, but I truly found sitting on that machine forging my way between narrow rows of fruit trees a real pain—utterly boring after living on the edge for so many years—a life of adrenaline highs.'

Summer gave Mick a sideways glance. 'But I thought that was what you wanted—to take a step back from that life and get away from crime.'

'Not exactly, dear. I wanted to escape the dreadful shifts—working into the night in the thick of it, confronting the underworld head-on. I'm a long way off retiring and never envisaged giving up fighting crime altogether.'

Summer appeared flummoxed. She shook her head, frowning. 'I don't get it, sorry.'

'When I was a lad, I was obsessed with getting into the police force and fighting evil—ever since my father was stabbed to death in broad daylight after a mistaken identity attack. He was a senior police officer.'

Summer's mouth dropped open. 'What on earth? You've said nothing about that until now.'

'Well, with all the suspicions going around after Tony's death, I thought it best to wait a while before I mentioned it.'

'That's a terrible thing for you to have experienced. Were you with him?'

'No, but my mother was, and she never really recovered from it right until her death. I was at school—the darkest day of my life.'

Summer's stomach formed a tight knot. She felt a little betrayed that Mick had never disclosed this trauma.

She held his arm, searching his face. 'I thought we had grown close enough to tell each other everything—especially those things in our past lives. I've been an open book for you and wondered why you never said much about your family.'

'They were all the kin I had—an only child, as you know.'

Summer suddenly realised why Mick had always appeared so distant all those years she and Tony had socialised with him.

'There's something else I must mention, now that we're getting into the deep and meaningful,' said Mick.

He didn't mince his words. Summer held her breath ready for his next revelation and he seemed to be on a roll.

'Hayley informed me her team gave up looking for the culprit who threw the brick at your window. As I guessed—they suspect it was a teenage prank, but I think it was related to me staying here. Someone has it in for me and I could have been the target after all.'

Summer glared at him. 'Why are you suddenly bringing all this up? Hadn't we got past all that?'

'Perhaps it's not safe for you to have me living here. I'm afraid something bad will happen to you.'

A jolt ripped through Summer's heart. Was she going to be let down again? The penny dropped as she visualised Mick as a boy being told his father had been killed. He must have set out in life to protect his mother—and keep everyone safe. That would explain his obsession with solving Tony's death.

'I can't let anything happen to you.'

'I understand that, Mick, but I will not up and abandon the guest house and my grandparents' memory because of an unfounded notion that you have been targeted. As you say, it's not what your colleagues concluded.'

Summer never thought she would have to convince Mick to continue staying at the guest house. To her, their relationship was signed and sealed, and he was there to stay, but now her dreams appeared to be falling apart.

'I can't take the risk of being responsible for any harm coming to you. It was bad enough worrying myself sick after Tony's demise, thinking a hitman was out there and you would be next,' Mick said.

'But that wasn't the case, and it didn't happen!' Summer blurted, holding back tears at Mick's sudden about turn.

'So, what do you propose to do, may I ask?' she snapped!

'I don't know ... perhaps I've been rather presumptuous in moving so fast. I'm sorry for raising your expectations.'

Summer's mind was in turmoil. All her hopes and dreams were shattered in minutes.

'Look, Summer, I care about you a great deal—more than you can imagine. But we can't be together in this house right now. I'll have to move into my place in Devonport. We can still see each other, and further down the track, perhaps we could both run my place as a B&B. There's a police station two doors along, so I doubt if any troublemakers will dare try anything on there.'

Summer's brain struggled to digest all that Mick dumped on her out of the blue. Did she have to choose between keeping hold of her guest house or moving into Mick's Devonport home for fear of losing him? It seemed a drastic measure to take for a random attack on her house. She would rather believe the original theory of the police officers who reported it as a teenage prank.

Now Mick had blown it out of all proportions. Did he get cold feet and then use this incident as a smokescreen to avoid their relationship?

Although downcast, Summer let it go.

'If you think you should move back to your place, then that's what you must do.'

Mick sat back, staring at the wall, his face devoid of expression.

'I guess that's why I'd decided not to marry all those years, avoiding putting women at risk.'

'Mick—I'm not worried about my safety—I have faith. If anyone wanted to harm me, surely it would have been while I was living with Tony. He was also with the CIB, like you, and rubbed shoulders with dangerous gangs involved in organised crime. But trouble never came our way—so I think you should let it all go.'

'No—I'd never forgive myself if I brought you into danger and I owe it to Tony to take care of you.'

'Well, that's your call, I suppose. But I can't abandon my guest house. This is my life's dream, and I thought you and I could do it together, but that was silly of me—a pipedream. Guess I'll just have to continue running it myself with staff.'

'I'm not saying I want to end our relationship and still want to marry you but would like you to think about my proposition. A B&B in Devonport by the sea will be popular. I'll move there this weekend and give you time to think about it. We could always shift further out of the city and sell both houses further down the track when we … you know … get hitched.'

It was confusing for Summer to hear Mick speak in contradictions. On the one hand, talking about moving out into his own house and then discussing marriage. He was saying "Come here ... go away".

Long before Summer had met Tony, she'd dated a troubled man. Her psychologist told her about the dance of intimacy. He explained that when a child can't escape the anxiety caused by their environment or be soothed by a parent, they can develop fearful attachment. They seek closeness and intimacy and yet want to withdraw.

Summer recognised that Mick fitted this description. He must still be suffering delayed trauma from the loss of his father.

She loved him dearly and couldn't bear the thought of him moving out, having got used to his companionship. She thought they'd shared all their hopes and dreams, but it appeared not.

39

It had been nearly a month since Mick had moved back to his house in Devonport, and Summer missed his company dearly, but he didn't abandon her.

One evening he called around to take her out for dinner and a movie. He had also invited her for an evening meal at his home another day, which highly impressed her.

Most of the time, Mick was going flat out in his new role as an Interpol Case Investigator—spending much of his time working from his home office on their Tracking System.

Summer was relieved he no longer patrolled the streets on the graveyard shift, which was often dangerous. They still planned to get married, but Mick avoided the subject, occasionally remarking that it would all happen in due course, which kept Summer hanging as usual.

~

It was a full house the morning Summer received a phone call from Mae and Lily's refugee resettlement officer. She had rung to arrange for the girls to visit.

'Hi Carmen—Are they no longer living in Cambridge with Elma and Dougie?'

'Oh, no. That was only a temporary arrangement until we knew it was safe enough for them to return to Auckland. They prefer to stay up here to be near their friends, and now that Rob Dean and his henchmen are locked up for good, we're looking to rehouse them in Auckland under the Refugee Resettlement scheme.'

'That's great—I'm thrilled for them.'

'The only problem is—we don't have sufficient housing for everyone and there's a long list of people for whom we need to find homes.'

'Oh, I see. How can I help?' Summer replied.

'It's the reason I was coming to see you— not only because the girls want to see you but also to ask if you might know of anyone who could help with temporary accommodation in Auckland until their names come up on the list.'

Summer had her serious face on. 'The poor girls. I feel so sorry for them being shunted from pillar to post. Look—give me two or three days until the guest house empties, and in the meantime, I'll rack my brains and see what I can do.'

'You're a pearl. I didn't know what to do, as the poor girls have already been through so much. I just want to get them settled somewhere.'

'Oh, I didn't mean they could stay here permanently, but perhaps if it quietens down I could fit them in for a short time.'

'It would be marvellous if you could give them temporary accommodation.'

'Okay, Carmen. I'll be in touch at the end of the week. Give my love to the girls.'

~

Jeremy's progress while working for Summer maintaining the grounds around the guest house was remarkable. Even his personality had changed. She could clearly see how beneficial his therapy sessions had been. He'd not once shown himself to be a nuisance.

Rosie had also come to the party in more ways than one. She was a busy girl studying part-time and working in the B&B. Summer was impressed with her amenable personality—easy to get on with and eager to help.

Summer knew not to become so dependent on her as she had done with Petra. Before long, Rosie and Liam could fly the coup unexpectedly and buy a house, leaving her in the lurch.

Although Summer was grateful for the amazing staff who had graced her B&B, the constant turnover of employees unsettled her. She had thought, once Mick had moved in, that he would take up most of the slack when Liam gave up his job as caretaker, and also fill the gap when Petra left—but it wasn't to be so. Perhaps they weren't meant to run the guest house as a team after all, to her extreme consternation.

The guest levels had dropped by the following week. Summer had texted Carmen to say it would be convenient if she could bring the girls to visit on the Thursday. That was when Mavis and Rosie were on duty together and could take over while Summer entertained Mae and Lily.

~

Carmen drove up to the guest house with the two refugees while Summer excitedly raced to greet them before their driver had barely come to a standstill.

There were hugs all around, and Summer could scarcely believe the changes in Mae and Lily. They were no longer the timid, emaciated waifs she had witnessed before they went to stay with Elma and Dougie. Although they had only lived with the middle-aged couple for a short time—a matter of months—they had evolved into vibrant, happy and healthy young women with plenty to say.

Summer directed them to an outside table and chairs under an umbrella so they would have privacy from any guests coming and going inside the house.

Following a full-on spread for morning tea of various savouries, fresh scones with jam topped with cream and club sandwiches together with cups of tea, the girls expounded on their cherished stay in Cambridge.

'Elma and Dougie breed horses and took us trekking on horseback. Like you said, they also have kayaks, and we went out on the lake several times with them. I would love to live there forever, but of course, it's not possible,' Mae blurted.

Summer sat and listened to Mick, grateful he had organised the girls' stay with Doug—his ex-colleague and friend.

'I wondered if you had any ideas about emergency housing near the city?' said Carmel. 'The thing is—our organisation has on-the-job programs lined up for the girls in a large city hotel that has a training scheme. They have also been offered a grant for the Diploma in Hospitality. Mae has extensive experience as a sales manager at a substantial beach resort in Thailand already, and Lily's background was in restaurants.'

'Oh, really—that's amazing! I could have given them some coaching here, but now I have Rosie working with us. Where is the hotel?'

'On the North Shore along the waterfront.'

'I see. Well, I'm still asking around—waiting for a friend to get back to me. In the meantime, I could put you up, girls.'

Summer had told Mick about the plight of these two migrants and said he would give it some thought but was too busy to get back to her. She would have to follow it up.

Mae and Lily's eyes popped out at her offer.

'You're so kind—thank you!' Mae got out of her chair to hug her while Lily followed suit.

'Give me a copy of your study rosters so I can get you to help Mavis and Lily in the guest house sometimes. You can learn to take bookings on the computer too.'

'Thanks so much, Summer,' said Carmen. 'You don't know how much this means to us as an organisation. There's such a scarcity of emergency housing in Auckland. We have the girls' names down for an apartment on the North Shore, but there is a hefty waiting list. The Refugee Centre is also overloaded.'

This conversation upset Summer, as the impact of what Carmen had said shot arrows through her heart. She realised how blessed she had been to inherit such a substantial home from her grandparents in an affluent location—one that could house so many. People would probably say she was born with a silver spoon in her mouth, but the death of her beloved Tony had taken the joy out of it. One thing was for sure—people who knew her had often commented on what a humble person Summer was, including Mick.

'When can the girls move in?' Summer asked.

'Anytime that suits. They're in one of our emergency hostels nearby but they can't stay there—it's usually only for overnighters.'

'How about you take them to collect their luggage and bring them back here today? I'll warn Mavis and Rosie to get the room ready. They can share one of the family suites for the time being. They're quite spacious.

~

After the girls had finished their meal that evening, they retired to their suite to watch television. Summer hovered around, offering supper to the handful of B&B guests who lingered. She always mixed and mingled with her patrons whenever they were in the living room.

When the guest house was quiet later that evening, Summer sat in her quarters relaxing in a recliner.

She picked up her mobile phone and rang Mick. Even if he was at home working in the evenings, he would always stop and talk to her.

Summer elaborated on the urgency of Mae and Lily's dilemma—their accommodation problem—and explained how they'd been offered in-house training for a Level 5 Diploma in Hospitality Management at a prestigious hotel on the North Shore, part time.

'They must do two shifts per week that can include weekends, so we'll have to cover them for those days.'

'How will they get to work from St Heliers Bay? They don't have a car—or do they?' asked Mick.

'No, neither of them drives yet. They'll need to take two buses.'

'I see,' he replied. 'It's strange you called right now as my tenants upstairs have just given their notice. Their parents have offered them a deposit for a house which they have already purchased, and they move out in three weeks.'

'What are you trying to say, Mick?'

'I'd like to help the girls out—knowing how much they've both suffered.'

'Carmen said her organisation can help with their accommodation expenses until they have permanent jobs. Market rent is unaffordable, so they'll also need a top-up from the government.'

'Why not send them over here once the family upstairs has left? Perhaps I can offer a low rent in return for housekeeping if they're interested.'

'What happened to Paula—the tenant who was taking care of your place?'

'She was only supervising my place while I was away and before I began advertising it as a B&B. Now she, too, has bought a house and gone to live with her mother—moved out last week.'

'Goodness, Mick, you've got your work cut out for you now that she's gone.'

'I've sorted it already. Remember, I told you an old friend of mine from the Force looked me up recently?'

'Ted, I think you said his name was—the old guy who recently retired.'

'That's the one. His wife ran off with a neighbour a few years back and it emotionally crippled him, so I'm trying to give him a leg up.'

'Oh, yeah—how can you help him?'

'Actually, it's a two-way street. We're both benefiting each other. After his divorce settlement, he couldn't afford to refinance his house, so now I can assist him with a place to live and an income.'

'How can you do that?' Summer replied.

'He has offered to be my caretaker—you know—look after the lawns and weeding in return for free accommodation. Having him there adds more security to the place as he has moved into the single room downstairs. I've shifted back up top.'

'Marvellous! Perhaps Mae and Lily would like to learn how the B&B works and then you could up the advertising and try to get the place filled up. The girls could set out the continental breakfasts each night before they head off for the day. You could also teach them your booking system.'

'Mmm. Great minds think alike. But until they've completed their diplomas, we would have to keep up with all the domestic duties. Maybe when the girls have finished their studies, they might be interested in running our guest houses.'

'What an excellent idea! Imagine if they took everything out of our hands,' Summer replied, thinking she and Mick would eventually tire of cooking, cleaning and laundry.

Mick shrugged. 'I'm not sure—let's wait and see. Working in a B&B won't pay much compared to big city hotels.'

His last remark burst Summer's bubble— just as she got excited.

'Anyway, how is the work with Interpol going?'

'Somewhat stressful at present. I didn't intend to get dragged into anything hands-on, but the Auckland crew are trying to rope me into going on the field. They know my role is purely consultancy, but they are short-staffed.'

'Oh no, you're not going back to police work—I hope,' Summer's voice croaked unexpectedly. She cleared her throat.

'No, it's not what I want. I just meant I'm getting pressure from the team at Unchained to pitch in. I'm digging my toes in, and this present case involves highly dangerous drug traffickers who will stop at nothing if anyone stands in the way of their multi-million dollar operation. Some of them are up for murder already.'

'Yikes! What is the Operation called?'

'You know I can't disclose that, Summer. I've got to be super careful. These rackets are going on all the time in big cities like

Auckland, but this particular organised crime ring is even more brutal and cruel than Kiwi Gold and associates.'

Summer heaved a loud sigh. 'Oh, Mick. I wish you would get away from the criminal world altogether. Surely it must get you down dealing with all that darkness each day. Life should be enjoyed and not merely endured. You seem to have lost the joie-de-vie you once had when you hung out with Tony—fishing, kayaking or hiking. Where is the old Mick we used to know?'

After Summer had offloaded her burden of concern on Mick, he smartly got off the phone afterwards, saying he would be in touch when the family upstairs vacated the place.

Summer had prayed hard that night that her wise words would sink in, and Mick would give it serious thought. But she also had an invested interest in what she said—longing for him to move back in with her. How did he think they could stay engaged to be married if he went back to active service fighting organised crime in the field? That must never happen, or their relationship would be doomed.

40

Jeremy had taken to the job as caretaker of the St Heliers Bay B&B like a duck to water and was proud of it. In exchange for Summer sending him home to Olive with fresh berries, or nectarines from her trees, his aunt would in return send Jeremy back with a cream sponge or chocolate layer cake. No wonder her nephew never wanted to leave her.

The guest house ran smoothly, and most days Summer didn't notice Mick was no longer there—although she still missed his company terribly.

'It's freezing this morning—there's a chill in the air,' said Rosie, arriving in the kitchen ready to help Summer with cooked breakfasts for those who had ordered them.

'I'm afraid so. It's still autumn—it shouldn't be this crisp—just a cold snap, I guess,' Summer replied, opening the fridge. 'Mae and Lily prepared the continental breakfasts last night. They'll be out soon. I said they could sleep in this morning as they have a day off from the hotel.'

'Oh, okay, Rosie replied.

'Would you mind taking the items from the fridge and putting them on the buffet in the dining room? The guests will be along soon.'

Mae and Lily had filled the large canisters with cereals the night before, which stood in a row on the walnut wooden buffet.

There was Summer's granola and a variety of commercial cereals. Lily placed a tub of homemade yoghurt on the sideboard along with a bowl of chopped fresh fruit, a platter of grain bread with butter and a small dish of Summer's homegrown jams. There was even a jar of lemon curd and for the health-conscious, homemade peanut butter.

Summer carried a bread basket containing warmed croissants and an array of different pastries to the dining table.

'Mmm they smell good,' said Rosie.

'Haven't you had breakfast?' asked Summer.

'No, not this morning. I slept through the alarm and Liam had already left early for work.'

'Go on then—take one,' said Summer, passing her a plate.

'Are you sure? Gee, thanks.'

Rosie's hand went out quick as lightning for the French delight, relishing every mouthful.

'There are almond croissants on the other plate if you'd like one,' said Summer.

'No, this will be fine, thanks.'

'How's the house-hunting going—any luck yet?'

Rosie wiped her fingers on a paper napkin.

'Oh, no, it's far too soon yet. We have a specific amount to save as a deposit, so our mortgage payments will be manageable. We're not there yet.'

~

In the evening when the guest house had emptied, Summer stood at the kitchen bench observing her cat in the backyard who had set off the security light. She watched as Petal sniffed around the pool at the bottom of the fountain, which was full of large goldfish. The cat knew she would be in big trouble if she landed a paw in the water and furtively sidled around the edge of the rockery with one eye on the pool and the other on Summer's front door—for fear of a female tornado rushing out the door emitting a nerve-wracking shriek.

Summer didn't rocket out the front door yelling at Petal, as the pond was covered with plastic mesh, preventing the cat from doing any harm.

As she leaned on the kitchen bench, continuing to watch her feline friend, a bright sensor light fully illuminated the fountain and the courtyard where Tony had met his demise. It was as though he was still with her in spirit and the fountain was now a memorial for him. It was her late husband's shrine, and she hoped to never leave this

432

house. While remaining there, Summer would always be one with Tony. But in the future, if still going ahead with marrying Mick, she'd have to let him have her heart and let go of Tony—but never his memory.

It was late before Summer got to bed, and the early morning starts were wearing her down. When Petra had been with her as live-in staff, the girl had become competent enough to prepare the occasional cooked breakfasts on her own—especially when Summer needed a break. Even though Rosie was still in training, she was eager to prepare light meals with help from the others who could pitch in if they were free.

Summer was about to turn in for the night but before going off to sleep, sat up in bed to see the evening news On Demand from her TVNZ phone app, as she had missed it earlier.

Zooming in on some shocking images, Summer's gut tied itself in knots.

A young female police detective had been stabbed to death while accompanying a maritime police officer onto a recreational vessel called Neptune moored in the harbour.

The crew was suspected of being involved with a drug trafficking ring working the Crystal Road maritime trade route. When the officers stepped inside the vessel, someone had grabbed the detective and knifed her.

Summer tried to catch the police officer's name who hailed from the same city station where Mick had worked. To her shock and horror, she heard the name, Detective Sergeant, Samantha Evans! It was Sam, Tony's rookie, who had worked with him before his death and partnered with Mick more recently. Summer remembered Mick telling her that Sam had recently passed her sergeant's exams.

She slumped back in her chair distraught—mulling over the upsetting news, thinking how devastated Mick must be.

Summer had a powerful urge to call and offer him solace but knew her words would only be cold comfort. Still, she couldn't just do nothing while he sat alone in his room struggling with the tragic press release.

She looked at her wristwatch—it was nearly midnight. She should message him first in case was too late to call him.

Hi Mick. I saw the tragic news tonight about Sam. I'm so sorry. Would you like to chat? She texted.

Waiting for a reply after a good half hour while cleaning her teeth and getting ready for bed, she couldn't stay up any longer—climbed under the blankets and turned out the light.

~

Since hearing the devastating news about Sam's murder, Summer phoned Mick repeatedly without success. She had also

434

tried getting his attention by email—to no avail. He was keeping under the radar.

Summer did her best not to take it personally, thinking he must have been too cut up emotionally to cope with talking about it. There couldn't be any other explanation.

After a week, Summer practised being more assertive by paying Mick a visit to Devonport. She texted him she was going to drop by and asked if he was going out, to let her know.

Mick didn't reply, so she gathered he must be staying in. He wouldn't be so mean to let her drive to Devonport for nothing.

The guest house was half empty that week. Mavis and Rosie worked well together, which gave Summer more time to herself or to run errands for the B&B. She could trust them both to manage the place without her when it wasn't operating at full capacity.

Summer made her getaway soon after breakfast. It wouldn't have mattered what time she left as the traffic was always heavy on the harbour bridge.

She just had to put her mind at rest that Mick's real reason for remaining incognito wasn't because he'd changed his mind about their relationship or had gone right off her. She realised it was probably her wild imagination plaguing her, but regardless, cast that doubt out of her mind once and for all.

Oak trees lined Mick's street with autumn leaves of pink and yellow adorning the footpaths like a fairy's carpet. His massive, stately Devonport villa stood out from other homes in the area with its brightly coloured flower garden bordering the front lawn. The sign above the villa's door—*Seashells*—stood out, too.

Summer spotted Mick's private SUV Outlander parked in the driveway's turning bay and pulled in behind his vehicle.

She waited in her car with her engine running to see if he would hear the commotion and come to the door, but there was no sign of him. Now a twinge of unease rippled through her spine.

Summer got out of the car and knocked on the front door. Ted answered.

'Is Mick in please? I'm Summer, his fiancée,' she said, watching the man's face for signs of surprise. 'Oh, hello, Summer—I've heard so much about you. I'm glad you're here. Nice to meet you at last. Come on in.'

After Ted's response, the tension in her neck muscles relaxed. He directed her into the kitchen for a quick chat.

'I'm worried about Mick,' said Ted. 'He hasn't been accepting guests and there's nobody here apart from the family upstairs who are moving out soon.'

'What do you mean ... sorry ... I don't know why you would be worried.'

'It's his demeanour this past week—so gloomy. I thought maybe you'd broken off your engagement.'

Summer's face dropped. 'Not so far as I know. He has mentioned nothing to that effect. But I believe he has just received some extremely distressing news. A close friend has been killed.'

'Oh dear, I knew nothing about that. He didn't say a thing.'

'He wouldn't—it's a private matter. So where is he now?'

'In his living quarters probably and he's hardly eating anything. It's only this week he's been like this.'

'It's called grieving. But I'll see if I can humour him. Maybe a little tender loving care is what's needed. I haven't seen him lately—we've been so busy.'

'Mick told me two friends of yours are moving in upstairs after the family leave. He'll be running a B&B offering continental breakfasts,' said Ted, taking Summer by surprise, as Mick didn't say he had told anyone else about his plans.

'He asked if I would help the girls settle in when they arrive.'

'I see. So, he is still planning to go through with it. Unfortunately, this tragic incident has knocked him off his perch, I'll bet.'

'I'll leave you to it, then. It was good to meet you finally, Summer. If you need me,

just knock on my door. I'm at the end of the
hallway on the left.'

41

Summer knocked on Mick's door, pounding harder and harder each time until finally it opened. The sight she beheld was one she would never forget. The tall, robust specimen of health she knew a few weeks earlier had become an emaciated, quivering wreck in a matter of days since Sam's death.

He stood, blocking the door to his room. 'What on earth are you doing here?'

She took a step back. 'I messaged you on your phone saying I would drop by today and to let me know if you were going out. You didn't respond, so I gathered you didn't mind me coming to see you.'

Mick appeared flummoxed. He knew he would offend Summer by sending her away and reluctantly invited her in, motioning towards a chair. He plonked himself down on his usual couch opposite her.

'Look, Mick—before you say anything else, I heard the terrible news about Sam and I'm ever so sorry. I knew what a great team you both were.'

With those kind words, Mick broke down—head in cupped hands, sobbing.

Summer couldn't bear to see the distress in her once-perceived pillar of strength and protector. Now he appeared as a mere shell of a man—the epitome of deep pain.

She got out of her seat and sat next to him, ignoring his obvious need to be alone in his anguish, and placed an arm around his broad shoulders, leaning her head against his so their cheeks were touching. She bristled as warm tears trickling down his unshaven face and just held him without speaking.

Mick suddenly sat up, pulling himself together. He took out a handkerchief from his trousers and wiped a tear-stained face before blowing his nose. Summer did the same with a tissue she carried. Drying her moist cheeks, she took Mick's hand, holding it tight.

He threatened to break down crying again, stiffened and snuffled.

'I'm sorry, Summer. The news about Sam crippled me. I feel it's all my fault.'

Summer searched Mick's tear-stained face. 'How can it be your fault? That's ridiculous.'

'No ... you don't understand .... I should have been there.'

Summer struggled to grasp what he was saying. Was this his grief talking, making him confused?

'You no longer work on the beat. What do you mean you should have been there?'

'If I had been still with the Force, I wouldn't have let Sam go into the boat. I would have stepped onto the moored vessel and asked her to stay back.'

'But you told me Sam was now a detective sergeant—a senior police officer—so she wasn't your rookie and would have made her own decisions. I can't see how you can blame yourself for her death.'

'No, Summer—you don't get it! Let me explain.' Mick described his work at Interpol at length—how he'd been online tracking the movements of a drug trafficking ring in Auckland Harbour that had links to a container ship. The investigation was called Operation Scorpion.

'Interpol wanted me to take an active part in the drug bust of the launch, Neptune, but I refused, as it wasn't part of my contract— remembering I had promised you I wouldn't take an active part on the field in my new role. When Interpol asked the city police crew to assist them in storming the vessel, I didn't know Sam would be the detective assigned the task, having only recently been promoted to a senior detective. I should have asked at the station which officers they had assigned.'

'There's no way you can be responsible for what happened, and you can't admonish yourself for something which would never

441

have been preventable by you since leaving the Force.'

Mick raised his head and said feebly, 'I guess you're right. I just can't get over the fact that Sam had died such a painful death. At least a gunshot mostly kills outright, but stab wounds can cause indescribable pain.'

'How about we go along to your favourite Bistro down the road and grab some food? I'm hungry and I'm sure you haven't eaten either—it's almost lunchtime.'

'Sorry, Summer. As you can see, I'm in no fit state to venture onto the street. Everyone will see I'm cut up and there are people around Devonport who know me.'

'Well, I can't just sit back and let you wither away.'

'Here—take this card and order a pizza from the Pizzeria a few blocks away. I've got a bottle of red wine open—oops you're driving so instead we can have a ginger beer with it.'

Summer glanced at the business card and phoned the pizza outlet. Afterwards, she quizzed Mick on what he was going to do now.

'How do you feel about working for Interpol—with drug cartels and traffickers?' Is this the work you wish to continue?'

Mick took a deep breath, then let out a loud sigh.

'No, not the way you put it. I thought I would have a distance from them, but didn't think it through enough, I guess. I never thought Sam would be caught up with drug traffickers. It was me who got her team involved in the tragic fiasco in the harbour.'

'Where did the drug smugglers bring cocaine in from?'

'A yacht moored off Kawau of all places. They would have sailed in from the Islands after collecting the cargo from a South American container ship in the Pacific Ocean. The contraband must have been transferred to a recreational yacht heading to New Zealand, and from there onto the launch called Neptune.

'Is that how they do it? So many sea vessels involved. I wondered how they got it onto the boat in the Hauraki Gulf.'

'Unfortunately, using multiple carriers is an age-old trick used to put trackers off the scent. Organised criminals are experts at covering their tracks. Luckily, the Maritime Police had received an anonymous tip-off about the Neptune—not for poor Sam, of course.'

Mick caved in again. He sniffed loudly, wiping his cheeks with his sleeve.

Summer leaned over and kissed his cheek. 'We don't need to continue this conversation. I'm worried about you. How about coming back to my place for a few days until you feel back to your old self again?'

'I'm not sure about barging in on you like that mucking you around. You've got your worries with running the guest house. But we could go out for a walk after we've eaten and get some fresh air.'

At that moment, Mick's doorbell rang.

'It's the pizza courier. Would you mind going to the door, Summer? I look a sight right now.'

'Of course, I'll get them.'

By the time Summer returned with the food, Mick had already set out plates and cutlery.

He poured their drinks. 'Do we need a pizza cutter?' he said, taking the boxes from her and lifting the lids. 'Ah, no, we're all set—let's eat.'

Summer was relieved to see Mick had perked up a little. The muted sadness she'd often observed in him when he'd lived with her still reared its head—a recurring emotional bluntness. She often wondered what was behind it all, although she could recall him once saying he often felt numb.

It was a sultry day, making the idea of walking the promenade in the cool sea air rather inviting.

'Leave the dishes, Summer. I'll do them later. Let's get out the door.'

It had been ages since they'd gone walking by the seaside together and Summer had missed it—something she wouldn't often do alone.

When they'd got to the end of the seafront, they sat down on the stone wall and before she could say anything, Mick suddenly began pouring his heart out to her, unexpectedly.

'When I was a teenager, my father died, and I went off the rails—getting into trouble at school, hanging out with rebellious kids. I know it made my mother terribly unhappy, and the strain caused her fragile health to get worse. As I grew older, I suddenly realised the slippery slope I was on and decided that I would devote my life to convincing others to avoid lawlessness. Mum passed away following a heart attack shortly after I left home to join the police force. Ever since then, I've blamed myself for her death after not doing more to support her.'

Summer searched his eyes, which averted her gaze. She honed in on the pain behind frozen tears, pinpointing his unfelt, unresolved grief. But that happened decades ago. Why has he never accepted it? He's full of self-condemnation.

She caressed the back of his head. 'Oh, Mick. You haven't been blaming yourself all these years, have you?'

'I don't think you understand, Summer. Instead of acting the victim, I could have helped my mother cope after Dad's death ... you know ... do more around the house and take the load off her. If I had done, perhaps she wouldn't have had the heart attack.'

Summer felt his pain while he continued to offload.

'When Tony died, I couldn't take that it happened the day I left your house to go fishing. He had told me he was going to do some digging to prepare the foundations for your new fountain that day. I can't believe I was so selfish and didn't offer to stay back and help him. He might still have been here if I had given him a hand. Perhaps I'm just self-centred and a living time bomb to be around.'

Summer could see by his face that Mick was burdened with self-condemnation, which she hadn't until this day discerned.

'I think you're being excessively hard on yourself. It would have happened even if you hadn't stayed over, so it wasn't your fault.'

'It's true, though,' he added. 'Tony had offered me his hospitality all evening—a bed for the night when we had both been drinking and a cooked breakfast. He asked me to accompany him for a coastal walk before he started digging, but because I had looked forward to going fishing that morning, I left him to it.'

It was as though, for the first time in their relationship, Mick desperately needed to unburden himself and bare his soul. He had picked the right person—Summer was an empathetic listener.

'Oh, Mick—please! Get rid of the sledgehammer and let it go. You weren't responsible for either of their deaths. I can't believe you've carried this misplaced guilt for so long—it's time you forgave yourself.'

Summer wrapped one arm around him and snuggled in close. 'Now I know why you left my home. I think you're afraid you'll cause something bad to happen to me.'

Mick gaped at her. 'You've certainly got that right.'

'I was worried you had changed your mind … about us … getting married, I mean.'

Mick turned towards Summer and took her hands, keeping eye contact.

'My dearest Summer—that is so far from my mind, it's just the opposite. I've missed you immensely, but all I wanted to do was protect you.'

'Surely, if anything bad was going to happen to me because of Rob Dean, it would have done by now. I don't think he and his cronies saw me as a threat,' Summer replied.

'You're right. I've come to the same conclusion lately. I was going to drop by to discuss it with you until this terrible incident with Sam on the boat occurred.'

'What were you going to say?'

Mick's face suddenly became animated. 'Actually, I was hoping you wouldn't mind if I moved back to yours. Why don't we get married this year—in the spring, perhaps? Because of what happened to Tony and Sam, I've decided to leave crime work altogether.'

'Goodness! This is a bolt from the blue. What will you do instead?' Summer replied.

'How about you and I run our two guest houses as a combined business? You have sufficient staff now to help at St Heliers Bay. Mae and Lily could operate my Devonport place when they move in, and I'll oversee it regularly—that's if they agree.'

Summer threw her arms around Mick's neck. At last, she could see the healing unfolding in his heart and soul—signalling a future she could live with. Now all she had to do was take a risk.

42

It only took a short time for Summer and Mick to have both their guest houses up and running smoothly with a full quota of staff. The rooms filled up most weeks, and they shared the responsibility of overseeing both accommodation facilities.

Mae and Lily took to managing Mick's Seashells guest house in Devonport like ducks to water—Lily with her restaurant experience and Mae her management skills. They were on familiar ground and coped well with Mick or Summer checking on them regularly to help where needed.

Summer held Mick to his idea about a cruise, but this time he intended to make it a honeymoon for their impending marriage, which was a complete distraction for her from running the B&B.

'Yay! It's only a matter of months before we tie the knot,' she blurted to Mick. 'I'll have to phone and invite the children together with their partners.'

Ava was in a stable relationship with James whom she'd met at University, and

Pete had recently been seeing Faith—a novice solicitor in his Law practice. Summer was eager to tell them her news.

'I hope you can all come,' she blurted, after announcing her plans to Ava and Pete on their WhatsApp group. 'Make sure you invite Faith, too, Pete,' she said, remembering he had a new partner whom she hadn't yet met.

'Awesome, Mum. I'll make sure James and I get the time off at work. I'll put in for it once you give me definite dates,' said Ava.

'Great! But I have something else I need to share with you.

'Oh—more positive updates, I hope.'

Summer was about to tell Ava the story about Jake and Connie's dramas and their connection to Tony but changed her mind.

'A woman whom your father had once supported in a difficult situation when he was a police officer has offered me the use of a lovely holiday home at Cooks Beach on the Coromandel. It sounds private, with plenty of native bird life.'

'Really? That coast is awesome for a holiday. You're so lucky,' said Ava.

'With the best fishing spots,' Pete added.

'The thing is—after our honeymoon cruise in the Pacific, Mick has suggested we have a long-overdue family holiday at Connie's bach, if you're all keen. Hopefully, you can take extra leave from work.'

'Mum, that's amazing—thanks! But what about your guest houses?' Pete asked, being an astute businessman.

'It's no problem. We just have to put up the *No Vacancy* sign at the gate and on our websites for those two weeks. We'll be fine.'

'I can't wait. Do you have a date for the wedding?' Ava asked excitedly.

'No, not yet—it'll be in spring, but Mick and I will set it soon. I'll let you both know in time to organise your leave.'

'Sounds wonderful—we'll all look forward to it,' said Ava.

'Got to get to a meeting, sorry,' said Pete, waving goodbye. 'Brilliant plan, Mum. Talk soon.'

'Well, I'd better go now, too,' said Summer. 'I'll be in touch with you all once the arrangements are set in concrete.'

~

Mick came in from picking Granny Smith apples in the orchard. He placed the basket on the kitchen bench where Summer was busy rolling out pastry.

'You've got a splendid crop out there. They're only just ripe and should keep you going for at least another two or three months. What do you do with them all?'

Summer lined up her pie dishes at one end of the bench and wiped her hands on her apron.

'I usually freeze them in slices ready to use for pies.'

'Do you want me to peel this lot?'

'I'd appreciate that if you don't mind.'

Summer gave Mick a rundown of how to place the peeled and sliced apples into a bowl of water containing lemon juice to stop them from going brown.

As they set about preparing the fruit for the pie cases, Summer stared out the window, watching Jeremy at work on the ride-on mower. He waved and continued driving up and down the rows of fruit trees.

The fellow had come a long way from when he had first been apprehended for his misadventure of not reporting Tony's accidental death.

It was as if he were serving a self-imposed penance as he went the extra mile, seeking Summer's approval of his work performance.

Jeremy had shown no further episodes of voyeuristic behaviour while in Summer's company, and so far had made a full recovery from OCD.

'What do you think about having a wedding ceremony here in the courtyard? Mick gestured towards the fountain. 'Didn't Ava and Pete say their father would have given his blessing for you to remarry?'

Mick's suggestion threw Summer off balance.

'I know what you mean ... it sounds lovely and something I would have dreamed of—a wedding ceremony around Tony's beautiful fountain—the one he had designed and planned.'

'Well, let's talk about it later. We don't have any guests in for dinner this evening. It'll be busy tomorrow, but tonight we are free.'

No sooner had Mick suggested a wedding in Tony's prized courtyard, Summer felt a shiver down her spine seeing Tony, in her mind's eye, lying with a cracked skull next to the fountain.

'Can we talk about it properly later over a drink? I just want to get these pies in the oven now and then take a shower,' Summer replied, slipping away.

~

After they had finished their meal of leftover lasagne and tossed salad, Mick and Summer retired to the lounge, which was devoid of guests.

'Mmm, that delicious aroma of those baked pies cooling on the bench is making me hungry,' said Mick, sitting on the couch with his legs stretched out with Summer lying with her head on his lap.

'I'll have to put them in the freezer before I go to bed.'

'Can we talk a little more about the wedding?' Mick pleaded.

Summer thought it odd that he would be so insistent on the topic. It was usually the bride-to-be who would be obsessively bringing the subject up, so she found it rather touching and sat up properly on the couch so that they could have a serious discussion. She weighed her answer to Mick's earlier suggestion.

'To be honest, Mick—although I would love for us to be married in my beautiful, landscaped gardens by the fountain, I feel it would be like walking over Tony's grave.'

Mick took her hand and squeezed it.

'It's all right, Summer, you don't have to explain. I just thought I would let you know you have my approval to have our wedding ceremony in your backyard. But that's only if you're comfortable with it, and I'd understand if you weren't.'

'I'd love to have it here, but I just can't do it. Sometimes I wonder how I've gone on so long living in this house standing at the kitchen window without giving the gory scene of his death a thought. I must have been in denial and pushed the memory far down. But when I saw Jeremy waving to me on the ride-on, suddenly Tony's face popped up and I saw him lying on the cobblestones by the fountain—a flashback I suppose. Imagine me reliving it during our wedding ceremony.'

Mick nodded, letting her speak.

'I understand, Summer. So when and where would you like to get hitched, then?'

Mick thought maybe she was getting cold feet and was about to change her mind.

'How about early spring? I don't want a winter wedding, and it's reasonably warm. No societal affair, either—only close friends or family. But where? Every other venue will be booked out for at least ten or twelve months in advance and will cost the earth.'

Mick took both her hands. 'Don't worry about the cost—I'll pay for the reception. I've got another idea which will not only cut down on expenses but will be close to our hearts.'

This was what Summer loved so much about Mick. The way he talked about the heart. He had a spirit.

'First, we can have the ceremony and reception at Seashells, and I think Mae and Lily would relish hosting it ... perhaps with help from Mavis and Rosie. My backyard is ideal—Ted has been manicuring the lawn and gardens so well they'll be fit for the purpose by then. What do you think?'

'Marvellous idea! But what about catering—shall we use our staff? It's a heap of work and we won't be able to enjoy our wedding if we're having to be in the kitchen supervising.'

'Ah ... I've also been working on that one. I've got friends—a couple who run the Devonport Tavern—who said they would be delighted to use their restaurant staff for any catering I might need at the B&B. Locals regularly book them for private functions, and I'll get a substantial discount. Years ago,

I saved their son from taking his own life, and they still kind of reckon they owe me.'

Summer threw her arms around Mick and kissed him. 'What a fabulous idea—it'll be perfect. We have a great deal of organising to do—I'm so excited.'

Mick stood up and stretched, arching his back. 'I'm going to hit the hay—early start tomorrow to help you with those folk who want cooked breakfasts before they leave at seven,'

'Oh, yes, it's Mavis's day off and Rosie isn't coming in until late morning,' Summer replied.

Mick trundled off to his room, got ready for bed and dashed into his Ensuite before returning to his bedroom and turning on the television.

The evening's entertainment was dismal, as usual, and the guest house did not have Sky. But he was happy enough with a smart TV.

He was about to watch one of his regular mystery series on Netflix when his mobile phone vibrated on the bedside table. It was Hayley Winters with an update on Operation Sea Wolf—the long-awaited outcome of the trial involving Rob Dean and his associates.

Mick was ecstatic when he got off the phone eager to rush along the hallway and tell Summer, but she'd turned in for the night.

43

Three months later

The onshore wind from St Heliers Beach was icy as Mick and Summer walked along the promenade towards the mobile food vendor who was parked next to the beach. Usually, the man was flat out selling fresh fruit ice creams in waffle cones, but during the chilly winter days, hot chips were in high demand.

Summer sat on the park bench a short distance from the van while Mick did the honours and got the food. He also brought back a cup of hot chocolate for Summer who wrapped her hands around it to warm herself.

'Gee, thanks—this looks good,' she said, sipping the sweet delight, while Mick started blowing on the piping hot chips.

'Isn't it great we get the afternoon off once a week to spend time together,' said Mick. 'We're like an old married couple, although we haven't even tied the knot?'

'Absolutely,' Summer replied. 'But at least we're practising—not long now. The children

have all got their leave sorted for our big day
and you just have to confirm the date with
the caterers at the Devonport Tavern—then
we're away. I'm relieved we're keeping it
simple.'

While Mick held a couple of chips in his
fingers, seagulls lined up on the sand in front
of him omitting the occasional raucous
squawk.

'Get away! Go on,' he roared at them. After
they guessed he was unrelenting, they flew
away.

'It feels strange without having Olive
popping in now and then—especially with
her fresh scones. She'll be sorely missed by
the community, I'm sure,' said Summer,
reaching for the fries.

'Yes, I'm sure. But Jeremy must be finding
the house dead quiet rattling around there on
his own,' Mick replied. 'It was unexpected,
Olive giving up her home to live in a
retirement village.'

'I think it was all the stress with Tony's
death and Jeremy being arrested that sent
her over the edge, poor woman,' said
Summer, looking downcast.

'Well, she must have had a bob or two to
buy an apartment and leave Jeremy the
house.'

'Actually, I was going to talk to you about
that. Something else has come up,' said
Summer.

'Oh, really ... spit it out. I hope it won't spoil our afternoon.'

'No, Mick, but I want you to think about this proposition. The other day, Rosie said something about the cottage being a little too cramped for her and Liam. They hope to rent a house in the area while saving to buy a home, but everything is way too expensive around here.'

'Sorry, Summer, I don't see where you're going with this. Have they given their notice?'

'No, they haven't. But I had an idea.'

'Oh-oh. Another one of your brainwaves, is it?' said Mick, grinning, passing her the cup of chips to finish, cleaning his hands on a wet wipe she handed him.

'I thought of asking Jeremy if he'd like to earn a good income from Olive's house and move into our cottage for free. In return for his services with our garden maintenance.'

'I don't know. Why would Jeremy want to give up a three-bedroom house to live in a tiny cottage?' Mick replied.

Summer stopped to think.

'It's something Jeremy mentioned about it being rather lonely and deathly quiet living by himself. He said that the house feels so empty now.'

Mick zipped up his parka. 'Shall we walk back slowly as we talk? It's getting quite nippy sitting here.'

'Good idea. I need to get Jane's room ready—she's coming to stay tomorrow night.'

Summer gathered up the takeaway cups and tossed them into a nearby rubbish bin.

'I see what you're getting at,' Mick replied. 'Jeremy may be happier with some human activity going on around him and at the same time earning an income from his house. But do you think it ethical of him to give up the home Olive had left him in order to make a financial gain?'

Summer thought hard. 'I don't think there are many people who would bequeath their home to a loved one then begrudge them the freedom to turn it into a cash asset.'

'I suppose it sounds okay if you put it that way,' Mick replied.

'And it could be in his best interest to benefit from the home which would please Olive, surely,' Summer added.

'Fair enough. I'll let you do the organising with this one. You truly are a charitable human, Summer. It's what first attracted me to you,' he said, taking her hand and walking her back to the guest house.

~

'Jane! It's great to see you. I can't wait for you to meet Mick. He's out on a kayaking trip with Liam, but he'll be back by dinner time.'

Summer took her friend's suitcase and showed her to a room. When she opened the door, Jane looked wide-eyed. 'It's so

460

beautiful and sunny—what a gorgeous Ensuite.'

'These are large rooms for families or couples, but I thought I would treat you. It's not so busy this week.'

'And a vase of sweet, little rosebuds. Thank you, Summer.'

'Why don't you freshen up and then we can have afternoon tea on the covered veranda.'

Shortly afterwards, the two friends sat chatting over coffee and cake, catching up where they'd left off since Jane's last visit. During that time, Summer had told her about Tony's mysterious death and the murder of the Port guard.

Summer took her time trying to piece together the chain of events leading up to Operation Sea Wolf.

'Mick attended the trial of that corrupt detective Rob Dean and his associates involved with human trafficking and money laundering. I'm sure I can discuss with you what he said, as it was a public hearing and in the news.'

I assumed you were going to be a witness. When we spoke over the phone during the inquest, you mentioned you had evidence to provide the police.'

Summer's face turned red. 'Yes, but the investigating officer couldn't use most of it. I got it illegally, without Selena's consent.'

'You mean all that trouble you went to front up to that awful woman's parlour,

Angel's Staircase and getting into her computer was in vain?'

'I'm afraid so—at least as far as criminal evidence in court goes. I felt like a right idiot when Mick told me it was inadmissible in court. But it still proved to Mick that Selina and Dean were in cahoots.'

'So, why were you so intent on tracking that dirty cop?'

'Because—at first—I suspected he was Tony's killer. Remember, I told you that his rookie, Sam, had seen him go unaccompanied into the evidence deposit room. Dean had manipulated the Property Officer to allow him entry while he ducked out to the toilet. That's when Dean did his dastardly deed, tampering with evidence. Ever since then, I suspected he had killed Tony to silence him.'

'Really? I would have run a mile,' said Jane, with a shudder. 'Getting involved with that stuff isn't for the faint-hearted.'

'Anyway—Mick used the information I gave him to investigate Dean.'

'Didn't you want to attend the trial yourself?'

'Mick had invited me to the High Court, but as I'd already made a written affidavit for my admissible evidence, I wasn't required to be a witness in the courtroom. They thought it best for me to stay out of Dean's sight. The trial was all over the television once he was convicted, and he was sentenced last week.'

Jane rubbed her hands together. 'Great! I followed some of it in the news in the beginning only but didn't hear all of it. How long did Dean get?'

'Oh, life, of course. He had multiple serious convictions on top of murder.'

'At last, Summer. Tell me what happened exactly.'

'Well, at his preliminary hearing, he pleaded not guilty, the weasel, but the prosecution had produced more evidence just before his jury trial that put the final nail in his coffin.'

'Thank God for that,' said Jane, reaching out for another Brownie, eating it excitedly like a small child listening to a bedtime story.

'Remember the bit I told you about the detective who saw Dean had got to the Port first?'

'Yes, but you didn't tell me the name?'

'I couldn't then, but now it is public knowledge—his name is Bernie Wright.'

'I wouldn't like to be in his shoes—so brave of him.'

'He testified about Dean being absent while he was working with him and three other officers on the graveyard shift. The DSS had told Bernie he felt peckish and had a yen for a bag of hot chips. He slipped out to the White Lady takeaway truck at the bottom of town after saying he would bring food back for them all. Dean had instructed Bernie to stay behind and write up reports.'

'Jeepers—he's so calculated, artful dodger, eh?'

'Absolutely! But there's more. Apart from Bernie being an eye witness after verifying that the DSS was already on the container terminal when he arrived in a car with other officers, a second key observer has now come out of the woodwork.'

'Wonderful! What a stroke of luck for the prosecuting police officer.'

'A senior constable from a different police crew who was working on an unrelated case at the waterfront drove past the container wharves while on patrol in the area. He had recognised Dean's vehicle exiting Queen Street and cruising the Port before the murder took place. The officer had wondered why the DSS was there, as this was before the Port guard had alerted the Maritime Unit. At his interview, Dean's only alibi was that he had stopped by the White Lady—an all-night takeaway truck—and this was confirmed by CCTV. The Prosecution believed he had already planned to be on standby for the traffickers, in case there was trouble.'

'Sorry, I've lost you, Summer,' said Jane, wiping chocolate from her mouth with a paper napkin.

'Dean must have already known about the trafficking incident before the Maritime Police had phoned the station.'

'Wow! So the second police officer dobbed him in at the last minute. He and Bernie must have been trembling in their boots, narking on one of their own,' said Jane.

'Yes, especially as Dean outranked Bernie who knew his testimony was the only way that the culprit could be convicted beyond reasonable doubt. Everything else was circumstantial evidence, and it would have been difficult for the prosecutors to convince the jury he was the killer. But now the DSS is completely out of the way with no parole.'

'That must put Mick's mind at rest. It was brave of him to sell a senior officer down the river,' said Jane.

'Selina and her brother each got six years' jail time, but they'll be out in four, I guess, with our pathetic judicial system. Anyway— it's not the reason I asked you to come. I've got a really special favour to ask.'

Jane's eyes lit up. 'Oh, that sounds suspect. What can I do for you?'

'It's about our wedding in September. I was hoping you could be my matron of honour. What do you think?'

Jane, holding back tears, threw her arms around Summer as Mick walked through the door.

'Hello, Jane, it's great to see you,' said Mick. 'I can't hug you just yet—I need to help Liam clean the kayaks and then freshen up after being on the sea.'

~

A short time later, Mick came into the lounge to greet her properly.

'You've chosen a quiet period to visit. I'm sure you two have a great deal of catching up to do. I'll see you at dinner—we're having a BBQ.'

While Mick was busy with Liam preparing the BBQ, Summer and Jane shared about their personal lives.

'I've recently met someone, called Marty,' said Jane sheepishly. 'He's the first man I've got close to since Brandon died.'

Summer had been subtly trying to encourage Jane to start dating again since her husband had died. She had been on her own for over two years.

'I'm just afraid that if I end up with someone new, I'll always be comparing him to Brandon, and then it will be bound to fail.'

It was as though Summer was hearing herself talking. She knew in every respect what her friend must be feeling, as she'd also gone through the pain of self-doubt when she began falling in love with Mick.

'Jane, I can assure you, life is full of risks. One could say I should never have married a policeman. We'd always been in love, and I thought it would never end, but in the blink of an eye my hero was ripped out of my life.'

'I kind of hear what you're saying,' Jane muttered feebly.

'And you'd risked marrying a man who—unbeknown to you—would be plucked out of your life falling victim to cancer.'

'So ... what are you getting at?' asked Jane.

'After putting myself through a heap of unnecessary anguish, the pain of attempting to steer clear of disappointment was far greater than the fear of letting go.'

'So, you just gave up,' said Jane.

'No, not at all. I finally gave in and let God run my life. Now, I have no expectations of the outcome of any situation. That's the conclusion after being married to a detective for almost two decades and about to go through it for the second time.'

'Oh, really? You can't be serious.'

'Although ... if Mick hadn't given up chasing criminals, it may well have finished us, as I was over it. To be honest, being married to an organised crime investigator is a roller-coaster ride and not for the faint-hearted. Most of them end up divorced or single.'

Summer cast Jane a glance, adding, 'But without these brave officers, our country would be in complete chaos—I do realise that, of course. It takes a unique character to tolerate such a tough, stressful frontline role—but to be married to a detective also takes a special person who'll keep the home fires burning no matter what. Unfortunately, when Tony's death was, briefly, a suspected murder, I just couldn't take the thought of living that life any longer.'

Jane's face beamed. 'Strange you should say all that. Guess what Marty does for a living. He's a Detective Inspector with the CIB in Coromandel!'

'Summer's mouth fell open. She shook her head in disbelief, as Jane burst out laughing.

'Why didn't you tell me before I went spouting off?'

Jane gave her a wry smile. 'It's okay—I already knew all that. Marty and I have been seeing each other for a while now and I'm slowly learning how to keep the home fires burning ... it was you who taught me how to do it.'

~THE END~

Contact: patricia.snelling.books@gmail.com

Website: patriciasnelling.com

Visit my website! There you'll find more Cosy Mysteries and Romantic Suspense books with a blurb or taster with each title.

All my novels are rated Clean Reads. Clean reads are stories without graphic violence, explicit sexuality, or strong profanity. Although I have written my books with a Christian world view woven into the narrative of each one, they are also suitable for a secular audience.

AUTHOR BIO

I get most of my inspiration from
interesting people I've met or adventures
I've had that left me with an impression. My
stories are based on faith, hope and love and
in particular, the ability of the oppressed to
rise above their circumstances and
overcome huge setbacks in their lives.

I'm passionate about social justice and
marginalised people overcoming the odds.
If you enjoy thrilling mysteries with a touch
of romance in small town settings, my books
are sure to entertain you.

My hometown is near the seaside in an
idyllic coastal part of New Zealand called
the Hibiscus Coast which I love, surrounded
by beautiful native trees and birds.

I enjoy the outdoors, and in New Zealand
we are spoilt with lakes, mountains and
forests full of wildlife. When I write, I try to
draw my readers into the surroundings.

If you enjoy reading books with encouraging
and positive endings, then my novels are for
you.

www.ingramcontent.com/pod-product-compliance
Lightning Source LLC
Chambersburg PA
CBHW020229110726
47898CB00004B/1199